# YELLOW FEVER

# Terry L. Vinson

# YELLOW FEVER

# GRAVESTONE PRESS

ISBN  978-1-78695-731-3

Gravestone Press
is an imprint of
Fiction4All

This Edition Published 2021
*Fiction4All*
*www.fiction4all.com*

Cover art by Deron Douglas
www.derondouglas.ca

# Prologue
### *Preordained Vigilance*

The Date: *Late summer, Nineteen Eight-Four*
The Place: *Just outside Fort Worth, Texas*

Strategically crouched with her shapely rear end facing the roadway, she secretly wishes her skin-tight blue-jeans were a size or two larger, though not to dramatically alter the desired effect. She peers at the rented Jeep Wrangler's flattened rear tire with a pinky finger lodged seductively between pouting, ruby lips, reaching with a free hand to push the narrow-framed Raybans up onto the upper edge of her forehead. If duly accused, she would argue a charge of entrapment. Her marks needed little in the way of enticement, though it clearly never hurt to 'sweeten the pot', in a manner of speaking.

Her gold-banded wristwatch reads six-twenty-six PM. Approximately an hour of daylight remaining, ninety minutes tops. Nearly choking from a mouthful of blowing dust, she comes to the conclusion that the next mark will definitely be the last of the evening. Despite its obvious advantages, foremost being the cloaking factor, she has never liked working in the dark. There is a layer of comfort in the daylight; a sense of security that the night air wilts away. As far as production goes, it has not been a good day.

Thus far, sixteen candidates since nine AM has equaled sixteen strikes. In truth, she cannot recall the last such day, especially with weather conditions so favorable for 'good Samaritans', be they sincere or inherently evil, to ply their merciful (or merciless) trade. As is the ritual whenever such an anomaly occurs , she allows just a flicker of hope within her fevered mind that perhaps…just perhaps, the good Lord above has deemed fit to place a permanent 'out of order' sign within her inner circuitry, thus eliminating the very source of her 'power'. Grunting aloud as an 'oversized load' blows by like a cloud of rolling thunder, she quickly voids such whimsical thinking. She knows better, as there have been numerous such 'false alarms' before. If nothing else, at least the weather has been accommodating. At just over eighty-five degrees with relatively low humidity, it wasn't your typical late summer day in West Texas. Certainly a pleasant change from Seattle's constant rains just a week earlier, or Miami's stifling heat and humidity from a month ago.

Bending down with a groan, she feels the vehicle's presence even before actually seeing it pull forward and park less than a half dozen feet away. She hears the truck's engine shut off just before a trio of semi's blow by in a thundering wave.

"Need some help there, sweetie?" a man's voice bellows, the word 'sweetie' drawn out into two separate syllables ('*Sweee-teeee*') in a husky Texas drawl. Before turning about and standing, she hears not one but two car doors slam shut. An adrenaline rush of epic proportions ensues, to be quickly dashed by a wave of soothing calm that reduces her pulse to near coma-status. Through the years and countless such encounters, her ability to both control the change and subsequently harness the effects has

6

become almost second-nature. Still, she understands the importance of ensuring that both men fit the specific criteria.

Strange as it seems, this is not always assured. Scum is indeed scum as a rule, but there are varying degrees and levels involved. Such cases are few and quite unusual, but like a rare archeological find, do exist.

"Bucky's road service, m'am," he continues, strolling over with a wide, toothy grin from which a well-gnawed toothpick protrudes, "pretty girl like you shouldn't outta frown like that. It might end up freezin' that'a way, am I right, Douglas?"

"Right as rain, Buck," the other man replies in a nasally tone, walking around the side of the massive truck to join his partner until they stand posed elbow to elbow less than five feet from the Wrangler's back bumper, "that would indeed be a heckuva shame."

Allowing herself a single step forward, she performs the equivalent of a body-scan of sorts, essentially inhaling both men's auras until they are distinctly separate entities. Sighing heavily, she is inwardly relived to have confirmed that both are indeed ripe for the picking.

"Might've been low when I left Arlington," she coos, still focusing on the tire but consciously aware of the men's roving, roaming eyes as they take in the whole of her.

As is the ritual, she instantly records two distinct mental notes that might well come in handy as things progress. First, mark number one keeps his hands tucked into his back pockets, thereby hinting of a concealed weapon of some type. Secondly, mark number two walks with a decided limp, favoring the right leg and hip.

"You got a spare, darlin'?" mark one asks, having finally removed his hands from the hind pockets of his jeans in order to lean back on the truck's massive grille.

As the initial stage of change shifts into first gear, she casually reaches up to replace the tinted Raybans. Other than the waves of intense heat her flesh will soon emit, an occurrence for which there is no precautionary measure to take, her self-checklist is now complete.

"Only one of those tiny ones...you know, the *donut* kind. I think it's flat too," she concedes with a girlish giggle. As always, she allows her natural accent to flourish, having found this especially alluring to such boorish, uncouth types.

Mark number two laughs hardily, revealing several missing front teeth. Both appear the stereotypical thirty-something West Texas 'shit-kicker' types, what with soiled baseball caps, muscle tees (though neither actually possess the build necessary to accent such a fashion choice), faded blue jeans and cowboy boots (mark number two's appearing to be of the imitation snakeskin variety). She finds this amusing, though in a decidedly sickening fashion. She'd run cross dozens of such men of all ages, from the plains of Kansas to the rolling hills of Tennessee. Though many had seemed sincerely helpful and the majority harmless in terms of setting off her inner alarm, such an appearance was hardly conspicuous if one did possess the evil seed.

"Tell you what, gorgeous. There's a Firestone garage 'bout three miles up the road off the Hicksville exit. We'll be more'n happy to get you set up with a new wheel or at least have 'em tow in your ride."

Mark number one nods in agreement while staring a hole through her bosom and exposed midriff.

Besides the aforementioned painted-on jeans, she sports a short- sleeved '*Dallas Cowboys*' halter that ends midway up her finely toned abdomen and two inch heels that leave her red-shaded toenails exposed while also increasing the natural curvature of her rear end. Her hair, pitch black and luminous, is tied into a tight bun at the back of her skull, held into place by a pair of tiny, mostly submerged hair-clips.

"Well, I don't…know if that's…I mean," she babbles, staring into the mostly clear skies with a hand poised atop each hip, "I really shouldn't…"

Mark number one steps over and past her, kneeling as to properly inspect the damaged tire.

"Don't see where ya got much choice, beautiful," he chides, squinting into the sun as he glances back up at her with the toothpick bobbing wildly between yellow-stained teeth, "sides, don't judge a book by its worn-out old cover now. We're basically harmless, right Doug?"

The other man replies while turned away to view the passing traffic.

"Right as rain once again, Buck-a-roo."

Pausing to again nibble a pinky finger, she then

9

crosses her arms across her chest and sighs.

"All right then. I...um... sure appreciate it."

Mark number two claps his hands cheerfully while rising, shooting his partner a sly wink.

"No problem, little lady. We'll get 'er back on the road for ya." "Just let me grab my purse," she says, ducking inside the Honda's minuscule interior and retrieving a tiny brown hand bag.

Moments later, she sits with her hands tucked tightly between her thighs with marks positioned on either side. While in such close proximity, as her shoulders and upper arms brush against both men, the increased body heat becomes a concern. She hopes neither questions or makes an issue of it until it's too late in the game to matter.

Mark number one pulls out onto the highway, spitting gravel as the truck's comically oversized tires spin out in a weaving lurch.

"Just hang on, cutie, ol' Buck'll get ya there in one piece," he howls, the pungent aroma of spilt beer and recently smoked marijuana permeating inside the cab's cramped confines.

\*\*\*

"Don' t fret, sweet thang. The Buck-Master don't go back on his word. We'll get ya to the auto mall soon enuff," mark number one pants, reaching over to fondle her left shoulder, "what's your hurry, anyhow? 'afraid you've already missed whatever appointment ya had."

Leaning in the opposite direction, she finds precious little room to maneuver as a result of mark number two's broad-shouldered body- block.

"Buck speaks the truth, lady. I see it as a might

10

fair trade, really.

Tit for tat, ya might say," he blubbers, and she feels a light misting of spittle coat the back of her neck, "more *tit* than tat though."

"You mean...both of you...at once?" she asks, careful to maintain a tone that rides the middle ground between startled and slightly aroused. As the men force their bodies ever closer, essentially forming a fleshy perimeter on either side, she welcomes a series of inner shutters akin to multiple orgasms.

"Well, a'course both of us, babe. Why, me an' the Doug-meister do *everything* together. We're *really* into sharing, right partner?" mark one blurts, his hand slowly working its way towards her left breast, the nipple of which grows instantly erect through the relatively thin cotton tee.

"Damn tootin', Buck," Mark two agrees with a looping nod, reaching over to rub the back of her neck.

"Seems only fair, honey buns. A little nookie in return for this here roadside rescue. Hell, every hero deserves a reward (pronounced 'ray- ward')."

"How about....just a...well....you know...," she mutters through rapidly moistening eyes, through which the overall scope of her vision has not only widened to twice its normal parameters, but views everything in a deep shade of crimson despite the sunglasses' darkroom effect.

Mark one's voice grows husky with lust.

"How's about what, cutie?' We're open for suggestion. The kinkier the better."

"Well, how about oral...I mean...a... blowjob

11

instead?"

The two men look past her at one another, giggling like schoolboys after a particularly amusing fart joke.

"What ya think, partner?" m ark one asks with a mischievous wink. "Truthfully, Buck-o, I was kinda hopin' for a slab of something a bit more substantial, buuuutt, what the hell? I've heard tell these oriental als can suck the chrome off'n a trailer hitch. I' m game."

Mark one's right hand shoots out and snatches her lower jaw even as his left increases the pressure on her breast. Miraculously, her sunglasses remain fitted despite the abrupt jarring.

"Seems we've struck a deal, girl," he whispers harshly through a tight-lipped grimace, "course, don't be offended if we change our minds half-way through the deed."

Mark two tosses his head back and howls like a baying wolf, his hand having departed her neck for the back of her jeans.

"Damn straight, Buck-O! It's a man's prerogative to change his mind!"

As their fondling grows increasingly frenzied, the girl flashes a seductive pout, running the tip of her tongue over each ruby-shaded lip.

"In here? Not enough room, fellas. You've got to give this girl some space to work her...magic."

"Not to worry, cutie," mark two says, twisting around to open the passenger side door, "we keep a nice, clean pad in the bed for just such a special occasion."

Exiting the cab, the girl rotates her head in a

circular spin. She then executes a similar stretch for each arm and shoulder as both marks study her with comical bemusement.

"Damn, girl, this ain't the Olympic trails," mark two blurts, and she can clearly see the building erection at his crotch.

"You one of them gymnasts?" mark one adds, openly massaging his own swollen manhood through his khakis while propping a booted foot atop the lowered cab door.

The girl flashes a brief smirk while scanning their isolated surroundings, realizing she'd have been hard-pressed to discover a more suitable spot herself.

"No, but I used to be a dancer."

Mark one cackles gleefully while extending a hand to his cohort and heaving him onto the bed, where a wide, cushioned pad awaits.

"Oh, I'm sure you were, cutie. Bet you could slide that greased pole like nobody's business."

Both men squat down to remove their boots, then quickly stand up and begin unhitching their belts.

"Well, c'mon up, woman. Don't get all shy on us now," mark two says, pulling his trousers and underwear to his ankles while giving the area a final scan and resembling every bit the nervous prairie dog.

By her calculations, they'd driven at least three miles since exiting the main highway onto the narrow dirt/gravel path. The clearing mark one had chosen was cloaked in shoulder-high weeds and a line of equally overgrown, horribly gnarled

13

shrubbery. The West Texas landscape, the girl muses, was the textbook definition of 'eye sore.' These two had definitely used this sport before, possibly several times, she decides, reaching back to remove tiny, twin hair-clips and thus allowing her shoulder-length locks to fall free.

In response, mark two practically moans in girlish delight.

"God damn, but yore a pretty one. Ain't never had me no slant-eye before. Hope yore as good as advertised, hon."

Both men fell to their knees as to some silent cadence while stroking their respective man-hoods.

"You boys ready for me?" she teases with still another tantalizing lick of each lip.

The marks nod like a pair of famished hounds over an overfilled food dish.

"Yeah, cutie. Question is, are you ready for a twin injection of only the finest Southwestern beef?"

"Oh, don't worry, boys. I think you're in for more than you bargained for."

She crawls slowly atop the truck bed on her elbows and knees with both fists clinched tight, all the while taking note of the multitude of terror-filled eyes swirling like cascading waves of misery behind each man's faux visage. The final confirmation complete, the girl sighs as a powerful surge of adrenaline fills her veins.

"Baby, I'm afraid I gotta make an early amendment to our original agreement," mark one croons, scooting forward on his knees with his swollen member leading the way, "I just gotta have a piece of that sweet caboose 'a yours.

14

Hope ya don't mind the lack of lubrication," he concludes as mark two laughs in the background while holding his position, "but just to be polite, I'll make sure I spit on it a couple'a times."

"By all means, big boy," the girl replies in a barely audible whisper, rising to her feet to allow the mark to scoot past her, "a man's gotta do what a man's gotta do, correct?"

"Damn straight, you slant-eyed whore, and what I'm about to do is plant about eight inches of West Texas' finest right up your fine little poop shoo-.."

Her movements are frenzied yet amazingly fluid; machine-like in their preciseness, they appear calculated yet also wildly spontaneous. Having taken but a single step forward, she uses full extension of her left arm to shove the first hair-clip forward in a straight jab that travels the length of mark two's prone body and penetrates his left eye with a sickening pop. Twisting about on her right heel, she executes a full about-face while simultaneously whipping her right arm around in a horizontal blur. Mark one has time but to widen his eyes before the second clip slashes his throat just below the Adam's Apple.

Gagging up a mouthful of his own bodily fluid, mark one reaches up and clamps a hand across the spewing wound as the girl briefly balances on her left heel, ballerina-style. Like a human funnel, her body twists but once, spinning the right heel around like a battering ram to impact at the center of mark one's breastbone, sending him pin-wheeling from the bed of the truck and onto the hard, dusty terrain.

Whirling back towards mark two, who rolls and

squirms about the now blood-soaked bed with both hands covering his wounded eye, she lunges forward and lands three vicious, lightning-quick blows to the man's throat, forehead, and finally the bridge of his nose, which implodes with a resounding crunch.

Mark two's arms fall limp by his side as a final huff of air escapes his blood-smeared lips. His remaining eye rolls into the back of his head as spasms wrack his torso and legs before falling motionless.

The girl exits the truck bed with a graceful hop and looms over mark one's still frame. Lying flat on his stomach, she can hear his muted gargles.

"(IN KOREAN) How you like them apples, you sick asshole..." she whispers between tightly-clinched teeth while raising her right food and tilting the arch slightly upward. The foot remains suspended for a full five seconds as the attached calf and thigh tremble with the building tension of an over-wound metal coil.

"(IN ENGLISH) Burn in hell, fucker..."

The heel descends like a red-hot piston, cracking the skull beneath like an egg shell. Death-spasms ensue as the girl casually removes her shoe and wipes bone fragments and brain tissue onto the back of the deceased man's shirt.

Less than ten minutes later, having used a strip of the same shirt as a fuse and packing one corner into the truck's gas tank, she crouches down on her haunches and watches the yellow and blue flame absorb metal, rubber, flesh and bone as the sky is enveloped in clouds of blackish smoke. A package of 'Wet-Ones' pulled from her hand bag had served nicely to remove the few streaks of blood on her hand and neck, while a fresh tee sporting the '*Dallas Mavericks*' logo replaced the stained one, tossed unceremoniously into the raging fire. Similarly, the specially designed hair-clips, a bit elongated at three plus inches with syringe-like tips, had also been sacrificed to the god of fire and replaced by a simple rubber-band.

Realizing a fire-truck or ambulance is more than likely on the way, she soon rises with a stifled yawn, removes her heels and performs a quick series of leg stretches before sprinting off in an easterly direction. At the five-minute mile pace she normally maintains, she figures her vehicle to be less than a half-hour away at most. As is normally the case, she'll steer clear of the highway for the first twenty minutes or so, even if forced to double-back later on.

While navigating a steep, rock-infested hill less than a hundred yards from the clearing, she hears the truck's gas tank explode in a single, ear-piercing shriek. Her pace remaining steady despite any and all obstacles, she begins calculating and approximating the mental checklist that is mandatory for successful mission follow-up. All told, she hopes to see Texas in her rearview mirror by no later than eight PM. Having dedicated a full month between its spacious borders, the impending exodus can't come soon enough. Arkansas awaits for a three week tour, followed by a similar agenda for both Tennessee and Alabama. Working her way east, the trek she has labeled 'The Eradication Tour' is now nearing a full year in duration. There are times she feels she has aged at least five winters in that same span. If such a thing were possible, she feels an 'old' twenty-four.

Though she neither visualizes nor hears anything tangible, she abruptly slows her pace to a casual jog. Turning about while jogging backwards, a brief but thorough scan of her surroundings reveals nothing out of the ordinary. As she turns about, the jagged terrain flattens and she descends a final hilltop leading into a wide clearing. She spots a series of what might be farmhouses a few hundred yards to the North, and immediately decides to veer hard to the left and thus a bit closer to the still hidden highway.

A sharp, whooshing sound ensues from her left, and she executes a textbook tuck and roll. Rising to her knees behind a grouping of gnarled shrubs, she reaches up with her left hand. Her forefinger and thumb find the prickly object wedged just behind her left earlobe.

Pulling it free with a single tug, she studies the striped dart's sleek, aero-dynamic design even as her vision grows blurry and her ears fill with the rumblings of a nearby chopper.

Collapsing onto her back, she becomes acutely aware of the thumping of heavy combat boots rushing in from seemingly all directions. Thick clumps of dust coat her face, lips and drooping eye-lids as typhoon winds blister about and the engine's hum grows ever louder. As consciousness betrays her, a single line of dialogue is heard, though the words are partially muffled and sound like a tape recording played back at a purposely slow speed.

"Lock and load 'er, boys,' it roars, the pronunciation of each word stretched to comical proportions, 'we got us a long flight ahead."

# CHAPTER ONE
## The Eyes Have it

Lei Hui Park was born in Pusan, South Korea on June 9th, nineteen sixty. Raised by a wealthy uncle, she attended one of the country's finest private schools for the 'intellectually gifted' from age six.

At the tender age of ten, Lei was sexually assaulted by a friend of the family. Though the man, an old friend of her uncles, was unable to complete the assault due to sexual impotence, the young girl was predictably scarred for life, and not just in the typical fashion. True, the main culprit had been the constant mental duress and the loss of trust in her elders, but also something more. Something buried a bit deeper. Something that had been...added. Several months after the attack, while being 'counseled' by one of her teachers, Lei experienced what she would later come to think of as a 'spell'. She began to feel the change as soon as the teacher, a male in his early forties, had called her back into the classroom after all her mates had departed.

Her stomach instantly began to churn, the flesh of her bare arms, neck and face flushed and fevered. Worse yet, it was more what she *saw* than what she felt. As the teacher had pulled her close, gripping her rail-thin shoulders in a vise, their eyes had met and locked firmly into place. The teacher's voice grew from a whisper to a shrilly whine as his grip intensified. Lei was haplessly oblivious by that point, however, utterly hypnotized by the swirling

20

mutations the man's hazel green eyes had become.

At some point during the incident, the young girl had lost control of her bladder, mesmerized by what she initially thought to be nothing more than a fear-induced hallucination. She'd ran home that day, her undergarments and school uniformed damp and tinted by the smell of her own waste, and dreamed of the teacher as a horned demon in disguise; a spawn birthed in hell's darkest cavern whose earthly assignment was simply to torment her at every turn. She also dreamed, amid a sequence of violent tossing and turning, of the eyes. The kaleidoscope of colors, sizes, and shades she'd envisioned through the demon's cold, unblinking stare. It was almost as if there were souls trapped inside whose only form of communication was to magically appear through the horned being's steely glare.

Less than three weeks following this episode, the teacher had vanished from the campus amid whispers from both faculty and student body alike. He was replaced by a young female teacher who quickly became one of Lei's personal favorites. One of Lei's classmates had heard the teacher had been 'dismissed' for what she called 'lewd acts' with one of the younger children. As days progressed, such rumor and innuendo were gradually confirmed.

Considering the adverse effects just being alone in the man' s presence had had on her, Lei felt predictably befuddled, but quickly dismissed the entire scenario as nothing more than a random fluke.

Having just turned twelve, Lei soon discovered otherwise. She had been attending a birthday party for a school friend when the girl's older brother had approached her and another girl behind the cover of thick shrubbery. Initially just startled, Lei had immediately begun to shake and convulse as the teenaged boy exposed himself to them with a maniacal grin. Her classmate having already fled in disgust, Lei found herself frozen in place, utterly paralyzed as the boy's probing hands began to slowly unbutton her shirt even as his erection grew. As her flesh grew hot and warm tears coated her cheeks, Lei saw the boy kneel before her. Somehow unable to close her eyes to the abomination, she instead locked them on her would-be molesters own set of dark brown orbs, which gleamed with mad, youthful lust. There she witnessed a similar transformation as two years earlier, as dark brown quickly became light brown and then a piercing blue, before reverting back to the original shade. Of one thing Lei was certain; hers were most definitely *not* what is commonly referred to as the 'windows to the soul', but instead 'windows to the tortured soul'; wide, terror- filled eyes brimming with fevered tears. Innocent eyes. Youthful eyes. *Children' s* eyes.

In descending order, the boy had reached the fourth button of her lily-white cotton shirt when Lei, whose upper body was wracked with a white-hot fever even as her arms and lower torso turned to ice, appeared to temporarily black out. Later that afternoon, while being questioned by her family physician, Lei would state that she recalled only brief flashes of what had occurred during the 'blackout' phase, tiny fragments of jerky, frenzied movement. In future years, such an episode would come to be known as a *'Crimson Rage'*.

The young man, having just turned sixteen, would suffer deep lacerations to his face and neck (scratch and bite marks), as well as lose the use of his left eye, which had literally been gouged out.

Lei would escape the incident virtually unscathed save a large red welt on her right cheek, possibly from a hard punch or slap across the face. Though her hair, face and neck had been drenched in blood, it became obvious from her attacker's many wounds to whom the spilled bodily fluids had belonged. An investigation would reveal that the young man had just recently been released from juvenile incarceration for an attempted rape on a thirteen year old girl two years earlier, for which he was still receiving treatment and daily medication. Lei spent several months in after-school 'counseling' before being deemed psychologically fit to properly resume her regularly scheduled childhood.

Just weeks following the completion of high school (six days past her seventeenth birthday), Lei's uncle sent her across the ocean to live with an aunt in San Diego, California; an aunt that had married an American GI and resided in the states since the Korean War. He included a five-hundred dollar a month allowance and the promise of a two-hundred thousand dollar 'gift' once she turned twenty-one. She was immediately enrolled at San Diego State University and began taking classes with an eye towards a communications degree. Near the end of her initial semester, while struggling to fit into her new surroundings, Lei met a fellow student named Kum Hui Chang, a sophomore that had moved to the U.S. at age fourteen.

Kum Hui essentially took Lei under her wing, helping the young immigrant with her English and assisting in the acclamation process. It wasn't long before the two became fast, virtually inseparable friends.

As weeks and months passed, Lei resisted the many male suitors who came her way, no doubt drawn by her exotic good looks and finely toned body-a body that endured daily three hour weight and cardiovascular workouts and would, within the short span of two calendar years, claim first and second degree black belts in two separate forms of the martial arts.

Early in her own sophomore campaign, but not before months of grueling soul-searching, Lei began dating a friend of Kum Hui's boyfriend named Chad Lynch. A book-wormish type with thick, black-framed glasses, skinny build and outrageous sense of humor, Lei found a soothing comfort zone when in his manic company. Though the four month relationship was never to go beyond the heavy petting stage, she had at least discovered that there did indeed exist a male specimen for whom lurid sex *and or* other felonious crimes were not an issue.

Their unceremonious break-up had been eventual; Chad simply could never accept such a beautiful, charming girl as his own, and slowly retreated back into the impenetrable shell from which she'd first found him. Moreover, Lei wasn't able to surrender herself to anyone, neither mind nor body. Not quite yet. Oft times she wondered if such a life-shattering, psyche-altering event was ever to be a part of her future. After a calm, relatively event-free summer spent working retail in a local mall, Lei's junior year began with renewed promise. She attended Kum Hui's college graduation a few months previous, followed by her friend's wedding to her long-time finance, Warren Josephson.

Busy with classes (both campus and martial arts related), Lei filled the role of the quintessential loner without her friend to fill the role of constant companion.

After a two and a half month absence, the newly christened Kum Hui 'Kim' Josephson re-entered her life around Christmas of nineteen eighty, though in a less than celebratory manner.

Having secured her own one-bedroom apartment just a mile from campus, Lei had been shocked to see Kum Hui standing outside her front door that cool, rainy afternoon.

Sporting a black eye and evidence of light bruising about her right jaw-line and neck, Kum Hui had fallen to her knees in tears within minutes of the two saying hello.

Her friend said she'd been mugged outside a shopping center a few days earlier, and had filed the necessary report with local police. Her husband Warren ran a small print shop a few miles east of the city, and had been out of town on a selling jaunt at the time of the assault.

The sudden tears, it seemed, weren't related to the aforementioned assault, but instead tied into Kum Hui's rapidly crumbling marriage.

25

Without giving specifics, Kum Hui said Warren had recently admitted several affairs, a few of which had been on-going during the engagement phase and were still quite active. He'd supposedly told her that 'marriage wasn't for him after all' and wanted it to end as soon as feasibly possible.

Fitfully shocked, Lei had always found her friend's husband to be the cordial, polite, easy-going type one would never even suspect of straying.

Without hesitation, Lei insisted that Kum Hui immediately move in with her, at least until the initial smoke of the separation cleared.

It took Lei several days to work up the courage to ask a question that had been burning a hole in her gut. Replying while wearing an expression utterly void of emotion, Kum Hui had denied, though anything *but* vehemently, that Warren had actually played the role of 'mugger' in accordance with her bruises.

Arriving home from Tai Kwon Do class the following afternoon, Lei could hear the muffled echoes of moaning sobs reverberate from her apartment's partially opened front door.

Racing up the front steps and into the cramped living room, Lei found Warren propped atop Kum Hui's chest, essentially pinning her to the carpeted floor with his knees. His clinched fists were wound into her hair, jerking forcefully as she cried out in anguish, kicking out and punching his chest and exposed face to seemingly no avail.

Leaping into the fray at full-bore, Lei had gotten but the briefest of glimpses at her friend's soon-to-be ex-husband and future inmate of the *Richard J.*

*Donovan correctional facility.* The predatory snarl on display, complete with bared, bloodied teeth and deep-grooved scratches beneath each eye, was hardly noticeable when compared to what she'd seen painted onto each pupil like some abstract inkblot.

The first set that flashed into view had belonged to Kum Hui, a rich, fluorescent hazel. The next two, sparkling blue and dark brown, had been unidentifiable save that fact that each had belonged to young females, possibly late teenage to early twenties. All three had one thing in common; a trait that Lei found nauseatingly familiar despite the passing years since her last such viewing; each was filled to overflowing with stark, primal fear.

Unleashing a warrior's scream, Lei instituting a solid roundhouse kick that caught Warren Josephson just beneath the right ribcage, sending him sprawling into and over the center portion of a wide sectional couch.

Rolling to his feet, Warren charged forward like a rampaging bull. Lei was unable to completely sidestep the rush, and was sent flailing back against a far wall, knocking several framed pictures to the floor before falling forward onto the kitchen's hard-tiled floor.

Shockingly, Warren had apparently left her for dead, instead opting to climb back onto his wife and continue the marital assault.

Sucking in several deep breaths while ignoring a bleeding gash at the back of her scalp, Lei scooped up a relatively small but solid glass vase from a nearby cabinet and sailed forward with her right arm cocked back like a baseball pitcher. She got to within two feet of Warren before letting it fly at full force. The squared vase, which was roughly the size of a pencil-box and had once held a trio of freeze-dried roses, shattered like a glass grenade upon impact with the back of the man's skull. Lei then closed ranks, landing a half-dozen short jabs to the sides and center of his face before sending him airborne with a wicked uppercut to the chin.

A half-hour later, Warren Josephson was escorted via ambulance to a local hospital before being sent packing to the county jail, charged with aggravated assault and spousal abuse. Within a week, the news broke.

Josephson was charged in the rapes of two local college girls, both incidents within a week of each other. Lei had seen the girl's pictures in the local paper. One was a black girl, age twenty, with piercing blue eyes. The other victim was of Vietnamese descent with eyes a dark shade of brown. It seemed the 'affairs' Warren had confessed to his wife had been less than consensual, but of the serial rapist variety.

Lei later learned from her friend that Warren, always a casual drug- user in college, had become well-acquainted with both heroin and cocaine while on several 'business trips' to LA. Kum Hui said the change in the man had been horrifyingly rapid in nature; that the drugs had in fact, 'stolen his soul'.

In a teary, sob-wracked confession, Lei's closest friend confessed that Warren had indeed began beating and raping her mere days following their wedding.

Over coffee several weeks after the incident, Lei

had come very close to confessing her extra 'sense' to her friend. As had been the case years earlier following similar 'incidents', the fear of literally being labeled insane kept her silent. Once, almost a decade earlier, she'd nearly told her uncle of the troublesome 'events', but had shied away for the exact same reason.

Following the tension-filled trauma of Warren Josephson's trail and subsequent sentencing, wherein he received a forty year sentence without the possibility of parole, Kum Hui Chang moved back to South Korea and Lei was again left to ponder an uncertain future.

She temporarily dropped out of school, citing 'mental fatigue', and even thought about a lengthy visit back to the homeland. Instead, she remained in town and secured a summer job working for a maid service that specialized in cleaning office buildings after-hours, figuring to resume her pursuit of a degree some months later. Despite weekly visits to her aunt, she felt herself growing increasingly inverted from society as a whole. Fear clung to her like an extra layer of flesh. She began to dread frequenting public places. Trips to the local grocer or gas station became torturous odysseys that left her emotionally drained.

Early on a Saturday morning in early May, Lei found herself visiting a small church less than three blocks from her apartment complex.

She'd awoken around five AM and had been unable to fight an overwhelming urge to do so, despite the fact that she hadn't attended a religious service of any type since leaving Korea some three years earlier. The previous day and for no discernable reason, she'd driven a different route home from work and had noticed the small structure, with its faded red brick and severely aged stained glass windows.

Located just off Thompson Lane, a squared wooden sign attached to the left side of two large double-doors had read '*Soul Searchers Methodist Church* – Come Inside and Begin the Cleansing' in large, bold Korean type.

She'd found the doors unlocked, and had practically tip-toed her way through the semi-darkness, taking a seat on a front pew facing the church alter.

Several moments of deafening silence had ensued, and she thought the place to be deserted. She'd never heard nor felt the preacher's presence until he'd addressed her in a low, soothing whisper. Despite the sudden intrusion, she'd felt not a single twinge of fright.

"Do you desire company, my dear?" he'd asked cautiously in an accent she instantly recognized as being heavily Seoul-tinted.

She turned about gradually, the calm, gentle gracefulness of her movements surprising even herself. It was only then she'd initially noticed that her own hands had been joined in prayer.

"I...I'm not...sure, father. Do I...call you f-father, *Otishe*?"

He was a long-faced, gray-haired Korean man of perhaps sixty, sporting a casual blue suit and button-up white dress shirt with a matching collar.

"Yes, young one, you may call me Father Cho.

30

Your accent is Pusan, correct?"

She nodded, temporarily hypnotized by his piercing green eyes.

Eyes that exhumed wisdom, having no doubt seen and thus absorbed their fair share of human conflict and misery.

"Yes, Father Cho. I'm...my name is Lei. Lei Park. " "How long have you resided in the states, Lei?"

"Arrived here in seventy-eight, Father. Soon it'll be three years, though it seems....sometimes....much, *much* longer."

The old man nodded knowingly, staring past her to the squared alter beyond, the background of which was bathed in shadow.

"I understand the longing, my dear. I haven't visited our beautiful homeland in almost twenty years. True, we can eat the same food, watch some of the same programming via video tape, but it just isn't the same as breathing the same air, now is it?"

"No, Father. It certainly isn't," she replied, lowering her head. "Pusan native, I take it?"

She looked back up and flashed a timid smile. "Yes, Father."

He nodded yet again, and she continued once a verbal response never materialized.

"Seoul, Father?"

"Why yes," he beamed, "you have a good ear, young lady. It's not often many of my own flock can properly identify my fading accent."

Both laughed briefly before reverting back into a rather awkward silence.

"Anything you'd like to discuss? I'm here to

console and advise, if need be."

Father Cho arose, his knees popping loudly, and joined her on the first pew. Her nostrils flared with the faint scent of Old Spice, a rather cheap American-produced cologne her uncle had often used.

"It's....not an easy subject to breech, Father," she began, her voice cracking with emotion, "I think....I *know* something's horribly wrong with me."

"There, there, young lady," he said softly, placing a hand gently atop her right shoulder, which trembled slightly upon contact, "it cannot be all that bad, can it?"

Choking back tears, she focused on a mural hanging on a nearby wall and sucked in a strained breath.

"Oh, yes it can, Father. I'm afraid...it can."

"I'll try to help if I possibly can, my dear. That is, if you do wish to discuss it. I certainly don't want to pressure you."

"Do you believe in curses, Father?"

The old man paused, removing his hand from her shoulder and placing a curled fist beneath his chin.

"Can you...be more specific please?"

"Do you...think some people are given the means to...feel and see certain things that others are not?"

"What types of things, my dear?"

"Evil things, Father. The...evil that m-...men do."

"Evil is indeed everywhere, my child. The seed

32

is planted within all men. One has but to turn on the evening news to wit-.."

Waiving him off with both hands, Lei raised her voice much louder than she'd intended, her final words lowering to a barely audible murmur.

"That's not what I mean, Father. I can actually…see the victim's eyes reflected in the men that perpetrated the act. I can…feel… *sense* the evil within the predator's being…how it cloaks their… very flesh like a second skin."

They locked eyes briefly, and Lei was both relieved and astonished that the older man displayed no signs of either shock or disbelief.

"Who are these victims you see?"

She paused, wringing her hands nervously. A part of her, the portion that had always prevailed in such situations, begged desperately for an immediate shutdown; a backing away or ever better, a frantic exit from the premises. For once in her life, Lei fought off the urge. Perhaps it was the spiritual surroundings. Perhaps it was the Father's calming influence. Or perhaps, and more likely, it was simply time to *let go*; to allow someone else a glimpse into her inner sanctum, an inner sanctum fraught with restless demons in desperate need of an immediate exorcism.

"Woman…a-and girls. Some of them very young. Some *…most* the victim of…sexual predators…others murdered in…cold blood."

The preacher laid his hand atop hers and gently squeezed, his tone not the least bit patronizing.

"So it's their faces you see in the eyes of the predator's themselves?"

33

"Yes…y-yes and n-no, father. Their…if the victims are many, I see a swirling rotation of eyes…not inside the pupils exactly, but a complete transformation. They…the perpetrators eyes become the eyes of the ones they've harmed.

Also…I change somehow. Mentally and physically. I become more aware…and feel an inner strength.

I…don't know where it comes from, but its strength I've yet learned to harness. It…it scares me, frightens me more than the ability to just sense the evil."

"I…see. How long have you been aware of this, my child?" "When…since I was a young child. Seven, maybe eight." "And how many such episodes have you witnessed?"

"Enough. Enough to know this isn't some hallucination-fueled fluke, Father."

"How have you reacted?"

"At first, I tried to brush it off. I was…just a child. Once I got older and realized it wasn't just some mental defect on my part, I tried to…I just hoped it would go away. The last time…I…the last time…" she paused, lowering her face into her hands and feeling the heat radiate from behind her moistened cheeks, which were coated in warm tears.

"Go on, my child."

"I felt a burning rage, Father. I felt a need for retribution. Fatal retribution, on the victim's part. For the victims. I wanted to kill him, Father. Lord help me, I've never wanted anything so badly."

After a lengthy pause, during which time Father Cho arose and began a slow, purposeful pace from one end of the pew to the other, Lei was able to quell the water-works and regain at least partial control of her emotions.

Wiping her eyes one final time with a shirt-sleeve, Lei looked up to see Father Cho poised behind his pulpit, his hands gripping either side as if prepping for a fire and brimstone sermon to an overflowing flock.

"Lei, you referred to this…power you have…this sense, as a curse.

Do you truly believe that?"

"What would you call it, Father?" she replied somewhat curtly, instantly regretting the malice in her tone, "a gift?"

"Well, have you ever considered that side of it?" She paused, tilting her head in utter disbelief. "Excuse me?"

"Lei, people are born unto this world with a purpose. Some purposes, a small percentage I'm sure, are clear-cut and readily defined almost instantly, while most are inanely vague. Some, actually *most*, never discover their purpose on earth, while still others spend a lifetime denying it.

I believe in fate, or *preordained destiny*, if you prefer. This…power you've been granted to envision these…sinful abominations of the flesh… perhaps you should consider moving past the acceptance stage and into the action phase."

"Father," she babbled, blinking madly as if attempting to refocus on a particularly realistic illusion, "what exactly are you telling me to do? I…I'm confused enough as it is…"

"Just this, my child," he chided with just a tint

of barely hidden sarcasm, "evil exists on many levels. Some, like myself, are preordained to deal with it on a spiritual level, using text and words to alleviate its effects on God's children. Others are called upon to eliminate the source...to... *eradicate* by whatever means necessary.

Make no mistake; the Lord recruits warriors for just such an honorable cause. Just as he has chosen me for the former, I believe he has chosen you for the latter. I know it must be hard for you to fathom, dear one, but this situation isn't that unusual."

Lei swallowed hard, rising from the pew in a tense, guarded crouch.

"*Eradicate*? You mean k-kill..."

"Tell me, young one, were you...sexually abused as a child?" "I... well, there was...I was b-barely ten..."

"This...traumatic incident no doubt served as your inner awakening. Because of the...nature of the assault, you were granted the power to see, to identify sexual predators of an extreme nature," the Father continued, his voice and mannerisms slowly transforming into full- blown sermon mode, "as times passes, the instinct, this... 'special sense' you've been granted will only increase in scope. It won't be limited to simply predators of a sexual nature...but also to those demons in human guise that relish in the act of taking lives. You'll be privy not just to rapists, molesters and the like, but serial killers and mass murderers. These spawns of the Dark God should not be viewed as your own species, Lei, for from both a psychological and spiritual standpoint, they no longer qualify. Alas, their false dialogue and clever disguises will be pointless in the face of your gift. I understand the temptation to…shy away from physical violence as a solution to any situation, such is the Korean culture, no unlike so many *western* attitudes. Do not fall into such a mind-trap, Lei. Hesitation, in any form, can prove deadly when facing such heartless, merciless beings."

Sitting back down as her entire frame jittered and shook from a tidal wave of fevered chills, Lei felt strangely discombobulated, her vision growing ever darker and bleary at the edges. The Father's words echoed in her mind as if he were speaking from a faraway distance.

"The alarms, the warning signs you receive, will be similar in terms of the evil you face, but also uniquely distinct in their own specific way.

You must prepare yourself, young one, both mentally and physically, for the path you tread will be as dangerous as it is infinite."

"But…I s-still don't…" she pleaded, her hands again unconsciously locked in prayer.

"You will, Lei," the Father said sternly, his raised arms and torso outlined in a dull, gold-shaded aura, "you *will* understand…and very soon. Do not fight the realization when it comes, young one. One cannot shrug off such a destiny without the vilest of consequences. One must surrender to it willingly. One must…embrace it."

Crumbling to the ground like a house of cards, the last image Lei recalled visualizing was Father Cho's levitating form floating up and over the podium, a pair of ivory-white wings protruding from his upper back like feathery sails.

***

Lei awoke in her own bed, naked and bathed in sweat. Her temples pounded like twin base drums as her breath escaped in labored huffs. The clock had read one-thirty PM on Saturday afternoon. Following a cool shower and several stiff cups of black coffee, she got dressed and departed her apartment on foot.

She arrived at the corner of Wilmen and Thompson Lanes less than five minutes later, her fevered frame gain soaked in fresh, odorless perspiration. Feeling her pulse rate increase at a frightening rate, Lei stood facing an empty parking lot which held only scattered bits of trash and knee-high weeds. A dilapidated wooden sign which read *'FOR LEASE- Contact Bill Jackson at REMAX, 546-6754'* had been inserted into the ground at the center of the relatively cramped lot.

"It…it was here,' she mumbled, repeating the same refrain until all sound was lost though her trembling lips continued to form the words.

She arrived back at her apartment a half hour later, managing to down another cup of coffee before rushing into the bathroom to vomit. Seemingly unable to form a coherent thought, Lei lay back down at around three PM and didn't wake until six AM the next morning.

Once her eyelids parted and she rose to a sitting position on the bed, staring out a nearby window into an early morning mist, Lei Park clearly realized two things. One, she felt better than she'd felt in years; her mind clear and refreshed, her very flesh

38

electrified.

Number two was a true epiphany. She had a purpose. A new purpose. A life-long commitment to adhere to; the rules of which she would be forced to make up as she proceeded. A true case of 'on the job training' taken to the extreme.

Releasing a sigh of pure, unbridled relief as she stretched out her arms and yawned, the smile she flashed was as radiant as her suddenly glowing complexion. Springing from the bed with a newfound lust for life, she caught a glimpse of herself in a nearby dresser mirror and paused. Oh yes, she was indeed different.

Something new and infinitely powerful had been added to the soup bowl, so to speak. She then shot herself a playful wink, nodded, and headed for the phone stand located in the living room. It was time to go to work.

***

One-hundred sixteen days later, she phoned her uncle in Pusan and informed him she'd taken a job as a financial advisor for a large San Diego based company; a job that would require extensive travel, keeping her on the road essentially eight months out of each year. Ever generous, her uncle made immediate arrangements to send her the two-hundred thousand dollar gift she'd been promised at age twenty-one, despite the fact that she was still four months away from that particular landmark birthday. In return, he only asked that she 'proceed cautiously' and visit the homeland (and more specifically himself) at least once per calendar year.

Five days later, Lei Park made her first

confirmed kill. She'd inadvertently bumped into the man inside a local drugstore and was literally taken to her knees by the physical symptoms that followed. Following the man (Caucasian; balding, overweight, perhaps low to mid-fifties) to a ramshackle apartment building located less than a half-dozen miles from her very own, she entered through an unlocked door and stabbed him repeatedly with an ice-pick taken from the man 's very own kitchen. The assault had occurred while the man showered, each fatal blow administered through a thin, mildew- infested plastic curtain. After a frenzied but thorough cleaning of the scene, she left him floating in a tubful of his own life-source, his right eye frozen permanently agape. An eye that, in death, had reverted back to its original guise from the multitude of former victims its owner had previously claimed.

Two days later, she read a two-paragraph blurb in the local newspaper concerning the man's untimely demise. Not surprisingly, Rory 'R.L' LeJoy had once served time for multiple crimes against society, and had only recently been exonerated for the murder of a nineteen year old prostitute from San Francisco. It seemed only Lei knew the truth about not only that particular case, but several similar homicides to which Mister Lejoy had been present and accounted for, many of which had *not* included sexual battery of any type. Feeling a rush of elation as her actions were duly justified, Lei strolled out to her apartment's tiny balcony and scanned the distant horizon through a searing, purposeful glare. So much to do, so little time, she mused.

Never had such a well-worn cliché been so very fitting.

Less than thirty days later, she said goodbye to her aunt and moved from the apartment, placing the majority of her meager belongings into storage.

Armed with a cache of homemade weapons, multiple-degree black- belts and precious little else, she would travel via rented car from city to city, town to town, utilizing only cash and the occasional travelers check. Hotels, boarding houses and bed and breakfast rentals would serve as her temporary 'home addresses', and she placed a strict thirty-day limit on stay durations.

The initial stop would be a Holiday Inn just off the interstate east of Phoenix.

Exactly sixteen months later, while booked in a similar room within the same chain, this time on the outskirts of Butte, Montana, Lei Park's official 'eradication' count matched her age. Sitting alone while lighting the twenty-two candles atop her store-bought birthday cake, she was unable to maintain the steely, ice-veined composure that had become her personal trademark. Her body began to shake and convulse as a torrent of warm tears coated her face and neck. The culprit for such an abrupt, intense outburst had nothing to do with guilt, shame or anything else remotely tied to what she'd began to think of as her 'line of work', but something much simpler. Loneliness blanketed her very soul like a stack of thick winter quilts. She was, after all, only human; tied to the same weaknesses while drawn to the same base desires.

Wiping away the gist of the tears in frustration, she sucked in several deep breathes and reinforced her inner iron will, thus halting what she considered nothing more elaborate than a pathetic session of self-pity.

"No time to play drama queen, woman," she croaked aloud, her voice hoarse with emotion, "waste of time, wasted energy."

After dousing the candle flames with a splash of ice-water, she then unceremoniously tossed the cake into a nearby trash can and spent the remainder of the evening splitting time between executing furious sets of push-ups, arm-raises and crunches with prepping her homemade arsenal.

By the next morning, all thoughts of loneliness had vanished in the wake of a single minded mission, at the core of which lay one simple word: *vengeance*.

# CHAPTER TWO
## Slant

She awoke to the heady smell of disinfectant, forcing herself to swallow several times before being wracked with a violent cough.

Blinking madly, it was as if her eyes were coated in syrup, for nothing tangible fell into focus through a dull, pinkish light.

With great effort, she attempted to raise her arms, though to no apparent avail. Much too groggy for full-blown panic to ensue, she quickly resigned herself to the fact that full-body paralysis was indeed a possibility, whether drug or injury induced.

After an unknown stretch of time, wherein she might or might not have passed out yet again, she became acutely aware of random movement, though haplessly unable to determine exact sources or locations.

"She...ing round et?" a distant voice chimed.

"out...of it...justment...-eight to sixty... hours..." a separate voice replied in Korean, this one a bit clearer and obviously female.

"...her with me. Alone, please....we've got...sensitive matters... discuss...' the first voice, of the husky male variety, commanded in English.

Another lengthy (?) pause ensued as she drifted in and out at random intervals.

"Hello? Anybody in there? Wakey wakey time….."

"Hmmmm? Wha……sssaaaa…uuuuu…" she stammered and spat, coating her chin in frothy salvia. Able to raise her head a few inches from the deeply creased pillow encasing it, she then reached up with badly shaking hands and began vigorously rubbing both eyes.

"Might wanna give your tongue time to catch up with your brain, darlin'. From what I hear, shaking off a couple'a days of 'conscious sedation' is a true bitch."

Allowing her leaden arms to descend, she stared wide-eyed as the figure slowly swam into focus, much like segmented puzzle pieces.

She immediately took notice of the man's gleaming white teeth, temporarily hypnotized by their perfectly squared formation.

"Hiya. We need to talk." "Wha…whooo…w-where…?"

"Whoa, there. One query at a time, sweet cakes."

Her reply turned into a series of garbled gags that lasted a full minute. Meanwhile, the man pushed his chair back with a loud screech and stood, allowing her rapidly clearing vision a full, unblocked view of her surroundings.

"Who…who are…you again?"

"Nope," he nodded negatively, "that's strictly need-to-know type info you ain't yet privy to. Next?"

The man stood in a 'parade rest' pose with his hands tucked securely at the pit of his back while his sizeable, black-booted feet were spaced at least ten to twelve inches apart.

Other than the bed she inhabited and the aforementioned chair, the room was utterly bare save a single light fixture overhead.

Reaching to scratch the tip of her burning, itchy scalp, she again studied the man's comically stoic stance before releasing a muffled giggle. No matter the majority of her mental faculties were still engulfed in a hazy fog; she had no problem whatsoever in identifying the man's fictional alter-ego. While the stocky, muscular frame, close-cropped Marine buzz-cut and five o' clock shadow were stereotypical soldier, it was the presence of the black patch cloaking his left eye that supplied the most vital of clues.

"Uh-huh. Wanna share the joke with the rest of the class?" he asked, his toothy grin wavering just a tad.

"I…my apologies. It's just that…you… re… remind…" she began, only to fall into a fit of uncontrolled cackling that led to yet another coughing jag. It was only then she called attention to the ankle- length white gown she donned; one usually associated with extended stay hospital patients.

"Shit must be a distant kin to laughing gas," the man barked, shaking his head sadly.

"Nick…Nick Fury, *Agent* …of S-*Shield* … I…presume?" she finally said, thin, watery streams gushing from each eye.

Lowering his head in apparent disgust, the man shifted a spit- polished boot from side to side.

"Oh Jeez, never heard *that* one before. Lady, original you ain't.

Didn't know you people were so big into Marvel comics."

"We read them in…grade school…," she said in a raspy whimper, "English class. I was…always partial to… *Captain America*…"

"How very patriotic," he spat sarcastically, folding his thick, muscular arms across an equally toned chest, "so do I assume the stories contained within provided an early influence?"

She tilted her head quizzically. "In…influence?"

"Yeah, you know…maybe that's where the seed was originally planted."

"I…don't…"

The man grabbed the chair and pushed it to the edge of the bed, taking a seat with the chair's back shoved against his chest.

"Aw, don't be purposely obtuse now. I'm talking about the *vigilante* seed, of course. Something sure crawled up your butt, pardon the term. I mean, let's be realistic about this deal. You're a rare bird, sister. Barely twenty-three, five–feet four, one-hundred twenty pounds…tops. Pretty as a picture, if ya don't mind me saying so.

Exotic. Super-Model looks, in my humble opinion. A former college student with above-average intelligence who was placed in 'advanced' course studies by the age of seven. Quite the impressive package, yes sir. Now…," he paused with a frown, squinting at her though his one visible eye.

"….how is it such an individual turns to a life of vigilante justice?" "…Vig…justice? D-don't understand…" she babbled, breaking eye contact as her accent grew increasingly pronounced.

The smile the man revealed was no longer cheery but tight-lipped and grim.

"Forget the 'me no understand' bullshit, lady. I'm runnin' short on time and patience. We've been trailing you for the past four months, starting in central Arizona up until that little escapade in the West Texas heat a few days past. We know what ya are, and what you specialize in. For an amateur, I have to give you due credit. We've tracked your kills all the way back to the spring of eighty-one, but you sure as hell didn't make it easy. Whoever trained ya, to them I give a tip of the cap. On the other hand, if you were *self*-trained..." he pauses, winking playfully, "well, then... you are de-fi-nite-ly one baaaad to the bone som' bitch."

Checking his wrist-watch, the man cursed silently before standing stiffly and headed for a knob-less, metal-framed door to their left.

"Nurses will be in to check on you in a sec. You'll be cleaned-up and fed before the official in-processing begins. We have a meeting set for sixteen hundred hours...approximately three hours from now."

Whirling back around on his left boot heel with shocking grace and fluidity, the man's jaw was set tight; his tone laced with awe, though she was unable to rate the level of sincerity.

"Confidentially, girl, you just gotta divulge some of your combat secrets. I mean, how in the hell does a pipsqueak lil' China Doll like yourself take out brutes like Curtis Willingham with a handful of sharpened bobby-pins, for fucks sake?"

"I...I don't know any William ...Curtis...ham,"

47

she muttered, staring down at her hands as she folded them across her abdomen.

The man she secretly referred to as 'Nick' continued unabated, waiving his hands in the air like a street magician.

"The man weight upwards of three-hundred pounds, and could pull trees up from their roots, woman. Or what about Jeno and Claudia Peters? You remember, that common-law couple outta Reno that was into kidnapping homeless kids off the streets, then raping and beating the hell out of 'em before tossing them onto the ol' barbecue grill?

Found those two fine, upstanding citizens brunt to a crisp inside a roadside dumpster a dozen miles from Vegas a few months back. Coroner report said their faces had been spared the gist of the flames, but that it looked like somebody had ran a cheese grater over 'em.

Goooood shit, dragon lady, ex-*cell*-ent! Have to award you some serious points for all the unconventional weaponry. And yeah, we know all about your martial arts mastery. Impressive as it is, Orientals possessing black belts are a dime a fuckin' dozen, right? I mean, to down such heavyweights on a consistent level without sustaining some serious scars yourself…you must be a *grand-fucking-master* at another art, that being the element of *surprise*."

Peering up gradually, she locked onto the man's deep-set eyes with an intense glare but remained silent, choosing instead simply to nod her head slowly from side to side.

"Okie-doke, lady. You wanna keep playing dumb, be my guest.

We'll see what tune you play once the boss gets his meat hooks into ya. Believe you me, girl, I'm Pope John the second in comparison. Better snap to and get with the program when that man dresses you down."

"Nick?" she asked timidly, raising a hand as if for permission to speak.

"Yeah, wise ass?" he replied cautiously, cocking his head to one side as to receive some vital, top secret information.

"I don't appreciate all the vulgarity, but....I just *love* the patch." "Un-real," he growled, biting his lower lip, "who would ever believe such a charming looker could double as a homicidal maniac with a purse full'a poison-tipped nail files?

Oh, and just for the record, lady, I consider you a ruthless, sadistic fuck. You'd do well to alter my opinion while you've got the chance.

You see....I'm gonna be the only back-up you got in this deal. Kayo (*English translation*: goodbye)."

The man performed a half-hearted 'about face' as Lei's head collapsed back onto the pillow.

Practically hyperventilating, she heard the sound of a faint buzzer before glancing back up to see she was indeed alone.

Moments later, as her breathing somewhat normalized, she raised her right hand to her face and literally willed it to stop shaking.

By the time a female nurse entered the room some five minutes later, accompanied by an armed guard whose uniform she instantly recognized as that worn by the South Korean army, Lei's calm, stone-faced demeanor was a perfect match for her inner resolve.

***

"Miss Park, there is no question of your guilt. Please don't waste my time with any tearful denials. We have over two dozen documented homicide cases in seven different states. Young lady, you'd be standing trail for five calendar years before your official sentences even begin. Thus, you either drop the innocent act or I'll have your murdering ass transported on the next available hop back to West Texas."

"Fine," Lei sighed indifferently, "then what exactly am I doing here?

Wherever, in fact, *here* is…"

Sporting a dark blue navy suit and wire-rimmed glasses, the grim, gray-haired man began flipping through a thick manila folder with thin, skeletal fingers. Following 'Nick Fury's' departure, Lei had been given a series of shots via a trio of loaded syringes, then escorted down a narrow, darkened hall to a community-type bathroom, where she was allowed to brush her teeth and shower before being given a gray, pocket-less jumpsuit to wear. She was then led back to her room, where the bed linen had been changed and a food tray left at its center. She ate sparingly, but did manage to choke down the majority of a tall glass of chilled orange juice. Several minutes later, she was again escorted down the hall, this time to a larger room containing a lengthy conference table with matching chairs and a classroom-style chalkboard.

"Your present location will be divulged soon

enough," the man replied curtly, "fact is, you might find it a rather pleasant surprise. Then again…perhaps not.

As for your presence here, that, as they say, is quite the complex tale. Get comfortable, Miss Park. This is going to take a while."

Hugging herself from an inexplicable chill, Lei glanced to the older man's left to 'Nick Fury', whose probing, emotionless glare seemed to scan her like a pricy slab of raw meat hanging from a meat-hook.

"Like the man said, Lei-baby, just open your ears and keep the trap door closed 'til otherwise notified, got it?"

"What can I say," she replied with a sour smirk, "I'm utterly enthralled."

'Nick' laughed aloud, causing Lei to cringe back as if he'd reached over to slap her.

"Told ya she was a pistol, sir. Not exactly what one would expect from such a highly skilled, cold-hearted terminator, huh?"

"Actually, such a flippant attitude might well be a major component in her arsenal," the older man replied without looking up from whatever piece of correspondence had captured his attention.

"Good point, sir. A bon-a-fide enigma, this one."

The room was eerily quiet, as if it were located in some underground cavern and constructed in thick, sound-proof walls. To Lei, even the slightest sound, as whenever the man turned to a new page, was akin to small arms fire.

"Okay, I believe I have the gist," he said, sighing heavily and closing the folder with a

51

resounding slap, again causing Lei to openly flinch.

Leaning back with his hands at the back of his thickly muscled, almost non-existent neck, 'Nick' was unable to hide his amusement.

"Jumpy…juuumm-py. Where are those legendary 'nerves of steel'? I 'm beginning to think we got us an imposter here, sir."

The older man removed his glasses before propping his elbows atop the table.

"If so, we'll know soon enough, won't we?"

"You got that right, sir. Ain't no room for cowards in this here chicken-shit outfit."

Feeling a rush of dizziness, Lei lowered her head and dozed, only to be snapped to attention by the booming sound of a closed fist slamming the tabletop.

"Up and Adam, Killer. Nap-times over," she heard 'Nick' spout with malevolent glee.

Forced to re-focus her still-shaky eyesight, Lei looked from one man to the other several times.

"Who *are* you people?"

The older man coughed into his hand before clearing his throat noisily, as if prepping for a lengthy seminar.

"Who we are, Miss Parks, isn't nearly as important as what we're trying to accomplish. Please listen carefully, as I've only time to provide a single in-brief.

"We have a situation, Miss Parks. A situation that we're hoping you can help us rectify. Once I've provided the details, you've but a single question to answer before we go into any further specifics. Depending on your answer, we'll either proceed or no longer waste our time on you."

"What are you tal-.." she began, only to be cut off in mid-word as 'Nick' had thrust the forefinger and pinkie of his right hand into the corners of his mouth and released a shrill, piercing whistle.

"Shut the hell up, woman, and listen to the man. The question and answer period will follow."

"(IN KOREAN) Asshole," she mumbled angrily, rolling her eyes in disgust.

Re-opening the folder, the older man began his spiel while retrieving what resembled a photo pack that had been tightly sealed and rubber- banded.

"Miss Park, we have a situation that requires someone with your...apparent skills. There have been a series of rather grisly homicides perpetrated, and all conventional methods of investigating have been thoroughly exhausted. The first of these..." he paused, removing the bands and black-plastic wrap from the packet, then tossing over a series of four by six inch glossy photographs, "...occurred just over five months ago. Those are the crime-scene photos for case one."

Holding the first of the pictures less than three inches from the tip of her nose, Lei was forced to blink several times to alleviate the bleariness.

Once the image cleared, she found herself twisting the photo at several varied angles just to properly define the content.

As the puzzle pieces fell gradually into place, there was an audible hitch in her throat. She swallowed hard before studying the two additional pictures in a similar fashion.

"As you can see, damage done to the facial area

53

of the victim was rather extensive. In two of the four cases we'll discuss, proper identification was by fingerprint. The other two by tooth imprint."

Lei coughed into her hand as warm, salty bile filled her throat.

Moments later, a separate trio of photos were slid her way.

"The corpse of victim two was discovered twenty-four days later. As you can see, it's fairly obvious the MO's match almost to a tee.

Mutilation patterns are mirror images."

"Almost looks like ... some kind of animal attack."

"At first glance, perhaps, and there were indeed bite marks present, though this assumption was quickly dismissed due to the ... urban setting of the crimes and the obvious lack of wildlife capable of inflicting such carnage. Here then, are stills of the third crime scene, taken seven weeks and a day after the second. Similarities abound."

Glancing only briefly at the first of still another grisly trio of shots, Lei again felt her gorge rise, looking away as her breathing became harsh and labored.

Leaning her head back and closing her eyes, she felt the latest wave of nausea subside only a notch. Bowing her head once again while reaching up to massage the back of her sweat-moistened neck, she became aware of a series of snickering, sarcasm-laced giggles permeate from 'Nick's' general area.

"Now how can someone whose chosen profession is butchering their fellow man possibly own such a weak stomach? Pathetic, lady. Either that, or its one hell of an act. An act I ain't buying. Not for a New York Fucking minute."

Gulping down still another build-up of stomach acid, Lei started to respond in a profanity-laced tirade before being cut off by the older man's mechanical, ever-casual rhetoric.

"Victim three's remains were found in a rice paddy less than fifty yards from her place of residence. Again, same MO… to the letter, seventeen days following incident number two."

"Did…did you say…rice paddy?" she asked, facing forward wearing a pained grimace.

"Patience, Miss Park. In due time. I have files on two other such murders, the last of which took place nine days ago. As you have probably noticed, the frequency of the kills is increasing at a rather alarming pace. We are, in fact, expecting another such incident within the next forty-eight to seventy-two hours. Obviously, Miss Parks, we hope to nip this pattern squarely in the bud."

A momentary pause ensued, wherein Lei's warped frown slowly melted into a fatigue-laden smirk.

"I'm…I'm sure you do. Good luck with that. I wish you nothing but the best.

"Now, will one of you storm-trooping assholes tell me *where* I am and why?"

"Well, Miss Parks…" the older man began, having already cut off 'Nick's' predictably excitable response with a simple nod, "First off, I can tell you where you're *not*. You're not in a holding cell awaiting extradition to one of the numerous states waiting to charge you with first degree murder. If I were you, I'd view this as a definite positive.

As for your usefulness in this particular situation, do you truly require an answer?"

Lei paused an additional moment before sticking her arms straight out with the palms facing up.

"Would you please stop talking in riddles? Am I to be…studied…*dissected*…or what?"

"Damn, you're thick as a proverbial brick," Nick spat sourly, continuing only when the older man didn't intervene.

"We can't nail down a suspect, Einstein. Physical evidence has been sorely lacking. Whatever slim leads that were established are presently exhausted all to hell and back. Enter little Miss Vigilante, who has demonstrated the phenomenal ability to both track down and exterminate some of the vilest scum roaming free within the borders of the good ol' US of A. Nobody knows how you do it, lady. You got eggheads from three noted law enforcement agencies as well as a handful of the country's most respected universities scratching their collective noggins in complete confusion. As far as we can tell, you haven't eliminated a single innocent along the way. Now, we ain't that concerned, at least right now, on the *how* part. We just want ya to ply those magical skills of yours to this particular fucking nightmare we've recently encountered. It's kinda simple to figure out, really, even for a 'storm-trooping' jackass like myself," he cackled with a pronounced wink of his lone visible eye, "The perp's out there, more than likely residing within or nearby the twelve mile radius where all the killings have taken place. You play the dual role of both tracker and bait. You flush, and/or *detect* the murdering fuck with that homemade radar of yours; we step in and seal the deal. How's that for the Reader's Digest version?"

"I'm...*bait*, then?" she asked, her complexion having grown eerily pale despite the natural yellow tint of her skin.

"Hey," Nick concluded with his arms spread wide, "look at it this way; it's a part you've definitely perfected over the years."

"What if I refuse?" she asked with a wicked sneer, the extreme slant of her eyes practically thread-thin.

"Not a problem, Miss Park. You'll then be re-sedated and handed over to the proper authorities," the older man stated matter-of-factly, peering over the top edge of his glasses as 'Nick' silently nodded beside him.

"Completely up to you. We're not about to force you into anything.

Actually, we are the ones taking the chance here. From an ethical standpoint, this could turn out to be the worst kind of nightmare. After all, you might well turn out to be utterly useless to the overall objective, even counterproductive."

After several tense moments, Lei fell back in the chair, clamping her eyes shut as her shoulders visibly slumped.

"That's....what we *thought* you'd say," 'Nick' chortled, reaching over and retrieving the folder and quickly flipping to a desired spot.

"Welcome to the team, sport."

"Okay, if I….if we do capture the responsible party, what then? Am I handed over to law enforcement like so much bagged trash?" she asked, nervously tapping her lengthy, perfectly manicured fingernails atop the slick tabletop.

The older man paused before clearing his throat.

"Miss Park, if you are in any way instrumental in helping capture said suspect, we've been given the power to grant you a full pardon. There will be conditions of course, the details of which are as of yet unclear."

"By the way, Miss Lei, if you don't mind my asking," he continued, cocking an eyebrow, "your accent isn't at all pronounced, and your dossier states you didn't arrive in the U.S. until the age of seventeen."

"I had tutors in Korea and when I got to the states. Tutors who were very well compensated to eliminate my accent."

"Well," 'Nick' said with mock cheer, "mystery solved, then. On to the task at hand…"

Lei bit her lower lip while gazing past the man's amazingly squared head to a butterfly shaped water stain on a far wall.

"Ho-kay, then. Here's the initial portion of our itinerary. No need to memorize it. This is just for protocol's sake, you understand.

For the sake of this mission, your codename will be 'Slant'.

I'll be your one and only official contact. My codename is 'Cyclops'."

Lei couldn't help but grunt in amusement. .

"Glad to see your sense of humor is back in

58

working order.

The mission itself has been deemed 'Operation *'Ville Ripper.'* Hokey I know, but damned fitting in this case. Mission completion will be determined *only* by the capture of a viable suspect or suspects who are duly tried and convicted of these specific homicides. "til then, *Dragon Lady...*" he concluded with a wink and nod, "... your pretty little ass is allllll ours."

Closing the folder and tucking it snugly beneath one arm, 'Nick' exchanged a brief glance with the older man before both pushed back their chairs and arose with remarkable precision.

"As for your present location, Codename *Slant*," the older man said, walking around the table and swinging his right arm around in a 'come with me' gesture, "if you'll be so kind to follow us, please."

The trio departed the makeshift conference room in single file with the older man on point and Lei between them.

After covering less than a dozen feet down a dimly lit hall, they turned left onto a stone-step stairwell and proceeded to ascend two additional floors.

While trudging up the moistened concrete, Lei had detected the faint odor of stale urine. In scanning the faded paint, cracked stone and rotten patches of wood within the structure, she could only imagine the varied species of vermin that called it home.

"In here, please," the older man said, opening a door to their right just as they'd cleared the stairwell exit.

It was obviously the top floor of the building, each wall lined with colossal, curtain-less picture windows in the old 'warehouse' style.

Temporarily blinded by the influx of daylight, Lei shielded her squinting eyes until they'd halted at the center of the room.

After an additional moment of stilted silence, she dropped her blocking hand and regarded each man with a questionable glare.

"Okay, now what? Is this when I meet '*Deep Throat*'?" she scoffed, wiping a fresh build-up of sweat from her brow.

"Not quite, smart-ass. Walk over and take a peek out the window," 'Nick' replied, pointing to their right.

Lei took a step in that direction, then hesitated, the hospital gown she wore sticking to her damp skin like Velcro.

She looked over at the older man, who nodded politely. "Go on, Miss Park. There are no booby-traps to fear."

Dragging herself forward, she could feel precious energy ebb away with each half-step.

Gripping the window seal as she leaned forward to peer through the window's wide metal bars, Lei instantly locked on a large wooden billboard erected just across the street near a similarly constructed warehouse building.

From there, she spotted a series of dilapidated shanties that appeared long-abandoned, followed by a half-block of similarly decaying storefronts, complete with tattered cardboard and paper signs which announced some ancient sale or years old daily ' *special*'. As with the billboard, the writings of each held one very distinct similarity.

"Where the-? Is…is this *Korea* town? San Francisco maybe…no, no, it's LA, right? "

"Try a little farther west, Slant," the man known only to her as 'Cyclops' blurted, "a whoooooole lot farther, as in eight or nine thousand miles."

Still gripping the window seal for support, Lei whirled about in a gradual spin that, despite its relatively slow execution, nonetheless triggered a brief dizzy spell.

"You mean…I'm….we're…oh…...oh god…" Cyclops took a bow.

"Welcome back to the homeland, baby girl."

Lei's next words, spoken in her native tongue and released in a hissed whisper through tightly gritted teeth, formed a tapestry of creative, over-the-top profanity that would've made any veteran sailor blush from embarrassment.

***

*From a physical standpoint, his sleep is fitful, uneasy He tosses, turns, twists, groaning aloud, though still manages to keep one at least one foot planted deeply within the mysterious, mystical realm of deep rim sleep. If awoken, he would surely rise if for no other reason than to seek out a form of pain relief, but it in pill or liquid form. As it is, the unyielding gatekeeper of his dreams strictly prohibits escape from the domain he presently inhabits. Reality, it seems, will have to wait. As for now, the alternate universe that is the subconscious mind has secured the lock and double bolted it for good measure.*

*** 

## THE FOLLOWING DAY 0900 HOURS

"Feeling your oats today, Missy?"

"Up yours, one eye," came the sardonic reply, followed by a low, horse giggle.

"Well, you are feeling better. Nothin' like a shot of B-12, ten hours of shuteye and a good breakfast to kick jet lag right in the kisser, is there? What say let's get started on the second and easily most vital part of your in-brief?"

Lei groaned, itching like mad at the armpits and groin from the black and red shaded skin-tight spandex body suit she'd been instructed to don upon awakening.

Sauntering up with one hand gripping his crotch through camouflaged combat pants, 'Cyclops' smarmy expression was one of pure, unadulterated lust. Though they inhabited the same conference room as the previous day, one significant alteration had been made; the addition of a wooden podium similar to what one would see in a school classroom or church. Additionally, the words 'Dancer' and 'Yobo' had been scribbled onto the aforementioned chalk board in looping, oversized letters.

"Ah, nothing like the unbridled enthusiasm of a new student to get me nice 'n hard. Hope you ain't easily offended, 'cause this man's the polar opposite of politically correct. In fact, how's about a blow-job while I'm on the subject? I mean, be a damn same to waste such a fine pair of pouting lips. Do a good job and I can guarantee you'll be teacher's pet."

"(IN KOREAN) Sick son of a bitch."

"Let you in on a little secret if ya promise not to tell. I tried to get 'em to shave your snatch when they had ya sedated. Just a personal preference of mine. Ahh, there's truly nothing finer than shaved Asian pussy."

"(IN KOREAN) Up yours, dick-head." "Extra credit if you swallow."

"(IN KOREAN) Go *fuck* yourself."

Backing away and folding both arms across his chest, 'Cyclops' cocked his head playfully to one side.

"Ya know, I've always pondered that particular insult. Don't really think it's physically possible. Another thing, what exactly is a *dick- head*? I mean, ain't that kinda redundant?"

"Big deal. You speak the language."

"(IN KOREAN) Fluently, my dear."

"(IN ENGLISH) Prerequisite for the job, I'd think."

"(IN ENGLISH) So very astute, my young grass-hopper. Darn if you aren't the sour puss this lovely morning. Hell's belles, woman. What *more* do you want? Here you are back in the country of your birth; safe, snug and secured from all those nasty law enforcement types that wouldn't hesitate to lock your pretty little caboose up and toss away the passkey. I mean, *shit*, we assigned you the best, least roach-infested room in the building. We fed you; bathed ya; filled your gut with vitamins. We even provided those hip new duds, which I gotta confess I find ex-treme-ly sexy on that tightly wound bod of yours. I ask you, what is there to complain about?"

Shoving her chair back with a loud screech, Lei stood with both fists clinched tightly at her sides, her face contorted in anger as her shoulders visibly trembled.

"Listen, you goddamn jackass....I get it, okay? I'm trapped....blackmailed... *ensnared*. I have no choice but deal with whatever horseshit you shovel my way. Now, can you *please*.... spare me your lame attempts at humor and the constant fucking baiting and just get ON with it? SHIT!"

With a loud sigh, 'Cyclops' shook his head from side to side before lowering his chin to his chest. When it arose, it was as if he'd literally morphed into a different person, the animation having completely left his face, replaced by a stoic glare that was almost comically dead pan.

"Bout *damn* time I saw some attitude,' he growled, reaching up to 'flick' his eye-patch before strolling over to the chalk board, 'gonna have to tone that Americanized vocabulary down a bit, though.

Dummy-up, so to speak. Alright then, let's begin...."

Over the next hour and ten minutes, Lei sat both motion and expressionless as her erstwhile partner broke down the impending mission in a stiff, robotic monologue, repeating several segments of the narrative in triplicate.

The gist was simple enough. Her new 'employer', or perhaps more fitting, 'permanent parole officers' were a special UN task force dealing in what were labeled 'extreme' cases of homicide that might well affect international relations. In this particular situation, four citizens killed in gruesomely sadistic fashion near an American military instillation.

Four murders in almost as many months, all within the same general vicinity; an area deemed '*GI Central*', located just three miles south of SunJon Air Force Base in a part of town officially known as the JunWon Villa, thus the unknown suspect(s) codename of '*The 'Ville Ripper'*.

The base had been constructed in the middle fifties, and served as but one of three major Air Force bases on the peninsula. Lei, had of course, heard of the base. It wasn't quite as large as Osan Air Base, while not quite as small as Kunsan. Naturally, where there was a base…there were G.I's. G.I's with a thirst for alcohol…in mass quantities. Lonely G.I's, thousands of miles from home. Horny G.I's, with a lust to blow off steam via the exotic charms of the local female establishment. Through these many elements were birthed U.S. Government backed 'townships' such as 'G.I Central'. Osan Air Base had its legendary '*strip*'. Kunsan Air Base had the even more infamous '*A-To*wn'. For the one-thousand or so American troops stationed at SunJon, '*G.I. Central,* or more popularly referred to simply as '*The Ville*', filled the bill.

A sixteen square mile maze of bars, bars masquerading as eateries, clothing shops and one to two room '*hooch's*' that were the equivalent to a four to five hundred square foot apartment, The Ville was a single troop's (or those many 'married but cheating' types) oasis away from the base, the single place he or she (for those female troops with a

65

similar penchant for heavy partying) could escape the long hours and constant 'war games', not to mention the very-real threat of eminent warfare between the North and South. Plainly put, the entire 'town' was built with two distinct acts in mind; inebriation and sexual deviancy. In other words; get drunk....get laid, not particularly in that order. As one Wing Commander had recently put it when grilled about the 'morale aspect' of such a place's existence: *anything for the troops'*.

The four aforementioned victims, all of whom had plied their trade as exotic dancers within the Ville, had resided within a three mile radius of each other, though it had yet to be determined if they'd actually known each other on a personal level. Thus far, no other link between the four had been established. Following the latest murder, it was decided that a more unorthodox, borderline reckless investigative method might well be in order. In discussing the case during a multi- agency teleconference, a high-level CIA official was the first to suggest that a 'wildcard' be brought into the mix. He'd recently became aware of a female vigilante of Asian nationality that his people were fast closing in on in the West Texas area. A vigilante whose unusual talent for tracking and eradicating human predators was as eerie as it was impressive.

Thus, once she was successfully 'bagged and tagged' (a term 'Nick' had used with great glee), a time-table of three to five days had been set to initiate the latest undercover operation.

Handing her a blue folder, 'Nick' instructed her (with a lesser dose of his usual sardonic wit) to spend the rest of the afternoon and night memorizing each and every syllable contained within. The next forty- eight hours would be dedicated to getting over her jet-lag while simultaneously 'getting into character' for the role ahead. Inside the folder lay her new identity, to include a wholly fabricated past and certain personality traits that would be uniquely her own. There was also a detailed map of G.I. Central, a large red circle drawn around her new digs serving as a reference point. As the seminar had drawn to a close, she'd calmly queried her lone contact concerning the availability of weapons 'in case things got hairy'.

"If things do indeed get hairy, Darlin'," Nick had replied straight- faced, "I'm afraid you're in for the grand-daddy of all Brazilian waxes.

Besides, from what I've seen, all you'd require is a ball-point pen and a pill bottle to wipe out a whole damn armed division single handed, misses McGyver. Seriously..." he'd concluded with a shake of his squared head, "handing you a loaded weapon of *any* type was the one argument we couldn't win with the big boys. This ain't Detroit or the Big Apple. Don't think you can walk down any street corner alley and find a pop-shooter. If fact, if you're caught trying, the mission is immediately aborted and your butt-cheeks and mine are officially hanging from a very cramped sling."

"But...what if...." she'd pleaded, her voice still noticeably ragged from fatigue.

"Not so much as a *butter knife*, sweetie. Sorry."

He then escorted her to her assigned room, where an armed man wearing combat fatigues

67

conspicuously void of insignia stood guard.

"Learn it. Live it. *Love* it," Nick quipped before departure, "better buck up and gird your loins, girl. You'll be entering a whole new world soon. I'm talking an alien landscape that would make 'ET' stain his drawers. You're gonna have to learn to adapt on the run…or should I say…on the *stage*. Not to worry, though…we'll be play acting together. The new Redford and Streisand, no less."

"For now, sleep well and I'll see ya dark and early."

As was the daily ritual, meals were provided at exactly noon and six PM, with no human contact in-between.

Lei divided her time between naps and studying the contents of the folder, still not quite able to shake the feeling that the entire scenario was all some sort of hallucinatory dream sequence born from a severe concussion.

In reaching over to pinch herself for at least the tenth time that very day, she was once again forced to begrudgingly dismiss such a wishful theory in lieu of the stinging sensation such an action produced.

\*\*\*

Around the age of eight or nine, mere months before her first 'encounter' of the sexual predator variety, Lei had been given a small part in a school play. Some sixteen years later, she could still vividly recall the severe case of 'stage fright' that had gripped her very soul like a pair of steely appendages, reducing her to a simpering infant that was essentially dragged from the stage by her grammar school teacher.

In reading over the typed notes that contained her newly assigned 'identity', she couldn't help but ponder if her drama skills might still be as pathetic. Certainly she had perfected the art of deception in terms of situational improvisation, having played numerous roles while baiting marked targets. Then again, playing a 'scripted role' was a new species of animal altogether, especially the definitive 'fish out of water' character currently at task. Regardless, she had less than two days to literally become another person, and not just for a few minutes to a half hour, which was normally as far as she'd been forced to stretch from an acting standpoint.

The personnel file, broken down in numerical order, read as follows:

**NAME**: Sukie Hui Kim

**AGE:** Twenty-one (*twenty-two* Korean years, wherein the nine months spent in the womb is counted as a full calendar year)

**Date of Birth**: Feb 11th, nineteen sixty-three.

**Place of Birth**: Pusan (the lone tidbit that wasn't fictionalized, due to regional accent)

**Occupation**: Newly hired Exotic Dancer, A.K.A, *'bar girl'* in G.I slang. **NOTE**: Dancers within G.I Central are not authorized 'topless' status, but wear custom-made two-piece costumes (provided by club owner); usually halter tops, thongs, and high-heeled shoes.

**Last Employed**: Danced in Pusan clubs near Naval Base. Before that, worked manual labor in factory setting (also Pusan). Factory salary was the

American equivalent of just under a dollar an hour (approximately eighty-nine cents).

**Current Employer**: The *'YELLOW FEVER'* club, one of seventeen such bars contained within The Ville. Club owner, *Chow Yun Jung*, has no idea of cover, nor do the other nine club employees, to include four other dancers and two female 'hostesses'. The 'Yellow Fever' is a relatively new kid on the 'bar' block, having opened its doors less than six months prior. The bar had previously been known as the *'Phoenix'* club, but poor business had led to its doors closing in late summer of nineteen eighty-three.

Unlike the 'Phoenix', with its disco flavored music, checkered dance floor and floating disco balls, the *'Yellow Fever'* has gained recent notoriety as the Ville's lone 'upscale' club, catering mostly to officers (mostly Captains to full-bird Colonels, with the occasional one or two star General) and visiting dignitaries. With this in mind, drink prices are elevated to double or triple what one would find in the other bars, and a 'cover charge' of ten dollars (roughly eight-thousand, six hundred Korean *Won*) is mandatory for entry. It employs a full-time DJ who plays a request-powered mix of top forty pop, country and classic rock tunes, the walls dominated by rock-star/celebrity posters and globe-shaped strobe lights.

Other notable clubs within the Ville's perimeter include (listed from top to bottom in order of popularity, as in 'most frequented'):

The *'Pacific Coast'* – Largest dance floor of all clubs; disco/pop oriented music. DJ on

Friday/Saturday nights only. Boasts seven rotating dancers, most of which were 'heavily recruited' from Korean- only bars in Seoul.

'*Head East*'– Heavy metal themed music. No DJ' s or dancers. The closest thing to a 'biker bar' within the perimeter. Town Patrol (roving pairs of on-duty Security Policemen) perform 'extra duty' on weekend nights just to quell the many skirmishes *slash* brawls that occur on a semi-regular basis.

'*Rising Tide*' – Pop/country mix with occasional DJ. Largest bar in terms of square footage. Employs four dancers (two on weekdays).

'*Western Edge*' – Country/Western only. Large dance floor. Employs three dancers (Friday-Saturday night only). Legendary as the 'rowdiest' of all the clubs, surpassing even the 'Head East', drunken brawls are not at all unusual, especially among the many TDY (temporary duty) troops who visit the base on weekends.

'*Blue Moon Junction*' – Pop/light rock, it is the only 'multi-level' club within the perimeter. Employs four dancers. Offers outdoor grille and balcony bar. Popular for its 'casual' atmosphere.

'*Paradise Cove*' – Light pop/country/disco mix. Employs no dancers, DJ on weekends only. Also a full blown restaurant offering both Korean and American dishes, it contains a large outdoor eatery. Widely known as the 'safest' of all clubs for married personnel (those of the 'faithful' minority) to congregate.

There were a handful of other clubs listed with such names as '*Wall- Bangers*', '*Serenity*', and '*Club Now*', all listed under the sub-heading 'dives'.

While casually sipping a cool glass of *Kin*, a Korean soda that looked and tasted suspiciously like Seven-Up, Lei studied the G.I. Central map with an expression of comical dismay. It was truly like trying to decipher some ancient treasure-map. The main road leading to and from the base (the main gate was less than four miles away) was a narrow two-lane listed as 'Route 110'. According to her notes, a bus line known amongst the troops as the '*G.I Track*' picked up and dropped off several times per day, with marked frequency on weekends. Also, there were two separate cab companies that possessed permanent base entry status, as well as a half-dozen such companies that served from outside the main gate area.

Taking a left from the bases main gate onto route 110, one would cover the four mile distance in scenic splendor before viewing a large metallic overhang reading '*GI Town*' in bold, black lettering that greeted all visitors upon entry. Once inside, the buses and multitude of cabs utilized a centralized drop and pick-up point at the center of a wide, paved lot. At least two dozen narrow road and passageways led into the heart of the club scene and past a series of clothing and discount stores that sold the local wares to eager airmen and airwomen looking for a cheap trinket.

Following a series of similar pathways, one could find as many as two or three clubs per street, accented by the occasional restaurant or retail shop. Behind the clubs, a series of weaving, zigzagging walkways led to a virtual bee-hive's worth of minuscule living quarters known popularity amongst

72

the locals as 'hooch's'. Squinting as if studying a rare microbe beneath a microscope's lens, Lei counted at least sixteen distinctly marked living quarters all within the same quarter-mile radius. Of course, she'd seen similar housing areas in and around Pusan, homes stacked upon homes like so much cordwood, but never so outlandishly cramped. Obviously residing in and traveling about America the past seven years had warped her view of her homeland's sometimes serious lack of living space.

Her own future abode was located several miles past the '*Swarm*' club on the Ville's east side, down a trio of winding pathways and into a makeshift cul-de-sac consisting of five such residences.

On a separate typed sheet, entitled 'QUIRKS and TRAITS', Lei was first offered keen insight on the individual she was to portray from a personality standpoint. Such terms as 'inherently stubborn (a trademark of her people as a whole)', 'standoffish', and 'a classic tease' were used to describe Miss Kim, who was also a 'loner' by nature who could claim few close friends in the span of her short life.

Reading further, she noted a second individual listed as '*Yobo* (Korean for 'husband' or 'boyfriend'). Details were sketchy but included:

**NAME:** Charles Whitt

**AGE:** Thirty to thirty-five

**RACE**: Caucasian

**MILITARY RANK**: 1st Lieutenant (Pay grade O-2 - Air Force)

**HAIR**: Brown, cut in 'buzz-cut' style

**EYES:** Blue

**DURATION OF RELATIONSHIP**: Three

73

months.

**CIRCUMSTANCES OF INITIAL MEETING**: Met as a result of her employment in Pusan club "*Ecstasy*" (fictional club; went 'out of business' two months earlier). Charles was TDY for training at Naval station; was then given permanent PCS orders to SunJon Air Base.

Sukie followed soon after, gained employment at the '*Yellow Fever*', where they secured a residence together in G.I Central.

"So, I got myself a Yobo. Club dancer with a live-in; stubborn as a mule and a tease to boot," she groaned between barely suppressed giggles, "Lord, this just keeps getting weirder and wilder by the minute."

The giggles soon turned to guffaws; rib-aching, full-blown banshee howls that forced her to her knees even as her eyes welled up with fresh tears.

Before she'd mercifully fallen fast asleep atop the carpeted floor, curled up in the classic fetal position, the laughter had long given way to retching sobs of misery. The following morning, Lei Parks, former student of advanced studies and vigilante killer, officially went missing; replaced by a reckless, rather hard-headed young club dancer named Sukie Kim with the Top Secret codename of '*Slant*'. As days and weeks would progress, it became increasingly difficult to tell apart what had been two distinct entities now merged so expertly into one.

# CHAPTER THREE
## Re-adaptation

"Why, top of the mornin' to ya, Miss Kim. May I offer you some coffee or tea just to help pull those pretty little slanted eyes a bit wider?"

"Had my fill, Left-tenant Whitt, but so kind of you to ask."

"(IN KOREAN) My, but you're a young one, aren't you? What, pray tell, is your date of birth?"

"(IN KOREAN) I was born on February eleven, nineteen sixty-three." "(CONTINUES IN KOREAN) Your accent sounds vaguely familiar, Miss Kim. Might I inquire from where is it you hail?"

"You certainly may, Lieutenant Whitt. Pusan City, born and raised." "Hope you don't mind all these personal inquiries. What's your occupation?"

"I currently work as a dancer in one of the local clubs." "And before that?"

"The same, though not locally." "City…name of club?"

"Pusan City. The *Ecstasy.*"

"Have you ever held a different position?"

"Did some factory work. The pay was for shit. I was living on Rameon noodles and rice cakes."

"So you gave all that up to become a combination stripper/whore for hire?"

"Not at all, Mister Whitt. I'm a highly skilled exotic dancer. An…entertainer. I provide a vital service to the community, especially geared towards our American allies."

"Uh-huh, so what's the going rate for a quality BJ these days? Ten bucks?"

"Afraid I wouldn't know. I'm…currently involved with someone." "Married?"

"No, but I do have a live-in Yobo." "American?"

"Yes."

"An Airman, I presume…" "Yes, a first lieutenant."

"Refresh my memory…what's their pay grade again?" "Oh-two."

"How's you two meet? Again, hope I'm not prying…"

"Not at all. We met at the club where I danced. He was serving TDY at the naval station in Pusan."

"Think he'll marry you and take you away from all this? You know, to the land of gold-paved streets and cash growing on trees?"

"I…I'd like very much to live in the states, but…we haven't really talked about it."

"Ever think about getting pregnant? Happens allllll the time in these parts, I hear. An 'oldie but a goodie'. That'll sure gum up the works. You'll have him by the short hairs then, won't ya?"

"I…don't think I'm ready for.."

"So you're just gonna keep letting him pound that tight little cooze for free?"

"Well, we have a good relation-.."

"Cheap bastard won't even pay off your bill at the club?"

"I…we need the money….and besides, I…I like my jo-.."

"He doesn't mind other men ogling his lover's

76

ass? Drooling over her perky little tits?"

"We have a...an understanding...there's no jealous -..."

"He ever let ya...make a little extra cash on the side...hmmmm? Maybe pull a train or two? Fess up, girl, you enjoy that big North American cock, don'cha?"

Breaking eye contact for the first time since the session commenced, Lei whirled about on one high heel with a hand clasped over her mouth.

"(IN ENGLISH) Crying? Are you actually cry...?" 'Nick' started to ask before a series of girlish giggles cut him off.

"Oh, so it's *funny*, is it? Damn it, woman, this ain't no comedy club. I can already see we have some serious issues ahead."

Turning back around, Lei slowly removed her hand while visibly fighting off a fresh wave of hysteria.

"I'm...I can't help it. I feel...it's like I'm on the set of a porno movie. A really, really bad porno movie. By the way, what's a... *train*? I mean, I know what a locomotive is, but in perverse terms, you completely lost me."

Donned in a tight green tee shirt that accentuated the muscular bulkinessof both his arms and pecs, her erstwhile partner studied her for a moment before dropping his head and growling in apparent exasperation.

"Tell me something, lady, are you...perchance, a virgin?"

"What?" she replied, all traces of humor having vanished from both her tone and facial expression.

"Simple question. Are….you….a…virgin? Ever play hide the sausage?"

Working her jaw muscles in obvious anger, Lei reached up to adjust the tight-fitting halter crushing her bosoms.

"Is the hymen still intact? Have you taken the tube steak? Been properly Rotor- Rootered? You know…*boned*…humped…penetrated by the muscle of love? Has anyone ever lain the fleshy pipe into your moistened pooter-pie?"

"What the fuck business is it of yours, Snake Plisken?" she finally barked back, lurching shakily forward and almost slipping on the slick tiled flooring.

"Ahhh, that's my girl…take dirty to me…"

"What's my sex life got to do with this mission, one-eye?"

"(IN KOREAN) Speak the native tongue, damn it. I can tell you're sadly outta practice. That accent is part Pusan, part California *Valley- Girl*. As for your question, I'm just concerned, that's all. It's just that, with all that school-girl giggling whenever a 'dirty ' word was said, I couldn't help but wonder how much experience you've had…you know… up close and personal. I mean, just cause you killed pervs for a living don't mean you ever did the deed yourself, and I'd just like to know what I'm working with here. Might need to start this training with a little sex education training instead…"

Leaning forward with her high-gloss nails perched atop the conference table that separated them, Lei's arms and shoulders visible tensed, revealing a taunt, muscular build.

78

"(IN KOREAN) Let's just on with this, pinhead. I *understand* the role. All this psycho-analysis BS is a waste of what I've been told is *precious* time. I already know how these girls are viewed by both Korean society and the troops they service. Hookers, whores, doped- up sluts, some still possessing the stereotypical 'heart of gold.' Most came from broken homes. Misfits from day one, estranged from their families. The majority are just looking for a fresh start, hoping for a free ride to the good ol' US of A, courtesy the first Airman that's willing to foot the bill. Did I miss something there, Plisken? If so, please feel free to enlighten my ignorance…"

"You know," he replied, stepping forward and leaning over the table until their foreheads sat less than six inches apart, "you're beautiful when I'm angry."

"What's the point of all this, Charlie? You don't mind me calling you *Charlie*, do you? I mean, I surely don't mean to breach any strict codes of conduct."

He backed away with a sigh, crossing his arms and staring into the brightly lit fluorescent lighting above.

"The point is, honey-pot, that you're gonna hear a lot of similar shit once you hit that stage every night. Not only that, depending on their level of drunkenness, those boys are gonna be pawing at those butt- cheeks and pinching those nipples at every opportunity. Most of the clientele that frequent the 'Yellow Fever' ain't your stereotypical horny airmen, they're high-level brass and rich Korean

79

businessmen who have a penchant for getting what they want, including copping a feel when the notion hits 'em. You're gonna have to develop a thick skin. There won't be no poppin' out their eyes with a sharpened heel or decapitations with a filed-off tampon. You're gonna have to deal with it. Service with a smile, so to speak. Some of 'em ain't gonna want to hear about some 'Yobo' you're faithful too either. They're not gonna want to take no for an answer. Think you can deal with that without either busting a gut laughing *or* ripping their fucking heads off? Fair warning, there has to be a middle ground."

"I...can't promise you anything," she replied timidly, practically collapsing into a nearby chair, "it...depends on...what I feel. What I...see."

Lumbering forward, the man slapped an open palm atop the table, causing Lei to openly flinch.

"What you *see*? What you fe-....hey, let's get one thing straight. Don't let that 'built-in' radar of yours talk you into attacking every Tom, Dick and Colonel Harry with a questionable 'vibe'. We're after big game here, sister, the *biggest*. You can...I mean, you are able to... gauge the *level* of discrepancy in a mark, right?"

"Of course," she replied with a weary roll of her eyes, "I can separate the truly evil from the moderately *warped*."

"Then believe me, '*Sukie*', you'll have no problem distinguishing our killer if you make his or her acquaintance. This boy or girl has a healthy dose of Lucifer's DNA swirling about the old bloodstream."

"So...what happens if I do happen across them?

I'm not armed, not that there's any room on this band-aid costume you've provided to stash one. Do I just woo them with my charms and then allow them to gut me as well? Might not be time to yell for help, you know."

"That's where I come in, babe," he blurted with an elevated level of machismo she couldn't help but find amusing, "you'll be wired at all times, even when you're on stage. Any sign of the 'Ville Ripper, we'll be on him or her like white on rice. You spot 'em, we'll take 'em down. Bank on it."

"Who exactly is we?"

"Town patrol. We'll have several units of armed SP's in place at all times, some Air Force, some Korean Army regulars. This is high-level, international shit, after all. Those girls were probably being scoped out for days, maybe even weeks at a time before the perp made his or her move."

"But…why assign me to the…this *Yellow Fever* club? Seems the killer might show up at a dozen other clubs and never step foot in the place. I can't detect what I never *see,* you know."

"Good damn question, Miss Sukie," he grinned, "glad to see you finally showing some interest. Anyhow, we've been able to determine a pattern of sorts. Might seem a little on the simplistic side, and it's just a theory for now, but one we're pretty damn confident in regardless. Check it out…"

Stepping over and back to the bulletin board, he reached up and lowered a pull-down map that covered the whole of 'G.I. Central' in bold black and white.

Four clubs were circled in yellow highlighter, with the names of each victim scribbled next to their former place of employment.

"....the four victims danced in clubs once managed by Chow Yun Jung, the present-day owner of the Yellow Fever. Coincidentally, or maybe *not* so damn coincidental, all four girls once danced at the Fever when it opened six months back, but were 'let go' as time passed for what Jung considered more 'attractive' models recruited from in and around the Seoul area. Ever the kind-hearted pimp, Mister Jung set them up with dancing gigs at the other clubs he managed. Said all four were 'nice enough', but that he required only the 'cream of the crop' grace the Fever's stage. Fever's got quite the rep, you know, and not just in the local area. Jung charges ten bucks for a glass of pink-colored Kool-Aid, and only those with either lofty rank or social status could afford to wine and dine on a nightly basis, not to mention placing an order of 'take out' pussy afterwards."

Crossing her arms, Lei regarded him with a deep, troubled frown.

"So you think the killer might've marked these girls when they danced at the Fever?"

"It's a sizeable reach, I know," he shrugged, turning away from the map and back towards her, "but it's also the only thing that makes sense. They might've been targeted later on, but just the fact that all four once worked there together is a bit too much to take for granted. Otherwise, I'm afraid useable clues are about as elusive as Mama Sun's long-lost youth.

82

As far as you and I go, we make up what I like to think of as the 'Guinea Pig' division, being that several within the chain of command don't buy a word of your so-called 'tracking abilities' claim. They really ain't expecting you to produce. Fact is, if it wasn't for Bill, um…that's Colonel Carver, we wouldn't be having this conversation at all."

"Was he…?""

"Yeah, you met 'im. He's the only one that went to the plate for ya, girl. Gotta admit, I was nay-saying right from the get-go."

"Don't bullshit me, one-eye. You people have nothing to lose tossing me out there like fresh meat on a hook. If I do happen to help, great. If I don't, you'll chalk it up as a failed experiment and ship me back for trial. No great loss."

"Have to vehemently disagree there," he countered with a raised forefinger, "If you *do* assist the capture in any way, shape or form, you're fully pardoned, my dear…that blood-soaked slate of yours wiped clean. Talk about your motivational tool."

"Yeah well…let's just say I trust you people about as far as I can sail you."

"(IN ENGLISH) That's…*toss* you," the man said with a toothy grin, "but I get the gist. (IN KOREAN) Hey, I can only pass on what I've been told."

Lei huffed, tossing her arms weakly into the air. "Let's just get on with this, then…Chuck."

"That's my girl…and I'd really prefer *Charlie*," he replied with an enthusiastic clap, "now let's get our game face on….dear."

83

"Dear?" she frowned.

"Might as well get in character, Yobo," he shrugged playfully, "How's about a little nookie later?"

Pausing, she cocked both eyebrows in comical dismay even as her jaw fell open like a cabinet with a shattered hinge.

"*Yobo*?…you mean….it's gonna be…*you*?"

Spreading his bulky arms as if about to receive a loving hug, '*Charlie*' flashed a brief wink with his lone remaining eye.

"Remember….learn it…live it….love it."

"Ohhhh shit," she spat sourly, lowering her forehead flush against the table.

***

Yun Hee Cho had just turned twenty-two. Born of a British Father and Korean mother, she'd been shunned by Korean society for the majority of her life, never finding a true clique until it became evident as an adult that her long legs, sizeable bust-line and exotic beauty held certain…financial advantages if utilized within the correct circles. At a going rate of seven-fifty per evening, three-hundred of which she herself pocketed, a prosperous month had been known to net her upwards of six-million Won, or approximately eight-thousand American dollars. Some years earlier, before discovering her 'hidden talents', she'd toiled as a seller at an Open Market outside Kwang Ju for mere pennies a day. In times of depression or shame, when thoughts of the personal price she paid in her chosen line of work crept to the forefront of her mind, she would console herself in the fact that a full year spent at such back-breaking menial labor was akin to a week spent refining her present occupational skills.

It was rare that she be asked to 'escort' in a different city, though denying such requests were hardly an option. Entering a bus stop restroom just outside the city limits of Sunyon, she studied her almost flawless reflection in a slightly cracked mirror and pondered the night to come. She'd heard the stories, of course. The news stations had purposely played it down, no doubt due to political ramifications with the Air Force base in such close proximity to the crimes. She'd also heard of the club with which she was tasked to meet her latest 'companion'. It had garnered quite the reputation of late as the weekend hangout of the rich and infamous, complete with dancers recruited from Seoul's top clubs and a full-time DJ that had once had his very own television variety show. All the tales of gruesome death and unknown dangers associated with the general area mattered little in the grand scheme of things. She had a service to provide. A service she was paid quite well to perform.

By dawn's early light of the following day, she assured herself with a nod while shooting the splintered mirror a final parting glance, nothing would matter but the most pleasant task of all; the counting of the cash.

\*\*\*

"Didn't they ever consider just closing the main gate...you know...making it off-limits to all G.I's until after the murders are solved?"

Lei and the man she now referred to as 'Charlie' stood at the center of a makeshift workout room, complete with scattered free weights, assorted dumbbells, several weight benches, and a trio of cushioned mats normally associated with martial arts classes.

"They did just that after the first two murders. Shut 'er down for six days after the first and ten after the second. The locals protested vehemently...on both occasions. That base is their life's blood, from the shop owners to the hook-...the girls of the Ville. Plus which, shutting the gate on a semi-permanent basis might give the impression that the powers that be figured the suspect or suspects to be G.I's. Not a good image to project. Hell, half the population of this country wants us out as it is. American troops get blamed every damn time a fruit cart gets overturned."

Barefooted and wearing a loose-fitting jump suit, Lei eyed a large punching bag hanging just to their left. Hung from the ceiling by thick, looping chains, she found its slight swinging motion strangely hypnotic.

"So what? What if an airman or...high ranking officer *is* responsible?

Surely that possibility hasn't been ruled out?"

"Not at all. Even had a few leads on some questionable TDY troops from the PI. Annual 'Team Spirit' exercise brings 'em in droves, brass included. These particulars were Marines with a penchant for

86

inflicting pain on the local ladies of the evening. Nothing panned out, though."

"Any local suspects?"

Nodding, he walked over and gave the hanging bag a light jab, accidentally snapping her frozen gaze.

"None worth mentioning. Korea ain't exactly the U.S. when it comes to sick fucks carving on their own kind for no apparent reason. Tell ya what though, this country is growin' more *western* by the day. Sad to see."

"For all we know, our perp hops off a bus near the Ville once a month, gets his kicks, then rides his or her happy ass straight outta town again. If that is the case, we've only got about twelve, thirteen million suspects. More buses and cabs in this country than California has queers.

Town patrol's had to step up big time. Double shifts for both the Air Force and South Korean SP's. Those boys are seriously dogged out."

"A few extra security guards? You're telling me that's the lone preventive measure that two military commands could come up with?"

"Well, that and issuing line badges to everyone working or residing in the Ville. Anybody caught after club hours without either a military ID or Ville ID is automatically busted and interrogated."

"How's that worked out?" she asked, cocking an eyebrow sassily.

He paused to watch his own steel-toed combat boots scoot lazily from side to side, and Lei was struck at how much he suddenly resembled a restless teenage boy.

"Oh, 'bout four-hundred arrests in the past five months. Mostly drunken Airman and locals suffering from chronic insomnia."

"(IN ENGLISH) Peachy. (IN KOREAN) What are curfew hours?" "Midnight on weekdays, two AM on weekends. Actually, until this murder spree, there was no set curfew in the Ville, at least not on weekends. Clubs stayed open all night."

"How'd you get so fluent in Korean?" she asked after a brief hesitation.

"I… was stationed here for several years in the mid-seventies.

Kunsan Air Base. A few years ago, the security liaison position for the peninsula opened up and I snagged it."

His expression notably distant, he twisted about and tossed another light haymaker at the hard bag.

"Why here?" "Why *not*?"

"You were married to a Korean once, weren't you, Chuck?" Snapping too abruptly, he whirled about with newfound exuberance, though his cheeks were slightly reddened.

"Hey…enough questions, probie, and quit calling me Chuck, will ya?

Makes me feel like I'm part of an old 'Peanuts' cartoon. Our government didn't finance all this…" he barked, gesturing towards the scattered equipment, "…for us to stand here and beat our gums over shit that doesn't pertain to the mission."

"Oh yeah, biiiig budget alright," she countered with a wry smile, "why, those rickety looking weight benches alone must've set 'em back ten or fifteen bucks apiece."

"Enough, smart ass," he growled, side-stepping over until he stood posed dead center at the widest of the cushioned mats, "now…get over here and show me what ya got."

Lei placed a hand atop her left hip while tilting her head in the opposite direction, her shoulder-length hair tied into a tightly-wound pigtail that roped over her right shoulder.

"Meaning what precisely?"

"Just get over here. I just need to see something."

Strolling over with visibly slumped shoulders, she fronted him while leaving a space of approximately two feet between them.

Though their height wasn't dramatically different, he was perhaps two inches taller at most, his thick, barrel-shaped chest and wide-angled back literally swallowed her whole from certain angles.

"Now what? You going to teach me some popular strip-club dance steps?"

"Not quite, sweetheart," he blurted, lunging forward in an attempt to grasp her by her upper shoulders.

Shocked but hardly frozen into place by his aggressive act, Lei quickly fell to one knee and executed a textbook 'tuck and roll' maneuver that left him grasping nothing but air.

Taking instant advantage of his awkward, off-balance pose, she whipped her right leg around in a blur, catching him at the backs of both knees.

Landing on his back with a muffled thud, he instantly crossed both forearms over his face in a blocking stance, effectively taking the brunt of Lei's subsequent elbow-drop.

Both rolled from the pad in opposite directions while bellowing separate but equally distinct warrior cries.

Lei scooped up a nearby barbell before bouncing to her feet and striking a defensive pose, casually tossing the twenty pound weight from palm to palm.

Reaching up to re-adjust his eye patch, which had pulled slightly askew in the tussle, he studied her momentarily while backing away with his hands raised palms out.

"White towel, babe..." he said between light gasps, "...you win by TKO. The belt is o-fficially yours. Now... drop the hardware."

Following a few additional tosses, Lei slung the dumbbell against a far concrete wall with a forceful, backhanded throw that sent chunks of masonry stone sailing airborne.

"(IN ENGLISH) And...just what the fuck...was that all about, Chuck?" she growled, kneeling onto her hunches.

"(IN KOREAN) Korean, *Sukie*...speak Ko-re-an. Don't break character, no matter what. Had to see for myself, that's all. Proof's in the puddin', you know. I'll say this much for ya," he said, gingerly massaged each elbow, "ain't no questioning either your quickness or aggressive nature."

"(IN KOREAN) What the hell qualifies *you* to judge my fighting skill, asshole?" she replied, though with noticeably less anger.

"Oh, I did some boxing in my time...attended a Tae Kwon Do class or twelve. Damn good thing

90

too... or that forearm smash of yours would've relocated the bridge of my nose to the back of my skull."

Bowing her head in apparent exhaustion, Lei cursed under her breath while slowly nodding from side to side.

"Hey, a man's gotta know who he's stepping into combat with," he shrugged unapologetically.

After a moment, she stood and strolled purposely past him and towards the hard bag.

"Are we done here?"

"I'd say yeah," he replied, not bothering to turn towards her. "Great. Then if you don't mind, I do believe me and this hard bag require a bit of face time."

"Not a problem. Knock yourself out. Initial in-processing is history.

Stage two begins at four AM sharp tomorrow morning."

He matched towards the exit door just as she began a series of furious jabs, hooks, and sidekicks that threatened to tear the seventy pound, sand-filled target from its sturdy chains.

Five full minutes later, she lay flat atop the cushioned pad, her breath escaping in harsh, strained sobs as her sweat-soaked frame left a circular outline on the pad's plastic surface.

"Stage *two*..." she huffed in exasperated wonder, "Lord, give me strength to cope."

***

Yun Hee Cho had noticed the old man standing

91

on the corner, nursing a cigarette while leaning on a shovel, his bright yellow shirt smudged with mud. She'd briefly considered how strange for someone to be indulging in such back-breaking work at just past one AM in the morning, and had even vocalized such thoughts to her date, who hadn't bothered to reply, remaining silently indifferent to whatever she deemed noteworthy. *Pour man,* she mused in silent misery while lying in a rapidly spreading puddle of her own precious life-source, *somebody's going to...lose a ...grandfather.*

Unable to even turn her head from the scene due to the numbing paralysis holding her captive, she watched the old man die a horrible death, the shovel having been ripped from his grasp and subsequently used as a tool for his own demise.

He'd no doubt heard her shrieking cries and ran blindly into the alley, wielding the garden implement like some magical, protective talisman.

Otishe (*English translation*: old man) had been sixty-five years old if he'd been a day. No doubt someone's grandfather, playing hero and paying an ungodly price for his foolhardy but noble actions.

As the stagnant, breeze-free air filled with the sickening aroma of split bodily fluids and perforated gut, Yun Hee Cho' s vision began to darken and grow increasingly blurred. On the very edge of passing into a merciful state of unconscious bliss, the final image she would clearly envision was the tips of her killer's spit-polished shoes parked mere inches from her own torn, blood-drenched face, followed by a series of moist, ripping sounds that seemed strangely distant.

*Such is the fate... of one so... lost*, she mused, coughing weakly as frothy, maroon bubbles formed at the corners of her mouth, *for...the most vile of sins must... be readily atoned if the... heavenly gates are to... be viewed.*

Her own grandfather had once passed on that particular jewel of wisdom, one she prayed was indeed gospel, for as separate geysers of blackish blood spewed forth from her ears, eyes, and mouth and her face imploded within itself like a deflated balloon, there was very little doubt that Miss Yun Hee Cho's own personal atonement could most assuredly be stamped '*paid in full*'.

\*\*\*

"So...how do you like the new digs, honey-pot? Best we could do on short notice."

Lei stepped up from a tiny foyer, which consisted of a sink, water barrel and trio of wooden shelves, and into the single room residence. "Oh, what can I say, Charles? Enchanting. Simply enchanting.

What more could a girl ask for? Got a rice paddy out front that's just a lovely spot for mosquito breeding, and a garbage-strewn alley in the back with matching trash cans, no less. Think I even saw, and *smelled* mind you, a decaying animal carcass lying near that storage shed across the street. Heaven, I tell you. Pure *heaven*..."

"(IN KOREAN) Native tongue, remember? At least when we're alone. Practice, practice, practice. Gotta get that damn Southern California lilt outta

93

your voice."

"(IN KOREAN) It's a dump, Sir Chuck. A flea-bag closet at best. Four walls and a roof, more than likely on the leaky side. What are the dimensions, anyhow? Ten by fourteen? Looks like they copied the design from Alchatraz."

"Bitch, bitch, bitch…. home is what you make of it, doll. At least Otishe did toss in the mini-fridge and the box spring. Hey….what do you expect for a lousy hundred fifty bucks a month, right? And stop calling me Chuck, damn it," he quipped, sitting aside his overstuffed duffel before heading back out to retrieve the remainder of their luggage. At barely six AM on a Wednesday morning, the sun had yet to completely rise in the Land of the Morning Calm.

"Why so far away from the center of things then, *Charles*? The taxi must've driven three or four miles once we passed under that overhang," she said once he'd reentered the cramped space, hoisting separate pieces of luggage under each arm, "felt like a rat in a maze."

"Overhang?" he asked casually, squatting onto his duffel while wiping the building sweat from his brow. His arms were noticeably pumped from hauling the luggage from the trunk of the cab, which had been forced to park several dozen yards from the entranceway.

"The G.I. Town sign," she huffed, scanning the papered walls, which were riddled with water stains. Donned in skin-tight, ankle-high blue jeans and a white halter with the words '*Go-Go's – We Got The Beat*' stenciled in black across the chest, she was at least dressed for the part of Ville 'night shift'

94

worker.

"Oh yeah. Well, we needed to keep a certain distance from your new...co-workers. The club is a good two mile walk from here. Make it real hard for anybody feeling 'nosey' to just drop in on us without warning."

"Wonderful, so I get to hike that distance to and from work every night, wearing three-inch pumps, no less? You going to hoist me on your back, big boy? After all, you are my *man*."

"Think cab fare, babe. Got 'em running up and down these winding streets all night like fire-ants headed to a picnic," he said, briskly massaging his own neck. Similarly dressed in casual slacks, a green tee-shirt and white tennis shoes, he appeared every bit the 'off-duty' serviceman, a plethora of partially faded tattoos adorning each bicep and forearm.

"Speaking of which, let's store this gear and head into town for some breakfast. I'll show you the sights, then we've got someone to meet back here at nine o'clock sharp. Tonight, we drop by the Club for formal intros."

"Do we have to do that *today*?" she whined, "I'm...not sure I'm up to-.."

"Listen, lady, your first scheduled shift is tomorrow night at five PM, and I have yet to see you 'boogie down', so to speak. You've gotta show these people some serious ass-shaking, or they're liable to be suspicious right from the get-go."

Lunging forward, she gave the luggage he sat upon a forceful kick, though not hard enough to completely budge him from his perch.

"Hey, excuse me for being neither a trained

dancer *nor* hooker. I didn't exactly ask for this shit."

"Calm down, sister," he grinned, refitting his rear end to its original position, "help is on the way, at least for the former. I'll explain on the way.

As for the latter, well….let's just hope it doesn't come to that."

Lei openly bristled while fashioning her hair into a tight ponytail. "(IN ENGLISH) *Hope* my ass, buddy-boy. It won't come to that…period."

\*\*\*

**Same Day**
**Sixteen hundred hours Sunyon Air Base**
**NCO BARRACKS #777**

"C'mon, SOS. Let's hit it…can't keep the booze or broads waiting," bellowed Staff Sergeant Milt Jacobs, peering into a tiny mirror above his barrack's room sink while attempting to pop a zit atop his pointy chin.

"Next bus leaves for the Ville in fifteen minutes, man. Let's boogie."

Buck Sergeant Jeremy Yeager, nicknamed 'SOS' as in '*Speed of Sound*', due solely to the matching of his last name with a certain, rather famous Air Force Flyer named *Chuck*, checked his wristwatch to confirm his roomies frantic claim while parched atop the lone available toilet like the 'thinker.'

"Police up those hormones and calm down, MJ. Give a man time to wipe his privates, for shit's sake."

"Rush it up, Sarge. I don't wanna have to fork out three bucks apiece for a cab."

"Go on ahead it you have to. I've got to meet the Colonel at the Yellow Fever at eighteen hundred anyhow."

"The *Fever*? Oh, is it 'break in a new dancer' night or what?" queried Jacobs, a stocky black man with broad shoulders and a matching beer gut.

"Fair bet. He never drags the staff along unless that's the case." "Ol' Full-Bird Bennett is a One-Star perv, ain't he?"

"Yep-per. Typical Senior Officer. Happily married for twenty some-odd years; two grown kids and a grandkid on the way, yet he still finds time to bankroll not one but two yobo's down at the Ville. Man possesses a true heart of gold."

"Yeah, with a *dick* to match. Bet lovely Miss Bennett and the kiddies would simply be thrilled at 'Big Daddy's' deviant behavior."

"Her and every other dedicated wife and mother sitting back in the states, MJ," Jeremy replied, turning about to flush before departing the john's cramped confines wearing only a pair of green jockey shorts with matching socks, "Bennett's served in the Pacific before, and Germany before that. Man's a veteran whore-monger. Don't think for a minute that his lovely wife don't know the score Probably makes the man wear a full body suit whenever they bump ugly's."

At six-three and just under one-ninety, Jeremy's cut, toned frame resembled that of a well-conditioned athlete; muscular but not overly so. Having just turned the ripe old age of twenty-eight

97

some weeks earlier, his mustache (labeled the 'Hitler brush stroke' due to its limited growth potential under Air Force regulation) held a surprising number of premature gray strands.

Pausing at the barracks door while spraying on what seemed like an entire bottle of cologne, Milt Jacobs then shot his roomy a mock salute.

"You got that right, brother. Well, I'm off and runnin' then, man. 'Sides, you'll be VIP-ing it all night long. Can't be hangin' out with non-commissioned trash like myself."

"Yeah, right. Meet you at the Pacific about ten or so, brother Milt.

I'll buy you an OB or three before curfew and we'll pour ourselves home."

"Got'cha. We'd better make it a good one too. They might be securing the gate locks after tonight."

"Lock down? For what?" Jeremy asked, pulling on a pair of jeans while following the other man out into the narrow hallway.

"Didn't you hear, man? The *Ville ripper* struck again last night...double-murder 'bout three miles north of the clubs. That's six in five months. Soooo, let's be careful out there, man..."

"Yeah....later," Jeremy replied timidly, having already shifted focus elsewhere as he re-entered their sixteen by eighteen foot quarters and closed the door behind him, thereby drowning out at least a half-dozen rock, pop, and rap concertos blaring from nearby rooms.

Having just recently arrived on station from a two year assignment at Tinker Air Force Base in Oklahoma, there were days Jeremy Dale Yeager felt as though he'd aged a decade in the previous twelve months. He'd received the official divorce decree just weeks before departing Tinker for South Korea, his second remote tour in less than six years wearing Air Force blue. He'd previously spent thirteen months in the Philippines, where he'd met and eventually married Flordeluna, so the '*work extremely hard, party extremely harder*' atmosphere infamous at such bases as Sunyon was hardly new.

As one of only four base supply technicians on station, his work schedule was long and rigorous, normally eleven to twelve hours a day, Monday through Friday, plus half-days every other Saturday. During the frequent (usually Bi-Monthly) wartime 'exercises' that were the norm at Sunyon, it wasn't unusual for the majority of the bases' permanently stationed airmen to put in an eighty-to-ninety hour workweek while tasked to don bulky (weighing up to thirty pounds) Kavlar vests, utility belts, gas masks and combat helmets, all while dragging around an overstuffed duffel filled with a protective chemical suit and its many accessories. After two relatively serene years (at least professionally) spent at a stateside base where his hours rarely varied from eight to four, Monday through Friday, Jeremy had quickly been 'reinstated back into the real military' upon arrival in the *Land of The Morning Calm*, an assignment he'd so far found to be anything but tranquil. In truth, he desired nothing more than to stay as busy as possible, thus blocking out the complete shambles his personal life had recently become. In that regard, working base supply at a remote tour was a Godsend; a whirlwind of never-ending activity as keeping the Wing's assigned personal supplied in both work-related and personal 'necessities' was truly a Herculean task.

On the minus side, working for Colonel Brad Bennett, the commander of base supply, had its drawbacks for someone attempting to (temporarily at least) quell certain hormonal urges. As his fun-loving roomy was so apt to say in their thirty-some days as barracks rats, 'SOS old buddy, you came to the *wrong* base to attempt celibacy."

The Colonel insisted that all troops under his command 'blow off steam' at least bi-weekly by accompanying him to the Ville for drinks 'on him', courtesy of the upscale 'Yellow Fever' club, *the* nightly hangout for high-ranking brass and wealthy locals.

The only excuse not to attend said gatherings, even for non-drinkers (few and far between at Sunyon) was literally a written Sick Call excuse from the base hospital. One could limit their stay to an hour or so, but to 'make an appearance' was pretty much mandatory in the Colonel's steely eyes. For Sergeant J.D. Yeager, this was to be appearance number three at the infamous 'Ville', the first two of which he'd managed to 'escape' early after only an hour or so spent sipping OB beer and ogling the scantily clad dancers on display, supposedly the cream of the crop that G.I. Central had to offer.

"Nurse the booze…avert the eyes," he mumbled several times while slipping on a black cotton tee and brown 'parachute' pants. He continued to repeat the same refrain while tightening the strings on his imitation '*Nike* ' tennis shoes (purchased a few days earlier for the bargain basement price of fifteen thousand Won in Sunyon City, American district) and combing a brush through the squat porcupine quills that served as his hair.

Glancing into the mirror to ensure the absence of any overgrown nose hair, he splashed a palm full of *Dakkar* cologne (actually, another cheap imitation from Sunyon City) onto his neck and upper shirt, concluding the oft repeated verbal reminder a final time in a noticeably sterner tone.

"Nurse…the booze (translation: stay *reasonably* sober)…avert…the eyes (translation: don't fixate on the dancers or other nubile Korean female forms)." Jeremy clearly understood that if rule one was strictly adhered to, rule two would then be much easier to follow.

"Ho-kay then," he sighed nervously, checking his wallet (imitation leather – still another Sunyon City special) to ensure he possessed sufficient Won (at least for a possible cab ride back to the base), "…let's hit it, and remember this …." he paused, checking his own reflection one final time while raising a single digit airborne, "…no matter *how* beautiful she is or *how* large the wave of horniness you feel….just ride the storm out, dude. Ride the storm out…"

Hopping aboard a large white bus with yellow striping (known base wide as the 'Ville coaches') a few minutes later, Jeremy secretly wondered how much longer he could hold out without getting involved with one of the locals. It wasn't just the sex he craved, but the constant companionship that served to buffer life lived within a military pressure cooker. Ten thousand miles from home and suddenly single once again, the odds of his soon becoming a 'live-in Yobo' were beyond favorable; it was, in gambling terms, the safest of 'sure' bets. Besides, the symptoms were all present and accounted for, despite his fevered self-denials. He was a heavy (weekends) to moderate (weekday) drinker who had been officially diagnosed with '*Yellow Fever*' some years earlier while stationed in the PI. The dreaded 'YF' was a mysterious syndrome not easily shaken, especially when stationed near a sex-drenched hot-box like G.I. Central. It was a lifelong urge; an attraction to females of the Asian persuasion that only those afflicted truly understood. The pull was relentless; unwavering.

As the bus departed the main gate and shot past several small residential villages and local shops, Jeremy Yeager felt his gut begin to tighten and his palms moisten with sweat. His self-control was waning, big time. The longing pulled at him like a physical presence. While primal *lust* was definitely on board for the ride, a much baser emotion known simply as loneliness was behind the wheel. Toss in the fact that the well-populated object(s) of his many carnal desires were readily available twenty-four-seven and just a bus or cab ride away, and it was simply a matter of time before the war would be hopelessly lost, no matter the number of little victories achieved along the way.

"Nurse the booze….avert the eyes…damn it," he whispered, garnering a strange look from the troop sitting next to him.

For distraction purposes, he scooped up a discarded 'Stars & Stripes' and forced himself to focus on the recent murder spree, a subject the brass was obviously trying to avoid publicizing with little success.

"Wild shit, huh?" his seatmate commented, pointing at the large, bold-printed headline which read *'Horrors Continue: Double Homicide Shocks Tiny Community Near Sunyon'*, "you'd think we were back in the states."

"You got that right. Place isn't any better than D.C. or Detroit," Jeremy replied with a sad nod, "Sunyon, murder capital of the ROK."

After a brief scan of the article, which was short on detail but long on tap-dancing from a public relations point of view, Jeremy quickly turned to the sports pages instead.

"How 'bout them De-troit Tigers, huh?" he blurted aloud, initiating yet another questionable glance from the stranger with whom he shared a bus seat for most likely the first and final time in both their lives. Such was the norm on a remote tour of duty; people came into one's life in fragmented segments and departed just as rapidly.

"I'm a Yankees fan," the other replied with a warped grin.

"Ah, the hell with all of 'em,' Jeremy practically yelled to drown out the buses' wining engine, 'let's go get drunk."

Both men nodded in silent agreement, not to mention commitment, to a task each knew was easily enough achieved.

*In fervently kicking free the sheet and blanket from his legs and feet with a surly growl, he manages only to briefly awaken his previously slumbering companion, who eyes him curiously through the dark haze before twisting about to face the opposite direction. Of late, she notes before falling into a deep realm of rim sleep that will fully possess her subconscious for the next six-plus hour, her lovers fits of nocturnal rage have increased beyond the merely bothersome to the problematic stage.*

*Her unconscious state of bliss is undeterred, however, as the wild ramblings and periodic wails that soon part his lips go unheard, as do the occasional groans of sadistic glee that otherwise might have both alarmed and frightened even the most faithful of companions.*

***

**SAME DAY**
**SIXTEEN FIFTEEN HOURS KWANG-OH VILLAGE**
(Located two and a half miles east of G.I. Central)

"(In Korean) You sufficiently psyched or what?" Charlie asked, studying Lei with a lusty leer, "I mean, this being your big debut and all."

Standing in front of a full length mirror attached to the hooch's inner door, she noticed his wide-eyed stare and frowned.

"(IN ENGLISH) Getting a pupil-full there, one-eye?"

"(IN ENGLISH) Hey, just double-checking the product before it hits the shelves."

She wore a mini-halter shaded in red, white and blue stripes, a dark blue thong which bit into both her butt-bone and waistline like tautly pulled fishing line, and silver-tinted pumps with three inch heels. Her hair was pulled back in a seductive swirl, held in place by a star- shaped, gold-shaded clip. She'd managed to keep her make-up relatively conservative save the purposely overdone dark Navy shaded eye-shadow and ruby-red lipstick.

"What time is it?" she asked nervously, reaching around to adjust the ill-fitting thong for at least the tenth time in the previous half-hour.

"Relax, Lei. We've still got ten, fifteen minutes. Mister Jung likes his girls showing up 'fashionably early', remember?"

"Smarmy old jackass. Did everything but feel me up."

"What did you expect? The guy considers himself the Ville *Hugh Hefner*. I hear he shacks up with two of his former dancers in a big ol' condo just north of Sunyon City."

Bending down in a squat as to loosen the thong's confining effect, she could practically hear his eyes widen and his tongue lop loose with the shock and awe of a Looney Tunes cartoon character.

"(IN KOREAN) He's nothing but a flesh-peddling pervert. His kind are the true disgraces around here. Selling out his own people like farm animals on an auction block."

"Um, yeah, if you say so. Hey, you mind doing a few more of those? I think I saw a seam rip."

"Get a grip, Chuck. On second thought, I'd better not temp you," she replied, straightening out with an exasperated groan.

"So the dance lessons went okay? I've heard Miss Mia is the best in these parts. Sure don't come cheap, either."

"She...clued me in on a few select moves. From what I gather, it's really just a matter of swaying with the beat. Patrons are mostly wasted and could care less. Besides, all they really want to see..." she paused, reaching back to slap her bare right hip, "...is some prime Asian female flesh on display."

"On second thought," he spat, gasping comically, "please do *that* again."

"My point exactly."

"Should be a good crowd tonight. Wednesday's both the regular and Kool-aid drinks are half-price. That always seems to bring out even the most tight-wadded of commissioned officers."

"Great...more dirty old men," she said, rolling her eyes, "I cannot believe I've got to pee *again*. I...can't remember the last time I was this wired."

"(IN ENGLISH) Oh yeah, that reminds me," Charlie said, rising from the room's lone chair, a cushioned 'bar stool' he'd managed to procure earlier that day, "stick with English for the rest of the night, but cut waaay down on the vocabulary. Most of the Ville gals speak only the 'broken' variety, though some better than others. Can't have you sounding like a Pac-Ten grad without raising some serious eyebrows."

Lei responded from behind the tiny bathroom's semi-closed door. "(IN ENGLISH) Okie-dokie, G.I. You number ten! I show you *oodly* time, okay? Me love you *lonnnnnnng* time!"

"Jeez, lady, I said cut down, not give yourself a lobotomy," he chuckled, checking his own 'cowboy' motif in the door-length reflection. From his black jeans and matching button-up shirt (complete with bolo tie) down to the imitation 'snakeskin' boots, the only thing missing was a ten-gallon hat.

"So how were they killed?"

He instantly froze, the hand he'd been running through his spiny buzz-cut halted in mid-comb.

"How'd you hear about that? We don't even have a radio in here." "You're kidding, right? Scuttlebutt in these small villages spreads like a viral infection. My dance instruct-.." "Lei, get into character, please."

"Oh…yeah…right. Um, Miss Lee, she tell me two found dead. One was a young girl from out of town, the other an old *hadibogie*…uh, grandfather. She say grandfather's daughter was talking walk and found the bodies. She say both chopped up very good. Grandfather's head was cut in half like ripe melon, and girl was sliced…uh…carved into six or seven pieces. This true?"

He paused, obviously stifling a giggle before responding.

"That's better. Ya still sound a little brain-damaged, though. Cut in half like *ripe melon*? Geez…..turn it up a single notch, but not *too* far."

"So what's the story, G.I. Joe? These killings

107

connected?" "Nothing's been confirmed, but from the damage inflicted on each victim, seems like a safe bet."

"Same MO?"

"Not really. Chick wasn't a local. She was a high-priced escort.

The old man's daughter said he was a chronic insomniac who was out digging in their flower bed. No doubt he tried to play hero and got his skull segmented for his troubles."

The toilet flushed noisily before Lei emerged in full regalia, though still tugging at the bothersome thong.

"Well, then…kind of blows the *Yellow Fever* theory out of the water, doesn't it? Then again…we most definitely still have a suspect to nab, right?"

"You, my lady, have a firm grasp on the obvious, yes. In fact," he said, handing her an ankle-length, maroon colored robe with the words '*Yellow Fever Club*' sewn onto the back in dark black lettering, "we have two witnesses who claim to have seen the female victim inside the Yellow Fever club last night around eleven PM."

"Could they ID anybody she was with?" she inquired while slipping into the robe's silken confines.

He shrugged his shoulders and sighed before reaching back to ensure his wallet was indeed accounted for and duly secured inside his jeans back right pocket.

"You would've thought so, right? No such luck. One said they recalled seeing her male escort from the rear, and then only briefly. None of 'em would know the guy if he walked up and gave 'em a big, wet kiss."

"Let me guess," she said, securing a thick belt across the robe's midsection, "these…witnesses were all male."

"Bingo, sister."

"Figures. So they only recall the female victim, and only then by her breast size and the shape of her rear end."

"You're as smart as you are gorgeous." "Any other useable clues left at the scene?"

He shrugged while casually checking his wristwatch.

"Nary a one, Nancy Drew. As usual, lots 'o blood and oodles of gore, but little to help nab the crazy loon responsible. On the positive side, and I know this is a reach, but at least the killings were farther out of the loop…almost four miles from the Ville…actually, closer to Sunyon City. "

"(IN KOREAN) One question: I know the odds are astronomically stacked against it actually happening but wha-…"

"Get into character, dear…in English," he scolded. "(IN ENGLISH) What if I do….sense the presence of…"

"Lose the thesaurus, Lei…*sense* and *presence* won't work." "Shit," she spat angrily, rolling her eyes, "okay….what if, I do feel the…*bad man* is near. How do I relay…(paused, waiving her arms about in frustration)… how do I tell you? Hand signals? Cross my eyes? Fart the Star-Spangled Banner? I mean, as much as I'd like to…I can't exterminate…(paused, huffed)…I can't kill the perp….the guy right then and there… in front of live witnesses, right, Joe?"

"That's a little better, but you still sound way too educated, and stop calling me Joe. This ain't some Vietnam war flick, for Cripes sake."

"Sorry, pal, that's about as basic as I can get without sounding retarded."

"We've inserted a tiny mike in the right shoulder pad of your halter. Simply tilt your head to the right and whisper. I'll…we'll hear ya, no matter how loud the rock 'n roll blares. Might as well give her a quick road test…"

"We? Got a mouse in your pocket?"

"You've been assigned a 'permanent' town patrol team, remember? …that's Security Police. They'll be stationed inside the Fever *and* wired for sound at all times. If for some reason I don't hear your distress call, they will."

Reaching into the robe, she probed about the shoulder area until a small, circular object caught between her thumb and forefinger.

Meanwhile, Charlie carefully inserted an earplug into his left ear and flashed a 'thumbs up' gesture.

"Charlie 'one-eye' is an asshole," she whispered in Korean.

He repeated the thumb's up before slowly twisting his hand about and playfully shooting her the finger.

"Loud and clear, smart ass. Bottom line is this, Lei…if that inner radar of yours locks on anyone even remotely resembling our boy, don't hesitate to sound off. We ain't worried about a few false alarms. Hell, we might even nail a few closet pervs or killers in the process.

Either way, we're not the least bit concerned about getting embarrassed by hauling in the wrong man…or woman."

"Not to worry then…I've never been one to hesitate," she shot back with a purposely mean grin.

"From your track record, I ain't about to doubt it."

"So, everyone's officially okay on the sunglasses issue, right?" "Yeah, Mister Jung thinks it's real stylish. Long as you can see okay. I mean, we don't want you taking a header off the stage." "Let's just say I'm used to dim lighting."

"While we're on the subject," he began, clearing his throat, "if you don't mind my asking…"

"But I *do* mind."

Obviously ignoring her curt response, he continued unabated.

"What's the deal with that? You have some kinda eye condition? If so, believe me, I can sympathize," he quipped, reaching up and tweaking his patch.

"When I spot a mark, there's a…visible change in my eye color, and certain…physical signs."

"Ya mean, like, *Mister Hyde* type shit? We talking blue flames…bulging forehead … swollen butt-cheeks or what?"

"Hey Jackass, if you're going to make jokes, you can-.." He waived her off apologetically.

"Sorry, soooo-ry. It's just that, I need a symptom I can spot…just, ya know, in case you're not able to respond verbally."

111

"Believe me, Ace...you'll know without me ever waiving my arms, yodeling or screaming out," she said with a stern nod.

"If you say so, ya stubborn shit," he sighed, "so...you about ready to vamoose?"

Lei paused, scanning her reflection one last time with a pained expression of utter disgust.

"As ready as one can possibly be who is forced into the fiery bowels of hades, I guess."

"C'mon now, *Slant*, accentuate the positive."

"(IN KOREAN) Go fuck yourself, *Cyclops*."

"Tsk, tsk...." He replied, leading them out the front door as to waive down the next available cab, "such loathsome garbage seepeth from such a gorgeous mouth."

"(IN ENGLISH) Eat shit and die, Shakespeare."

"That's more like it."

Less than a minute later, they loaded into taxi with interior space comparable to a Volkswagen Beetle and headed towards G.I. Central through a winding maze of one-room shanties, rice fields, and dilapidated farmhouses.

"Nervous, doll?" Charlie asked as they neared the unofficial eastern-most entrance to the Ville.

Lei turned to him, batting oversized, wholly artificial lashes. "Nervous? Naaaah. Scared shitless?" she sighed heavily, "you bet."

He studied her momentarily, leaning back as far as the cramped space would allow as to adequately size her up.

"Lady, I don't think you know the meaning of the word." "Mister," she countered grimly, "I've lived with it every day. In many ways, it's been the

112

only consistent thing in my life."

The cab driver, a bald, middle-aged Korean man wearing dark- tinted sunglasses, shot her a curious glance before returning his gaze to the narrow passage ahead.

"Dummy up, dear," he goaded, smiling through gritted teeth. "Oh…sorry, Yobo. Me do better next time," she countered whimsically, though the building tightness at her midsection was akin to a boa constrictor's deadliest squeeze.

# CHAPTER FOUR
## Fever Pitch

"Whoooa boy, check out the new meat. Tall, shapely glass of water, isn't she, Sarge ?"

"Yes, sir, Colonel. That she is."

"Think I'll invite her sweet little caboose over here for a drink or three," the Colonel leered, "get to know her better, whaddaya say?"

Colonel Brad Bennett's steely green eyes gleamed like a man twenty years his junior. Nicknamed '*Bird-Dog*' by those he supervised, Bennett's wild reputation as a boisterous, hard-drinking, woman chaser was as legendary as his temper, which could reach volcanic status in a matter of seconds if properly agitated.

"Lemme go nab her 'fore somebody beats me to it," he practically yelled as the initial guitar riffs of Ted Nugents' '*Cat Scratch Fever*' permeated the smoke-filled air.

As the Colonel strolled over to a far, shadowy corner to visit 'mamasan', Jeremy leaned back and scanned the club from his rear table perch. The Yellow Fever was one of only two clubs which possessed stadium seating from which one could survey the majority of the spacious seven thousand square foot structure, to include the stage, dance floor, and an oval-shaped bar at the far East end.

He saw several of his contemporaries near the front of the stage, ogling the club's newest 'attraction', including Airman First Class Sandra

114

Morton, a chubby, bespectacled young supply troop with less than two full weeks on station. Sipping a frosty OB, he couldn't help but be amused by her wide-eyed, '*where the hell am I and what am I doing here*?' expression. Other than the casual, laid-back atmosphere of the *Paradise Cove* club, the Ville didn't exactly cater to the female troops on station, at least not the straight ones. The majority of female G.I.' s considered all Korean females residing in or around the Ville as nothing more than 'parasitic prostitutes', while in-turn being viewed by the locals as unattractive 'she-males' who reveled in their own 'homo-masculinity,' in performing tasks designed by and for men.

Cultural conflicts aside, no one was immune to the oft-time severe effects of such a major relocation without a lengthy adjustment phase. Jeremy could definitely relate, at least somewhat. He'd felt a similar sense of disorientation his first few weeks spent at Clark Air Base in the PI some five years earlier, where he'd arrived relatively innocent, at least in terms of lives lived anywhere other than stateside USA. There was an initial period of awestruck wonder that was as weirdly surreal as it was overwhelming, not to mention the accompanying seven to ten days of jet-lag that could easily spark a major bout of 'sensory overload' in all newly assigned personnel.

A military assignment in South Korea was many things, as exhilarating and exiting as it was frightening; as challenging as it was frustrating. It included long hours, extended duty, and weekends spent crawling inside sewage-filled ditches wearing and/or lugging around forty-plus pounds of gear as war-time 'exercise' horns blared overhead. In comparison to most stateside assignments, the responsibilities placed on each individual airman were ten-fold. On the opposite end of the spectrum, tours to the pacific region were also legendary for their hard-partying atmosphere, while just as infamous for the high-rate of divorce once said assignment was complete. Many a happily married man had fallen victim to the seductive charms of the local ladies, be they exotic dancer, street walker, or simply a local searching for a way off the peninsula towards a better life.

Along those lines, Sergeant Jeremy 'SOS' Yeager had made it his personal mission to depart Sunyon Air Base the same way he'd arrived; single, unattached, and (for the most part anyway) emotionally stable. Then again, he mused, draining the remainder of his fast-warming brew while studying the shade-wearing dancer's finely toned rear end as she departed the stage to the familiar tune of Dire Straits 'Money For Nothing', there certainly wasn't any harm in looking, or *lusting* for that matter. In all actuality, within the realm of such a potentially dicey scenario, it was virtually impossible to have one without the other.

Lei stepped gingerly from the stage, greeted by a short, gray-haired man wearing a western-style shirt, blue jeans, and a broad, toothy grin.

"Honey, you are surely a welcome site to this colonel's worn-out old peepers. May I interest you in a tall glass of liquid refreshment?"

Taking his cool, clammy hand as she descended

the stage's final step, Lei hoped her weakened legs refrained from visibly trembling. In just over three hours since her arrival, she'd danced but four numbers but felt as if someone had been belting her kneecaps with a rubber mallet.

"Let me get my robe and I join you," she beamed while resetting the sunglasses as to prevent further slippage while hoping her overly dried lips didn't stick to her teeth. She slipped her arms through the robe and turned slowly about, glancing briefly over to her immediate left, where 'Lieutenant Whitt' caroused with one of her fellow dancers at the western edge of the bar.

Moments later, she followed Colonel Bennett's lead up a tilted walkway towards the rear of the club.

"What's your name, darlin'?" the Colonel asked as they joined Jeremy and Tech-Sergeant Josh Cowen at the table.

"Sukie, and yours?" she replied, hardly taking notice of the other two men as the act of simply sitting down provided waves of sweet relief. If nothing else, this night had proven had badly out of shape she really was.

"Just call me Colonel B," he answered, gesturing with each thumb to either side, "these two knuckleheads answer to Jeremy and Josh."

Jeremy nodded politely and looked away as if suddenly distracted, while Tech Sergeant Cowen, a balding, thin-faced, pasty-skinned twenty-two year vet enduring his last assignment before retirement, practically fell across the table in a drunken lurch while reaching to take her extended hand into his own.

"Goddamn, but you're c-cute (pronounced 'coot'). Colonel," he slurred, sitting back down with a huff, "I do believe I'm in love…once again."

"Settle down, Cowen. Remember that loving wife and six kids," the Colonel retorted with very little humor. Lei, having already grown equally annoyed and/or disgusted by the touchy, feely, flirty ways associated with the inebriated masses, had found the art of appearing interested while drifting into a 'comfort zone' all her own surprisingly easy.

"F-five. Five kids, sir. That is, unless the milkman's fathered one since I PCS'ed."

A middle-aged waitress with a grim, business-like demeanor sauntered up, seemingly from out of thin air, as they were wont to do whenever a dancer was on the floor soliciting drinks.

"Buy drink for the lady?" she asked in a stern, robotic monotone Jeremy found comically dry.

"Darn tootin'. One Kool-Aid special, a fresh round of brews for the boys here, and I'll have another belt of Soju on the rocks," the Colonel responded cheerily, his darting eyes never leaving Lei's person, most notably the area near or around her exposed neckline.

The waitress vanished after a slight bow, soon to be followed by Sergeant Cowen, who stumbled away mumbling something to the effect of having to 'drain the weasel'.

As the Colonel leaned in closer, Lei removed her shades but kept her sites trained on the young man sitting across from her, finding his distant glare and lack of attention towards her a refreshing change

118

of pace.

"So, gorgeous, where'd they find you?" the Colonel barked, his very aura seemingly entombed in the stout aroma of witch hazel and pipe tobacco.

"Pusan City," she responded, turning towards him as he tilted his head downward and instantly noting a bushy growth of grayish hair sprouting from his inner ear, "I... move....come here for a change."

"Well, let me be one of the first to bid you a warm welcome to the Ville. May I say, you are one beautiful addition to the community."

She had opened her mouth for the obligatory thanks, at least the tenth such required reply of the short evening, when she noticed the Colonel looking past her with a decidedly grim expression. Turning to her left, she saw the two uniformed security policeman, referred to within the Ville as 'Town Patrol' striding up the incline towards them.

"Colonel Bennett sir?" the first, an Airman First Class, asked cautiously.

"What it is, Airman?"

"We have a message from Wing Headquarters," the second responded, a Senior Airman with a horrific case of acne, "a Major Jenkins requests you contact him ASAP. You can use the car phone in our unit, sir."

Following a momentary pause, in which he and Jeremy exchanged a worrisome glance, the Colonel arose with a heavy sigh and followed the SP's down the carpeted incline.

"I'll be back, Sarge. Put the drinks on my tab."

"You got it, Sir," Jeremy bellowed through

cupped hands as Richie Blackmore's Rainbow cranked out *'Street of Dreams'* in chest- pounding, ear-ringing Dolby stereo.

Fidgeting like a nervous pre-teen, Jeremy alternating ringing his hands and tapping his fingers atop the table to the song's hard-driving beat, all the while avoiding eye contact as Lei studied him with great curiosity.

"You a Colonel too?" she finally asked, once the decibel level had subsided a notch.

"Me? Um, no, I'm…just a peon," he shrugged after a moment's hesitation, shooting her only a passing glance before returning his attention to the stage, where another of Lei's cohorts so expertly swerved and swayed to the rhythm.

"Pee-on? What's that?" she queried a bit louder, utterly fascinated by his total disinterest.

"Means…(cleared throat)…that means a nobody. Ugh… nobody important anyway. Just a sergeant," he stammered, pointing first at his left shoulder, then waiving a hand over his bicep area, 'four stripes and a star…no brass."

"I thought only officer allowed in club."

"We work….I work for Colonel Bennett…Brad….that is…Colonel B. He gives us passes to get in."

He reached into his shirt's lone pocket and pulled out a tiny, laminated badge, flashing it to her like a cop taking charge of a crime scene. In doing so, Lei noticed his hand had trembled just slightly.

Again, she couldn't help but be strangely enticed. Though he wasn't handsome in the traditional sense, there was an attraction she couldn't

120

quite place, at least, not yet. If nothing else, she conceded, at least it provided her a welcome distraction.

"You got yobo?" she asked casually, almost laughing aloud at his shocked, wide-eyed response. In the background, the opening notes to REO Speedwagon' s *Keep on Loving You* caused a semi-stampede onto the dance floor, which had gone mostly unused up until that point.

"Yo-? No...I...um...,yeah....well, kind of....long story that...," he stuttered, pausing as the waitress returned and began offloading their drinks onto the table.

"That be...ten thousand won," she spat with a bare palm upturned.

The *Yellow Fever* was as infamous for its overpriced drinks, most of which were at least twice that of other clubs, as it was for its high- ranking clientele. The ridiculously bloated pricing was but one of many reasons anyone under the pay grade of E-6 couldn't even seriously consider hanging out on a regular basis, the main being a mandatory cover charge of ten bucks just to step through the constantly guarded double-doors.

"So, you had Yobo but no more?" Lei continued once the waitress had departed, sipping a frosty pinkish-colored liquid from a long straw.

"Well, yeah...I guess you could say that," he replied after a long swallow of his own, "but...we...we're still trying to work it out."

As the blaring music temporarily faded into relative silence, Jeremy caught himself lingering within her searing gaze. Almost immediately, he felt

121

the majority of his uneasiness fall away. It was a change, however unsubtle, that he regarded as equal parts soothing and scary. They fell silent for a few moments while scanning the multitude of writhing, squirming bodies down below.

"How long you been at the base?" she finally asked, her dark ruby lips parting for yet another sip of a drink the troops called the 'Kool- Aid' special, which even the ladies agreed contained very little if any alcohol content.

He briefly considered another lie, as with the Yobo comment, but instead countered with "Just over eight weeks. How about you? Don't think I've seen you here before tonight."

"Tonight my first night to dance. I moved from Pusan last week," she said, forced to raise her voice as April Wine's '*Just Between You and Me*' blasted from the surrounding speakers.

"You...got yobo?" he blurted after they'd both paused for a drink and quick scan of the dancer presently on stage, a petite but immensely attractive young girl with unusually large breasts when compared to her peers.

"Yeah," she replied, gesturing towards the bar area with her right hand, "but he too much butterfly."

Leaning out and over from the left of the table, Jeremy squinted while using a raised hand to block out the effects of an overhead strobe.

"The guy with the eye-patch?" "Yeah, that's Charlie."

"He an officer?" "O-2."

Jeremy leaned back in, nodding knowingly. As

122

insane as it was, he could've sworn he felt just a twinge of jealousy tug at his midsection.

"Oh, a lieutenant. Muscled up dude, isn't he?"

"Muscle….up?" she asked with a mild frown.

"He must work out a lot. Looks strong as a bull," he replied, pointing at his own bicep.

"Oh yes…he goes to gymnasium every day Sometime I think he care more about his own body than he does mine ," she said, rolling her eyes, "anyway, he make great bodyguard."

"I can believe that," he said with a sheepish grin.

She shrugged, returning her gaze to the stage, where her co- worker was just finishing up her routine.

"Here come your friend, the Colonel."

"Uh-oh," Jeremy grumbled, spotting Bennett stiff-walking up the incline, "I can tell Pappy ain't the least bit happy."

"Pappy?" she quizzed with a girlish pout he found incredibly sexy. "That's just what I call him. The Colonel's kind of like … a father to ll of us," he explained, standing up as to depart as his boss grew near and David Bowie's '*Let's Dance*' kick-started a new wave of drunken, dance floor boogieing.

"Jeremy, I'm headed back to base," the older man said, reaching for his drink before downing the sum of its content in two lengthy swallows.

Pushing his beer aside, Jeremy stepped out from the table as to depart.

"I'll hail us a cab, sir."

"No, no, you can stay. Major Carson just needs a debriefing and insists the damn thing can't wait 'til

123

morning. Just don't be hanging about after curfew, Sarge, or both our asses will be in a sling come first light."

"Besides," the Colonel said tongue-in-cheek, "we can't leave the little lady here unadorned on her first night on the job, and there's nothing but the usual drooling wolves down at floor level."

"Well, um, she does have a yobo," Jeremy said, feeling a small wave of embarrassment as Lei flashed a hurtful look.

"You not buy me another drink? My rotation come soon, then I come back, okay?"

"Well, I'd better get back myself. Got an early day, right sir?"

Blinking rapidly, the older man's squinting eyes darted back and forth between the two subjects several times, as if awaiting further dialogue between the two.

"Uh, yes, I...that's right, yeah, Sergeant. Might be better if you come along at that...kayo (English translation: *goodbye*), young lady," he concluded with a slight bow in Lei's direction.

"Yeah, well...I'll be seeing you then," Jeremy added weakly, practically running into the other man's turned back.

"I'm here every night except Monday," Lei announced with a polite tip of her drink glass.

Jeremy nodded a final time, then strolled away at a double-time- march pace.

Watching his hurried departure while re-donning the heavily-tinted shades, Lei couldn't help but smile in utter bemusement.

*Do I really make some of them that nervous?*

*Perhaps I just made the acquaintance of the Ville's last surviving virgin. So cute and polite...and so very out of place.*

Moments later, she arose with a pained grunt, side-stepping several clutching hands and ignoring the various cat-calls while making her way towards the stage, where Bowie was about to give way to Rod Stewart's '*Maggie May*' , her pre-set signal to take center stage for a three dance set. A few hours later, she would concede, at least to herself while soaking her feet in a basin of heated water, that her first night spent 'entertaining' at the Yellow Fever club had, bar none, been the roughest, most physically challenging six hour stretch in her young life.

***

"Ziltch, huh? Not a single blip on that inner-radar of yours?" "Had a few minor surges, but nothing remotely felonous."

Lei laid across the badly sagging queen-sized bed with her feet propped atop a set of pillows, wearing only a loose-fitting pair of jean shorts and a sleeveless cotton tee-shirt.

"How many Kool-Aids you tally when all was said and done?" Charlie chided while peering out from between dust-coated blinds from the hooch's lone window, where an early morning fog had quickly given way to bright rays of sunlight.

"Let's put it this way; I've peed about sixty times since midnight." "Lucky there's no booze content, or I'd have had to piggy-back you ome."

"Regardless, a few more nights like that and kidney *slash* bladder failure is a definite possibility."

"So…," he said, turning back towards her as a trio of Korean-made transport vans whizzed down the narrow one-lane with their horns blaring, "what'd you think of the place overall?"

"For the record, I'm rigorously opposed to both legalized prostitution and/or slavery."

Strolling over to the bedside with his hands tucked inside his camouflaged pants, Charlie regarded her with a sarcastic sneer.

"I meant the atmosphere, your co-workers…the clientele. Wasn't looking for a political analysis."

"The other three dancers are pill-heads, Chuck. I'm not real sure at least two of them even know they're present most of the evening. Not a bad strategy, really…'" she paused, leaning up to prop her chin on a curled fist, "and most of the troops are just looking for something to grope, and don't give a good damn about the '*I got Yobo*' sentiment.

Got to admit though, quite a few of them backed away but good once they got an eyeful, pardon the pun, of my live-in love."

"You think those guys are bad?" he countered, temporarily unable to pry his eyes from the semi-stiff nipples protruding through her thin cotton shirt, "you outta spend a shift or three in the *Western Edge* or the *Serenity*. Those noncommissioned boys hit the entrance with full- blown erections and expect to hit the exit with a cure for that particular condition tucked on their arms. I've seen dancers and hostesses hauled outta there with black eyes, bloodied noses, or worse. Remember, it's usually

126

referred to as an 'Officer and a Gentleman' for a reason, sweetie."

"If you say so, Chuck, but I don't know how many more times I can take being called 'pooter-pie' and being pinched on the ass-cheeks without ripping out somebody's spleen," she moaned in a raspy tone that reeked of fatigue.

"Just maintain, Lei. You're tolerance level will increase, believe me. Besides," he replied in an equally weary voice, "we might only have a few more weeks before Operation *Ville Ripper* is permanently shelved."

Grimacing, Lei leaned up onto her elbows. "What's that?"

"Wing Commander is catching a shit-load of heat from some of the local politicians around Sunyon City. They're pushing like hell to lock down the base until the killer or killers are in custody. I've heard that PACAF's head honcho himself might institute the action any day now."

Feigning disappointment even as her heart fluttered with newfound joy, Lei huffed loudly before responding only to be drowned out by multiple horn-blasts from the nearby street.

"Um, you've probably covered this terrain before…but, what the blazes is Pac-calf again?"

"Sorry…*that's Pacific* Air Forces…as in command." "Right, so…if that does happen, then what?"

"Clubs would stay open, at least for a few days…maybe even a week, hoping for a few civilian stragglers. Obviously I'd have to maintain a low profile since I'm supposed to be stationed on-base. I mean, there is a chance our perp is a local. Slim as dental floss, but stranger things have happened."

Eventually though," he continued, side-stepping back over to the window, where the smell of grilled beef and bean curd permeated through the thin wire-mesh screen, "they'd close the doors and we'd be forced into plan B."

"Plan...B?"

"Yep," he said, having lowered his voice almost to whisper level, "street surveillance. Followed by a door to door Odyssey I'd rather not even think about. Always gives me a splittin' headache."

Lei collapsed face first back onto the less-than-firm mattress, essentially burying her head like a spooked ostrich.

"I can tell the possibility thrills you beyond words, darling," he said, studying her toned rear end for a brief moment before heading for the front door, "better get your beauty rest, dear. The bell tolls for round two in less than six hours. Meantime, I gotta check in with the powers that be, then I'll bring you back some lunch. Any preferences?"

"Double Whopper with cheese." "Try again."

"Big Mac...large fries, chocolate shake?" "One more time..."

"Pepperoni pizza...extra cheese...no anchovies. Side order of garlic bread sticks."

"Somebody certainly got spoiled on Western cuisine, now didn't they? How 'bout a nice, steaming bowl of kimchi soup and some dried octopus?"

He departed the tiny domicile to the sound of a pained groan and a tirade of mostly unintelligible

128

profanity.

***

"C'mon, partner, spill the beans. You can't fool Big Milt. We've been room dogs for coming up on five weeks, and I ain't ever seen you hit the Ville two nights running."

Sipping beers in the barracks dayroom, Milt Jacobs paced a circle around Jeremy's chair like a hovering vulture.

"You caught a whiff of something extra sweet in the Fever last night, didn't ya? C'mon now, give Uncle Milty the scoop."

"It's a sad tale, man," Jeremy finally relented, waiving a half-empty bottle of Budweiser in front of his own face as if attempting self- hypnosis, "the girl's got a live-in. She volunteered that info already. It's a waste of time, buuuuuut…."

Jacobs broke into a wild jig, tucking his own brew tightly against his mid-section while zigzagging in front of the room's lone black and white TV, which was presently showing an old rerun of '*The Adams Family*' , courtesy of the AFKN *(Armed Forces Korean Network)* network.

"But *what*? Talk to me, dude. It's a waste of time…but *what*?" "Oh, hell, I don't know. She was just so damn gorgeous, man.

And…the way she talked….I can't put my finger on it, but…"

"Uh-huh," the other man interrupted, collapsing onto a nearby couch with a resounding huff, "bet it wasn't just your *fingers* you wanted to lay on her,

129

am I right? Had some heavy-duty *pipe-laying* on your mind, didn't cha?"

His gaze gleaming and distant, Jeremy fell silent as his overly exuberant roommate stood up and began to gyrate wildly, pumping his arms and hips in opposite directions.

"Don't fight it, SOS. It's all about stress reduction, son! Take it from Uncle Milty, there ain't no shame!"

"Have you been listening?" Jeremy finally inquired in a high-pitched shriek, though unable to completely wipe the smile from his lips, "the girl is *with* Yobo. Big, hulky looking First Luey with an eye-patch, no less. Looks like he could bench-press South Dakota."

"So? They ain't married, are they?" "No, she didn't mention..."

"Well, then....that tells me both of 'em are probably gettin' a little on the sly, bro. It ain't love...just temporary lust, like most Ville romances."

Jeremy took a long swallow and belched loudly before flashing a winsome smile.

"Come to think of it, she did say the guy was the 'butterfly' type..." "You see? What did I just say? She's fair game, brother, fair fucking game," the other man said with a dramatic bow, accidentally spilling several drops of frothy brew onto the badly worn carpet below.

"Besides, you said the guy was a First Left-tenant, right?" "That's what *she* said."

"Officers don't ever get too serious over the filly population down at the Ville, you know that.

130

Those commissioned boys got too much to lose. Plus, if she's asking right off the bat whether or not *you* have a live in, that just means the girl's looking for a change. Yep, she's definitely in recruiting mode."

After a lengthy pause, wherein both men finished off their respective beers with similar gusto, Jeremy regarded his roommate with an angry stare, though he was completely unable to disguise the levity in his tone.

"Damn it, Milt. I only brought this up so you could talk me *out* of it."

"Sure you did, partner," the other man said with a wink, "just keep telling yourself that."

Leaning weakly forward, Jeremy bowed his head and sighed.

"I told myself I wasn't gonna do this, dude. Not after what I went through with the ex. Told myself I was gonna do my twelve months here completely incident free and hop onto that Freedom bird with a clear conscience and a refreshed outlook."

"Damn, boy, you're still human. You can't just turn emotions on and off like a garbage disposal, much less your hormones," Milt Jacobs replied in easily the sincerest tone Jeremy had ever heard the man utilize, "you're young...they're young. Enjoy yourself. Besides, nobody says ya gotta go get yourself hitched. Just have some fun and walk away, and make sure the girl knows it ain't never gonna get more serious than sharing bed-space for the next ten months. "

"You and your damn horse logic," Jeremy said with an appreciative nod, tipping the empty beer

131

bottle towards the other man, who replied in-turn.

The two shared another beer over an episode of 'The Munsters' before retreating back to their room, where Jeremy readied himself to catch the next bus headed to the Ville.

*\*\**

Lei could feel the man's anger radiate from his person in palpable waves as she finished off her soup with one final, purposely noisy slurp.

"Nice try, Sukie, but you ain't drowning me out on this. You need to find a way to brush this bastard off. He's an unwelcome diversion."

Using her chopsticks to ensnare a sizeable portion of bean sprouts, Lei remained unresponsive while casually glancing about the restaurant's deserted interior.

"You hearing me, woman? Nip this in the bud and be damn quick about it. We didn't set this up as a goddamn dating service. Put 'im on the trail of other game."

Shrugging, she forked in a mouthful of turnip kimchi to accent the sprouts.

"He's harmless. Besides, he's always good for two or three drinks," she said between chews, "I can't just push him away as long as he's offering. Might raise some eyebrows amongst the management."

"Don't bullshit me, sister," he raged, leaning forward and sharply slapping the tabletop with a bare palm, "I've been keeping this one good eye peeled but good. Last night you spent forty-five minutes nursing a single glass, and that ain't the first time. I've seen a definite trend in the past week or so.

Get this, lady, 'cause I'm only saying it once…"

Leaning back, he paused as the businesses lone waitress re- entered the cramped dining room of the '*Shrimp & Go*' to refill his water glass before sauntering back out of sight. At just past ten AM, the Ville population had yet to properly stir, thus the narrow streets were predictably desolate. Having arrived just before nine-thirty, they'd yet to see another customer enter the shop, the capacity of which would've been somewhere around the twenty to twenty-five range at best. Like most Ville eateries, the meat of their business was done between the hours of six PM and whenever the clubs closed, the majority of the clientele consisting of drunken airman and their female 'companions' searching for a quick snack. Most served fresh seafood and local dishes such as kim-bob, the Korean equivalent of Japanese sushi *minus* the raw fish, Chop Suey noodles, and of course, kimchi, the most popular and versatile of all local dishes. Whether it be eaten mild (preferred by most American connoisseurs) or blazing hot (pretty much any and all Korean nationals), and prepared with cabbage, turnips, or any other of a dozen separate recipes, kimchi was to the Korean people what bread was to those raised in North America; a garlic-leaden, extremely aromatic treat not for those with weak stomach's or sensitive noses. Together with rice, that of course being the official Korean 'Staff of Life', it wasn't at all unusual for those born and raised on the peninsula to consume the spicy concoction at breakfast, lunch *and* dinner on a daily basis for the duration of their life span. Not surprisingly, Lei had found that re-adapting to the foods she'd grown up on the easiest of tasks, her initial craving for 'American' type foods having grown increasingly weak as days passed.

"….you ain't here to be romanced, understand? Tell this jackass to take a hike or I'm liable to play the part of 'hard-ass Yobo' on the both of ya."

"My, my…" she cooed jokingly after a quick sip of water, "if I didn't know any better, I'd say my Yobo has been bitten by the green-eyed monst-.."

"You ain't here for the 'suckie-fuckie' action, kiddo," he barked back without a hint of good humor, "It's just an act, remember? Now…get your shit together or I'm liable to drop the hammer, meaning somebody's gonna be handed a one-way ticket to a federal penitentiary back in the states."

Her face turning a deep shade of red, Lei tossed the chopsticks against a far wall before shoving herself back from the table and standing tensely.

"*Eat shit*, one-eye. (IN KOREAN) This fucking charade was never my idea, remember?"

She took off in a wild sprint, a string of profanities trailing her out the double-door exit, which had been propped ajar.

"Wait…a minute, dammit!" he grumbled, struggling to pull the required Won from his wallet before jogging after her. Seconds later, the waitress watched him lumber down the winding passageway from the restaurant entrance, whispering aloud concerning what she'd determined to be nothing more than a lover's spout between a couple doomed to ultimate failure from a simple lack of communication.

***

His mind inhabiting a different plain altogether, Jeremy watched the man's lips move with virtually no interest in the meaning they relayed.

"I said...am I good to go?" the troop repeated for at least the third time, his brow creased in building frustration.

"Hello? Anybody *in there*?"

"Um...hang on, Sergeant...um..."Jeremy mumbled, his daze officially broken as he began separating the Master Sergeant's gear for at least the fourth time since the man's arrival at the *'Equipment Check-In'* window, "okay, that's one gas mask with inserts; one utility belt with canteen, Kavlar vest and helmet... black gloves and booties. Okay, Sergeant Wilson, sign on the dotted line there and you are o-fficially a free man, at least as far as base supply is concerned."

The balding, middle-aged NCO signed quickly and practically tossed the form back at him with a disgusted grunt.

"Thanks for the prompt service, Sergeant Yeager. Might wanna try some caffeine, or maybe a *hearing* aid."

Ignoring the sarcastic remark, Jeremy nodded blandly as the man lumbered off in a huff.

A Senior Airman with a shaved, pointy head and the physique of a bent toothpick approached the

135

window next, his broad smile exposing a horrific overbite.

"What say, ass-lick?" he cracked, tossing a comically overstuffed duffel onto the tabletop.

Jeremy glanced over the bag and grimaced, performing a textbook double-take.

"You gotta be shitting me. Earl?"

"Why, I wouldn't shit you, SOS, you being my fav-or-ite turd an' all."

"No way....you're short?"

"Twelve days and a wake up, shitheel," the freckled-faced airman beamed in a deep southern drawl, slapping a badly crinkled form atop the pregnant duffel, "read 'em and weep."

Wearing a deep frown, Jeremy scooped up the form and scanned the top portion.

"Little Rock Air Force Base, huh?"

"Damn tooting. Only a hop, skip and jump from the old stompin' grounds, old buddy."

"Didn't you hear, Earl?" "Hear what?"

"Effective immediately," Jeremy announced in his best news anchor voice, "PACAF has rescinded all orders for *in-bred* and certified *homo* personnel, and you, my boy, qualify on *both* counts. Looks like a twelve month extension for Earl the Pearl."

The younger man shrugged wearily and rolled his eyes.

"Oh, kiss my freckled butt-cheeks, Yeager, and out-process me already. I've done my time in this live-in sewer, and then some."

"Thought you liked it here, man," Jeremy said, reaching into the duffel with a sour frown, "Geez, this gear reeks. You take a piss in here or what?"

136

"Aw, it's all right, I reckon...I'm just fed up with Asia in general. The PI was okay, but this place is a pain in the ass. Nothin' but war game piled atop war game. Guess I just crave some home cookin' and down-home lovin '."

Jeremy pinched his nose with one hand while separating the mildew-scented gear, his tone predictably nasal, as if he'd ingested a lungful of helium. The two had been stationed together at Clark Air Base in the Philippines for several months before Earl's PCS to Sunyon, sharing several hundred San Miguel brews in the process, but hadn't seen much of one another since Jeremy's arrival on the peninsula.

"Really? Heard you were getting plenty of loving, Ville style." "Yeah, well, the Yobo was getting kinda flaky there at the end. I moved back on base a few weeks ago."

"Flaky? Don't tell me she started pushing you to take her to the land of the big BX..."

Earl shrugged good-naturedly, scrunching his nose as if just noticing the putrid scent emitting from his duffel.

"Along those lines, yeah. Funny thing was, she knew that wasn't ever gonna happen. We'd talked about it the day we shacked up.

Supposed to just be for kicks, you know? Four months later, she expects me to extend for a year and kick start the marriage paperwork. No noooo, not this boy. I get the feeling the US Air Force don't take kindly to polygamy."

Turning his head from the duffel's open maw, Jeremy side-stepped over to a nearby desk top and retrieved several blank forms.

"Yeah, kinda doubt your wife would appreciate the added addition to the family either."

"You got that shit straight, bro. Speaking of the Ville, I hear through the grapevine you're becomin' a real regular at a certain upscale night spot."

Though they remained locked on the forms he so effortlessly penned, Jeremy's eyes instantly squinted a shade. Lord, was it that obvious, even to outsiders? In such a close knit military community, the art of keeping a secret was definitely of the 'lost' variety.

Everyone seemed to know what everyone else was doing, whether the information be first, second, or third hand.

"Just killing time, you know," he replied tight-lipped.

"I hear ya talkin', son. How long you been here now?" "Just passed the thirty-five day milestone on the old short calendar."

"Yep, that's about the time I reached red-line status on the old horn-dog meter, if I recall correctly. Found myself shacked up with Mia a few months later."

Nodding vehemently, Jeremy pulled a wrinkled chemical suit from the duffel with his fingertips, as if handling toxic waste.

"Not gonna happen to this boy, Earl. I've been down that rocky road, remember? It's a hard lesson to learn, but I've earned my degree."

"Uh-huh. So your tellin' me your just hanging out at the Fever, coughing up ten bucks a drink for your health? I've heard their dancers were of the

138

super-model variety, with oversized melons and rear ends shapely enough to make a grown man drool."

"Urban legend, Earl," Jeremy replied while checking the gas mask for its proper inserts, "I just like the atmosphere. Sides, I got a membership card, remember? Get all my drinks half-price."

"Whatever you say, Hoss,' came the sardonic reply, 'just make damn sure she's worth the effort, hear? I recall you tellin' me about that first wife of yours. Little kitten from the PI turned into a hellcat on wheels once that green card slapped her palm."

Pushing the empty duffel forward towards the other man, Jeremy continued filling out the required out-processing forms even as his mind' s eye temporarily called up a bleary image of the ex-wife, her face contorted in anger, as was the normal expression during their final, turbulent months spent as a couple.

"No need to remind me, dude. I lived it, remember? Damned if I'll frequent that particular highway to hell again in this lifetime."

"I'll be rooting for ya, pal," Earl replied while signing the first of several pre-printed forms, a ritual he would repeat several times over before being allowed 'legal' departure from the peninsula, "cause the odds definitely ain't in your favor. Sooner or later, the little head takes charge. Just a matter of time."

Jeremy reached over and shook the man's hand as they exchanged a warm smile that spoke volumes without benefit of further vocal exchange. There was a tight, unspoken bond between those who served twelve-month remote tours; wherein personnel changes were a daily occurrence and interpersonal relationships oft times cut short from their full potential. Everyone assigned went through the same exact four step program; the in-processing phase (easily the most trying), followed by the 'learning the ropes' phase (the initial 'wetting of feet'), the 'comfort zone' phase (wherein adaptation to one's surroundings is complete and daily tasks finally become, for the most part, routine), and concluding with the 'out-processing' phase, a seven to ten day span that is easily the most joyous spent at a remote site.

"Ten and a half more months," Jeremy whispered mere moments after the other man's departure, "and I'll be standing on the other side of this damn gate."

Just the thought sent an icy chill racing down his spine. "Meanwhile, I got me some living to do."

\*\*\*

"Just what in the HELL do you think you're doing?"

Lei stood at the center of the one-room abode, ripping a multi- colored halter top into shreds as a steady stream of warm tears trailed down both cheeks.

Still gasping for breath from the lengthy jog that had proceeded his arrival back at their hooch, Charles leapt over and gripped what remained of the halter and tore it from her hands.

"You didn't *pay* for this shit, lady. It ain't yours

to destroy."

Backing away, Lei took up a decidedly defensive combat pose with her left arm raised in a blocking pose and the right cocked back to strike.

"What's this?" he asked with a malicious grin while backing up a step, "you're challenging me? Is that it? You really want a piece of the *rock*?"

Curling her bottom lip beneath a top row of bared teeth, Lei casually curled the fingers of her blocking hand into a snake-like 'come hither' gesture.

Visibly slumping, Charles placed his hands atop his hips and lowered his head before casually tossing the shredded clothing aside.

"Let's…both just calm down, Lei. I…know I can be a hot-headed bast-…"

Lurching forward at warped speed, she executed a forceful but slightly off-kilter reverse kick, the heel of her bare left foot impacting just below the right side of his rib cage.

Off-balance and unable to control his backward momentum, he pin- wheeled back until pummeling the far wall, his hair and upper shoulders coated in plaster fragments as the outline of his wide, muscular back was permanently engraved in the half-wood, half stucco wall.

"Son of…a…BITCH!" he bellowed, rolling onto one knee with both arms instinctively covering his face and head.

"Cut… it out, DAMN it!"

Though he managed to successfully block the first in a barrage of short jabs, several more connected solidly with his lower jaw and forehead until he was sent reeling by a vicious uppercut, the sound of the blow overshadowed only by the gnashing of his own teeth.

Bouncing from wall to wall like a ricocheting pinball, his size twelve boots shattered everything in their path, to include a small coffee table that was perfectly halved in a single stomp.

The vision in his one working eye badly blurred, he was still able to brace himself at least somewhat while gauging her location by the constant stream of profanities spewing forth.

Once a front kick only grazed his outer left thigh, he jumped straight up with bended knees to avoid the follow-up leg sweep. Upon descent, he easily blocked her attempted 'clothes line' blow, gripping her right arm by the wrist and elbow before slinging her to the hardwood floor as gently as was feasible.

"Settle…down…Lei….just stop it now….STOP IT!" he screamed, hugging her close and essentially pinning her back and shoulders with his massive bulk.

He felt her struggles transform in to a weakened series of tremors, her upper body shaking uncontrollably as shrill cries echoed from the back of her throat.

"It's okay. I'm…I'm sorry. Do you hear me? (IN KOREAN)…I'm *truly*…sorry. I didn't mean to…talk to you…or treat you…that way."

Her words were accented by the intermediate sob, her voice cracking with equal portions of immense sadness and a barely controlled rage.

"(IN KOREAN) I…don't want

142

this…shit…anymore. I can't….I just…want…out. Out…let me…*go*…just let me….go."

"I wish… I could, darlin'," he replied, slowly easing the pressure of his body weight while loosening the grip on her wrists and arms, "it…just ain't in my power."

He rolled gently off of her as her pants gradually subsided.

Eventually they both lay atop the floor, staring into the moisture stained ceiling through glassy reflections.

"I dream…" Lei said after several moments of strained silence, "that this, what we're doing now, will be the only life I'll ever know from here on. I dream…that ten years from now we'll still be looking for the same killer, only to find out he was right under our noses the entire time. Not a G.I…not even a local, but a specter; an evil entity birthed from this…this place that breeds sin like maggots on a dead carcass.

You want to know the truth? The unvarnished, honest to God's truth? I'd *rather* die than know my future lies here…" she concluded, rolling towards him and tucking her body against his, "…I'd rather have the killer find me before I…find him."

"Lei, I...listen, we'll find hi-..," he began, cut off as she thrust herself upward, clasping her hands atop his shoulders as their lips impacted with a firm wetness. Their tongues danced and probed like electrified antennae, and he was instantly intoxicated by not only the sweet smell and taste of her, but also the feel of her lithe, athletic body pressing so desperately against his own. One of her hands found his groin and began a gentle, rhythmic massage, even as her cupped her heaving right breast, her passionate moans fueling his frantic movements.

Forcing her hand from his building erection, Charles rolled from her grasp in minute segments, the parting of their mouths serving as the final break.

"Lei...Lei, I can't....I can't do this," he whispered in a tone ripe with lust while keeping her at arm's length.

Rising to her knees, Lei's regarded him in silent despair as her lower lip quivered in random spasms.

"I...I'm sorry....," he continued, hanging his head in apparent shame, '...I can't do that to...to her."

A nearby horn sounded from the street, triggering a full three minutes of silence between the two. Lei eventually arose to take a seat on the corner of the mattress as Charles walked gingerly about, collecting broken chunks of the shattered table and placing them in a plastic wastebasket near the front door.

"So, you *are* married. I suspected as much," she finally said after blowing her nose into a napkin.

"Nine years." "Children?"

"One daughter. She just turned six." "Korean?"

He adjusted his eye-patch, which had been pushed slightly askew in the scuffle, then cocked an eyebrow her way.

"You really have to ask?" "They in-country?"

"We rent a house just outside Seoul. They...split time between here and the US."

"I take it you were stationed here once."

"Ten years ago this month, I arrived at Kunsan

Air Base. Met Kim just a few months into my tour. I ended up extending at the Kun, then getting orders to Osan for another year. Got out of the service a few years later, but haven't been back to the states on a permanent basis since."

Lei nodded knowingly before collapsing back onto the bed and effectively cocooning herself within the mussed sheets.

"I...um...apologize for...the scene...and...," she mumbled, her head pressed deep inside a foam pillow, "well, I can't remember ever feeling more like a horse's rear end...at least not lately."

"No apologies necessary, lady. There's something...I've gotta...I need to say," he said, walking over and placing an open palm atop her exposed right shoulder, "been holding back for too damn long. First off, my last name's not Whitt; it's *Rutherford*. Figured you earned the right to at least know that.

Yeah, I blew my stack back there 'cause we can't afford to have our covers blown by you getting chummy with any of the local airman, but...it's more than that (pauses, sighs heavily). I've... felt an attraction to you since day one. A damn strong one. It's not just the close proximity the past few weeks either. You've....you intimidate me like no one ever has, be it a man in a combat situation or a beautiful woman with an open invitation. I was scared at first...'cause I wasn't sure why I was so...drawn to you. I mean, there ain't no man alive that could resist your looks, but...it was more than that. Knew it right away. Felt it, like some kinda physical ailment...draining me, making me misplace my

145

priorities. At first, I thought it might just be the danger factor. I mean, wild as it sounds, this...power of yours...this mystery radar you possess...is quite the enticement for a regular Joe like myself. Once we... moved in here and set up camp..." he paused, turning from her and facing the open window instead, "... the magnet to steel effect only intensified. This may sound loony as hell, but...you can't know the jealousy I feel when we're at the club and those guys are...ogling you and...telling me how sexy you are and how they'd like to.....*shit*. I've come... real close in the past few days to backing out of the mission altogether.

Did some real soul-searching, in fact. But, I knew if I did that, the powers that be would cancel the program and send you packing...back to the states and...right back into federal custody. In the end, I just couldn't... force the issue, despite not trusting myself a single second in your presence."

Freeing herself from the binding sheets, Lei leaned up and blew weakly into still another facial tissue, her eyes horribly bloodshot.

"(IN KOREAN) Don't be afraid. I don't *love* you, Charles, but I'm not looking to *waste* you either," she said, smiling wearily as he turned to face her.

"I didn't mean..." he stammered, taking a cautious step forward. "(IN ENGLISH) No harm, no foul. The thing is this....I've been alone most of my life, and....and the things I've...I've done. Things I...thought were...justified...the right thing to do. These days, since I've been here...I'm not so sure anymore. Years ago, a man I came to think of as an

146

angel once showed me the way. He…showed me my…destiny.

Lately…especially since I got here…I'm beginning to think he wasn't an angel at all, but more…like a demon in disguise."

"Lei, you've got a chance to wipe the slate clean. If we can catch the murdering bas-.."

"Charles," she scolded politely, standing stiffly and stepping forward until they were posed less than a foot apart, "I think we both know the odds of that happening. I haven't had the faintest glimmer….not even a single shiver or symptom in the two plus weeks we've been playing the game.

Maybe…I don't know, maybe the shock of the capture and my placement here…affected me somehow. Maybe the batteries ran dry. Maybe it's the 'homeland' effect. Or maybe…just maybe…" she concluded, placing a hand lightly atop his left shoulder, "… the curse has been permanently lifted. It isn't as if I haven't prayed long and hard for such a miracle. "

Reaching to cover her hand with his own, Charles crouched just slightly as to even their height, his one good eye scanning each of hers.

"You were given this…power for a reason. We read your file, Lei… several times over. Studied it and dissected it. I lived with the damn thing for two solid weeks. Everyone you took out was bottom-feeder scum, the lowest of the low. Some of 'em didn't even have criminal records, but *did* have a history of acquittals or major suspicion. These weren't minor offenders. All were major league sick-O's who were way beyond any kinda

147

rehabilitation. Make no mistake, you did society a favor. I ain't supposed to approve, and I sure as hell ain't supposed to tell you so, but I think you and I are beyond the BS stage. I'm in your corner, Lei, maybe the *only* one there, but I'm as committed to you right now as I am the mission itself."

"But...what if I have...lost it? What are we even doing here?" "Well, maybe it isn't that your...gift is out of order, at least not completely. Maybe it's just biding its time, preserving its resources." "For what exactly?"

He leaned forward until their foreheads gently met, then stepped back wearing a sad, pained smile.

"So it can hone in on the biggest, baddest, vilest mother of them all. Maybe it's just done detecting what it considers small fish. Maybe this time...it's after a fucking *whale*. "

"I...it's just...."

"We have to believe that, Lei," he said in a gentle but stern voice, gripping her by the upper shoulders, "face it. We've got nothing else to believe *in* at this point."

The two then embraced, and Lei's overworked tear ducts released a final torrent as Charles held and comforted her, adapting quickly, and with great personal relief, to the role of brother-figure.

\*\*\*

Nursing his third beer of the evening, Jeremy reached over the table and gave Lei a playful slap across the top of her hand in an attempt to pull her focus from the sparse crowd occupying the dance

148

floor. As was the norm on Friday nights, it was barely six o'clock and the tables below them were already filling up.

"Hey, want another drink?" he asked as she turned back towards him with a distant look.

"Annyo (English translation: *no*)," she said, waiving him off, "I already ojum (English translation: *urinate*) too much."

"You okay?" he asked cautiously, temporarily glancing past her and to the bar area, where her Yobo inhabited his usual seat while consuming a bowl of Jungle Juice ( a potentially lethal mix of Korean Soju and Peach Oscar wine ) with several of the club's nubile young hostesses.

"Yeah, just tired. I don't like Fridays. Everybody got Mechaso (English translation: *crazy*) look in their eyes."

"Yes they do," he nodded, watching her sip halfheartedly from a long straw, "and it's payday to boot."

She nodded without reply, rotating the straw between the forefinger and thumb of her left hand.

A pair of troops lurched by in a comically inebriated lurch, each eyeing Lei like ravenous wolves while trekking clumsily towards the dance floor.

"Some just get started earlier than others," Jeremy quipped, pointing a thumb in the direction of the stumbling pair.

"Mechaso," she repeated with a scowl, "Soju just makes them crazier."

Seconds later, the opening guitar licks from The Eagles' *'Hotel California'* was greeted by several drunken cheers.

"Hey, hey, hey," Jeremy beamed, shooting the bar area another quick glance to ensure Mister 'Yobo at large' was indeed still parked atop his assigned stool, "they're playing our song. You up to it?"

"I'd better not. Better save my energy. Got to dance five or six rotations tonight."

They exchanged a brief, inexplicably awkward glance before Lei turned away and trained her sites directly onto her live-in, who had stepped away from the bar to slow dance with one of the aforementioned hostesses. In response, Jeremy instantly felt a burning sensation fill his chest and lungs like a toxic gas.

"You sure you're all right?"

"Good as it can be, I guess," she replied wearily, taking a final sip of the Kool-Aid concoction before rising in a similarly fatigued manner.

"I see you later, okay? I'd better mingle some after this rotation.

Mama sun get real angry lately."

"How about Yobo? He pretty pissed off too, right?" he shot back in an irritated, accusative tone he instantly regretted.

She walked away without either a verbal or nonverbal response, her expression visibly unchanged.

Jeremy departed halfway through the second song of her third dance rotation, a hard rock ballad from the Super-Group 'Asia' that he'd learned to despise merely from recent overkill. Lei had merely

150

been going through the motions on the dance floor, but had managed to consistently flash those pearly whites at whoever had been providing drinks, not to mention *propositions*, in-between.

Arriving back at the barracks at just before ten PM, Jeremy nursed a trio of beers inside the abandoned TV room until just after midnight before crashing within the peaceful confines of his similarly deserted room. His roomie, Milt Jacobs, was no doubt still frequenting the Ville's many watering holes, and rarely reclaimed his side of their barracks room before the next morning.

Tossing and turning like a man possessed, Jeremy Yeager found sleep a virtual impossibility despite the relatively tranquil surroundings. He could not force this woman, in reality a complete *stranger*, from the forefront of his thoughts, no matter the effort.

Self-brainwashing had been a pathetic failure, as in thoughts of permanently banning himself from the Yellow Fever while trolling the other bars for a similarly ravishing target of his never-ending lust, preferably one *not* already possessing a live-in lover. Sounded simple enough, at least until he dwelled (whether consciously or not) upon Lei's natural allure or enigmatic personality, the latter of which was maddeningly impossible to gauge as being either sincere or a meticulously well-refined act. He'd spent literally every free moment in the previous three weeks at the Ville, tossing away a nightly average of thirty-five thousand won (roughly forty American greenbacks) while chatting with and lusting over a girl he still knew virtually nothing

151

about, to include actual name or age. They had danced (something he wouldn't normally even attempt sober), both the fast and slow variety, talked, laughed, and found a comfortable middle-ground dialogue despite some predictable but minor lapses in communication. His roommate, he of the 'happy marriage' and multiple Ville sex partners, had attempted his own brand of warped 'counseling', referring to Jeremy's condition as the 'pre-whipped' phase, the man's personal advice limited to 'find a LBFM that isn't already under warranty, dude (*'LBFM'* being crude G.I lingo for *'Little Brown Fucking Machine'* )." It wasn't as if Jeremy didn't realize the wisdom of such a statement, however crude. It was far from Mister Yeager's first rodeo. He'd been around the block, and then some, in dealing with these mysterious, exotic temptresses of the Far East.

Had even gone as far as marrying such an enigmatic entity and bringing her to the states, wading through mountains of red tape government paperwork to do so while (foolishly?) ignoring the constant badgering and negative dialogue that birthed from such a decision.

Less than two full years, a rather unpleasant divorce, and several unhealed scars later, he still found himself haplessly susceptible to their ravishing charms, his inner gut experiencing the same familiar fluttering; his thoughts and actions easy distracted as her image constantly flooded his inner mind's eye.

He awoke the next morning with just a twinge of a hangover, his desire for Sukie hardly abated.

Jeremy Yeager attended a Methodist church service that morning, a rare occurrence indeed. While there, he prayed for strength. The strength he most definitely need for the days and weeks to come.

\*\*\*

Charles Rutherford assaulted the hard bag with a flurry of combinations, concluding with a solid left hook that sent it spinning like a top, threatening to snap the connecting chains that held it airborne.

Taking a seat on a nearby weight-bench, he balanced his elbows atop his knees and lowered his head, spattering the floor beneath with a heavy coating of fop sweat. Unlike the previous two weeks' workouts, he no longer felt as though he was simply going through the motions. There was a renewed vigor, a fiery grit. No longer saddled with a sense of impending guilt, however unjustified, it was as if he'd awoken to a series of miraculous injections that had revitalized both his mind and spirit. Against heavily stacked odds, he'd renewed his vows of faith to his loving wife while managing to find the inner- strength to avoid temptation. Realizing he'd been mere moments away from an adulterous act that more than likely would've spelled the end of both his marriage and career only served to make the innocent outcome all the more rewarding. Though he could still taste her sweet, succulent lips and re-imagine the intoxicating scent of her, the obsession phase had passed without consummation. The crippling effects of her natural allure had diminished considerably the moment he'd backed away. There would be no more sidetracks; no more detours, no more distraction. It was again the mission itself that sat at the forefront of his every waking thought. That said, a new attachment of sorts had been added to the mission checklist. An attachment that added an extra task to his ever-growing list of responsibilities. He was Lei's mentor, true, but also her protector.

He'd know it from day one, but had purposely shied away from the prospects, remaining cold and distant as to avoid any type of building relationship. He realized he could no longer label her merely as 'extra baggage'; a tool to be used and casually discarded.

She now fell under the heading of his personal 'Holy Grail.' He would lay down his life for hers without hesitation, a claim he couldn't have made even a week earlier, and though it was impossible to verify, he somehow knew she felt the same way.

Obviously, he hoped such an occasion never arose, and certainly in the light of recent news, such fears might well be infinitely futile.

Leaning back, he clasped the heavy bar in the widest grip possible, heaving it from its stand with a loud groan. Three strained reps later, the last of which he'd practically bounced from his upper chest, he replaced the bar and leaned back up with a resounded grunt.

Reaching up, he removed the eye-patch and hung it from the weight bar's rounded edge, all the while pondering a precariously uncertain future. Just that morning his superiors had informed him that operation '*Ville Ripper*' would be unceremoniously aborted in two weeks unless evidence surfaced to validate its continued usefulness.

He'd argued, first politely and then more vehemently of the Ripper's one-kill-per month pattern, and that aborting too soon might well preclude the next murder by mere days. Rebuffed at every turn, he had eventually fell silent and sullen, even when ordered to avoid accompanying Lei to the Yellow Fever on an everyday basis when it was decided such behavior might well serve to 'tip off' the suspect if he or she was regularly casing the club. Though he understood (and even begrudgingly agreed) the logic of such a decision, the thought of leaving Lei's welfare in the hands of the 'town patrol' was less than comforting. Still, there was no winning such a weak argument, so he'd let it pass without even a token effort. He could only hope Lei would take the double-barrel issuance of bad news with less negativity than himself, though a blasé attitude wasn't likely considering her very fate lay in the balance. Two more weeks without results and she'd most likely be shipped back to the states for immediate indictment, only her cooperation in the project helping to eliminate the distinct possibility of a death sentence being handed down.

Scooping up a set of forty pound barbells, he began a deliberate series of curls, the pump in each bicep becoming more pronounced with each completed movement.

"We'll get you, ya bastard," he spat from between tightly gritted teeth, staring into a mirrored wall as the veins stood out in his neck like cable cords, "one way or another, your psychotic ass is gonna be alllll mine."

***

Strolling up the winding passage at a snail's pace, Lei inhaled greedily to the smell of grilled beef, boiled crab, and mandu dumplings emanating from a nearby street vendor. She stopped long enough to order a thousand Won worth of the kimchi mandu, eating it from a paper dish while detouring from the main path onto a dirt runway that split two massive rice paddies.

At just before ten AM, there still existed a slight chill in the air, perpetuated by a stiff breeze that was slowly warming beneath the sun's glaring intrusion. She covered an additional hundred yards before squatting down at the fields' northern edge, peering down from a steep bank into endless rows of sitting water from which the country's number one commodity would soon spring forth. Flaring her nostrils, she could just make out the faint scent of cherry blossoms in full bloom. Covering her eyes with the flat of her left hand, she scanned the perimeter and spotted a small grove of young cherry trees approximately two to three hundred feet to her left. Barely eight years removed, only now was she beginning to realize just how much she'd missed the sights and smells so common to her country of birth.

She scooped up pebbles from the dirt bank and casually tossed them into the water, all the while attempting, with minimal success, to properly organize her jumbled thoughts.

First there was Charles Rutherford, the gruff, one-eyed man fate had seemingly chosen to fill the newly cast role of savior, mentor, and all-around authority figure. The only person she'd ever met whose belief in her at least appeared sincere. The man who had, albeit temporarily, saved her from a life of incarceration and media-driven mythical status as the most prolific of female serial killers. True, in hindsight she deeply regretted the sexual aggressiveness she'd displayed, though she felt no shame for urges that, in the end, separated her from the cold, robotic killer most would logically assume she was.

Then there was Sergeant Jeremy Yeager; sweet, lonely *Jeremy*.

She'd easily detected the puppy-love in his eyes the very night they'd met, and by the fourth or fifth such occasion, watched it mutate into full-blown obsession. In turn, she'd also witnessed the deep hurt the night she'd attempted the *'cold shoulder'* maneuver, per Charles' direct order, a nasty little episode that had left a decidedly bitter taste in her mouth. Jeremy Yeager held all the scars of a recently failed relationship, and obviously viewed her as a possible healer. The irony of such a notion would've been amusing if it hadn't been so damn tragic. The poor man didn't possess a single clue, she mused. If he was only allowed even a slight glimpse into the person he viewed as some sort of walking, talking goddess, he'd more than likely go screaming bloody murder into the dark of night. Still, she couldn't help but reserve a soft spot for his dogged determination, and read his intentions,

157

however foolish, as both flattering and genuinely sincere.

She couldn't deny enjoying his company, being that they both shared a similarly warped sense of humor. Toss in the fact that, if given the chance, she'd physically *ached* to jump the man's bones, and the situation become increasingly complicated. Carnal cravings aside, she understood the gravity of allowing such a doomed, damned relationship to bloom. Plus, there would always be the remote possibility of positioning Jeremy directly in the line of fire, something that simply couldn't be allowed, no matter the personal sacrifice. All that said, young mister Yeager wasn't going to give up easily, this she knew without a shred of doubt, and she certainly hadn't helped matters by painting Charles as an insensitive, uncaring playboy. In regard to Sergeant Jeremy Yeager, she was going to have to tread very, *very* carefully.

Last but definitely not least, there was the growing concern over the sudden ineffectiveness of her so-called *'powers of detection'*. It was as if walking the grounds of her home country had somehow severed an essential wire or tripped an internal circuit breaker. In almost three weeks of entertaining countless male cliental within the Fever's squared walls, both military and civilian, nary a single symptom had emerged. She'd initially chalked up such unlikely results to an unusually high number of what she referred to as 'normals', defined as individuals possessing both clean criminal records (at least felonious- wise) and souls. It became apparent, however, after the first week or so, that something wasn't quite kosher. Over the past year, her 'power' had evolved to the point of being able to detect even the slightest level of past debauchery. There was simply no way everyone frequenting the Yellow Fever was that squeaky clean, especially those twenty to thirty year 'veterans' of the service who'd served tours in such infamously sinful locales as Germany, Thailand, the Philippines, or even South Korea. Simple logic dictated that even if such individuals were clean from a sexual standpoint, many long-term vets would have certainly had combat experience, either from Vietnam or other conflicts. Thus, despite such violent episodes being 'justifiable' from a wartime standpoint, she surely would've picked up a negative vibe of some sort. Thus far, in twenty-plus 'shifts' spent entertaining anywhere from four to five hundred clients, the inner radar screen had displayed not a single blip.

Rising from her squat in a stiff-legged stretch, Lei undertook a deep-breathing regimen in an admittedly feeble attempt to clear away the cobwebs. On the stroll back to the hooch, she purchased and consumed a cool bottle of Kin soda and a bag of 'shrimp-flavored' chips, all the while fantasizing that such leisurely, tranquil treks might someday be a regular morning ritual.

\*\*\*

"Hey, I don't like it any better than you do, but they didn't exactly give me a choice," Charles said in-between noisy slurps of beef- flavored rameon noodles, sitting across from Lei as they shared a

159

light lunch over a recently purchased serving table that sat less than a foot from the hooch floor.

"Wonderful. On the oft chance I do come face to face with Jack the Ripper, I have two pimply-faced SP's to watch my back," Lei replied, chomping on a vegetable dumpling in-between sips of steaming green tea.

"Listen, I'll be monitoring a two-way less than fifty yards away. I rented a shack just past the Fever's rear entrance. Couldn't be any closer if I was stationed under the stage."

"I don't know why I even care. The killer could probably be sitting in my lap and I'd never suspect a thing."

"It'll be there when you *need* it, Lei," he said sternly, adjusting his knees from the cramped 'lotus style' position he'd secured for the past fifteen minutes.

"If you say so, boss," she shrugged, "thirteen more days and it really won't matter anymore."

A truck wheeled by outside the window, announcing 'fresh fruit for sale' over a static-filled bullhorn.

"What do you think they'll do with me?" she asked after pushing away from the tray and leaning her upper back against the mattress' box spring, "I mean, straight from the button-hole, soldier."

He laid his chopsticks aside, wiping his mouth and inhaling deeply. "Lei, we'll worry about that when the time comes, okay? I know it's onna be damn hard, but try not to dwell on it. We'll...I'll come up with something," he said, bowing his head briefly, then looking back up with a newfound gleam in his lone eye, "working on it already, in fact."

"Are you now?" she replied with a tight smile, placing her hands behind her head. Without the required pancake makeup that her nightly 'trade' required, Charles thought, she resembled a girl of high school or early college years.

"Lady, guys like me just *live* for Plan B."

Rising from the floor with an audible creak from both knees, Charles stepped over her protruding legs and peered out the open window, balancing his elbows atop the narrow wooden ledge.

"Before the two weeks are completely up," she said after stifling a yawn, "you and I need to add a fresh coat of paint to this town, you think?"

"That can be arranged. You got anything specific in mind, lady?" "Yeah," she said dreamily, "I'd like to take the downtown tour. I hear they've got some really classy eateries and night clubs on main street Sunyon, just a few blocks from the American district. We can have a nice dinner, maybe share a dance or two to a live band before getting loaded to the gills on OB and Soju. Maybe even a little wine."

"Anything but Peach Oscar, right?" he snickered.

"That or colored water that tastes like watered down Pepto-Bismol." "You got it, gorgeous. Bank on it."

Though neither broached the subject, it was brutally obvious that just such a conversation might well be typical for someone facing a lengthy prison term.

161

After a short pause, Lei arose and instantly began a series of leg, back and arm stretches.

"My god, I haven't felt this out of shape in years."

"You're welcome to accompany me back to HQ and hit the workout room with me anytime you desire, ya know. It ain't the Y, but it sure beats the hell outta nothing."

"Thanks, but no thanks. That building as a whole gives me the creeps," she grunted, "like some kind of nuclear fall-out shelter *after* the fact."

"Understood. Long as you know the offer stands."

He turned, watching her twist and contort into various shapes that he could only imagine successfully executing with torn ligaments, ripped muscle, and pre-shattered bones.

"Oh yeah, you're as stiff as the proverbial board, alright. Damn woman, you've gotta have *elastic* bones."

He heard her giggle as the tip of her scalp brushed the floor from a stiff-legged stance.

"Listen, I've gotta get back, but…there is one more thing."

She froze in mid-stretch, a wishbone-like split with her torso lying atop her extended left leg.

"Oh shit, don't tell me…you saved the *really* bad news for last." "No, nothing like that."

He walked around to front her as she lifted her head and gracefully slid both legs beneath her.

"Hit me, big boy. I'm braced."

"Just this…" he hesitated, cupping his squared

chin in the fingers of his right hand, "from here on in, for however long the duration, if you feel….that is, you don't have to be alone."

Frowning, Lei leapt to her feet in two fluid movements and began a rather casual series of jumping jacks.

"Meaning…what exactly, chief?"

Staring down at his spit-polished boots, Charles locked on his own warped reflection displayed across the gleaming tips.

"Listen…I can't even imagine to know how…lonely you've been. I would think trust has been a real commodity for you these last several years, and of course there ain't time for any serious relationship building, but all I'm saying is….your time might be limited here, so…"

"Are you saying…get laid while I've got the chance?" she interrupted, halting in mid-stride and stepping up to him until her bared feet sat mere inches from the aforementioned boot-tips.

"Have my *ashes hauled* before being introduced to a gas chamber or being permanently locked away in a ten by twelve?"

"Well, yeah, I would've put it so blunt-.." he stammered, jolted back playfully by a two-handed shove.

"Why Charles, I made such an attempt just days ago, but was so cruelly rebuffed by a horny yet happily married hunk, remember?"

After a brief moment of awkward silence, during which time Charles Rutherford's rugged visage transformed from ghostly pale to a light shade of pulsating maroon, the two exchanged shy smiles and a warm hug.

"I appreciate the thought, Charlie, I really do," Lei said, pushing away from him before starting a fresh set of jumping jacks, "it's just...I don't want to leave anybody....hanging on the possibilities, you know? I don't want to hurt anybody like that."

"The Yeager dude, right?"

Her eyes instantly widened even as the pace of her movements increased.

"He seems like a sweet man, but he's recently divorced. Married a girl from the Philippines and she left him just eight months after they hit the states."

He took a seat to her left, the aged mattress sagging almost to the floor beneath his bulk.

"He's got it bad for ya, does he?"

"Unless I've got my signals severely crossed, yeah. Strange, but in a different life, the two of us might really have made a go of it. I've caught myself falling out of character several times when we're together. He's...he asks me about you constantly, hoping I'll eventually walk out on my *playboy* yobo. What can I say? A born seductress, that's me."

"You think you're joking, sister? I've seen a platoon's worth of tongues dragging the floor whenever you're shaking that cute little butt on stage."

"He's...he's different. He's looking for something else. Something within the cursed categories of meaningful and long term.

Something this girl obviously cannot provide."

Rising from the creaking bed, Charles patted her

164

lightly on the right shoulder, lingering just long enough for a brief massage of same.

"Tough call, no doubt, but maybe it's about time you considered your own feelings for a change, whadaya think?"

He turned once more before departing, his head lowered just a tad while regarding her through a single, tightly squinted eye.

"Tell ya this much for damn certain; if I were the good sergeant Yeager, I'd trade a bout of temporary heartache for a night with the likes of you."

In weakly waving him off, Lei found an appropriate rebuttal impossible to forge.

# CHAPTER FIVE
# Condition Black

Fighting off every combat-related instinct she possessed, Lei uncurled her clinched fists while dissolving the Tae Kwon Do 'blocking stance' she'd so naturally struck. Meanwhile, the drunken troop lurched forward with a wobbly gait, roughly grasping the whole of her right breast in his right hand as his buddies literally bent over in raucous laughter in the background.

"C'mon, ya slant-eyed tease, I don't give a rat's *fuck* about no Yobo… give Cap'n Rogers some'a that fine, tight Or-i-en-tal nookie. I didn't fly eight thousand miles for nothin', *goddamn* it. I wanna slab of Ko-rea's finest… "

She had endured similar abuse while on stage during her last scheduled set, to the point of watching a half-filled plastic cup sail by her head while being referred to by such regal monikers as '*slutty slope*' , '*Asian sperm-bank*' and, her personal favorite, '*slant-eyed cock-inhaler*'.

"Get away from me, mechaso *sheip-seckia* (English translation: *Crazy fucker*)!" she wailed, slapping his hand away and ripping away a tiny portion of her black-striped halter in the process.

"Oh, you got a real fighter there, Rodge," one of his equally soused cohorts announced with a pronounced slur, "bet she's a real hellcat in the sack."

"I'm plannin' on finding out that very thing,

166

Jake," the other man blurted, white, frothy spittle shooting from his lips as he leaned hard to the left before gripping the side of a nearby table for support, "hell,

I've a mind to drop trowel and hump 'er little brown ass right here and now."

"Think again, asshole," a voice chimed in from Lei's immediate right just as a streaky blur shot by her and impacted at the center of the drunken man's chest, sending both bodies barreling into an empty table like runaway freight cars.

"Jeremy?" Lei mumbled, briefly falling out of character as she attempted to leap into the fray, only to be hauled back by the upper arms by one of several SP's who'd arrived on scene in a mad sprint.

The two squirming bodies were quickly separated by a trio of similarly camouflaged troops, the drunken Captain quickly hauled outside while Lei's erstwhile savior was led to the far end of the bar.

Jeremy stood between a pair of SP's with his hands raised palms up, calmly shaking his head from side to side, his breath obviously labored. His black Polo shirt sat slightly askew and was ripped at the collar.

Joined at the edge of the stage by two of her fellow dancers and the club DJ, Lei watched the two SP's take turns lecturing Jeremy, who remained silent while gradually dropping his hands to the side, his breathing normalizing somewhat. Lei took a step towards them before being hauled back once again, this time by Mister Jung, who was ordering everyone to 'straighten up' the tables and chairs that

167

had been overturned during the melee.

Several minutes later, the opening chorus to Cheap Trick's *'Dream Police'* echoed a return to semi-normalcy. Lei had seen the SP's lead Jeremy outside even as several of the gathering crowd had returned to their respective tables.

As Lei departed the miniature 'dressing room' behind the stage just moments before the club was to close, Jeremy sat at the far end of the bar nursing a fresh bottle of Oscar.

"Hey there," he said, smiling broadly between gulps straight from the bottle.

"My knight in shiny armor," she quipped, walking over while cloaking herself in an ankle-length robe.

"Have to admit, that was a first," he replied, pushing the half-empty bottle to one side while standing somewhat shakily, "I'm just glad the Calvary showed up when they did. Plastered or no, that Captain was stout as an oak."

"*Oat*?" she asked with a pout, tilting her head just slightly as to strengthen the effect.

"Oak. O….A…K, as in tree."

"Oh. No, I think you take him easy. He way too drunk. Barely stand up."

"Don't be too sure. Think I've had a pretty sizable snoot-full myself. Besides, this boy's a lover, but not much of a fighter," he said, scanning what remained of the sparse crowd as they headed towards the exit in small groups and the stage lights were dimmed, "I… uh, don't see Lieutenant Yobo anywhere. He dessert you this fine evening?"

Glancing about as to avoid both the question

168

itself and intense stare that accompanied it, Lei found few avenues with which to properly stall. She turned and spoke briefly to one of the dancers and a hostess who passed by with their personal effects in hand, then waived at the DJ as he soon followed suit.

"Well, guess I'll pour myself onto the bus," he said weakly, hesitating a bit as he stepped by her, as if awaiting a sign or word that would halt him in his tracks. Once it appeared no such action was forthcoming, he started forward in a half-step before pausing yet again, speaking in a low, guarded tone.

"You...um, need an escort home or is...he...(cleared throat)...the Lieutenant com-.."

"Hungry?" she blurted frantically, having reached over and grabbed his right forearm.

"Well..." he replied wide-eyed, "yeah, but everything's closing for curfew here in a few min-.."

"I could heat up some rameon noodle," she injected, though with noticeably less anxiety, "and I have some packaged kim-bop that isn't too bad, just a bit dry."

"You mean, at your...?"

Walking around until she fronted him, she barely avoided stepping on the tips of his tennis shoes.

"Yobo gone for the weekend to Osan. He say for 'extra duty', but I don't think so," she said with a shy smile that, for once, was completely natural and not even remotely manufactured.

Jeremy nodded politely, the dim lighting unable to shade his blushing cheeks.

"So, it's okay if we...if I... I mean, there won't

be any trouble if…"

Hoisting herself onto her tiptoes, Lei's leaned in until her lips lightly brushed his right earlobe. The scent of his cologne was pleasant without being overly stout.

"No trouble. Charles won't be back until late Sunday. You…can stay if you like."

She leaned back, taking in the whole of him; the frazzled, just-got- out-of-bed hair, ripped shirt, and 'can't believe what I just heard' expression, and was forced to cover her mouth with one palm just to refrain from laughing aloud. It had been years since Lei had wanted anyone so bad, and the individual she'd chosen presently resembled a slightly dazed survivor from some sort of natural disaster.

"Let's…uh…go find a cab, then," he said with a warped grin before visibly tensing, as if acutely aware that he'd just inserted a size thirteen boot firmly between his own lips.

"Waitaminnit," she said in a comically accusing tone, reaching over to insert her left hand into his own, "how you know we need a cab to get to my place?"

He waited until they departed the front entrance and had walked out onto the narrow street to respond, their locked arms swinging loosely in tandem.

"Promise you won't get mad." "Mad at what?"

"I….um…followed you both home a couple of times, you and….the Lieutenant, I mean. Took a cab and had 'em follow behind once you left the club."

This time, it was Lei's turn to blush beneath his steady gaze.

"Oh, you stalker-man, huh?" she jibed, playfully elbowing him in the side.

"Just wanted to make sure you made it home safe with all the craziness going on around here."

"You think my yobo not protection enough?"

A box-shaped vehicle pulled alongside them just as he'd started to respond, what the troops referred to as a 'kimchi cab', a Korean made vehicle barely large enough to accommodate the driver, much less the passengers it was tasked to haul.

"Hey, for all I know," he replied, opening the back left passenger door for her and watching her slide gracefully inside, "your yobo is the man responsible. Everybody's a suspect, you know?"

"Even you then?" she whispered as he shoved his way inside the mobile sardine can as the driver awaited directions.

"Why yes, and even *you*, my dear."

They shared a laugh, their shoulders and legs having little choice but rub together like kindling sticks being prepped to ignite some pioneer-style blaze. Lei then spat the directions in Korean, and the driver sped off with a silent nod.

\*\*\*

Sitting across from one another in the center of the room, Jeremy felt his legs begin to go numb from a lack of blood-flow. He'd never been much for 'Yogi' type sitting positions, his ex having constantly referred to him as the 'stick man', though the meaning she conveyed was 'stiff' in lieu of 'stick.' Then again, he deduced, when in Rome. At

171

the present moment, nothing less than an M-16 round fired directly into his skull could affect the wave of raw elation he felt; a rush of lust-fueled adrenaline that he could only compare to the night he'd lost his virginity. She had changed directly in front of him (though in truth the limitations of space left her little choice), donning a white halter tee (braless) and a pair of dark red short-shorts that accented her perfectly shaped bottom, while pinning her lengthy locks into a tight ball at the top of her head.

Lei's state of mind was similar, yet still strangely guarded. She hadn't felt a man's touch, at least of the gentle, loving variety, in what truly seemed like an eternity. In truth, her last (and only) lover had been on the campus of San Diego State, a young man she'd dated on and off for a semester.

Neither had proclaimed love, nor even a semblance of, thus their abrupt separation had been less than traumatic. In dealing with a wide variety of sick, sexual deviants of all shapes, races and religions since, she had begun to think of her own personal urges as nonexistent; locked in permanent 'off' mode without hope for repair. Alas, the brief interlude between herself and Charles, however embarrassing, had belied such thinking. In retrospect, it had served as an awakening, a much-needed boost of humanity for a soul thirsting for just such a wake-up call to rejoin the living.

They each ate roughly half a bowl of noodles and a scant few of the rolled seaweed kim-bop, speaking infrequently while exchanging awkward glances. Jeremy had instantly been taken aback by

172

not only the room's limited dimensions, but also the lack of material possessions housed inside, though he managed to refrain from letting on in either a verbal or non-verbal manner. There was no TV present, only a small combination radio/cassette player of the twenty to twenty-five dollar variety, and no furniture to speak of other than the dresser, bed and small make-up mirror and stand. The last thing he desired was to express pity, and sincerely doubted such a knee-jerk response would be either welcomed or understood. He had, in his few short months on station, heard all the cliché-ridden hard luck stories surrounding the Ville girls, most of which were similarly themed to those involving their sister bar-girls from the Philippines.

"Yobo's house goods have not arrived yet. We hope any day now," she eventually commented, as if reading his very thoughts.

"He even talk about getting a bigger place closer to the Ville."

Standing, Jeremy wandered over to the window and peered out through open blinds onto the darkened street, where only a single light blazed from a distant pole.

"Sure is peaceful enough out here. At least you're away from the clubs and store fronts. Almost like farming country," he said, turning back towards her as she leaned over to collect the dishes, "I can almost hear the crickets."

"Just a bit down the path are several rice fields...even some wooded area. I like, but we probably move soon. Charles wants to be...near the action. Sometimes he just like little boy."

She joined him at the window and began gently stroking his back beneath a thin cotton shirt, feeling him initially tense and then melt beneath her touch.

"Sukie, I...um..." he began, reaching back to clasp her right thigh, "...you can't know how much I've wanted this, but...I don't want it to be just a one-night deal. I fe-..."

"Jeremy," she whispered huskily, her warm breath tickling the back of his neck as she reached around with a free hand to massage his rapidly hardening manhood through his khaki pants, "Sheeto (English translation: *no*). No talk now, okay? No more ... talk..."

He whirled around with a loud moan, wrapping his arms around her lower back and lifting her airborne as their lips connected and their tongues performed an introductory dance of sorts.

By dawn's early light, each felt a similar rebirthing; a reconnection of sorts with feelings both long buried and long-abandoned. For Lei, such blatant repression would no longer be possible. Jeremy had, in essence, unlocked the key to her very soul; a Pandora's Box overflowing with decayed baggage ripe for permanent disposal. She studied her lover as he slept, the rising sun piercing the window's thin blinds weaving a striped tapestry across his face and bare back. Soon, she would quietly depart for coffee and rice cakes at a local market, returning to him for what she hoped would be a quick breakfast followed by an early morning tryst. A tryst that just might serve to be her very last.

\*\*\*

Kim 'Kimmy' Sanders had been adopted and brought to the U.S. at age five, meaning that vivid memories of her birth country were practically non-existent. An honor student (valedictorian) at West Bay High in Little Rock, she'd earned a degree in communications by the age of twenty, and graduated from the ROTC less than three years later. Promoted from 1$^{st}$ Lieutenant to Captain in less than three years, she planned on retiring her commission before the age of thirty to start her own private security firm. In fact, her assignment to Sunyon was to be her very last wearing the Air Force blue, as she'd already announced her intent to separate just prior to departing the peninsula.

There had been very little mystery behind her placement in this latest task. Though her language skills had been practically nil (corrected by an intense, if somewhat rushed, crash-course), there was no doubting her nationality. With her pitch-black hair, severely slanted eyes (her subordinates referred to her as 'flossy'), dark complexion and tiny, pug-like nose, she fit the role to a tee.

"Travis, I'm turning onto the alley behind the *Head East*," she whispered, lowering her chin as to close the space between her lips and the tiny mike inserted inside her shirt. Master Sergeant Doug Travis was her transparent partner for the evening, a stone-faced, by the book type possessing no apparent sense of humor and very little in the way of human sensitivity. In other words (at least for this particular mission); the perfect choice to have watching one's back. It was a quarter 'til one in the

175

AM, and the clubs had been duly closed and/or abandoned for the evening. A slight fog filtered the narrow, dimly-lit passage in random, floating rifts, and Captain Sanders couldn't help but be grimly reminded of every corn-ball horror flick she'd ever seen.

"I'm coming up on a series of hooch's to my immediate right…and an abandoned vendor cart to my left. No movement to report," she mumbled, acute aware of the sidearm strapped to her outer left thigh as she reached over to ensure its presence for at least the fifth time in the past half-hour. The bright yellow skirt she sported was at least a size too small at the waist, as was the dark purple silk shirt that served to constrict her chest until her breathing was actually strained if overly exerted.

She made a left past a fenced-in cul-de-sac before passing an empty lot overgrown in waist-high weeds. As had been the case for the past month, her 'after curfew', thrice-a-week stroll through the Ville's Western edge covered a three-plus mile stretch, its oval-shaped perimeter encasing two-dozen or more 'hooch' complexes and countless potential 'hideaways' for prospective suspects. A former paratrooper and wily veteran in the ways of stealth, Sergeant Travis would trail her from two paths over, or from a distance of less than one-hundred total feet.

"Coming up on snake pass," she relayed, squatting next to a trio of horribly gnarled shrubs and taking the opportunity to adjust her left high heel, which had already rubbed a pea-sized blister from its incessant slippage.

Squinting through the foggy murk, she spotted a recent addition to the path, at least from two days previous. A row of large metal barrels had been placed at the corner of a sharp bend in the path, referred to by the locals as 'snake pass', just before a series of deserted, dilapidated shanties and equally abandoned store fronts. Sucking in a deep breath, she cleared her throat noisily before coughing into her right palm. The smell of human waste filtered into the surrounding air in thick, nauseating waves from the narrow binjo (open sewer) ditches dug into either side of the pathway.

"Moving again," she announced, clapping her heel onto the roadway as to sufficiently mask the dialogue.

She'd taken barely three steps forward before hearing a muffled thumping noise to her left, perhaps a dozen or so feet to her rear and at rooftop level.

*Travis playing roof-monkey again*, she deduced, no doubt hopping from one building to the next like a flying Ninja.

Regardless of his methods, she'd never felt less than safe with her assigned sentinel. The man had supposedly seen combat numerous times during two tours in Vietnam, while also serving as a 'hand to hand' combat instructor for potential paratroopers, the Air Force equivalent to the Marines' Green Berets.

She stepped strategically into the center of the path as the bend neared, putting a good three foot distance between herself and the wide-mouthed barrels.

Twisting her head as to give the last several barrels a token once over, she faced front just as a swirling cloud of fog seemed to swallow her whole.

Remerging from the levitating bank while sweeping her arms about in a frantic 'in-out' motion, Lieutenant Sanders froze in mid-step, coming dangerously close to toppling forward onto her hands and knees as her left heel had slipped on the moistened pavement.

Just as she'd pushed her way free of the fog, she could've sworn she'd detected a whooshing sound at her back, as if a sudden, stout concentration of wind had blown across the passage in a strictly horizontal direction. It had repeated itself but twice before she'd hit the brakes, a possible third such entry drowned out by the squeaking shriek of her sliding heel.

"Travis, if you're ground level, give me a signal," she murmured, gradually twisting her head about while instinctively reaching for her left thigh and gently cupping the twenty-two revolver held there. She heard metal clank together in a brief drumbeat, most probably the afore-glimpsed barrels, followed by a trio of sounds that were impossible to define; moist, ripping noises, not unlike semi-frozen meat being pulled apart by force.

She paused but for another split-second before backing clumsily into the nearby wall of an abandoned storefront, pulling the revolver free from its Velcro strap as her hair, neck and shoulders were coated in a sprinkling of dust and cobwebs from a protruding window seal.

"Show yourself, Sergeant Travis."

178

In the far distance, she heard canine howling, followed by a shrill, human voice screaming for silence.

"Sergeant, be aware I'm now armed and retracing my steps."

Pushing herself free of the wall, Lieutenant Sanders peeked out onto the winding passage she'd just covered and noted that the wall of fog had magically vanished, having possibly been effectively disintegrated by the same mysterious gust of wind or alley 'funnel' she'd first detected.

"Making my way back through the pass," she said, no longer bothering to whisper as she executed purposely wide, deliberate steps while allowing her gun hand to blaze the trail.

As the barrels swam gradually back into view, she immediately noticed that the last two in line now sat wildly askew, as if shoved back from the rest with great force. A third was turned completely over and continued to rock back and forth, seeking a semblance of balance.

"Sergeant Travis?" she asked, creeping forward at a snail's pace as the revolver began to shimmy in a weirdly circular motion despite her two-handed grip. Whether it be her imagination or an actual occurrence, the alley seemed to grow increasingly darker with each passing step. Though her head remained locked in a front and center position, she allowed her eyes to briefly roll upward, and noted a glowing full moon just off to her left.

"Travis, front and center," she spat, her lead foot less than a yard from the first barrel.

The startled gasp that escaped the back of her

179

throat was barely audible even in the relative silence, akin to a feline purr. Utilizing the more stable right heel, Lieutenant Sanders spun about in a complete three-sixty, rotating the revolver in a downward arc even as a new chorus of canine howls sounded off in the distance.

"Show yourself, damn it!" she yelled, haplessly unable to refrain from refocusing on the set of splayed, blood-spattered combat boots laying barely two feet to her left.

"I won't....issue another warning, whoever you are! Now step out into the open with your hands up!"

She took a single, shaky step forward, her eyes darting wildly from one side of the street to the other, unable to lock onto a single object until an oblong shape came bounding into view from the alleyway to her left. Having leapt back in delayed shock as the thing began to slowly lose momentum, Lieutenant Sanders' first thought was that it resembled a burst melon that had somehow rolled free from a nearby cart.

"Oh....oh    shiiii..."    she    stammered, unconsciously pointing her weapon directly at the object, which had slid to a halt on the pathway's far end, tittering on the very edge of the binjo ditch's steeply sloped bank.

Much like a doll's head pulled from its base by an angry child and subsequently tossed aside, Master Sergeant Doug Travis's severed head sat in an upright pose, looking as if his body were somehow embedded into the concrete like a man buried in neck-deep sand. His left eyelid had been jarred open

180

and stared straight ahead, the pupil lolling about like a loose marble. The neck, face and head were mostly bloodless save several visible spatter marks on the left cheek and atop his bared forehead.

"Oh g-god...Doug...."

Side-stepping over, she felt the sensation of moist, cool metal pressing against the bare knee and lower thigh of her right leg, all the while keeping the revolvers sites trained on the disembodied head of her former partner.

In flinching back, she accidentally tipped over the barrel her leg had inadvertently touched while her attention had been focused solely on the winking skull propped less than a half-dozen feet away.

"T-this is L-Lieutenant Kim Sanders of the...the United States Air Force...and I' m...I'm armed!" she shrieked, twisting her head around to her left just briefly as a bent soda can rolled into view from beneath an abandoned wooden pallet. Taking advantage of that single split- second of distraction, a form spilled forth from the overturned barrel as if forcefully shoved from the inside, executing a trio of combat-roll perfected spins before springing to its feet less than a full yard to the Lieutenants rear.

"I...I'm not...fucking a-around here now! Don't make me search you ou-.."

The Lieutenant's words froze just as she caught a blur of movement from the corner of her left eye. Biting into her own tongue, she whipped the revolver around with both hands even as her lower body remained virtually motionless.

The blunt trauma that ensued was executed with such speed, precision, and brute force, that Kim

Sanders had not a single clue anything was seriously amiss until she raised an open palm to her scalp and cupped a handful of her own grayish-colored brain tissue. Peering through splayed, gore-coated fingers, she found the task of properly identifying her killer a sad impossibility as her vision rapidly faded to black. In the three to five minute span to follow, the sound of flesh, sinew, and bone being systematically sliced and sawed into segmented cutlets was easily drowned out by the baying of neighborhood dogs and the piercing screams of their respective owners.

***

Charles pushed the steaming bowl away with a frown, then leaned back and massaged his midsection with both hands.

"So it's official as of when?" Lei asked before spooning in a heaping helping of seafood soup and quickly chasing it with a similarly bulky mouthful of brown rice.

"As of this morning at six AM sharp, per the Wing honcho himself," he replied, regarding her healthy appetite with wide-eyed awe, "these latest killings pounded the final nail in the coffin. I'm damned surprised it took this long, actually. If ya ask me, they waited 'til an officer got axed to really give a shit."

Following yet another humongous bite, wherein Charles watched in stilted amazement as she sucked down a lengthy serving of boiled squid tentacle, Lei paused to reply as the eatery's lone waitress strolled by to refill their tea.

"So, what are the rules again?" "*Condition Black* rules apply, basically."

She tilted her head in apparent confusion, still gnawing on the chewy contents of the last bite.

"Whenever there's a base exercise...wartime exercise, like Team Spirit or the ORI...ugh... that's Operational Readiness Inspection, they close the main gate whenever Condition Black is implemented, usually after a chemical attack scenario is triggered by higher headquarters. Condition *Red* is attack mode...duck and cover...*Black* is the aftermath... don the chem gear and find a hole to inhabit until the 'all clear' is sounded."

"Yeah, um...could you possibly delete a large majority of the military lingo?" she asked, playfully cocking an eyebrow before shoveling in still another bite.

"Sorry, babe...flashbacks. I forget sometimes what's plain English to some is ancient Aztec to others.

Bottom line, off-base is off-limits to all personnel 'til further notice.

In this particular case, 'til the sick fuck perpetrating these killings is sufficiently caged and or terminated."

"Okay," she said between loud smacks, "what exactly does this mean to us?"

Peering out from the eatery's dust-laden picture window onto the deserted street ahead, he leaned forward and crossed his bare forearms.

"SSDD for now, but only for a few more days...three at the most, I'd venture to guess."

Pausing between sips of freshly poured green tea, from which she drank from a large brown mug, Lei regarded him with a bemused frown.

"Oh…sorry again. SSDD….*same shit, different day*. They'll keep the clubs open for civilian clientele for a day or three before the owners shut 'em down for the duration of the lockdown. Luckily for us, the Yellow Fever is the one club that actually draws a decent crowd of non- military types, otherwise I'd say we have a night or two tops before the plug is pulled."

She nodded amiably enough while seizing a sizeable portion of cabbage kimchi from a tiny porcelain bowl.

"Sooooo… what then? One way plane ride back to the west coast for yours truly, complete with wrist and ankle restraints?"

With a deeply furrowed brow, he studied her momentarily. "Damn, you sure are blasé about the whole thing. Gotta admit, I was expecting the worst."

Forking up a fresh bite of rice, Lei shrugged without comment. "Well, I be da-…" he blurted, smiling broadly while slapping a flattened palm across the tabletop, "Thick as a brick, that's me." "What?" she replied, grinning briefly before successfully masking it with a quick sip of tea. "You did it, didn't you?"

"Did what, Cyclops? What exactly are you accusing me of?" He then used the same palm to gently slap his own forehead. "Had a sleepover, didn't you?"

Lei's eyes darted about as if stricken by a

sudden wave of shame, and she began waiving him off with a flailing hand.

"Took my advice and got laid, did ya?"

"Do you mind lowering your voice, motor-mouth?"

"No wonder you've been scarfing down this second-rate grub like it's your last meal, not to mention taking all my bad tidings in such happy- ass stride," he continued a t full volume, ignoring her half-hearted pleas.

"Jesus, Chuck, why don't you just grab a bullhorn?"

Leaning in, he peeked around as if to ensure their privacy despite the obvious isolation.

"So talk to me, how was it to get the old ashes hauled after all this time?"

"No comment," she grinned, her eyes gleaming with mischief. "Young master Yeager, I take it?"

Peering out onto the street as a pair of stray dogs whizzed by, she remained mum by spooning in still another mouthful of rice.

"Lucky buck. You're really fond of the dude, aren't ya?"

"Like I said, in another life…" she finally replied, dropping her spoon into the soup bowl and leaning back with a resounding groan, "….who knows?"

"I'm really happy for ya, Lei," Charles said after a short pause, reaching over and patting the top of her hand, "you…deserved the distraction."

"I just…hate hurting him. With Jeremy, last night wasn't just about a roll in the hay. He's looking long-term. He's been fighting it, but after…our time together, he'll likely be trolling jewelry stores for an engagement ring. Like I said…maybe in another life."

"He ride the early-bird back to the base?"

"Yeah. Said he'd see me at the club about six."

"Not gonna happen now. Main gate's shut and triple-bolted as of about three hours ago. There won't be any G.I' roaming these streets for quite a spell. That is, unless we catch one helluva break in the case, which even I've gotta admit ain't likely."

"Murphy's Law craps atop my shoulder once again…with relish," Lei said after a final sip of tea as they both pushed their chairs back and arose, "I have to admit…that boy was really beginning to…grow on me. Had me…feeling things I didn't even know I was capable of. It had been a looonng time, and I'm *not* just talking about the sex."

"Sorry, Lei," Charles said, following her out of the open-door entrance after leaving a ten-thousand Won bill on the table, "maybe you two can hook up again before…well, before whatever's gonna happen *happens*."

"It'd be nice," she sighed, donning her ever-present sunglasses as they stepped onto the concrete pathway, "but at the same time, it would just make a permanent parting more painful. Better just to nip it and…be done with it.

"So," she continued once he caught up with her and they walked stride for stride, "any workable clues this time around?"

"Colonel's gonna brief me in a few hours. Prelim I got was more of the same. MO identical to the others in almost every aspect. Crime scene was a goddamn slaughterhouse, with both victims sliced 'n diced like prize hogs at an open market. Being that neither victim was a local, our initial theory involving former Yellow Fever dancers is officially shot to hell."

"And you say one was an officer?"

"Yeah, young female lieutenant working undercover. Korean born but U.S. raised. I saw a photo; a real knockout she was. Damn shame."

"As opposed to the *other* victims?" Lei spat sourly, her stride instantly slowing.

"No, I mean…yeah, I didn't mea-.."

"Strange, isn't it? It takes the loss of a military member, an officer no less, for the big wigs to take drastic action. Seems it was much less of a concern when it was only a handful of hookers and a local farmer being butchered."

"Now, wait a second. I didn't say-.." he barked, stepping in front of her until their chests practically bumped.

"I'm not blaming you, Charles," Lei said, lowering her head, "but doesn't that strike you as being damned obvious?"

"I'm not saying you're wrong. Hell, just the opposite. Just wanna clarify that we're still on the same side here."

Smiling, she reached up with one hand and tugged gently on the underside of his eye-patch.

"(IN KOREAN) Sorry. Didn't mean to accuse. Genuine trust doesn't come easy for one such as I. You're definitely one of the good guys, Chucky."

Bending down until they were eye-level, Charles placed both hands atop her narrow but well-toned shoulders and implemented the gentlest of head-butts.

"Hey, consider me your personal *venting* bag. I got no problem with it, long as you don't get physical again, Tigress. Besides, ain't no arguing your point. The powers that be didn't go def-con on this 'til they lost one of their own. Par course, sad to say. Anyhow, I'll let ya know the details this afternoon. Who knows, maybe we did catch a break. Maybe the nut-ball bastard left a slug trail of some type."

"That's what I like about you, Charles. Unlike me, you're a *'glass half full'* kind of Joe," Lei replied as they continued down the long, winding trail back to their assigned hooch resembling long-time partners; hand-in-hand and almost perfectly in step.

\*\*\*

*Heavy of foot and bleary of vision, she treks the deserted streets of 'G.I Central' in a bleary daze, unable to properly focus as a virtual 'tour' of sorts ensue. Her movements are weirdly stilted and mechanical, and it becomes readily apparent that she is hardly the captain of her own ship, thus haplessly unable to determine a set course to whatever final destination has been chosen.*

*Lei treads the very heart of the Ville, the nucleus of the Sunyon, South Korea version of 'Sin City', like a recently assigned specter tasked as a permanent 'Sentinel'. She spots brief, frenzied flashes of faces both familiar and alien, and Ville landmarks easily recognizable and utterly obscure.*

*While the dimly illuminated streets remain bare and lifeless, void of even the most minute of movement, as if she were actually maneuvering within the confines of a framed still painting or photograph, the clubs themselves pulsate from ear-splitting waves of rock and pop tunes, the gist of which she finds soothingly familiar.*

*Bypassing the 'Paradise Cove', it's the smooth, flawless vocals of Phil Collins belting out 'That's all' with his Genesis band-mates.*

*A half-dozen yards up to her immediate right, Mick Jagger and The Stones kick in the final chorus to 'Start me up' behind the closed double-doors of the 'Rising Tide'.*

*Levitating approximately ten to fifteen yards up a steep, jagged grade, she hears the unmistakable crooning of Mister Tom Petty and his Heartbreakers, whose rocking rendition of 'Breakdown' bends and expands the red brick walls of the 'Head East' club like an elastic bladder on the verge of explosion even as Molly Hatchet's hard-edged 'Flirtin' with Disaster' reverberates from the opposite side (the 'Western Edge' club) with the bone-jarring force of detonated explosives.*

*All the while, Lei catches but spot-flashes and fragmented imagery of those enigmatic entities seemingly tasked to litter her path like pre- set board pieces in some nightmarish chess game, the faces of which radically mutate or transform just as a positive ID seems imminent.*

*She is steered through a steep left-hand curve, past a combination shoe-store/novelty shop that in truth serves mainly as a cash to Won money exchange, and watches the Yellow Fever's open-door entrance swim hazily into view on the right. In peering down at her own feet, she notes that she is donned in her dancer's shoes, and that each foot is inexplicably missing at least two toes.*

*The entrance is blocked ajar, as is normally the case on Friday and Saturday nights, weather permitting, and the 'ID' booth is barely visible within the darkened foyer.*

*Approaching from a sharp angle, she closes to within a dozen feet from the entrance (Dire Straits' 'So Far Away' echoing in the foreground) when she spots Kim Lee sprint out from the alleyway that separates the 'Fever' from the 'Blue Moon' club. Kim, a fellow Fever dancer, is completely nude, her oil-black hair streaked in silver and standing out like porcupine quills. Lei willingly embraces her co-worker, to whom she has never truly shared a sincere conversation, and only then notices the multitude of seeping gashes that envelope the woman's upper torso, most notably the neck and breasts.*

*Yellowish pus leaks from the tip of each horribly bloated nipple, and a dark red stain runs from the woman's breastbone down to a thick patch of straight black public hair at her groin.*

*Despite the plethora of garish, open wounds, Kim Lee appears ecstatic almost to the point of dementia, announcing that she will soon be accompanying her G.I Yobo to the States as her passport has been duly signed, sealed and approved. Displaying a rather gruesome grin that seems to*

190

stretch literally from ear to ear, the woman's teeth are stained a dark gray, her sluggish, reptilian tongue possessing a trio of sharpened forks that periodically shoot out and probe the night air.

As the volume to Kim Lee's words begin to mysteriously fade like a muted radio transmission, Lei briefly turns around to re-envision the Fever's entrance doors, which are now closed tight as muffled guitar riffs from Foreigner's 'Blue Monday' are overheard.

Whirling back around as if magically spun atop a child's merry-go- round, Lei is forced to blink several (hundred?) times in order to even marginally accept the image on display. Kim Lee's headless body maintains its earlier pose, the woman's arms and hands as animated as ever while her severed head sits upside down, perfectly balanced between her bare feet and spewing forth fountains of crimson from at least three separate sources that coat Lei's legs in a sticky cascade of blackish, coppery-scented fluid.

The naked, headless horror continues its silent speech unabated, hands gesturing wildly, even as Lei turns about and approaches the club entrance. She unceremoniously wipes her blood-stained feet on the thick 'Welcome' mat provided before leaning forward to grasp the first of two large metal handles.

As she pulls the door ajar and steps inside, a warm puff of escaping air slaps her face. Instantly taken aback as her eyes are forced to adjust to the onslaught of stage and strobe lighting, her gag reflex kicks into high gear from the overwhelming

191

*stench.*

*addling forward on legs that seem extremely hesitant to do so, Lei looks to her left to see every table in the house occupied to the tune of one customer per table, each equipped with their own personal tabletop dancer. Peering to the left towards the bar/stage area, she spots Mia and Susie, the remaining two members of their dancing foursome, performing a 'double-dip', always a popular act among the troops for its lesbian-ish implications. Songs seem to intermingle in a surreal mish-mash, each individual tune playing no longer than five to ten seconds before skipping forward to another. In the span of perhaps two minutes (five? ten?) she hears brief snippets from ZZ Top ('Sharp Dressed Man'), Pink Floyd ('Another Brick in The Wall'), Survivor ('Eye of The Tiger'), Heart ('These Dreams') and Toto ('Hold The Line'), all from the Fever's nightly 'Play-list' of requested favorites.*

*Standing at the center of the wholly unoccupied dance floor, she alternates her focus from the stage to the club seating, where separate dramas play out with equal portions of morbid fascination.*

*Sitting motionless at each table is a single form; a masked entity wearing black, skin-tight leotards and matching toboggans without eye, nose, or mouth-holes to allow free breathing, the masks stocking- like fit giving each a skull-like appearance. The accompanying dancers gyrate wildly for their audience of one, at times appearing to actually float two to three inches from the circular tabletop, levitating in mid- air for impossibly long stretches without missing a beat. Upon closer inspection, Lei*

192

notes that each of the dancers appear to be missing at least one appendage, a few of which hop about on a single leg while others waive twin nubs into the air, severed cleanly past the elbow or, in some cases, the shoulder. Still others have large sections of their hair either shaved or torn away, leaving raw, seeping sores in their wake.

Switching her sights to the stage, she watches Susie lay flat on her back and moan in apparent ecstasy with Mia's head buried deep within her exposed groin. Just as Mia arises and assumes a 'doggie-style' pose with Susie preparing to insert a comically oversized dildo, a shadowy figure appears seemingly out of nowhere, creeping up on the women from the rear of the stage.

The slimly built, lithe figure wears a long, flowing red (velvet perhaps?) cape and a similarly tight-fitting mask as the rest of the club's mystery cliental. As it approaches the ladies, gliding forward without benefit of taking actual steps, it pulls a short-handled tool of some sort from inside the cape.

Lei attempts to scream out; to yell a verbal warning to her co- workers, but much like the earlier failure in controlling her own movements, finds the power of speech no longer a viable option.

The figure sweeps past in a blur, hoisting a shiny, silver-bladed machete airborne with both hands just as both Susie's stroke and Mia's guttural howls increase two-fold. With shocking grace and fluidity, the figure spins about in a ballerina styled three-sixty, the exact trajectory of the blade impossible to detect, though it had apparently been whipped forward at warp speed.

As the figure dances a spinning silhouette back towards the front of the stage, Lei blinks rapidly as a light misting impacts her upper chest, neck and the left side of her face. Glancing downward at her own, now completely nude form, she detects numerous spatters from her belly- button to between her breasts, the nipples of each standing sharply erect.

Refocusing on the stage as the club patrons begin to chant an intelligible chorus at her back, Lei watches Mia's head slide smoothly from her neck and bounce twice before rolling onto the dance floor, a virtual crimson geyser spewing forth from the cleanly sliced stub. Meanwhile, Mia's left arm continues to pump unabated, actually increasing its furious pace as the torso, legs and feet are soon bathed in a torrent of spillage.

Susie's bowed head is then forced upward by a vicious tug, the figure having curled a large handful of hair in its left palm while swinging the blade around in an upward arc with the right. As with Mia before her, Susie's rhythmic wriggles are seemingly unaffected even as her severed head is tossed from the stage with casual aplomb.

Performing an impromptu 'break dance', the shadowy figure flips the blood-soaked weapon from palm to palm, flipping it airborne while rolling from one side of the stage to the other, only to catch it at chest-level upon its speedy descent.

The crowd's chants grow ever louder as Lei finds herself pulled towards the stage like a steel sliver towards an industrial strength magnet.

As the figure ceases its endless gyrations and strolls directly towards her, the lyrics to the ear-

*splitting chorus become chillingly clear. They are chanting a name over and over, emphasizing the last name in the exaggerated, drawn-out manner that is Korean custom. As the shadowy figure kneels over her at the edge of the stage, the perfume it exhumes eerily familiar, Lei is finally able to fully comprehend the chant.*

*The figure reaches up with a gloved hand, gripping its mask at the scalp while simultaneously cocking the blade into striking position with the other.*

*The name they chant is Lei's own.*

*The mask is peeled away like so much rotting flesh to reveal the same. She is finally able to scream...from both sets of faces simultaneously.*

*One scream is birthed in primal fear...the other in devilish glee.*

\*\*\*

"Just calm down for a minute, will ya? I didn't...c-can't...I'm not...*chill out,* dammit!"

Struggling beneath his vice-like grip on both her upper shoulders, Lei's red-shaded eyes darted back and forth like that of someone watching a lightning-quick tennis volley from mid-court. They stood at the center of a wide, trash-strewn alley located directly behind the club At just past eleven PM on a clear but humid Friday night at the Ville, the surrounding air permeated with drunken, bellowing voices and at least a half dozen separate rock and pop tunes, all of which combined to create a shrill, strangely ominous concerto.

"Why are you… just standing here, goddammit? Chase the bastard down!" she screamed, whipping her head from side to side, "they…they're *all* getting away, can't you understand?"

"Lei, chill… the hell… *out*! We've already detained the first two outside the guard shack," Charles countered in a harsh, shushing tone, "for Christ's sake, we ain't got the manpower to arrest the whole town."

Her struggles weakening, Lei bowed her head until her chin rested atop her upper chest. A fine mist of perspiration coated the whole of her heavily made-up face, the corners of each eye smeared in dark mascara, the blackness illuminated further by a maroon aura circling each pupil.

"That last one….he…I saw rape, m-murder…incest… s-so many victims… young…old…men, women, *b-boys, girls*…my god…*infants..*"

Placing a forefinger beneath her trembling chin, Charles gently raised her head until his one working eye peered into her own, which were finally beginning to lose a portion of their reddish hue.

"Lei, are you… *sure* about all this? I mean, over a month without so much as a tingle and now…now everyone who bought you a drink tonight is a raving psycho? Believe me, I don't wanna doubt ya, but you gotta admit, that's some weird shit."

Slinging her left arm in a circular 'uppercut' motion, she broke his loose grip and stalked away several steps before whirling back around wearing an angry sneer.

"I'm not imagining this, Charles. God knows I

196

wish it were that simple. I'm not crazy. I…saw what I saw."

"But Lei, that last man…" he countered, walking up behind her and placing a gentler hand across her right shoulder, "the one whose face you practically peeled away with those razor-nails of yours, he's a full- bird colonel in the ROK army…a twenty-five year vet. The guy before that was a respected business man; owns a large insurance company in Seoul. You gotta admit, they're not exactly your stereotypical serial killers…"

"I don't give a shit if they were ordained priests! Look into my eyes, Charles…these are not specially colored contact lenses," she countered, holding her right arm airborne and briskly rubbing the forearm with an open palm, "feel my bare flesh…that's not your everyday, ordinary fever, now is it? We're talking the volcanic variety. I can't turn this on and off like a light switch, and I sure as hell don't enjoy the aftereffects."

"Lei, listen to me. It's gonna be my ass and yours if-…"

"Are you hearing me, Charles? Are you hearing me *at all*? " she pleaded, feeling his grip intensify. Someone had scribbled '*Mama Sun gives the best head in the Ville – call OU812*' in magic marker on the wall before her, and beneath that, in different handwriting, '*Lying asshole - Mama Sun WON"T SWALLOW*'. .

As usual, such crude indifference to this place and the people trapped within its vile perimeters induced a twinge of sadness. Over time, she'd come to respect the locals to a greater degree than those tasked to protect her home country's borders. Though there was little doubt that loyalty to one's own race and nationality played a part in such an opinion, a definite loss of respect for the other faction was equally responsible. Over the past five weeks, she'd been cursed out, groped, and generally regarded like so much street trash by men assigned to safeguard her welfare. Try as she might, it was becoming increasingly difficult not to place all those assigned to the peninsula under the same glaring microscope.

"We may just have our man out of this bunch. The *butcher of the Ville*, yes indeed. I may have just handed him to you on a silver platter, just as I was tasked to do. Why are you fighting this? Why exactly would I be making this up?"

She felt his hand depart her shoulder, then turned about slowly to see him facing in the opposite direction, his hands tucked at the pit of his back in full 'parade rest' mode. In the brief interim between verbal exchanges, the two way radio at his belt squelched loudly in a series of static-filled belches.

"I'm not saying you are, Lei, just…cool your jets and hear me out for a second. Maybe it's just a subconscious thing. Could be th-…"

"Come again? A sub-…*allow me to repeat…I am NOT imaging this*! I don't have *false positives,* Charles, not in terms of detecting walking scum like those old perv-…"

"That's not what I'm implying, Lei. Give me a sec, will ya? I'm not doubting you think it's real, and I can plainly see the symptoms of this…crimson rage thing you'd told me about. But, don't you think it's at least possible that you might *want* it to be real...I mean, want it so badly that it...becomes so?"

"Wha-?"

"Think about it...the bad dreams you've been having...the night sweats. Deep down Lei, you know the end's near, and that your immediate future lies in the balance. A future that's about as stable as a bottle of nitro sitting on a fault line," he said with just an undercurrent of sarcasm while remaining turned away from her, "you gotta admit, such thoughts can prey on the mind.

Every brain has a built-in fail-safe, Lei, even that specially wired noggin of yours."

The pounding at her temples and throat increasing two-fold, Lei held tightly clinched fists at each side as her frustration level reached new heights, the fervor of which continued to mutate in light of her supervisor/alley/friend's casual indifference.

"Son of a...*bitch*," she whispered, suddenly no longer able to muster up the required strength for a suitable shriek, "now *you're* going to doubt me? Can't say much for your timing, Charles. What exactly do you expect me to say....or better yet, confess?"

Charles bowed his head, his broad shoulders visibly slumping. "I'm not accusing you of faking anything, Lei. I'm just saying its possible this might've been triggered by stress. You ain't a machine, woman, thus ya ain't beyond frying a circuit or two in the old brain pan."

Yet again, the two-way sounded off just as Lei was readying a response, as if purposely rigged to do so. This time, however, there were actual words accompanying the static.

"*Cyclops, report to guard shack immediately. Cyclops, do you read? Report to main guard shack, over...*"

"You gonna respond, or did I just imagine *that* too?" Lei finally blurted after a moment's pause.

"Listen, Lei," he replied, ignoring the radio while resting his hands on his hips, "you're getting bent all outta shape over nothing. Maybe you're right and you have nailed the guy... but three suspects in less than an hour? Ya can't blame me for a touch of skepticism."

Leaning against the cool stone wall, Lei could slowly feel the symptoms of fatigue take their inevitable toll, shoving all evidence of fear and anxiety away like so much shredded confetti.

"*Cyclops, do you read? Please respond. We've got a situation here that heeds your assistance, over,*" repeated the voice from the radio, obviously a bit more irritated.

"Charles? That guy's starting to sound a little perturbed."

"Fuck 'em," he growled, still facing away from her, "they're grown men. I can't be there to hold their peckers for 'em. Now, as I was saying, you've gotta listen to reason..."

"*Cyclops, this is Town Patrol CQ....please respond, over.*

*We've...we've got a...Colonel Yow Kil Park in custody that is requesting your presence immediately, over. Please respond, Cyclops, over.*"

Frowning, Lei planted both palms against the

200

flat, slick stone and pushed herself from the wall.

Charles practically jerked the radio free from his belt, tilting his head to the left as he planted it against his left ear.

"Hold your goddamned water, CQ. I've got issues of my own at the moment, over."

"Did...did he s-say, Park? *Yow Kil* Park?" Lei half-mumbled, shuffling forward on unsteady legs.

"Yeah, I think so, what of it?" came the sardonic reply, "from where I stand, ya see one Park, Lee or Kim and you've seen 'em all.

Same MO, no matter the moniker. All of 'em sport the same short, stocky build, straight black hair, sloped foreheads and pug-noses. A chink's a chink, more or less. Always amazed me about this ass- backward country. How can the majority of the female population be so damned gorgeous and the men so butt-fucking ugly?

Anyhow, what's the deal? This particular gook ring a bell?"

"As a matter of fact, you hypocritical fuck, it...m-most certainly does. Th-that's my...uncle's name..."

"Ya mean the same rich uncle that bank-rolled your stateside killing spree?"

"Yes...n-no...I mean, he never knew that I...was-..."

"Sure, sure. I hear ya squawkin', lady. Sweet, innocent Uncle Park. Never knew what a demented little beastie he had for a niece."

"Wha-what did you say?"

Crossing his arms across his chest, Charles took a casual step forward and flashed an accusing sneer.

"(IN KOREAN) 'Fess up, Lei, did Uncle Yow ever knock off a piece of that fine caboose a' yours? Hell, maybe dear old Unc is actually the one most responsible for your... shall we say...*distrustful* attitude towards men, hmmmm?"

"(IN KOREAN) Why...w-why you miserable...asshole...how dare y-...," she managed, her entire frame a-tremble.

"Planted the twin seeds of hate and rage at an early age, maybe?

Unconsciously motivated those first few kills that set the stage and whet the appetite?"

"Sh-shut up, you...worthless...fu...fuck. Just...shut up..." "Think I've got the picture now," he continued, raising a finger irborne and playfully waiving it back and forth, his grin mutating into a pained grimace, "oh yes, indeed, the clear, unvarnished Polaroid.

It's been lovable ol' Uncle Park the entire time, hasn't it? You've been taking out all that anger and pent-up frustration on male society in general, all due to Uncle Stinky-Fingers....

"I said...s-s-shut up, mother...*FUCKER!*"

"(IN ENGLISH) A little payback for all those midnight visits into your room after Aunt Park was fast asleep, am I right?"

"(IN ENGLISH) Are...are you fucking craz-..."

"Or maybe...," he concluded with a wink of his one remaining eye, "just maybe... deep, *deep* down inside, little miss Lei Park actually *enjoyed* those sinful little sessions. Every...fucking...minute of them."

With tear-filled eyes, Lei fell silent, her horribly

weakened legs prepping to spring even as her neck, shoulders, and arms visibly tensed.

"After all, once a slut...*always* a slut, right sweet-cheeks?"

Lei leapt forward with a primal scream, throwing a flurry of wild, unfocused punches that the man either easily side-stepped or blocked with minimal effort.

"Always...craving that...physical contact...ain't ya darlin?" he cackled, backing away defensively as his forearms absorbed the brunt of the blows, though a few did manage to ricochet off of his neck and lower jaw.

Regaining a sense of self-control, Lei backed away a step and slung off both her tennis shoes before striking a defensive pose of her own.

"(IN KOREAN) Fight...back...you....son of...a BITCH!"

Still flashing a toothy, if not somewhat warped grin, he raised both hands in a surrender type gesture.

"Sorry babe. Chuck's a lover...not a fighter. With that in mind, how about you come over here and show me what ya got..."

Reaching down with one hand while the other remained poised airborne, Charles slowly unzipped his jeans.

"...in terms of your one *true* talent."

"Now, asshole," she growled, rotating both arms in a frenzied, windmill-like motion, "I'm going to have to kill you."

"That's my girl," he replied, standing prone with his exposed manhood cradled in one hand, "come to Papa."

While an initial front kick barely glanced off his left thigh, the follow- up impacted just below his breastbone, sending him spiraling back against a trio of stacked wooden crates.

As he momentarily struggled to free himself from the mangled pile, Lei pressed the attack. She first executed a spinning sidekick, spun back around with a 'clothes-line' elbow, then completed the combination with a solid left hook.

The first blow had bounced harmlessly from his left shoulder; the second landing with greater impact just below his left ear, while the hook had served to shatter his nose with a resounding crunch and send him sprawling onto the concrete with a loud groan.

With Charles lying on his back, quietly clutching his face with both hands as thick streams of blood seeped between his fingers, Lei quickly stepped forward and planted the bare heel of her right foot across his throat.

Incredibly, the man continued to snort and giggle in apparent amusement, no matter the level of pressure applied.

"What's so…damn funny, you sadistic prick?" she huffed, her chest heaving mightily as she shifted the majority of her one-hundred ten pound frame directly onto his Adam's apple.

As he continued to make wet, gargling noises, Lei kneeled down with her left fist cocked back as if to administer a final, fatal blow.

It was then she noticed his eye. Not the working eye she'd grown so accustomed to addressing, but the socket that had been so effectively cloaked since

204

their initial meeting some forty days previous.

Apparently one of her blows had knocked the patch askew, as it now sat directly at the center of his forehead like some alien orb.

Gasping aloud, Lei hopped away as if her foot had suddenly submerged into a smoldering mound of red-hot embers.

She always imagined Charles' handicap as either containing an ivory-shaded pupil, or 'dead eye', or perhaps just an empty socket. Instead, what she'd witnessed was a swirling kaleidoscope of varied colors and shapes resembling a stack of flashcards being flipped forward at a rapidly accelerated rate.

'Ohhh…s-shit…y-you?   B-but…how?" Lei babbled, having unconsciously backed against a far wall.

As he rose to his feet, Charles pulled the eye patch free and casually tossed it aside.

"Well, guess I won't be needing that useless little jewel anymore, huh?"

Closing the distance between them, he massaged his injured throat even as his grin grew wider and increasingly predatory.

"Figure it out for yourself, Brainiac!" he spat with no small amount of sardonic wit, pointing to the afore-uncovered eye, "*this* is the fake one. Nothing but colored glass, though I gotta admit their making them more life-like all the time. Ah, modern technology… even came up with a completely transparent patch. Simply a-ma-zing, ain't it?"

"Then, it's been…*you*   all…this time?" Lei queried weakly, dropping to her knees as if a

205

mysterious paralysis was gradually taking hold.

Nodding enthusiastically as his mutated eye blazed forth a hypnotic mix of yellow, dark green and piercing blue, Charles pulled a long-bladed knife (machete?) from beneath the snow white, ankle- length lab coat he suddenly sported.

"Ah yes, Misses Einstein, it most definitely has, and I have to confess, it's been a real kick."

Crouching down, he placed the top edge of the hooked-shaped blade flush against the moistened flesh at the base of her throat.

Lei released an involuntary moan as the chilled steel peeled away several layers of skin in perfectly segmented slices and a warm stickiness coated her neck and upper chest.

"Shhh, don't be afraid, Dear Lei," he cooed, hovering over her trembling frame like a preying insect preparing to cocoon its latest meal, "though the pain will be extreme, I promise to shorten the duration as much as possible...just for *old times'* sake."

Staring directly into the pulsating mass of victim's past as the landscape surrounding her faded mercifully to black, the last set of suffering eyes Lei Park clearly visualized was her very own...

\*\*\*

She awoke shrieking with both arms flailing wildly, the blanket and sheet that had covered her upon sleep's inception some seven hours earlier lying in a sweaty, crumpled heap on the floor. Cursing under her breath, she arose with a tapestry of horrid images still freshly embedded in her inner mind's eye, a condition she hoped and prayed would quickly fade as the morning progressed and reality-based endeavors ensued. As days passed and the deadline for operation 'Ville Ripper' approached, the nightmares were becoming more frequent, not to mention graphic.

One hour, three cups of steaming green tea and a heaping bowl of kimchi and rice later, Lei departed the hooch dressed in a pair of cut-off jean shorts and a long cotton Tee with the words *'Studio 54 Party Girl'* stenciled in broad, glittery lettering across her chest.

One day before they permanently parted ways, she promised herself, she'd give Mister Charles Rutherford a piece of her mind concerning the less-than-stylish wardrobe he'd so haphazardly picked out for her 'cover'. She'd told Mia she'd be over around ten for their version of 'brunch', and was already a half-hour late. Luckily, promptness amongst the 'Ville girls' was a personality trait rarely adhered to. Schedules and appointments, social or otherwise, were a nuisance easily ignored. In their little corner of the world, 'daily routine' meant showing up for work on time and very little else. While there, perform the eighteen to twenty required 'dances' with at least a semblance of enthusiasm, while simultaneously maintaining a painted- on smile and semi-cheery disposition while milking base personnel of their weekly paychecks via watered down drinks that were nine parts coloring and one part actual alcohol. Despite some early (and rather stringent) reservations, Lei had managed to form a kinship of sorts with her fellow co-workers, all of whom shared a common bond in that their lives before the Ville had been less than satisfactory. Most were, at the very *least,* considered the black sheep of their respective families, while others were suspected to be either in fugitive status or former law breakers attempting to settle into a new identity, far from the restrictive nature of 'normal' Korean society. Certainly, Lei often mused, none had more to hide than herself, a former serial killer of deviant scum adorned with the 'gift' to sniff out evil doers and eradicate the source with extreme prejudice.

Following a light lunch consisting of vegetable mandu (dumplings), bean curd soup and rice and boiled broccoli spears, the girls spent the next several hours nursing several chilled OB beers apiece while discussing an array of 'hot bed' subjects, most of which fell under the heading of 'SSDD' in terms of life inside the Ville.

They spoke without nary an ounce of respect or reverence for their elders, more specifically their boss, Mister Jung, he of the perpetual, borderline perverted grin and penchant for girls less than half his age. A man whose soft, clammy touch was almost always sickeningly moist.

Susie, the optimistic dreamer of the bunch, announced that her yobo, Senior Airman Gil Bryant, had received his orders and would soon be hopping aboard the 'freedom bird' back to the states, all the while planning on flying back to 'initiate' their marriage paperwork sometime in the 'distant future'. Lei had met Bryant, a skinny young man with a shaved head and baby-face, but once in passing, the vibe she'd received of the less than positive variety. He'd supposedly told Susie, his yobo of almost eight months, that his extension paperwork had been 'lost' by base assignments, thus dooming any chance they'd had at marrying within the confines of his tour dates.

Though a relative newcomer to such complicated scenarios, even Lei recognized such an outrageously bogus claim for what it was. The man had obviously had no such plans, as marriage paperwork between G.I's and locals normally took no longer than three to four months at the outset, and Bryant had been spouting the 'not enough time' refrain for over half his assigned tour. Like many philandering troops, he more than likely had either a wife or significant other already at home, and had simply used Susie as a pleasant diversion, an amusing curiosity that would, for future years, serve to induce a lustful grin his loving spouse would never truly comprehend.

On the flipside, Mia was enduring her third straight yobo-less week, as her former companion for the previous six months, one Master Sergeant Larry Bates, had since departed for the states. She said Bates, a twenty-plus year man close to retirement, had informed her from the outset of their living 'arrangement' that he was married with children, and had no aspirations whatsoever in altering that fact. She said their seven-month relationship had been 'nice' if not a bit bland, even hinting that Sergeant Bates had occasionally been afflicted with erectile dysfunction issues (though mistakenly referring to them as '*penal malfunctions*').

With the main gate closed indefinitely, there was little in the way of financial relief in sight, and Mia claimed the bills were beginning to pile up without the added 'cash flow' a regular yobo provided.

When asked, Lei would describe her relationship with 'Lieutenant Whitt' as predictably problematic at times, but otherwise fine. As per the set script, she stuck with the story that neither was seriously thinking marriage, and that Whitt might or might not be considering a year's extension on his present tour. It had taken Lei weeks to properly mold the character of 'Sukie Kim', right down to the Pusan accent and toning down of her English vocabulary.

For the most part, she'd been accepted in the role, though for now a bolded asterisk would no doubt forever accompany her as the 'new blood ', thus meaning never to be completely trusted.

She departed Mia's three-room hooch (complete with a small kitchen and fairly spacious living room that was separated from the bedroom by a sliding glass door) at just past two while cultivated a pleasant buzz. Though the 'Kool-Aid' specials served at the club held little alcohol, the average night's consumption of at least a dozen or so had managed to build up her tolerance level to an all-time high, not to mention having weakened her bladder considerably. Thus, the four beers ingested after lunch had little effect except to create a rather mild, light-headed sensation that would pass all too quickly.

Feeling no sense of urgency, it took her a full hour to cover the mile and a half trek back to her own abode. She perused several small clothing and food shops along the winding, curvy path, even stopping momentarily to munch a bag of fried shrimp while sipping from a frosty bottle of Kin.

Arriving at the hooch at just before three, barely beating a light shower that had begun to fall, she wasn't at all surprised when Charles greeted her at the door.

"Well, good afternoon, Yobo. Come by for a quickie?"

"Shhhhh," he replied, pressing a forefinger against his lips, "I'm not supposed to be here, remember? Off-limits and all that."

She side-stepped by him and he quickly closed the door behind them.

"Oh, yeah, sorry. You know how hard it is for me to stay in character after a morning with the girls."

"Been over at Susie's?"

"Nope. The mansion of Mia, actually. Good food, spicy talk, cold brew. You know the routine."

"I can only imagine. Cutting somebody up pretty good, I'd wager." She grinned, collapsing atop a recently purchased bean bag.

"Safe bet. I'd say there are at least a dozen people strolling about the Ville this morning with ears aflame."

"Yours truly among them, by any chance?" he asked, taking a seat on the mattress.

"Not a chance, lover-boy. Nobody bad-mouths

211

Sukie Kim's man and lives to tell about it."

Leaning back against the bare wall with his hands tucked at the back of his neck, Charles flashed a weak smile that faded all too abruptly.

"Uh-oh. How bad is it, boss?"

"Ain't gonna fib to ya. It could be better," he sighed, his exposed biceps involuntarily flexing with each spoken word.

"Then again, it ain't like we didn't see this coming."

He paused to lean forward, balancing his elbows atop his knees. "Spill, Charles. How much longer do I have before being shackled nd shipped off?"

"Most of the clubs have closed as of last night. From what I've gathered, Old Man Jung is shutting the Fever's doors starting this Sunday."

Lei struggled to rise from the bag's deflated condition, each of her knees popping like brittle tree branches.

"So…my fledgling dancing career ends in just forty-eight hours." "Looks like."

"Bummer. I was just beginning to master the triple-titty spin. Ah, the cruelty that is show business."

He laughed despite himself.

"Triple-titty….damn, that does sound mighty intriguing."

Lei stood by the window, peering out into the misting rain as a gathering of townsfolk shuffled by, a few of which held crumpled newspapers over their heads for cover.

"So what now, Mister Rutherford? The dreaded one-way ticket back into the waiting arms of U.S.

Law Enforcement?"

Charles joined her at the window, playfully jostling her with a forearm.

"Not so fast, lady. You ain't about to get rid of me that easily. I've given the Colonel several alternatives to mull over. He's gonna get back with me this Monday in the AM. 'Til then, try not to stew on something that might not ever happen, okay?"

"Easier said than done, yobo," she replied curtly, twisting her head about until his patched eye was mere inches away. Recalling a recent nightmare, she fought the urge to reach up and peel it away.

"How'd the meeting go, anyhow? Any new leads develop from that last twin killing?"

Stepping away, he fell onto the pre-sunken bean bag with a loud groan.

"As of this morning, the boys at the lab are still squinting into their microscopes, but so far nothing earth-shattering to report. Same old roadblocks as all the others, except…there was one thing, though. Not sure if it means anything, buuuut…"

"What's that?" she asked excitedly, practically hopping into his lap.

Reeling back in apparent shock, Charles almost fell back before regaining his balance by cupping a hand beneath each of her bare knees and shifting them forward.

"Damn, you *are* solid, girl," he huffed in a strained tone, "gonna have to start rationing your meals."

"Thanks for the ego boost, muscles. You seem to be growing bulkier every day while I gain an extra layer of flab. Anyhow, enlighten me on this new evidence…"

"Wouldn't go as far as to label it evidence just yet…"

"Whatever. Spit it out, will you?" she pleaded, wriggling from his grip and taking a seat on the bed.

"Okay, but again…don't set your hopes too high. From the outset, it…kinda sounds better than it really is."

He paused yet again, causing Lei to toss her arms up in silent, open-mouthed frustration.

"There was a witness to the killings…."

"An…eyewitness?"

"Well, kinda…sorta. It's complicated." "How exactly?"

"Mister Jae Won Luk. Retired farmer and market owner. Lives less than two hundred yards from the crime scene. Was taking his nightly stroll through the realm of chronic insomnia when he… walked up on the killings."

"And you're telling me this isn't *evidence*?"

Charles quickly waived her off, having seen her expression begin to mutate from slight frown to deep-creased scowl.

"Two distinct factors work against such an obvious assumption, my dear. Number one; Jae Won Luk is eighty-seven years young.

Number two; the man possesses eyesight the equivalent to your basic fruit bat wearing a lead blindfold. Therein lays the problem with labeling him an 'eyewitness'."

"Well, what is the old geezer *saying* he saw then?"

214

"Prepare yourself…" he replied, raising both hands palms out. Folding her trim arms across her breasts, all symptoms of her previous OB-induced buzz having waned, Lei nodded stiffly, as if preparing for a physical jolt. "I'm braced."

"He signed an affidavit stating the assailant was… female."

To Charles' dismay, Lei's expression remained unchanged, at least for the most part.

"Based on…?"

"He said…the body shape of the assailant was slender, small-framed, and held the…distinct curves of a young female. Also, Farmer Luk said he heard both a weakened but pained scream, and also a cry more normally associated with an assailant…a warrior's yell, he called it."

Briskly shaking her head as to dismiss the previous comment, Lei stood up and began pacing the tiny room like an over-caffeinated storm-trooper taking part in a heated interrogation.

"So he did get a look, however unclear, of the attacker?"

"So says Stevie Wonder's Korean counterpart, yes. I met the man, Lei. He stuck his hand out and practically tried to shake my groin in lieu of my hand. Walked into the wall at least twice on the way to the interview room.

It gets better. Luk said it appeared the attacker was wearing all black, you know…*ninja* type duds."

"Nin-…all right then. Now I'm beginning to see where the lack of credibility comes in," she said, slapping her own forehead.

"Then again, it ain't completely out of the realm

215

of possibility," Charles countered, practically lying on the floor as the bag had been sufficiently flattened by his massive bulk.

"The old man did see *something*, however blurry, and as far as we could tell, his hearing's fine. It ain't as if a woman couldn't execute such crimes. Hell, look at yourself for example..."

The last few works had tapered off, and Charles instantly broke eye contact, instead preferring to glance down at his own intertwined hands.

"Sorry, Lei. I didn't mean to....you know." Lei shrugged, flashing a tight-lipped smile.

"No apologies necessary, chief. You make a good point. It most definitely could be the fairer sex. Whoever it is, they sure know their cutlery. Kind of tosses a wrench into the investigation, doesn't it?"

"You bet your sweet ass," he answered, reaching out to grab her ankle as to halt her frenzied pace, "lemme ask ya, does that built-in radar of yours work on... I mean, have you ever run across a *female* tha-.."

Lei bent down with her hands balanced on her knees.

"Never felt the first twinge, no. Of course, that doesn't mean the curse doesn't bend both ways... maybe I just haven't run into any women who properly qualify. Remember, I have spent most of the last decade in the company of men."

"Oh yeah, forgot about that."

"I guess I'm supposed to turn lesbian now?"

"Little late in the game for the old switch-a-roo," he said, lightly patting her naked calf.

"Yes, I suppose. Great time to find out that we

216

might've been checking out the wrong sex all this time."

"Don't you know it, sister. Still, I have my doubts. Ol' Rip Van Luk couldn't find his butt-cheeks with both hands, but it's the female cries he heard that give it some merit."

They fell silent for several moments before each took a seat on opposite ends of the small mattress.

"So I guess for now we continue with Plan A?" Lei finally inquired, folding her hands into her lap.

"No other option, buttercup. I'll be performing surveillance from my usual hiding spot in case one of the SP's lets out a yell. Crowds still pretty sparse, I take it?"

"Understatement of the year, boss. Had a grand total of sixteen customers last night. We didn't even bother to dance out our last three routines, and for once, jackass Jung didn't seem to care one way or another. I guess he's counting on a few more customers, what with the weekend coming up and all."

"Greedy is as greedy does, my lady."

Scooting over until their hips touched, Lei turned to him and cocked an eyebrow.

"What?" he said with a warped grin, leaning his head back a tad. "Humor me, Chuck."

"If it don't involve adultery, to which I'm greatly tempted as it is. I can tell ya miss this Jeremy character already."

"As a matter of fact, I do, but it's nothing like that." "What then?"

She swallowed hard before replying somewhat tentatively. "Give me just one peek underneath that patch."

Squatting behind a small metal storage unit, Sergeant Jeremy Yeager removed his head gear and ran a hand through his short, matted hair. Despite its thick inner netting, the combat helmet never failed to grove a substantial crease around the perimeter of his skull. As much of a hassle it was to haul around and/or wear thirty pounds worth of chemical gear, it was the helmet he despised the most. Then again, in a real World combat situation, such minor annoyances could no doubt be easily dismissed in lieu of losing one's head in a literal sense.

He could smell his own body odor drifting up from the small opening provided by the Kavlar vest, a putrid mix of fresh and ancient perspiration. With less than an hour remaining on shift, he silently prayed that it pass peacefully and without further incident. Day three of this particular wartime exercise was, mercifully, drawing to a close. No one had been the least bit surprised when the Wing big wigs, in their infinite wisdom, had decided to coincide the mandatory base closing with a round of 'let's play war '. No doubt the powers that be felt the troops had little else to concentrate on at the moment. In Jeremy's personal case, the long, mostly uneventful shifts left him little to ponder on save a certain female of the Asian persuasion and the magical night they'd spent together just four days previous. No matter the level of stench his body currently held, he could vividly recall her sweetly

218

intoxicated scent and the electrically charged feel of her warm, tender flesh. Once married and hardly green in such matters, the whole of the experience had nonetheless left him feeling almost virginal. True, it had been his first sexual encounter in over a year, so such an emotional roller-coaster ride wasn't at all unexpected, but the hangover effect was as if he'd just been forcibly separated from a life-long love. His chest ached and groin burned with equal intensity at the mere thought of her gentle yet expert touch or the exquisite taste of her slender neck, succulent lips and probing tongue.

Reattaching his helmet after a final, rigorous scratching session performed with the fingers of both hands, Jeremy was snapped back into cruel reality by the sound of the base Klaxons, which sounded off in unison in a lengthy (three minutes to be exact) high-pitched wail.

"Shiiiiiit," he moaned, tossing his chem gear bag onto the moistened clay and digging both hands inside, "....Condition Black when I'm fifty-five minutes from freedom.

Lady Luck, you are one cruel, sadistic bitch."

Moments later, he lay prone in a grassy ditch, his breathing harsh and wheezy through the skin-tight confines of the M-2 gasmask.

*Lord, I hope this isn't another three or four hour session, or I'm gonna end up taking a whiz in my chem pants. At least this hole is deep enough to keep me outtta sight from all the QC spies.*

As moments passed and the base fell conspicuously silent, Jeremy's thoughts again turned to Sukie and her alluring, seductive ways. He held

219

out little hope of the Ville being put back on limits anytime soon, as the latest scuttlebutt from Wing HQ was that until the killer or killers were captured and subsequently convicted, the base would remain on permanent lockdown.

In the meantime, he mused, tucking his gloved hands beneath his arms and assuming a semi-fetal position within the knee-high weeds, he could remain happily focused on the sweet memories of night's past, more specifically the night a certain dancer both stole his heart and re-ignited his weary soul.

\*\*\*

"Anything? A buzz….a twitch… an orgasmic tingle?"

"Orgasmic tingle? Ugh, not quite, but there was this supposed college professor from Seoul University who had my gag reflex working overtime."

"Prof get a little suggestive, did he?" "Only if you regard bestiality kinky." "Bestiality? You're shitting me."

"Apparently, he has a Persian cat he's very, *very* fond of."

"Oh, how very wholesome. He make you an official offer, monetary wise, I mean?"

"Quite substantial one, in fact. Somewhere along the lines of one million Won. Have to confess, boss, if I didn't possess a severe allergy to feline furr, we might not be having this conversation."

At half past the Witching Hour, they walked

220

arm-in-arm down the dimly lit passage, with only the sporadic beam of light shining from a nearby hooch window or glass door to illuminate the way.

"How many customers all told?"

"Fifteen…maybe twenty. Most of them on business trips from Pusan, Kunsan or Kwang Ju. Big spenders, for sure, but not enough to keep old granite jaw Jung happy. Then again, the change jar can't ever get full enough for that skin flint."

They proceeded past a wide clearing that served as the half-way point from the Ville to their hooch, leaving a full mile yet to cover.

"Did I tell you the wife is coming up for a visit?" Charles asked off- handedly, essentially stopping Lei in her tracks.

"Hey, that's great. How often do you manage to get together when you're playing Mister Espionage?"

"Not often enough. It isn't much, just twenty-four hours, but it beats the hell out of nothing. We're meeting at a restaurant in Dwan- Jae and booking a hotel for the night."

Smiling, Lei shifted her high-heeled feet from side to side before reaching up and slapping him lightly across the shoulder.

"Good for you. You deserve it, you big lug. She bringing your daughter? "

"Yep. Haven't laid eyes on little Tish in four, almost five months."

Charles shrugged, pausing to look skyward in the star-free blackness.

"I…want you to meet them, Lei" "What? Really?"

"Yeah. I've thought about it a lot since we arranged the meeting." "Damn, Charles, I'm…honored."

"Of course, I won't be able to introduce you as anything other than a co-worker. You know the routine…can't be divulging anything stamped *Top Secret* to anyone, family included."

With Charles in the lead by a half-step, they resumed the trek back home at a noticeably slower, more casual pace.

"Oh, understood."

"I'll introduce you as Agent Ling. You don't have to worry about the wife grilling you for details. She knows the score."

"Sounds great, Chuck. Where and when? You said…Dwan Jae?" "Yeah, there's a restaurant downtown…here's the address…" he replied, pulling a small piece of folded yellowed paper from his front shirt pocket and laying it into her exposed palm.

Lei gave it a quick glance, holding it eye level and at a tilted angle as to catch the glimmer from a nearby street lamp.

"I was on assignment in Dwan Jae a few months back. That place has the best seafood platter on the peninsula. Damn fine barbecued pork, to boot. I've bought you a round-trip bus ticket. It's only about twenty clicks east of here."

"I…think I visited an aunt in Dwan Jae once when I was a kid, but I barely remember it."

"Wish it were possible to drag young Sergeant Yeager along…we could make it a double-date."

"That is wishful thinking, boss," she said, her

222

eyes temporarily lighting up at the mere mention of the man's name, "but it's…really better in the long run that it ended when it did. The hurt…it's just less painful that way. Jeremy….we had a night…that's more than a lot of people can say."

"Well, regardless, I'd be proud to have you."

"I…don't really know what to say, chief," she said, shoving him playfully forward, "I just hope it works out like you've planned."

This time, it was Charles who stopped cold in his tracks. "Now what exactly does that mean?"

"She's the jealous type, right? The wife, I mean…" she asked, striking a sassy pose as she peered up at him with her head tilted to the side and her hands propped atop her hips.

"Matter of fact…yes, I'd have to say affirmative."

"And somehow, someway, word leaked out that you were working with a young Korean female on this latest *confidential* assignment, yes?"

"You're betting a thousand thus far, Little Miss Smart Ass," he replied, bowing his head in comic shame.

"So basically it's the old 'clear the air once and for all' thing by introducing me as your attractive yet distant and cool 'completely by the book partner.' I take it, in this new incarnation, that I'm happily married with….let's say…two young children?"

"Just one," he consented with a good-natured scowl, "and that's a definite affirmative on the happily married part."

After a moment's silence, both broke out in a fit

223

of giggles, stepping forward until they fell together and jostled one another playfully.

"Can't thank you enough for playing along on this one," Charles said as they continued down the path arm-in-arm.

"No problem. Might well be my last opportunity for a good deed in this lifetime."

"Nah, don't say that. We don't know what's gonna hap-"

"Don't sweat it, Charles. I've already accepted the fact that it's just about over. No need to keep sugar-coating bitter reality."

They continued on in silence for the remainder of the trek, then took a stance near the hooch entrance as Charles waived down a cab.

"See you in Dwan Jae then, two o'clock sharp," he announced while pulling the cab's passenger side door ajar and sticking a leg inside, "and hey…"

"What's that, muscles?" Lei blurted black, leaning half-in, half-out the hooch's open door.

"It *really* would make me proud to have you meet them, you know.

All BS aside, you've been one of the better partners I'd had."

"Well, Konsomnida (thank you), Otishe," she said with a slight bow, "I can honestly say the same. Then again, I don't have a whole lot to compare by, partner-wise."

They shared a final smile just as his head vanished into the tiny cab's cramped interior.

That night, for the first time since her arrival in country some thirty- nine days previous, Lei Park slept without either continuously awaking or being mercilessly bombarded with horrid nightmares.

# CHAPTER SIX
# The Unraveling

She departed the Ville for Dwan Jae at just past noon the following day, taking a cab to the Sunyon bus station and then hopping aboard the one PM bus for the eighteen mile jaunt.

Arriving at the Dwan Jae station at twelve-forty-five, she flagged down still another cab and provided directions to the *'Ling Chow Palace'* located at two-six-three East Main street. The driver, a mostly bald, chubby, middle-aged man wearing oversized sunglasses (despite overcast conditions) and sweating profusely (despite relatively cool temperatures) had regarded her with a questionable look before navigating them into and through the crowded lanes headed to the downtown area. Dwan Jae, with a listed population of just under one-hundred eighty thousand, was roughly half the size of Sunyon, though not nearly as spread out. Like many of the mid-sized Korean towns, square footage in terms of both living and business space was at a premium, resulting in overcrowded roadways (a mishmash of bicycles, buses, and vehicles both privately owned and business oriented) and sidewalks teaming with mobs of unemotional, stone-faced people who appeared to be trapped on an eternal treadmill with no clear-cut destination.

Despite a relatively short absence from her home country, Lei nonetheless caught herself marveling at the cold, indifferent attitude on display from the majority of the citizenry; an apathetic 'big city' remoteness that she couldn't recall being so prevalent in her youth. It was as if each township, no matter the size, harbored a secret grudge while the inhabitants went about their daily routines with a sizeable chip balanced atop their shoulders. Koreans as a whole were legendary for their inane stubbornness; a preordained birth-right that rarely allowed for compromise in terms of personal beliefs, be it family related or governmental. Enduring centuries of forced slavery had engraved this into the generational DNA pool, an 'us against the world' credo that was strictly adhered to when dealing with outsiders, though in-fighting amongst the nationality was a relatively common and accepted practice. No doubt the effect of being separated by mere feet from one's most ardent enemy, not to mention said enemy having shared the same tragic past and being of the same blood. Still, Lei had detected an extra layer of descent since her return onto the peninsula of her birth; an inexplicable sense of interracial segregation in the people that seemed to have little to do with the economy, politics, or the thirty-eighth parallel. Perhaps the alteration was more about herself than those around her, she'd mused. After all, she hardly resembled the naïve teenaged girl from that other life, though a single day hardly passed that she didn't wish for a time machine capable of making that so.

Approximately twenty minutes after departing the bus station, the cab dropped her off on a corner marked two-six four East Main Street. Lei handed him the fare, which included a five-hundred won tip, then stepped from the vehicle and scanned her surroundings, utterly oblivious to the curious stares of many passerby's.

Just as the driver began attempting to work his way back into traffic, temporarily stifled by an elderly man riding a bicycle at a snail's pace, Lei ducked down and addressed him through the front passenger window.

"Can you tell me where the Ling Chow Palace is from here?"

The driver rode the brake, turning back to her with a soured expression, his chin dripping fresh sweat onto an already soaked striped tee shirt.

He nodded, apparently gesturing directly behind her.

"No idea lady, but that's two-six three Main right behind you."

Standing straight, Lei whirled about, barely avoiding a young female bike rider who still managed to run over the big toe of her left foot.

Quickly scanning the unlit marquee, she heard the cabbie gun the engine at her back and pull away with a blaring of horns earmarking his hasty departure.

The sign, spelled out in large, multi-colored bulbs on a squared, ivory-glass backdrop, read 'CHANG'S SPECIALITY HOUSE'.

Having arrived forty-five minutes early, Lei thought about taking a casual stroll to kill some time, but quickly reconsidered once it became apparent the general area consisted of little save a series of crowded open markets and several rundown bars. Nearing a side entrance to the restaurant, Lei paused to consider limited options. After a moment, she decided to simply nurse a few cups of tea while waiting for Charles and his wife to arrive. Being that 'Chang's' was an indoor/outdoor eatery, Lei took a seat at a small glass table just beneath the corner of a wide awning.

Minutes later, a young male waiter took her order for a cup of Green Tea, his thin face seemingly frozen in a permanent scowl.

Sighing, Lei bent to place her purse next to her left leg, which faced away from the street.

She spent the next hour sipping lukewarm tea (refilled only once in that time), nibbling rice cakes (provided as a service) and studying the passing hordes with great fascination. After a time, one could easily imagine the pulsating crowd as nothing less than a mass colony of ants at work on some colossal construction task, their stoic expressions and stiff body movements wholly interchangeable. Few customers came or went in that time, at least to dine outdoors, though she had seen a few dozen depart the interior dining area.

One-hour and eight minutes into her vigil, the cheap Timex watch Charles had provided reading exactly two-sixteen PM, the narrow- faced waiter re-approached her in the same bland manner as before, his finely-slit eyes never meeting her own as they darted about wildly.

"More tea, miss?" he asked robotically, his slight voice possessing a rather annoying nasal whine.

"Um, yes...no...I mean, could you make it coffee instead?" she replied, reaching up to remove

229

several strands of hair which a stiff breeze had blown into her eyes and across the bridge of her nose.

"Yes, of course,' he stammered, fast-walking away as if to avoid an offending scent.

Forty additional minutes and two coffee refills later, Lei's scalp and the tip of each of her fingers began to tingle from a building caffeine overdose.

She decided to order a substantial meal to quell the shakes, and would stick around for another hour before catching a cab back to the bus station.

As the waiter was about to depart after taking her order for a serving of fried mandu (dumplings) and a bowl of fish soup, Lei caught his attention one final time with a raised hand.

"Did you work here when it was the Ling Chow Palace?" The man titlted his head, his brow creased.

"No. I think that's been a long time back. Old place closed down and new owners took over. Not sure exactly how long ago, maybe a few years even."

"So, this Ling Chow Palace didn't just relocate?" she inquired, feeling a sudden hollowness in the pit of her belly.

"Not that I heard about. I think the previous owners retired and moved away."

"Thank…thank you."

The stick-thin man bowed, having still managed to never lock eyes. "You're welcome, miss. Your food will be out very soon."

She hardly picked at the meal once it arrived, having already filled up on tea and coffee. While she nibbled a few of the dumplings, the soup remained virtually untouched and went cold in the half-hour she remained on the premises.

Leaving the waiter a five-hundred Won tip, she walked to the street and hailed a cab at exactly three-thirty. Strangely, several empty cabs had slowed to apparently give her the once-over before eventually passing her by for other fares farther up the street.

Reluctantly, she loaded onto the bus headed back to Sunyon at four-thirty, left to ponder not only her cohort's mysterious no-show, but also the following day's decision concerning her fate. As the bus had pulled away with what appeared to be a full load, Lei was once again oblivious to the peculiar looks she received from several fellow passengers, a few of which even going as far as to purposely relocate to a different section as the trip progressed.

At roughly the half-way point of the journey, the bus was slowed and eventually halted by a horrific traffic-jam. The driver soon came over the PA, speaking of a bad wreck up ahead that left little doubt of the culprit.

As minutes passed, Lei found herself growing increasingly drowsy. By the time the bus began to again move forward, albeit at no more than a snail's pace, she was fast asleep with her left cheek pressed against the window glass.

*** 

*Turning over onto his stomach, his flailing left arm barely avoids impact with his lover's upturned face, but instead grazes the very tip of her scalp and rolls harmlessly away. A thin line of spittle leaks from his lower lip, pooling onto before saturating into the pillow's cotton interior even as each eye alternates a spastic tick. Periodically, he reaches for his groin and gently squeezes, as if subconsciously ensuring all equipment contained therein is present and/or accounted for. As hours pass, his overall movements and full-body shifts became less frequent, though the twitches and ticks increase at a furious pace around both eyes and his ever-trembling, horribly chapped lips. As facial gestures go, he runs the gamut between nervous smiles and pained grimaces, each occasionally accompanied by either a low giggle or animalistic grunt.*

\*\*\*

She awoke with a start, gasping aloud while pressing a closed fist against her own heaving chest. Following a split-second of total disorientation, she realized it had been the insertion of a key and the subsequent creaking of the front door being pushed ajar that had awakened her.

"Coming in..." a voice chimed, and she could make out a massive shadow outlined within the blinding rays of sunlight streaming into the room.

Charles stepped inside as Lei attempted to blink the bleariness from her eyes while leaning up onto her elbows from the sagging mattress.

"Hey, hey sleepyhead...rise and shine," he chastised, walking over and propping a boot on the bed frame as she struggled to set up, "somebody slip you a Mickey or what?"

Clearing her throat loudly, Lei was forced to

swallow hard several times before being able to vocalize a response.

"Don't... know. God, I'm so...tired. Feel really...fatigued for...some reason."

"Weird. You seemed fine last night. Maybe you're coming down with the creeping crud. I hear it's going around."

"C-could be," she croaked, fighting off a coughing spell, "wh-what time is it, anyway?"

Charles backed away, hitching up his blue jeans before taking the seat in the middle portion of the sectional couch,

"Just past ten. You up to brunch?"

Tilting her head hard to the left, Lei lightly tapped a palm against the right side of her head, as if so shake out excess water from her ear.

"Ten...AM?"

"Ughhhhh, yep," he said with a weary roll of his eyes, "that is unless we've been magically transported to the North Pole, where I understand sunlight in the PM hours is downright normal, depending on the season.

You're about as sharp as a butter-knife this morning, aren't you?" "S-sorry. Maybe it was all that...caffeine. That reminds me, where were you?"

Charles studied her for a moment, wearing an expression of comic bewilderment.

"Come again, sweets?"

"I waited for...almost two hours."

"Waited? Hon, I haven't a blessed clue what you're babbling about, but condition yellow sounded off about seven this AM. Had to drag my gear from the bomb dump back to the shop and then out-process for the day."

Completely nude save an extra-long cotton pullover with a color image of *'Tweety Bird'* pasted across the front, Lei sat on the corner of the bed with her hands folded into her lap.

"Just…give me a s-second here…to gather my…wits."

"You got it, babe. Meanwhile, I'll check the ol' grub box. My guts empty as the first keg at a squadron cookout."

Inhaling and exhaling with equal labor, Lei observed his semi-blurry form rise from the couch in a single, energetic leap and side-step over to a dark-colored, double-door, mid-sized refrigerator.

"We got any eggs, perchance?" she heard him ask just as her bare feet struck the surprisingly cool tile. She stood shakily, temporarily forced to widen her stance and use her spread arms for balance.

"Damn, girl, you aren't one to stock the fridge in my absence, are you? Nothing in this bad boy but a jar of turnip kimchi and a bowl of week-old rice. Well, get that pretty little rear in gear, babe. Looks like we're eating out, after all," the voice stated as its originator straightened, shaking his head from side to side while continuing to investigate the cooler's mostly hollow interior. Her eyesight finally beginning to clear, Lei studied Charles' stiff-legged stance even as she became acutely aware of the change in both the man's accent and tone.

"Di-…did your wife make it in?" she muttered, still blinking rapidly as he whirled around to face her.

"My wife…make it in?" he repeated

234

sarcastically, "I dunno…enlighten me. Did *you* make it in…what?"

Feeling the fine hairs of her neck immediately stand on end, Lei suddenly envisioned a flood of warped, distorted images as the entire room seemed to expand, bend and melt away around her.

"Char-….Jere…Jeremy?….wha?.." she blurted, collapsing backward onto the bed but somewhat able to remain upright.

Though she saw his lips moving in what at least appeared to be normal speed, his words were stretched out and radically altered, much like an LP record or taped recording stuck in slow mode.

"Suuuuuuuukieeeeeeee……wwwwwhhhhaaaaa aaatttttt'ssssss wwwwwrrrrrooooooonnnnnggggggg?"

The individual standing in front of her was no longer Charles Rutherford nor Jeremy Yeager, but a mutated version of *both* men; as if they'd somehow been cloned within the same test-tube and spliced into a single being.

As the hybrid moved gradually forward with its arms spread wide, she noticed it possessed the facial features of Yeager but the hair style of Rutherford; additionally, while the left eye was dark brown (Rutherford), the right was a sparkling blue (Yeager). The torso, while still muscular, was less bulky than toned (Yeager), and the legs were thick and stocky (Rutherford).

"Cooooommmmmmmmeeeee tooooooooooo ddddddaaaaaaaaddddddddddddy nnnnnoooooowwwwwww…" the hybrid spat through a wide, toothy grin that displayed the long, squared teeth of Charles Rutherford behind the thick, full

235

lips of Jeremy Yeager. As the thing's movements slowed almost to the point of halting altogether, Lei shifted her focus to the room itself and certain objects and items that were weirdly out of place yet strangely familiar at the same time.

*Example one*: the bed she sat upon appeared to be of the King-sized variety, not the tiny bunk-like mattress she'd suffered so many sleepless night upon in the last five-plus weeks.

*Example two*: The walls were painted a dark green in lieu of the hooch's badly faded brown, and were no longer bare but littered in various murals that, despite never swimming completely into focus, also seemed vaguely familiar.

*Example three*: Besides the aforementioned sectional couch and refrigerator, both of which seemed to have teleported there since her awakening, was a three-tiered bookcase with a burnt finish tucked into one corner of the room, while a black leather love seat adorned still another.

"*Heeeyyyyyyy...ssswwwweeeettttttiiiieeeeee....h hhhooooooowwwww bbbbbooooouuuuutttttt.......ssssssoooommmmeeee.... nnnnooooookkkkkkiii iieeeeee* ?" the Jeremy/Charles thing asked with a gruesome leer, looming over her suddenly paralyzed frame. Lei could only manage to fall back onto the mattress as the thing's nude body crawled forward as to envelop the whole of her. Peering down in horror, she noticed it possessed two distinct sets of sexual organs that split at the center and forked in separate directions, each penis fully erect and sharpened at the tip like fleshy spears.

Despite feeling a tangible layer of disgust

centered at the hellish abomination readying itself to penetrate her, Lei couldn't deny experiencing a small twinge of desire as well.

As the thing fell atop her, pumping its hips forward with a guttural growl that sounded neither human nor animal in origin, Lei bit down hard on its left shoulder and tasted a sickeningly sweet sensation coat her lips and tongue. Searing pain cloaked her entire frame as a rough, clumsily executed double-penetration ensued, and try as she might, the fearful, gasping shriek at the base of her throat failed to materialize into anything other than a passion-filled groan of pure, gleeful ecstasy.

*** 

"You sure you're all right? I didn't even know it was possible for yellow skin to turn so .... *pale*. Hell, you're practically Caucasian."

"I'm...okay. Just another in what's been a steady stream of nightmares lately. Just let me grab a cup of coffee or two and I'll be as good as new."

Charles had arrived at just past six PM, waking her from the latest in a mind-numbing series of sweat-inducing, chest-pounding dreams that, at least in their initial stages, had given the impression of being nothing less than reality based. She could, after all, recall smells, tastes, and specific details in vivid, painstaking detail. What remained a mystery were the symbolic ramifications involved, if any. It wasn't as if the sensation of Déjà vu was a rare commodity in such brain- twisting ordeals, but lately it seemed as though the script doctor dwelling inside her subconscious had drifted from Edgar Allan Poe territory to a surreal mix of H.P Lovecraft and Robert Bloch in terms of creating both an atmosphere of dread and the subsequent pain-filled, gut-wrenching payoff. Whatever the instigating factor, Lei could only hope the pattern was soon discontinued.

"Oh, my head," she grumbled, massaging her temples as she arose, mummy-like, from the twisted contents of the bed-sheet holding her captive, "Funny. I can't even remember crashing."

"I take it you made the trip to Dwan Jae."

Lei hesitated to respond until she was able to perform a quick scan of the hooch to ensure no added furniture or similar objects had magically appeared. Once satisfied the room was sufficiently bare, she released a loud yawn, stretching out her arms while slumping on the edge of the bed.

"I hung around until about…three-thirty, then hopped the bus back," she said, grimacing as she massaged her biceps, "actually, I feel like I ran the whole way. Maybe it was food…or all the caffeine. What happened? You steer me to the wrong eatery?"

Lowering his head, Charles' tone was suddenly as weary as his expression was haggard. Leaning forward, Lei placed a hand atop his right shoulder and lightly squeezed.

"What is it, boss? No offense, but you look like I feel." "Kim…never made it, Lei. She was supposed to meet me in Kae Won, a little village about ten miles north of Dwan Jae. I met the bus, but…she never got off. I backtracked to Kwan Ju, but she'd checked out of her hotel at ten AM this morning."

"What about Tish?"

"Tish?" he asked sourly between nervously chewing the fingernails of his left hand.

"Uh…yeah, your daughter?"

He slowly dropped the hand from his mouth and looked over with a deeply furrowed brow.

"Lei, I…Kim and I don't have any children."

"But I could've sworn….my *god*," she huffed, slapping her own forehead, "must've come from one of my warped dreamscapes. No doubt about it, I'm in line for some serious therapy."

Charles crossed his arms across his chest and said nothing. "I'm sure she… Kim's all right," Lei blurted awkwardly for wont of nything else to say, now clasping both hands atop his muscular shoulders, "can't your…organization track her in-country?"

"Track…? Lei, as of this morning, the entire *organization* is sitting right here in this room. The Colonel will be hopping a freedom bird out of Kimpo tomorrow morning. No doubt I'd be occupying the seat beside him if not for my missing wife."

"You mean…we…I…it's…"

"Word came down this morning. They didn't even bother to wait for the scheduled meeting set for tomorrow morning.

As of six AM this date, we officially… no longer exist," he said sternly, his uncloaked eye lifting to lock on her own, "the powers that be have decided to take a harder stand on the case. There's even talk about a permanent base closure and relocation of several mission- essential units to Kunsan and Osan until the killer's apprehended. Not exactly unexpected by any means, but still quite the *pisser*, I must say."

He sighed heavily as Lei strolled over towards the window and propped an elbow atop the seal.

She responded only after several moments of awkward silence, the likes of which the pair hadn't shared since their initial meetings.

"So…what now, boss? You bring the cuffs or are the local authorities taking the reins?"

"Lei…."

Still staring out the open blinds, she locked her wrists behind her back as if waiting to be secured.

"No need to sugar-coat, big guy. I've….been trying like hell to prepare myself mentally for this very moment."

"Lei, I need your help. I…want you to help me find Kim."

Executing a textbook double-take, Lei regarded him with dumbfounded awe.

"Is that….I mean, permissible? I just figu-.."

"Officially? Not on your life, sister. Unofficially, right now I couldn't give a rat's ass about protocol."

"So what you're telling me is, you're going against direct orders?" "Pretty much," he nodded, cupping his chin under a clinched fist, "transport van is supposed to pick you up at eighteen hundred hours tonight and take you to Kimpo. Following a brief stopover in Anchorage, the 'official' itinerary calls for you to arrive at LA international some fourteen hours later and be escorted to a federal prison outside Phoenix. There you are to be held over for trail, tentatively scheduled for approximately six weeks from now."

Though shaken to the very core of her soul, Lei managed to refrain from showing it, save a barely noticeable crack in her voice.

"(IN KOREAN) That's gratitude for you. I take it the head honchos decided my efforts in this little fiasco rated nothing better than a '*fuck you very much*' brush-off, followed by a quick media crucifixion and public hanging. Can't say I'm exactly shocked, but I *am* mildly disappointed."

"Forget it, Lei, and forget them," he replied curtly, now pacing the room like an expectant father outside a maternity ward waiting room, "I'm hereby amending their orders. Insensitive bastards didn't give a good shit about my wife's vanishing act. Had the balls to hand me a plane ticket and assign me to a new case starting tomorrow.

*Tomorrow,* for shit's sake! This is my wife I'm talking about. Sooooo, I'd say that leaves it up to you and I, my dear, that is…if you…don't mind my using you one last time."

"Hey, big man," she said calmly, walking over and gripping him by the elbows to halt his frenzied stride, "I'll help anyway I can."

"Appreciate it, Lei. More than you'll ever know," he replied with an exasperated sigh.

"Of course, keep in mind that so far I've been about as useful as tits on the proverbial boar."

"Beggars can't be choosers, babe," he replied as they exchanged smiles, "and as it turns out, since my so-called allies have essentially turned their backs

241

on me, I'm feel damn fortunate to have ya."

"Glad to be of service, Charlie, but this does beg the question…what happens then?"

"Let me worry about that, Lei,' he nodded sternly, 'suffice to say, the aforementioned transport is gonna contain a conspicuously empty chair this evening, as is a certain seven-three-seven bound for the City of Angels."

"Charles, you do realize you're not only jeopardizing your career, but more than likely committing several felonies to boot.

I realize your wife's worth the former, but I'm not so sure I rate the latter…"

"Make no mistake, lady," Charles countered sternly, "you're both worth it. Now, pack up with little provisions you have and we'll blow this Popsicle stand. We've got some serious backtracking to do."

Lei's only reply was a brief nod, her mind already racing as if a silent alarm had been set and she was suddenly thrust onto the clock, her every action and movement vital to their endeavor's ultimate success.

"Tell you what," he continued, pacing once again, "I've got a couple of quick errands to run and I'll meet you at down at the Farmers Market in two hours. I just don't think it's a very good idea for you to be hanging out here just in case the goon squad shows up early."

"Sounds like a plan, boss. Plus which, that'll give me time to drop by Susie and Mia's and say my so-longs."

"Okay, just don't drop any hints as to the master

plan."

"No problem, Chuck," she grinned, "you can't speak of that with which you have no direct knowledge."

"Good point," he said, rolling his eyes in mock embarrassment before quick-stepping towards the door, "see ya in a few…partner."

"You'll find me mulling about in vegetable section at the market," she said loudly, watching him vanish and the door subsequently swing shut, "never could stand the raw fish row."

"Got' cha, (IN KOREAN) see ya there," came the muted reply.

All told, it took Lei less than twelve full minutes to pack (a medium sized satchel/purse), dress (jeans, cotton tee, imitation 'Nike' tennis shoes) , and hit the door running.

*** 

She first spotted Charles through the surging crowd while picking out ripe plums and placing them in a plastic bag. Having arrived at the open market some ninety minutes earlier, she'd already filled out the remaining space in her tote bag with various samplings of fruit, to include grapes, persimmons, and Asian pears.

Dropping the plums back into their assigned cart, she attempted to side-step an elderly couple that had temporarily blocked her view.

Forced to peek around, over, and in-between a sudden rush of shoppers, the glimpses she captured of her soon-to-be partner in federal crime were fragmented at best. Still, despite the briefest of imagery and considerable distance between them, Lei became instantly aware of something being oddly askew about Charles' overall appearance, something she was unable to place a finger on at the moment from such limited visuals.

The lingering horde temporarily parted, allowing for a two to three second window from which she gained her first semi-clear, unobstructed view.

Lei's initial reaction, however fleeting, was to cover her mouth with an open palm to refrain from giggling aloud. In addition to a pair of comically oversized sunglasses, Charles was draped in an unbuttoned, snow-white, ankle length lab coat that swayed and swirled about like ivory ocean waves with every stride.

Just as she was about to step into the open, a fresh wave of browsers filled the gap, effective blocking the path once again. Inadvertently shoved aside by an elderly woman hoisting at least a half-dozen overstuffed plastic bags, Lei paused beneath a makeshift awning, effectively dodging the latest surge while leaning against an abandoned cart.

While waiting for the last of the stragglers to pass through the narrow opening between carts, she peered past the awning's thick metal brace and spotted Charles less than a hundred feet down the muddled pathway.

Upon further inspection of her erstwhile partner, Lei's eyes narrowed even as her flesh turned clammy, her face and neck instantaneously flushed from a sudden hot-flash.

244

A pair of armed, uniformed troops flanked Charles on either side, the first two easily identifiable as Air Force SP's and the others Korean Army.

Instinctively crouching down until her elbows balanced atop her knees, she watched groves of shoppers scatter and/or side-step away as the troupe marched forward, all five having donned equally stoic, tight-lipped expressions.

*My...god... could this be...what it...looks like? He did mention something about...a goon squad...but why... why is he...with them...leading them here...and even blazing the trail?*

Duck-walking to the rear of the approximately three-foot high cart, Lei's mind raced with potential options, the least attractive of which was to simply stand, give away her present position, and essentially surrender without incident.

Discarding the tote bag, she fell to all fours and crawled past a series of similarly abandoned carts, oblivious to the many wary looks pointed her way.

Halting at the far end of a series of scattered carts, she stood with her back pinned against the cool, moistened stone of a warehouse building which sat adjacent to the market's western edge. From the angle she'd chosen, it was virtually impossible to be spotted from the street while being allowed a three to four foot wide horizontal 'window' between the top of each cart and the lower edge of the lengthy awning.

Her pulse pounding at her temples and throat, Lei inhaled nervously and held it, trying her best not to blink as folks straggled by, as not to miss the troupe's impending passing.

*Shit. Why...how could he do this....after... after all that we talked about? Why would he...be a party to such...blatant trickery? Certainly never read him as the traitor type. Unless...he was forced...his career, maybe even his life threatened...or perhaps even his wife's... at least then I could... understand...and accept somewhat.*

She saw a light flash through the squared porthole, like a white sheet carried along by a stout gust, to be followed by an equally conspicuous snapshot of military camouflage. With her gut gradually winding itself into a taunt knot that felt basketball-sized, Lei hesitated only briefly before dashing down a nearby alley at blinding speed.

Winding her way down a series of deserted, maze-like passages, her nostrils flared from a constant onslaught of pungent odors, from the pleasant stench of cooking meat and boiling soup to the gag- inducing smell of rotted garbage and open sewers. After what seemed like a full five minute wind sprint, she topped a series of steep, rain-slicked grades and emerged onto a two-lane side street, barely avoiding the grille of a small truck as it whizzed by her with its horn blaring. Peering back over her left shoulder, she was able to visualize a large portion of the path she'd taken as a mix of residential hovels, ancient storefronts and mostly deserted warehouse buildings.

Her breathing predictably labored but not overly so, she whipped her head about in all directions in order to choose the most logical route.

*So... what now? It isn't like I'm gonna remain*

246

*anonymous for long. By the time the evening news and newspapers get wind of this, there will exist no such place to run nor hide.*

Huffing aloud, she spotted a tiny clothing shop just down the street to her right.

*Well, it isn't like I'm beyond a little 'five finger discount' when my ass is in a sling, now is it? Lord knows I've done a hell of a lot worse. What's a stolen shirt, pullover or floppy hat to someone with two dozen homicides under their belt?*

Turning sharply, she had barely completed her first stride before being bear-hugged from the rear and hoisted airborne, her lungs instantly voiding what precious little oxygen they'd previously held.

\*\*\*

"W-ha…who…. *shiiiit*, h-how?" she croaked in a barely audible whisper, her hands still pressed flat against her would-be assailant's upper chest.

"Long story, babe, and this sure isn't the time or place to get into the details. Priority one is to find a suitable safe-haven. We can do the question and answer bit once we hunker down and wait for the furnace to cool a bit. "

After literally being accosted and carried from the street, Lei had been hauled into a nearby building with her arms pinned to her sides in an iron-tight grasp while unable to muster even the most minute resistance, be it physical or verbal.

"I…I thought the base…was on permanent lockdown," she gasped, flailing her arms about to alleviate the numbness, "...were you…*following* me?"

Reaching up, Jeremy cocked his head sharply while pressing a forefinger tightly against her lips.

" Shhhhh. Tone it down a notch, babe," he whispered grimly, "even the thickest of walls have ears, ya know."

Wearing a cautious expression that screamed skepticism, Lei leaned in until their noses practically pressed together.

"Excuse me, but do I know you? You resemble a young Buck Sergeant named Yeager, but I'm thinking some blood tests might be in order just to verify."

"I could ask you the same thing, darling," he chimed back, gently pushing her back several inches, "seems your vocabulary has improved about two-fold in the five days since we last jawed. Attend a crash course in proper English, did we?"

"But, how did you… find me here? Are you in on...all this?" "Damn, girl, could be postpone the interrogation? They'll be plenty of time to play twenty questions once we find a clear path out of town."

Though thoroughly mystified at her one-time lover's sudden appearance, it was the marked difference in both his physical movements and manner of speaking that had instigated Lei's questioning the man's very identity.

"There's a shit load of hiding places here in these old warehouses, some of 'em nothing more than twenty, thirty thousand square foot mazes. Take a five-man team six months to check all the nooks and crannies."

After a short, stilted silence, wherein the only sounds reverberating inside the abandoned, dimly lit structure were muffled voices and the occasional car or truck horn, Jeremy gestured towards a wooden staircase to their left.

"Let's head upstairs. Probably have the offices up there. We can use the windows for surveillance."

"Whatever you say, oh-oh-seven."

They stood as one and ascended the winding staircase, which groaned and creaked in spots as if on the very verge of total collapse.

Once upstairs, they discovered a row of six offices, a few of which lacked entrance doors while others appeared to have been gutted from the inside out.

"Let's check that last one there," Jeremy suggested, pulling Lei along by the crock of her left arm, "the one nearest the exit."

The spacious office held but two surviving pieces of furniture; a battered, rust-coated filing cabinet and a metal office chair with badly bent front legs. Though hardly the textbook 'hiding place' they'd sought, it did provide an excellent view of the adjoining street from a two by three foot window that was missing a 'v-shaped' section of stained glass.

"Anything?" Lei whispered, using the file cabinet as a lean-to as Jeremy peered through the opening.

"Couple of stew bums sharing a bottle of Soju in an alley across the street and a stray dog humping a trashcan. Nothing else moving."

"That mutt better be on guard, less those bums

249

get the munchies. You know how we Koreans are about Kagolgi (Translation: dog meat)."

"Nerves of steel," he quipped, flashing a broad smile while keeping his attention focused on the street below. A broad, infectious smile Lei instantly recognized (with no small degree of relief) as being all Jeremy Yeager.

"All right, Mister International Man of Mystery, let's talk turkey," she whispered, crouching against the wall after joining him at the window.

"Be forewarned, Lei Parks; it ain't the least bit pretty."

"Buddy-boy, it's hardly been a slice of caramel cake up to now.

Spill already...."

"In a nutshell," he said with a heavy sigh, rubbing his eyes with a thumb and forefinger, "lady, you were set up like a ten-pin from the word go."

"Set up...as... what?"

"Why, what else? *The Ville Ripper.*" "How do you know my real na-.."

"Not important right now," he said, flashing the palm of his right hand.

"But...I...I didn't arrive in country until after the fact. They're been...three...four murders committed already. How could I be framed for crimes that occurred eight thousand miles away?"

"Paperwork...passports, visas and such, can be easily altered, Lei, especially when those doing the altering have the right connections.

*Believe* me, by the time your capture hit the newswires, the dates would've conveniently jibed."

"I still don't...but why the act... why not just

250

transport me here and begin the framing process right away? Why bother with at all with the Yellow Fever 'exotic dancer ' bullshit?"

"Only thing I can figure is that they thought you might actually help find the real killer, then once the killings resumed without a capture, toss you onto the flames and let the media wolves feed."

"But…that doesn't *solve* anything. The murders will continue whether I'm locked up here or shipped back to the states."

"It's a band-aid, Lei, a smokescreen. The kind of cruel, merciless sleight of hand usually reserved for purely political reasons.

"Think about it; that base gate can't continue to stay in lockdown mode. Local merchants are pissed at the loss of revenue; the G.I population is suffering a major outbreak of cabin fever…and the two governments are walking on some seriously cracked eggshells.

Besides, they can always blame any further instances on copy-cat killers. You're here now…and you possess the… past credentials to legitimize the whole set-up."

Lowering her chin, Lei briefly closed her eyes and remained perfectly still for a full thirty seconds, as if in deep meditation.

"So…Charles…Charles Rutherford was…in on this from the beginning?"

He nodded solemnly, refusing to meet her gaze even as her head arose and her gleaming, moisture-filled eyes seared into his own.

"Afraid so. Real name's Petersen. Clay Petersen, codename: *Slant- breaker*. He's been an

Asian-based operative for over a dozen years. Former military brat who has spent half his life in Southeast Asia.

Can't say the man isn't good at what he does. Stays in character like no other. Hell of an actor, wouldn't you agree?"

Leaning forward with a look of mild distrust, Lei hugged her knees tightly to her chest.

"Who's to say *you* aren't the actor, Jeremy…or whatever your name really is? I' m supposed to believe everything you say just because we shared a bed five nights ago? Why should I buy into your act any more than I did Rutherford's?"

Glancing from the open window back into her tightly squinted eyes, the man's expression was one of comic befuddlement.

"Correct me if I'm outta line here, babe, but who was that you just saw stalking the open market with four armed soldiers?

Don't think they were down here looking for the lowest price on bean sprouts or fried squid, lady."

The intensity of her stare vanished almost immediately, replaced by the lifeless, vacant look of the soundly defeated.

"So…now we're both fugitives, is that it?"

"For better or worse, I'd say yeah," he answered, turning from the window to lightly tap her right shoulder with an open palm, "and for the record… the name *is* Jeremy."

She nodded weakly, though unable to muster even the tiniest of smiles.

"Jeremy….Stiles. Glad to meet you…again."

The frown that followed was half-hearted at

252

best, and his innocent, 'sorry about that' shrug managed to void out whatever lukewarm anger she'd managed to drudge up.

"Hey…at least I was only *half*-lying."

"Oh, I' m supposed to give you credit for only being partially deceitful?"

"I'd say yes," he grinned, "Miss Sukie. By the way, I really enjoyed your many wild variations of 'broken English' during our 'courting' phase. Give you a friendly tip, though. Bar girls slash dancers should never, *ever* use the word 'moderately', especially without the accompanying accent. Talk about your Webster-related snafu's."

Despite a valiant effort, and regardless of the anxiety-laced fatigue wracking her entire frame, Lei found it impossible not to smile.

"I actually used the word 'moderately'?"

He peered through the window while scratching a light growth of black stubble atop his pointed chin.

"Several times….unabashedly. Guess you thought I was drunk and wouldn't notice. Other than that, a fairly flawless performance, to include the dancing, which I found both gracefully executed *and* erotically charged. I will say this, Miss Parks, you rarely just 'went through the motions' up there. The true sign of a great entertainer."

"Not sure if I should thank you or punch you out, smart-ass," she replied, blurting out the final word in a nervous screech as she'd seen his eyes widen with apparent shock.

"Awww, shiiit. Un-be-lievable…fucking *un-real*," he spat angrily, ducking down until his scalp brushed her knees, "two dozen empty warehouses in a six block area and the son of bitch hones right in. Jackass must have a built-in radar. Either that, or he's bugged you somehow."

"What?" she asked in a barely audible croak, overlapping his bowed head with her own, "You mean….is it… Charles?"

"Yeah, Char-…Clay and his gang just exited the building across the street."

"You…think they'll…"

"They were making a b-line to the back entrance. Come on…"

After duck-walking to the door-less entrance, they posed on opposite sides, pausing to tilt their heads dramatically.

A low scraping sound ensued, followed by a jumbled series of muffled footsteps, as though the originators were putting forth only a somewhat half-hearted effort to conceal their presence.

"You may as well show yourself, Lei," a husky voice boomed, "I know you're here. All these cat and mouse games are such a waste of both our time. It's only delaying the inevitable, my dear. You *must* understand that deep in your heart of hearts."

Sucking in a raspy breath and holding it, Lei instantly felt a surge of static electricity that caused the short hairs on both her neck and exposed forearms to stand out like quills. Though the voice was unmistakably that of the man she'd come to know as Charles Rutherford, the vocabulary and manner of speaking being utilized was that of a complete stranger, a weirdly surreal phenomenon much like the one she'd just experienced with Jeremy Stiles just a few moments previous.

As she eyed him with renewed interest, Jeremy gestured towards the end of the hallway, where the afore-visualized exit was located.

With her legs tensed and lower back arched as if prepping to spring forward, Lei paused as Jeremy bolted around the corner in a semi- crouch.

As she dashed forward, briefly peering down the shadowy hall at their back, she heard distant footsteps growing ever closer as they thundered forward at sprinter speed.

\*\*\*

Despite looking back for but a single ticking of the clock, Lei had somewhat lost sight of Jeremy. The door they'd original thought to be an exit was, in reality, nothing more than just another bare space, in this instance a gutted conference room, its back wall having collapsed inward and leaving a rectangle-shaped, manhole sized, rectangular shaped gap into the open air. The last room at the end of the hall, it essentially served as a dead-end to any potential escape. Figuring she was simply following her newest protector's lead, Lei had sprinted inside without hesitation, coming to a skidding halt at the hollowed out room' s center-point, where her left thigh bumped the rounded edge of a lengthy conference table. Twisting around on the balls of her bare feet, she scanned the perimeter in a slightly bent combat pose with clinched fists rotating expertly in front of her face, though without effectively blocking her vision.

"Jeremy?" she whispered harshly, the stout

scent of boiling cabbage penetrating the wall chasm while more than likely drifting in from the street below.

"Jeremy, where are you, *damn* it? They're coming…"

Through gritted, grinding teeth, Lei cursed under her breath. She'd clearly seen him turn the corner and dart forward, and there had been but one single route to travel. So where exactly had he vanished *to*? There were no inner doors save the entrance and the ceiling was solid wood. Had he perhaps crawled through the gap in the wall and leapt to the street? Not likely, since a quick peek out and down revealed a series of tin awnings that would've been badly dented and/or flattened upon his descent. Did her former nightclub suitor *turned* one-night stand lover *turned* secret agent have the power of teleportation?

"(IN KOREAN) Alone again….naturally," she sang badly out of key, no longer bothering to whisper.

Shoving the surprisingly light conference table aside in frustration, Lei clearly heard an object slide from its dust -coated top and land atop the hardwood floor with a resounding thump.

Strolling around to far side of the table, which now sat badly askew as a rear leg had collapsed inward from the force of her shove, Lei bent down and retrieved the mystery object, holding it up to the foreground of the wall gap as to properly gauge its shape against the streaming daylight.

"Drop the weapon, please. Let us put an end to all the needless bloodshed," a calm yet stern voice chimed from what seemed like an impossibly close proximity.

Whirling about, Lei maintained her crouched pose as she swung the blade about in a wide, arcing slash, the follow-through creating a vacuum-packed whooshing sound, like that of an air-tight container being breeched.

"Cha-…Charles?" she croaked, rising only slightly while gracefully flipping the eight-inch serrated combat knife from palm to palm, the sparkle from its slick, marble handle reflected on the water-stained ceiling above.

"Clay. Clay Bennett. Now, please lower the shank….I *implore* you.

Whatever you may think, I didn't come all this way to see you harm yourself or anyone else…"

The lab coat was now buttoned at the waist, but still appeared comically oversized. While the man calling himself Clay Bennett did indeed still don a black patch over one eye, he held little of the muscular bulk of his alter-ego, instead appearing thin, almost *gaunt,* and though a man did indeed flank him on either side (both short, stocky and obviously Korean), neither wore a uniform, but instead white windbreakers of similar design and style as their apparent leader's ankle-length coat.

"You want me, you traitorous piece of shit, come and get me. It isn't as if I'm got anything to lose, right?" she growled, taking a step forward while straightening her stance.

"This needs to end right here, right now. We…I can get you the help you so desperately need. I… just don't want you to hurt yourself," the man replied desperately, holding out both of his hands palms out.

"Hurt *myself?* Not exactly what I had in mind, asshole. Better call your soldier-boys, mister. I'm not planning on going easy, not after….learning what you've done…and what you really are. I…trusted you, you lying son of a bitch. Trusted that you'd….do right by me if I …did right by you."

"Please listen….it's not what…"

"(IN KOREAN) *FUCK YOU!* (IN ENGLISH) I don't want to hear anymore lies! I'm fed up!" she screamed, whipping the blade viciously from side to side while taking still another half stride forward, "you know what I'm capable of, Bennett. Better yell for the Calvary while you've still got a tongue."

The man bowed his head sadly as the men at this side remained unmoving and essentially expressionless, resembling posed mannequins in a storefront window.

"You, um, follow someone in here? An invisible ally of sorts?" "Hey, you're the super-spy, Bennett. Figure it out for yourself.

Better yet, step forward about three paces and I'll whisper it in your ear as I carve *out* your liver."

"What exactly is it you think you're threatening us *with*?" he asked, regarding her with what appeared to be a healthy dose of sincere pity through his lone working eye, "A machete? A warrior's broadsword perhaps? Take a closer look, please. *Concentrate* and look much, much closer."

"Can the double-talk, you two-faced bastard," she spewed angrily, "I've thought about this long and hard, and I' m not about to spend the rest of my

258

days locked in a metal cage for something I believed, and *still* believe was right."

"Please," he pleaded, gesturing towards the hand which gripped the knife, "I implore you…look….closer…"

Sliding her left foot back as to alter her stance, Lei then pulled the knife across to eye level, though still pointing it forward like a protective talisman.

The gleaming blade with the slick marble handle was no more, replaced by a six to eight inch shard of jagged wood with a decidedly pointed edge, its makeshift handle littered in tiny splinters that had embedded themselves into her palm and the base of her tightly-curled fingers.

"Wha-what the…he-? But….I kn-know what I saw," Lei gasped, blinking madly as to magically transform the shattered section of treated maple back to the finely-honed, sharp-edged steel weaponry of just moments before.

"Correction …" Bennett injected while casually reaching inside the lab coat as if to scratch a bothersome itch, "you saw what you wanted to see. In your case, I'm afraid there always seems to be a radical difference."

Backing slowly away, Lei's eyes darted wildly from the wooden piece to her protagonists, who continued to maintain their respective positions without a hint of concern in terms of her actions.

"You d-did this….some kind of trick….hypnosis maybe." "Allow me a brief synopsis, as to help clarify what has to be a rather muddle mass of confusion on your part."

Removing his hand from its previously cloaked

state, Bennett pulled on a pair of tight-fitting rubber gloves and took a cautious step forward even as his two stone-faced allies remained frozen in place.

"Carving knife or splintered kindling, you come a step closer and I'll find a suitable orifice with which to bury it," Lei countered, striking a defensive pose with her free hand in 'blocking' mode and the other wound back to strike with the sharp-end facing forward.

The two men started to walk forward, but froze in mid-step as Clay Bennett lifted a single gloved hand.

"(IN KOREAN) Brute force won't be necessary. Just give me a moment, please."

The pair shot each other a brief glance and nodded in apparent compliance.

In response, Lei lightened her fighting stance, if only slightly.

Looking past the still trio, she first caught glimpse of a medium-sized black briefcase propped against a far wall, near the open entrance.

"Smart move, two-face. I'm afraid that in my present mood, I'd show very little restraint when putting a serious hurt on Mutt and Jeff Chang there. Loyalty to one's race only goes so far, you know."

Folding his arms across his chest, Bennett momentarily eyed the open section of wall before refocusing his attention back to her.

"Still believe yourself to be the ultimate warrior, I see. The avenging angel with a built-in homing device: The serial killer of serial killers and rapists.

Allow me the simplest of questions, in order to....know where we presently stand, so to speak.

Please state both the present year and who you believe *me* to be, or have been."

Lei cocked an eyebrow, peering into the man's lone uncloaked eye with steely intensity.

"What the...what is this *bullshit* ? You've got the audacity to play...mind games at a time like this? Mister, you are truly an extraordinarily...sick...fuck."

The man flashed a rather weak, sad smile.

"Humor me. It isn't as if any of us have an appointment elsewhere. The year and exactly whom you identify me with."

"Eat shit (IN KOREAN), you lying son of a bitch. Just take me if you're going to..."

"I'm guessing..." he continued unabated, cupping his chin within a gloved hand, "you'd more than likely answer late summer or early fall in the year of our Lord nineteen-eighty four, and as for me....I' m none other than Charles Rutherford, former Air Force noncommissioned officer *turned* undercover agent of some international spy network *turned* merciless traitor to your personal cause. Am I at least in the ballpark, my dear?"

"I'd say that pretty well sums up the shit-sandwich you fed me these past several weeks, yeah," she growled angrily as her fists began to shake and shimmy with a barely restrained rage, "is this your official retraction, jerk-off?"

"And your aliases included both the Korean moniker Sukie Kim as well as the codename 'Slant'..."

"Why do you insist on questioning the obvious, Bennett? You were *there*, remember? You fed *me*

261

this information, not vice versa!" "Fine. So far so good ," he conceded calmly, "Mister Lee, if you please," he continued, reaching back with an outstretched hand as the man to his right slapped a rolled newspaper into this open palm.

Side-stepping over, Bennett unrolled the newspaper and laid it atop the conference table before backing away.

"Again," he politely pleaded, gesturing towards the paper with a sweeping motion, "Just humor me. This could be...to use the vernacular, a real...eye-opener...at least for starters."

Creeping forward while maintaining a combat-ready pose, Lei peeked over and down, where the folded top half of the paper was displayed.

"It's your dime, pinhead. If you insist on wasting our time with parlor tricks, I'm in no position to stop y-.."

Dividing her focus between the bold-black print just above the headlines and the trio of statuesque individuals standing less than a dozen feet away, Lei's arms, legs and torso began to instantaneously tingle as from a mild electrical shock of unknown origin.

"Feel free to read it aloud. Believe me, each discovery and subsequent admission falls under the heading of much-needed therapy. There's no such thing as 'jumping the gun' in terms of a proper start time."

"This...can't be right. It's just a...trick. That's...that's why you're talking like some second-rate shrink.

You...you're fucking with my head again,

that's all. Pushing my buttons. This…garbage doesn't mean a thing," she raved, flinging the paper to the floor and retaking her previous stance.

"I take it this particular set of numbers doesn't jibe with your personal calendar."

"Hey…I know what year it is, jackass. That is, unless this room is some kind of magical time portal."

With a heavy sigh, Bennett leaned against the far side of the conference table and casually crossed one leg over the other while looking his thumbs beneath his squared chin. Suddenly wide-eyed, Lei was besieged in a tidal wave of flash-images; a déjà vu-filled head rush that seemed to indicate she'd witnessed the exact same movements countless times before.

"What I'm about to divulge isn't going to be any easier for me to say than it is for you to accept. My initial advice to you is to relax that incessant fighting stance, as it is as unnecessary as it is useless. Once again, I reiterate…we are *not* here to fight you.

The second is to listen to what I have to say not only with her mind, but with your heart. In your present state of mind, the temptation will be to twist everything I say in a negative way. All I ask is that you hear me out. Again, I reiterate. We aren't here to hurt you. We're here… to help. Now, are you willing to at least hear me out before attempting some aggressive, ill-advised act?"

"Do I really have a choice, *Clay?*" she replied with a scowl, dropping her guard only slightly, "what the hell? I might as well get a sneak preview of what my future court-trail's going to sound like. Proceed by all means, counselor. This girl understands her rights. Guilty until proven innocent... which is about as likely to happen as a pig sprouting wings and crapping on the Embassy building, right?"

Shaking his head from side to side, Clay Bennett turned briefly to address his cohorts.

"Did I every truly think this would be easy? Ah, reality is such a cold hard slap across the face for those of us cursed to see the glass half full..."

"Just get on with it, mister," Lei commanded, having crouched onto one knee with the wooden shank still clasped tightly in her left fist, "to paraphrase it in your own tight-assed lingo, this constant barrage of psychobabble grows increasingly tiresome."

Nodding somewhat reluctantly, Bennett inhaled deeply and began.

*For the present, in order to help maintain a workable level of tension, I'll address you by the name typed on your Korean birth certificate slash ID card, that being Misses Sukie Hui Kim. If you find this objectionable in any way, shape or form, perhaps I should then utilize your married name, Miss Sukie Whitt.*

"Soooo...we're back into role playing again, huh Chuck? I thought we were beyond that..."

*Please, Sukie, or...Lei if you prefer, the less interruption, the better. You were born in the city of Pusan in April of nineteen fifty-nine and, following the tragic death of your parents in a bus crash, were raised by an Aunt and Uncle on your father's side.*

*This uncle began molesting you when you were but the tender age of nine, infrequently at first but at an increasing rate as you grew of age. In addition, your stepbrother, three years your senior, also began sexually assaulting you around the age of fifteen.*

"Pardon me, Doctor Clay, but is this little stage drama scripted or are you just making it up as you go along?"

*Suk-...Lei please. I' ll provide you ample rebuttal time at the conclusion of my presentation. Now, realizing that revealing such a dark family secret might not only mean being ostracized from the local community, but also the possibility of incarceration for all involved, including your aunt and even yourself, you managed to conceal these personal horrors until you eventually ran away from home at the age of seventeen.*

*Your first stop was Kwang-Ju, where you toiled as a plant worker for a full year and a half, scraping by on a scant fifteen dollar a week salary. One evening, a roommate mentioned certain...job opportunities she'd heard about near some of the local American military bases, to include Osan, Kunsan and Sunyon.*

*A few days later, the two of you traveled to Sunyon and were instantly hired on as 'exotic' dancers at the Yellow Fever club, located in what was referred to as 'G.I Central' to visitors and simply 'The Ville' to those permanently assigned.*

"Are you deranged, Bennett? I'd never even stepped foot in '*The Ville*' until that day less than six weeks ago when you yourself provided a personal tour. Then again, maybe that was your evil, more muscular clone."

*Less than three months after beginning your 'tour of duty' at the Fever, you met an Air Force Sergeant, struck up a rather heated relationship, and the two of you moved in together. Two and a half months later, after growing impatient at watching his lover being ogled and propositioned by other troops on a nightly basis, the good sergeant paid off your bar fine. Five months following that, having just turned twenty years of age, you were married and subsequently flown to the states to begin a tour of duty in West Texas. This lasted just over two years, when your husband, one Jeremy Whitt, received PCS orders to return to your homeland for still another remote assignment at Sunyon Air Base. In truth, you'd both hoped for either Osan or Kunsan, but were reasonably happy just to make the return trip.*

"Jeremy…Whitt did you say? Jeremy…Whitt? What kind of horseshit are you spread-.."

*Jeremy Rutherford Whitt, to be precise, named after a grand grandfather Rutherford who served as an officer in confederate ar-…*

"Damn, if you aren't the creative one. And who're you again, Charles Clay? Chuck Rutherford? Soupy *Fucking* Sales? How exactly is mixing up the characters' names within the screenplay adding validity to your story?"

*It'll come to you, Sukie, believe me. It's simply of matter of my finding the correct trigger, be it a name, phrase or combination of both. Be patient, my dear. To continue, this second tour of duty wasn't nearly the happy, carefree experience the first had been. Oh no, far from it. It seems your marriage had become strained at the conclusion of the Texas assignment, and the problems had carried over with a vengeance once you two again graced Korean soil.*

*Good Sergeant Whitt, much to your chagrin, began to frequent the Ville's many night spots on a regular basis, and usually without his bitter better half in tow. Well, it wasn't long until Miss Sukie found out the horrible truth. Sergeant Whitt had begun to carry on affairs with not one, but three separate bar girls, one of which you'd even called 'co-worker' in your days atop the Fever's stage. A woman who had, in fact, traveled with you to the Ville searching for employment some four years earlier. This woman's name was Mia...Mia Park.*

"Mia...*Park*? Jesus wept, there he goes again with the name merging. I take it you mean the Mia I danced alongside these past six weeks. Got to confess, I' m starting to need a scorecard here."

*Have no fear. We'll get to that, and I promise all these names you deem... hybrids of some sort will fall neatly into place as the session continues.*

"Session? As in psychiatric? I guess all we need now is a few framed diplomas and a couch. Well, like I said, it's your dime..."

*Around the five month point in your husband's tour, a local dancer, the 'Ecstasy' club I believe being her employer, was found brutally murdered less than a mile from the center of the Ville. Local authorities had barely begun a thorough investigation when still another killing occurred with a frighteningly similar MO. This time, it was a bar girl from the 'Head East' club. Exactly two weeks after the second homicide came a third. In this particular case another dancer and former employee of the...Yellow Fever. You knew this girl very well, Sukie. Had even shared an apartment together at one time, not to mention similar dreams of escaping the horrible lives you'd both once lived. The woman's name, was...yes indeed...none other than the aforementioned... Mia Park. Within a week of her death, local and military police sought out and questioned your husband, as he'd been easily linked to her via the affair they'd been having.*

*I must say you're looking a bit piqued, my dear. Is any of this beginning to... ring a bell?*

"I...um...no... *hell* no, of course not. How can it be, numb-nuts? I spoke to Mia...the *Mia* I know anyway, just yesterday in fact.

I...I just...I'm weak from...lack of f-food, I guess. Can we....please just...sum this up? It's getting harder and harder to concentrate on your droning dialogue."

*Yes, of course. I do apologize, Sukie. It's just that, I find staying the course in terms of chronological order is mandatory for a successful session conclusion. I hope you understand...*

"What...who are you *this* time, Char-...Clay? Are you playing doctor... head shrinker, for Christ's sake? What the hell gives you the right...and...and what's the purpose anyway?

This isn't the least bit fair, you son of a bitch! I don't even know...tell me my part, *please*....I...need to know my part if I'm going to...be able to play along. I feel so damn...so lost..."

*It will come to you, Sukie. I promise you this. It will... come to you. For now, just play the part of listener, for that's all that's required of you.*

*All right now, to continue...*

*Jeremy was questioned and subsequently released, and as I understand it never seriously considered a suspect in Mia's killing. Indeed, as the investigation into the killing spree progressed, authorities found it a virtual impossibility to narrow a list of possible suspects. You see, the victims had more in common than just their line of work at the time of the slayings; it seems all three lived alone and had temporarily been without a significant other. In Ville terms, they were Yobo-less; meaning recent lovers had been plentiful, both of the American G.I and local variety. All had suffered the loss of long- time yobo's in the previous months leading up to their deaths; victims of PCS moves that had ended the relationships and left them searching out new avenues of personal and financial gratification. Of course, such a cold, heartless phenomenon is far from being anything new in places like the Ville. Not all the girls end up married with a free ride to the 'land of milk and honey'. Most discover that true 'knights in shining armor', or should I say khaki camouflage, are a rare breed indeed.*

*The majority , in fact, are lied to and cheated on, then discarded like so much bagged trash, receiving little pity from both the local community that feeds off their livelihood like flesh-consuming parasites or the military establishment that 'unofficially' constructed such communities for the 'recreational well-being' of the troops. Sad but true, as are the countless number of 'Amer-Asian' born to G.I's who flee the country, leaving behind a child that endures a lifetime of rejection for being a half-breed.*

(Long Pause)

*I... truly apologize. Afraid I sometimes stand atop my soap-box and lose all sense of priority.*

"I'm not saying I disagree, Bennett...but please...I beg you...just get *on* with it. If... your goal was to physically drain me with this speech, consider it a rousing success."

*Again, my apologies. Now...to the meat of the story, so to speak. Believe it or not, Sukie my dear, it was you who was instrumental in the eventually capture of the perpetrator deemed 'The Ville Ripper' by the local media.*

"Oh, hopping back into the time machine again are we? Set controls to 'near future' Scotty, and...engage at warp speed!"

*Sukie, please, wasn' t it was you who requested an expedited end to this?*

"Just finish this goddamn fairy tale, will you? I'm beginning to think I'm *already* serving time."

*Long story at least semi-short the, my dear, poor Sukie.*

*Mere days before Sunyon Air Base was permanently locked down due to the murders, you made quite the horrifying discovery, oh my yes, indeed, quite dreadful it was. Personally, I cannot even fathom the level of trauma you must've suffered. Truly, such an incident would surely have to be experienced in order to comprehend the level*

270

*of misery and stark terror endured.*

*(Short Pause)*

"Well, go on…what the hell did I do…capture Big Foot?"

*Prepare yourself, Sukie, for I' m fairly certain that this is when your…self-awakening begins.*

# CHAPTER SEVEN:
## Mind-Fillers and Wholly Fictional Fragmentations

"So spit it out, one-eye....for shit's sake...spit...it...out..." Lei barked angrily, wearily tossing up her arms in frustration. Minutes earlier, she'd unconsciously discarded the jagged sliver of wood, dropping it near her left foot as she'd just as obliviously assumed a 'lotus-style' pose. Despite being able to maintain a suitably irritated tone of voice, her entire frame appeared on the verge of fatigue-wracked collapse, her badly drooping eyes periodically rolling back into her head.

"How are you feeling, Sukie?" Bennett asked timidly, his hands pressed flat just beneath his chin. Every few seconds, he would spread them and pause for several seconds before re-connecting the palms.

"Fit as a fucking fiddle for someone being slowly bored to death in the literal sense, smart-ass. Thanks for the concern...."

"Can you see the flower, Sukie? Do you see the blooming flower?" "Yeah...yes, I see it. Of...of course I...see it. Its right there in front of me, isn't it?"

"Why, of course it is. Now Sukie my dear, I want you to continue observing the flower's magical bloom as I speak. I' m going to mention a date in time. A date from the recent past I believe you'll recognize as very familiar. When I mention this date, you will...see things. You will visualize crystal

272

clear images from that very date.

Things you…experienced on the specific date in question. These images will serve to… jog your memory on many varied levels. Do you understand?"

"Damn it, yes…I understand. Can we please just get on with it? My god, I do believe I'm sprouting moss."

"Very well then, my dear. The next words I speak will initiate a memory teleportation, as it were. This particular journey can only end with the sound of my hands clapping together.

Sukie, The date in question is….October sixth, nineteen eighty-four."

Resembling a victim of a sudden electrocution, Lei suddenly jerked and wriggled about in a spasmodic fury, eventually rolling onto her back and growing motionless except for the fingers of each hand, which danced and darted about as if she were tapping atop an invisible keyboard.

Throughout what was to be a four-plus minute ordeal, her eyes rolled beneath their lids like loose marbles, only occasionally flashing the milky whites of each like rotating beacons on a misty beachfront.

\*\*\*

**Part One:**
*Blind Pursuit*

From the edge of the darkened alleyway, the *pursuer* watches the young woman depart the '*Paradise Cove*' club' s double-door entranceway,

273

the subject pausing briefly to replace her dancer's shoes with a pair of purple-shaded sneakers. The dancer's sparse ensemble glitters in neon, the effect enhanced further by the moonlight's dull yet intrusive reflection.

Careful to maintain at least a twenty to thirty yard distance between them, the *pursuer* darts gracefully from alley to alley, utilizing the occasional fruit cart or trash can for added cover.

The young woman strolls casually forward without ever turning about, her pace only quickening as alleyways, storefronts and residences give way to open rice fields on either side.

The gap widening between them, the *pursuer* temporarily loses sight of the quarry, as the girl has vanished over a distant hillside after detouring off the beaten path by taking a sharp left through the paddy to their immediate left.

Feeling a sudden surge of panic, the *pursuer* seems to literally levitate forward at blinding speed without benefit of any actual steps being executed in the natural sense. The *pursuer's* breathing feels mysteriously constricted from some as of yet unseen source. Though the *pursuer* can clearly visualize the frosty air escape from between its pursed lips, the overall sensation is of a rather uncomfortable stuffiness, as if woefully overdressed even for the cool, crisp night air.

Cresting the hill at warp speed, the *pursuer* enters an overgrown path that appears only recently beaten down, the 'trail' possibly two feet wide at the outset. Marching through knee-high weeds, the *pursuer's* overwrought nerves are hardly soothed by

274

the presence of thick, gnarled growths of mutated shrubbery that engulf the path on both sides.

Halting abruptly, the *pursuer* then spots the quarry's prone body lying less than two dozen feet away, the outline of the girl's fallen torso creating a rather gruesome variation on a 'snow-angel' within the tall, flowing weeds.

The *pursuer* falls to one knee and immediately begins scanning the area for a possible third party hidden nearby.

Satisfied in the fact that there doesn't seem to be anyone else present near the general vicinity, the *pursuer* crawls to within a dozen feet of the fallen quarry.

The young girl lays utterly motionless; a discarded rag-doll in glittering sequin whose chest and midsection refuses to rise and fall as a symptom of normal breathing.

Scooting closer, the *pursuer* becomes aware of a faint yet vaguely familiar odor. It is a scent not associated with either the surrounding countryside or the nearby city, yet it awakens a familiarity whose origin isn't quite within reach.

Kneeling over the body with great trepidation, as if inspecting an ultra-sensitive explosive device, the *pursuer* is finally able to properly identify the odor, as well as its source.

The quarry lays in a fast-spreading pool of her own blood, having been gutted slaughterhouse style from the base of her neck to her lower abdomen.

Leaping up onto weakened legs, the *pursuer* gasps aloud, though the end result sounds strangely muffled. Attempting to back away, the *pursuer's* feet become tangled in an unknown obstacle, resulting in a clumsily executed fall, complete with wind-milling arms and kicking feet.

Reaching down, the *pursuer* discovers the culprit wrapped around both ankles like a fully constricted boa. A high-pitched shriek ensues as the *pursuer* pulls, jerks, and tugs in frantic hast to peel away what seems like a never ending roll of warm, gore-drenched intestine.

It isn't until the *pursuer* is able to balance on one knee and subsequently stand that the girl's body swims briefly back into view, revealing a hollowed out midsection whose contents now lay scattered like a nest of slumbering snakes just past her naked, blood-spattered feet.

Whirling about to flee, the *pursuer* is greeted by a trio of slumping figures standing less than a dozen feet away, their faces concealed in shadow.

Frozen in place, the *pursuer* endures temporary paralysis, praying a motionless state will somehow create an aura of invisibility from this newest menace.

Despite the frigid conditions, the trio all wear similarly skimpy costumes as those associated with the exotic dancers of the Ville, though in the gloom of night all related colors default to hazy black and white.

Following an undeterminable span (a minute, five? A half-hour perhaps?) locked in suspended animation, the *pursuer* side-steps cautiously to the left in hopes of eminent flight. Peering to the left down towards a steep, gravel covered incline, the *pursuer* quickly maps out a mental escape route of sorts. Before the *pursuer* is able to properly twist about to execute the pre-planned sprint, the three figures begin to twitch and convulse, performing what is essentially a grisly death-dance in amazingly choreographed sequence.

Again frozen (involuntarily?) into place, the *pursuer* is hapless to act, again regulated to the role of terrified witness as the three continue to juke and hop about, their faces revealed in the sparse moonlight as blank slates; featureless drones whose shiny, pitch-black hair serves only to illuminate their yellowish flesh.

Reaching with both hands towards their own chest cavities, the faceless trio begin to unceremoniously tear away the costumes, revealing wide, vulva-shaped slash wounds beneath their tiny, perk breasts. Clinching their hands into makeshift claws, they then proceed to bury their fists up to the wrists in their own exposed midsections before ripping out handfuls of steaming viscera.

With Herculean effort, the *pursuer* is able to break free of the trance, practically leaping head-first down the side of the hill and rolling end over end until the base of a lifeless elm halts all further progress. Soon after, the *pursuer* sprints atop the hard clay path between rice paddies, a chorus of vaguely familiar voices ringing out in the background. Voices that sing in English, though with a decidedly Korean-accented slant; their wispy, misery-filled tone as haunting as the words themselves.

*"We'll be with you...always... always just....a whisper...away...a whisper away.....'* they repeat

277

over and over in a harmonic, curiously seductive whine that the cool night breeze scoops up and carries along like a static-filled radio transmission.

The *pursuer* has but to cover the same ground in reverse to return to the outskirts of the Ville, where an endless series of back passages and narrow walkways seem to breed and expand in a convoluted maze seemingly void an ending point or escape route.

Seemingly at trek's end, the *pursuer* keys a door lock and tiptoes inside a tiny foyer, careful not to tip over a stack of ondol bricks sitting nearby.

Passing through yet another door, this one of the sliding glass variety, the *pursuer* is able to distinguish certain shapes within the darkness even while pausing at the entrance to remove a pair of black workboats coated in wet shards of displaced grass. A wide, square box adorned with 'rabbit ears' sits in one corner atop a two foot high oak stand, while an 'L-shaped' sectional couch centers the room, backed by a three-tiered bookcase with comically overstuffed shelves and a glass 'knick-knack' case housing several dozen ceramic, stone and wood figurines.

As if literally walking on eggshells, the *pursuer* nears still another sliding glass door in stocking feet, being extra cautious as not to slip or slide on the heavily waxed hardwood floor.

Placing bare palms on the door's cool exterior, the *pursuer* is gripped by a tidal wave of anxiety. Regardless of how strong the urge to flee the scene, the *pursuer* holds firm in the realization that the answer to a great mystery lays beyond; the final puzzle piece unveiled in all its enigmatic glory.

Exhaling in huffing spurts through whatever obstacle so annoyingly blocks the normal regulation of oxygen, the *pursuer* gently slides back the glass just enough to provide entrance space.

Stepping through with the right foot, the *pursuer's* heel has yet to make impact on the other side when a loud clicking sound and subsequent blinding light shatters the tranquility like an exploding grenade.

\*\*\*

**Part Two:**
*Unmasked*

Shrieking with tightly-shut eyes from the nova blast of brightness, the *pursuer* falls back into the living room in a spiraling lurch, ultimately taking a seat on the far edge of the sectional.

A form bursts forth from the light, and the *pursuer* performs a textbook double-take in wake of the shocking imagery revealed. As the form poses less than three feet away, waiving the object it so firmly grasps in its left hand back and forth like a synchronized pendulum blade, the *pursuer* catches a slightly distorted reflection in the glass door's grooved pane.

*It can't be*, the *pursuer* screams in subliminal denial, *how can such a…an abomination exist*?

The black stocking's fit is beyond simply snug; it is an extra layer of flesh pulled wickedly taunt. It is no small wonder the simple act of breathing has

279

been such a strain! It is truly the 'Iron Maiden' mask in cloth form! Beneath such a torturous, skin-tight fit, proper self- identification is not a viable option.

As full-body paralysis again sets in, the *pursuer* quickly refocuses on the naked horror standing a simple reach away.

*But...it        isn't...this        simply        isn't possible....she's...she's...*

Sukie is completely nude, her neck, breasts and abdomen coated in semi-dried blood to which leaves and specks of dirt and gravel stick like feeding parasites. Flashing a vacant expression and an equally bland, toothy smile that is the definition of hideous, Sukie hugs what appears to be a bone-knife tightly to her chest, the slightly curved blade at least eight to nine inches in length and stained in a blackish/red coating. The sudden incursion of bright light only serves to add several distinct exclamation points to the obscenity on display, not unlike observing particularly gruesome crime scene photos beneath a microscope's probing eye.

"(IN KOREAN) What's the matter, baby?" Sukie asks with a childish pout, "surprised to see me?"

The *pursuer* can only manage the weakest of nods and matching sob as Sukie's slim, lithe form glides forward and plants the sharp edge of the blade firmly against the bottom edge of the black stocking, just below the chin.

"(IN ENGLISH) I won't apologize, if that's what you require, or desire, of me. They all deserved what they got. Those devilish whores took what belonged to me, you understand. There is a high

280

price to pay for such treason, lover. A high price for *all* parties involved, including yours truly. Isn't it about time we balanced the universal checkbook, so to speak?"

"Can't be….you…I'm not…a killer. It's a dream…that's all….I…I'll wake soon enough…god help me…this nightmare has to end," the *pursuer* mumbles in a robotic, emotionless monotone normally associated with those under heavy medication.

"Awww, don't cop out on me now. Take a closer look, lover," she coos, leaning down to plant a light kiss at the center of the *pursuer's* forehead, "Take a good, *long* look. Remember, only when we learn to accept what we cannot control, can true healing begin to take root…."

"But…you can't be…" the *pursuer* manages in a harsh croak, "….you just…*can't be*…"

Keeping the blade firmly planted against thin nylon, Sukie then reaches up and palms the tip of the *pursuer's* scalp, firmly twisting as to properly position their respective reflections in the glass pane.

"Buck up, gorgeous," Sukie snarls while jerking the stocking free with a single, ferocious tug, "for what we have here, I believe, is a classic case of *mistaken* identity."

Instead of the stereotypical wide-eyed, open-mouthed expression of pure terror or the wailing screams that would accompany such a knee-jerk reaction, the *pursuer* is able to maintain an astonishing level of calmness in the face of such a shocking, repulsive revelation. Perhaps it is simply a matter of overkill, of the system growing immune to further atrocities to an already frazzled inner core. Or perhaps, just perhaps, this final, shocking 'twist' wasn't completely unexpected after all. In fact, as hindsight would later bear out, it was the only solution that truly made sense, at least from a logical point of view.

"So...I'm...not you...after all," the *pursuer* said, tilting his head in awestruck wonder.

Sukie giggled girlishly, vigorously rubbing a hand through his mused up hair.

"Why, of course not, yobo. You never *were*, you silly goose."

For a frozen moment in time, their faces joined together in soothing tranquility as if posing in a family photo shoot, one would've labeled them the atypical loving couple, albeit of vastly different nationalities and backgrounds. *'Announcing Mister and Misses Jeremy Whitt'*, the divorce decree might read, *'what once might have been marital bliss has, alas, taken a horribly wrong turn'*.

Even the glass pane's warped reflection was unable to mask the sincerity of their matching smiles, a freeze-framed Hallmark image quickly and effectively obliterated as Sukie ran the razor-sharp blade across Jeremy's exposed throat, spewing forth a fine red mist that cloaked their distorted features like some demented piece of abstract art.

\*\*\*

*His eyes roll from side to side beneath tightly clinched lids, his fists curled tightly at his sides as he lies sprawled atop the bed posed as stiffly as a*

282

*fallen mannequin. His entire body is bathed in a fresh coating of warm, sour-smelling sweat that forms a moist outline not unlike that of a crime scene victim. At some point, a labored sigh bursts free as his chest implodes in apparent relief. It is only a matter of moments before it will again expand as his lungs refill and every fiber of his being winds as taunt as an overextended rubber band on the verge of snapping.*

***

**Part Three:**
*Brain Fragments*

"Are you with me? Snap to…are you back *with* me? " a voice inquired from what sounded like a faraway distance, accompanied by a sharp clapping sound that echoed like multiple gunshots.

"Whe-..wha-? I….where?"

"Everything's fine, just calm down. You're safe. Now, look over here. Look into the mirror…*Jeremy* ."

"Jer-Jere-my? I do-..b-but… I don't unner-…understand…" "Trust me, Jeremy, as you always have. Just take a look…."

Posed on all fours, he peered into the oval-shaped mirror and openly winced, as if staring directly into a blazing sun.

"But…I don't under…it makes no sense."

"Certainly it does, Jeremy," the man exclaimed calmly, lowering the mirror while crouching down, "let us reflect for a few moments. We'll fill in the

283

blanks as we go, what say?"

"D-Doctor...Doctor   B-Ba-Be....awww   s-shit...."

"Bennett. Jeremy Whitt allow me to reintroduce myself. Clay Bennett at your service. See? You almost had it. It's coming back to you slowly but surely. Within a few hours the fog will have completely lifted."

"Cla-Clay Bennett?" came the shaky response, its originator tilting his head in confusion while gently scratching his sweat-slick hair with both hands, "but...I knew...know a Bennet. Colonel Brad...Brad Bennett. Full bird type. My...my OIC in base...base supply...called 'im 'Bird Dog' for how he loved to...chase the skirts."

"Afraid not, my boy," the other man said in a fatherly, consoling tone that was to be the normal for the duration of the session, "that particular Mister Bennett was just a fictional fragmentation, a minor *role* player if you will. Pardon me while I obtain the required script, for want of a better term.

Mister Lee, if you would hand me the briefcase please."

Moments later, he pulled several manila folders from the case before handing it back to his cohort, a short, stocky, middle-aged Korean man who then quickly retook his original position at the rear of the room.

"Okay, just hang with me a few precious moments, Jeremy," Bennett said, studying the fronts of each folder as to apparently place them in the proper order, "if I'm going to do this, I may as well do it right and start from the beginning. Have to

284

admit, I possess neither the energy nor patience to repeat myself."

Rising shakily to one knee, Jeremy Whitt scanned his surroundings with great caution, an overwhelming sense of displacement essentially handcuffing all other emotions. Foremost on the scorecard of surreal variations was the very room itself, which had altered quite dramatically from the one he'd recalled entering while trailing along behind his virtual twin. For one, the lengthy conference table had been replaced by a thick, circular wooden stand at least four feet wide and two dozen long. Obviously having once served as a bar, the dark- stained, genuine oak stand was backed by a wall-sized mirror that had been shattered at the center, leaving only a few jagged strips glued into place. Reaching up to touch its outer edges, Jeremy Whitt pulled himself to his feet with a pained groan, his knees and elbows sounding off with equal fervor. Just as telling if not more so in the ' *it was just a hallucination*' sweepstakes was the fact that all the interior walls were completely intact, the gaping hole of earlier no longer visible, nor the street odors that had accompanied it.

Glancing into a pyramid-shaped piece of broken mirror, he studied his distorted image with the curiosity of a toddler discovering his own reflection for the very first time. Leaning his elbows onto the bar, he had fallen into a rather soothing, déjà vu-induced haze before being forced back onto the hard plain of reality by the other man's booming voice.

" Bingo! Got it. Chapter one, page one in the Jeremy Whitt chronicles, as it were," Bennett announced with mock cheer, having taken up position directly across from Jeremy on the 'serving side' of the bar.

"First off, Jeremy, since there has to be a starting point…a point 'A', we'll call it, please take in the surroundings and identify our present location, if you can."

"Well, I…I'm not…it looks vaguely….just not s-sure…"

"No *pressure,* you understand," Bennett injected, holding up a palm as to halt the other man's nervous stammer, 'this isn't a test, mind you. Just want to get an idea of where we stand, memory-wise, before I go off on some exhaustive tangent that is only partially necessary. Bottom line is, I want to make this as easy as possible for the both of us. Given ample time, the majority of the transition would take care of itself, but I'd much rather cover as many bases as possible now to avoid potential conflict."

"It…the bar…" Jeremy said timidly, patting the dust-covered top with both hands, "it…looks vaguely…familiar. But then…I've…frequented many… similar spots over the years."

"This much is true, I'm sure, though I would think this particular spot might ring the proverbial bell over all others. We are standing, dear Jeremy, inside the gutted remains of the club once referred to as….the *Yellow Fever.*"

"This? This is…the Yellow Fever? But…it can't…I was….*she* was just there y-yesterday."

"No, Jeremy, you weren't. Fact is, no living soul has frequented the walls of this particular

286

establishment in quite some time. You see, the Yellow Fever closed its doors over two years ago, along with every other night spot with in what was popularly known as the 'Ville'.

"Closed? B-but, the base…"

"Ah, Sunyon Air Base…home of the 11th Fighter Wing, better known as the *'Shark Attack.'*. Sadly, a victim of government budget cuts, Sunyon permanently closed its gates some twenty-six months ago.

The official closing date was…." he paused while flipping through a separate folder, "July eighteen, nineteen eighty-five. Says here it remained a temporary 'training station' for three additional months, even though the majority of the three-plus thousand assigned personnel had already been reassigned. The effect on the local community, as you can plainly see, was less than positive. The base had been the main source of income in these parts. Without it, the region quickly became the dried husk now on display."

"B-but…this…that just c-can't be," Jeremy countered with a frown, "Sukie…was….just there. I saw…I watched…"

"You witnessed your loving spouse play the dual role of exotic dancer slash undercover spy?"

"H-how did…you…what do you know about it…th-that?"

Reaching over the bar, Bennett lightly tapped the topside of the other man's left hand.

"Let's just say I'm very familiar with the entire scenario, Jeremy, other than whatever… recent developments have transpired."

"What's that…supposed to…mea-…?"

"Trust me, Jeremy. This will all make sense in time.

These…memories of yours, however reality-based they may seem, are nothing more than a hodgepodge of fragmented facsimiles of actual events. Once we conclude this…session, I promise the many discrepancies that surface will bear that out. Bear with me, son.

Believe it or not, you and I have been down this stretch of road many, *many* times over."

"Please…feel free to…enlighten me," Jeremy replied between hacking coughs, the last of which practically doubled him over with his forehead resting atop the bar.

"At the moment, I'm…I seem to be struggling with the whole…notion that we're really even… standing here."

"Completely understandable. First off, I'll offer you the condensed version. After which, we'll cover whatever specific details you desire. At the same time, you can update me on any….new developments of interest."

Raising his head, a fresh coating of whitish dust adorning each bushy eyebrow, Jeremy turned to give the interior of the desolate structure a final, forlorn glance before nodding in acknowledge.

"By all means…fire away. Gotta confess though, I…won't be the least bit shocked if you and your…talkative pals over there simply vanish halfway through the spiel."

Temporarily discarding the folders, Bennett flung his head back and laughed.

288

"I realize this must seem *ultra*-surreal, Jeremy, but in the next few minutes you'll see that all the elaborate fantasies and their accompanying dreamscapes have…in effect… taken a powder. It'll be… kind of like watching a picture puzzle disappear one piece at a time.

There are already signs of normalcy cropping up. Even now, your natural way of speaking has returned."

"If you…say so, chief," Jeremy said sourly, stretching out his arms while fighting off a yawn, "Enough of the prelims already. You'd best pick up the pace or I'm liable to nod off between syllables."

"Oh, I doubt you'd find this the least bit boring, Jeremy. Now, kindly follow along as I begin. The key word here is concentration."

Jeremy's right arm arose weakly as he gestured with a thumb and forefinger.

"Ready when you are, Doctor B."

"See?" Bennett beamed, "that's how you came to address me in years past. Already the puzzle's first piece free-falls from the board. I'd suggest the next item on the agenda be that we take a little stroll…."

\*\*\*

**Part Four:**
*The Phantom Village*

"Not exactly how you remember it, I'd wager," Bennett remarked, walking several steps ahead of the pack as the four men slowly made their way towards the center of the Ville.

"This is…G.I. Central? Shit, it…it *can't* be. No…freaking…way…" Jeremy mumbled, twisting about briefly while looking past the two men flanking him towards a crookedly hanging, cob-web infested sign proclaiming the '*Head East*'.

There was a stilted silence as they rounded a sharp curve between the former '*Rising Tide*' club and a deserted store front that had once been used for money exchange.

"Base closures mean no more troops. No more troops equal a rapidly vanishing cash flow. Simple economics, Jeremy. Cruel but true. As I understand, it came down to a choice between Kunsan Air Base and Sunyon, and the '*Kun*' survived by a whisker, or a more substantial bribe, if you prefer."

"It's…it's a goddamned ghost-town," Jeremy mumbled in shell- shocked disbelief, "I feel like this…all must've happened overnight.

Like the whole damn place was…alive one minute and dead and buried the next…"

"Actually, it took all of two years to create the nuclear holocaust *aftermath* look it now carries. From what I gather, the place dried up gradually, the clubs being the initial casualties. They petered out one at a time by pecking order of previous popularity. I believe the *Yellow Fever* was considered middle of the pack, thus it held on for three or four months after the base closure before finally caving in. Most of the club and store owners fled to Seoul, Inchon or Pusan to start over."

Over the next few minutes, they sauntered past a half dozen former Ville 'hot spots', including the

'*Western Edge*', '*Blue Moon Junction*', and the '*Pacific Coast*', all of which held the same desolate, haunted look, as if they'd been abandoned for decades instead of merely a few short years.

"Looks like the old stomping grounds are more like…burial grounds these days," Jeremy quipped, though his downtrodden tone was utterly devoid of all humor.

"Sufficiently convinced, Jeremy?" Bennett asked, placing a hand on the larger man's shoulder.

"Yeah, that is unless this is just another brain-twisting mind *fuck* and I'll be waking up in my barracks room any second now."

Bennett gently massaged the man's shoulder before removing his hand and side-stepping away.

"I think you know better than that, Jeremy. If not, you soon will.

This isn't some Hollywood back lot that we secretly altered in order to mentally torture you into submission.

Now, let's head on back to the Fever and close this out.

Afterwards, we'll get a hot bowl of soup and some herbal tea into you. You're…looking a bit piqued."

By the time they'd circled back around to the Yellow Fever's previously boarded-over front entrance, Doctor Bennett had witnessed a subtle but dramatic change in Jeremy's overall demeanor, as blatant disbelief slowly transformed into a begrudging acceptance. Reality, however cruel it may be, was gradually beginning to clear away the fog.

***

**Part Five**:
*The Cruelest of Deceptions*

*I am indeed a doctor of psychiatry, Doctor Clay
Gilmore Bennett.*

*You, Staff Sergeant Jeremy Whitt, have been a
patient of mine since November of nineteen eighty-
five, roughly one month following the arrest and
conviction of your wife, Sukie Whitt, on four
separate charges of murder in the first degree.*

"Four char-...why can't...can't I remember any
of this?"

*You will, Jeremy. It's simply a matter of delving
further into the tragic, rather grisly details. Let it be
stated from the outset that the following information
is taken from your personnel file. Be advised, I
covered similar ground less than a half hour ago,
while you were....suffering an...identity crisis,
though I'm not quite sure how much you truly
absorbed, subconsciously that is. Once again, please
bear with me.*

*A quick synopsis; Sukie and yourself were
married in March of nineteen eighty-two during
your initial tour of duty at Sunyon. Sukie had been a
dancer at both the 'Paradise Cove' and "Yellow
Fever' clubs, where you had originally met. After a
brief courtship, you paid off her bar fine at the
'Fever' and set up housekeeping within the Ville.*

*The marriage and Sukie's required Visa were a*

292

*done deal less than three weeks before your required departure back to the states.*

*Following a brief two year assignment at Eakker Air Base outside Fort Worth, Texas, the two of you returned to Sunyon for still another remote tour. You had originally planned on extending an extra year this time around, but alas, this simply wasn't to be. You began cheating on Sukie almost immediately upon your return to Korea, frequenting the Ville on a three to four night a week basis while using the ' drinking with the boy's' excuse to deflect your spouses' concerns. Evidently Sukie had grown increasingly suspicious and had begun trailing you from the clubs, hence discovering the numerous marital improprieties.*

"I...why is it I can't remember any of these...supposed...other women? I mean, I've got...nothing. Not even a fucking blur, man..."

*Patience, son. Perhaps specific names will trigger a response. Mia Park. Se Ri 'Susie' Pak. ¯Lei 'Leah' Chang. Eun-Ju Bae. All employed as exotic dancers at the following clubs, Park and Sei Ri at the Yellow Fever'; Lei Chang at the 'Paradise Cove', and Eun-Ju at the 'Ecstasy.' Not coincidentally, all four were victims of the 'Ville Ripper'.*

"You mean to say I...I was banging two...two girls from the same club? The *same* club where I'd met my ex? Damn, I was either one hell of a playboy or the dumbest bastard ever to step foot on the peninsula."

*Obviously, Jeremy, it was a combination of blatant recklessness and total disregard for the state of your marriage that set this tragic chain of events into motion. To proceed with the unraveling, the first murder had occurred less than four months after your arrival back at Sunyon. By your seventh month back on station, the body count had grown to four. The last of the victims, Miss Eun-Ju Bae, was murdered on a brisk October night, her mutilated remains left on a weed-infested hill overlooking two colossal rice fields. She had supposedly been...eviscerated.*

*On that same faithful night, you stumbled home at just past one AM to find Sukie inside, her naked body drenched in blood, though without any visible wounds of her own. Apparently, when you questioned her about the origin of the mystery bodily fluids, she proceeded to attack you with the same marble-handled bone-knife she'd used to end the lives of all four girls.*

"Oh....oh God...she...good God, her *eyes*. I can....picture them the way they were that night. They shone a darker red than even the blood stains dripping...from her body. Demon's eyes. Over the years Sukie had...shown the occasional tendency for erratic, even violent behavior, but....never like...this...like that night. May sound cliché as hell, but...I...she was like a ...a total stranger. Somebody I'd...never really known at...all."

*I believe the exact word you used in the incident report to describe your lovely wife that night was 'possessed'.*

*To continue, from what I gather from the aforementioned reports, if not for the timely intervention of a trio of Security Policemen, who had heard the ruckus emanating from the hooch while on routine patrol, you might well have served as the 'Ville Ripper's' fifth and final victim.*

"I...I tried to reason...to talk to her, but she c-came at me so fast, and with so much...goddamn determination. Of course, I doubt being drunk off my ass after a Soju binge helped my cause. Then again, my reflexes always have been for shit. She must've cut me a good dozen times before those SP's busted in, but I can't recall feeling much pain. I guess the booze acted as a pretty stout anesthesia, though I do remember a hell of a stinging sensation, like I'd backed into a live hornet's nest."

*Though the medical report listed the majority of your injuries as superficial, there were two deeper slashes that could've proved fatal if left unattended, one to the upper left thigh and another just beneath your left breast. The former required eighteen stitches and the ladder some thirty-one. In addition, you had sustained a concussion and slight separation of your right shoulder.*

*In Sukie's case, she had steadfastly refused to drop the bone-knife despite repeat requests and was ultimately fired upon with rubber bullets and subsequently cuffed and taken to the base hospital before being placed in temporary custody at the base SP station. Meanwhile, you spent two full days in a downtown hospital receiving treatment for your wounds before being transferred to the base medical facility. .*

"They must've kept me doped up to the gills. I can't drudge up a single memory of being treated *off*-base."

295

*Within a full day of incarceration, Sukie Whitt signed a full confession in connection with the four 'Ville Ripper' killings, providing investigators particular details in each case that had yet to be made public, thus vilifying her guilt.*

*Due to both my many years served as a resident psychologist at Osan Air Base, not to mention the close proximity to Sunyon, I was... brought in to interview Sukie several days after her arrest in order to determine if she indeed possessed the mental capability required to be tried in a court of law.*

*It was...at the conclusion of our initial session, during which time Sukie had seemed relatively calm and certainly not the least bit aggressive, either verbally or otherwise, that I learned a hard, excruciatingly painful lesson about letting one's guard down. Having earlier dismissed the assigned SP from the interview room in order to cut down on any potential aftereffects fueled by anxiety, I had... momentarily turned my back on Sukie while studying my own hand- written notes. I can only recall having my arms pinned to my back and being spiked into the tile floor head first. I thank the Lord each and every day that I have no recollection whatsoever of having a ballpoint pen jammed into my left eye. I awoke in the ER some twenty-hours later and was immediately besieged by a double-dose of rather horrid news, the least of which being that Sukie had escaped custody and was subsequently placed at the top of the peninsula's 'ten most wanted' list. No, I'm afraid not even such an admittedly shocking revelation could quite hold a candle to losing half of one's eyesight.*

"Damn, you mean...she...Sukie was respon-...she did *that* to you?"

*Yes, it would be another five months before I began my sessions with you. By then, I had grown quite accustomed to the patch.*

"You...never told me."

*Purposely, no. I figured it would be detrimental to your treatment. I didn't want to...add to the trauma you'd already suffered.*

"Jesus, how could she...I mean, change that much...to do such things?"

*I'm afraid we may never find such an answer, Jeremy.*

"Hey, you're the goddamned brain-pan expert. You get all those fucking diplomas digging around in cereal boxes?"

*Calm down, Jeremy. Remember, I never got the chance to evaluate Sukie. No doubt she would've made a fascinating subject indeed.*

"More than even my severely cracked ass?"

*Neither a rational nor quite fair question, that. It is good, however, to see you...more at tentative, more... alert. To continue as concisely as possible, you remained in a dazed, coma-like state for several days following the assault, and placed under psychiatric care. I took over as your primary caregiver and counselor approximately four and a half months later. You were quite delusional at times, even to the point of assuming your wife's identity, though these periods were episodic at best. In stark contrast, you'd have two to three day stretches of complete normalcy. Fact was, on several occasions I came tediously close to recommending your release. It was around the sixth month of therapy when, to use the vernacular, things went south in a hurry.*

*Though your physical wounds were completely healed, the bouts of multiple personality disorder increased at an alarming rate. Under hypnosis, a technique that wasn't always successful in your case, I discovered what I believed to be the catalyst of the transformations. Simple really....as it is the root cause for a large majority of mental disorders, that being guilt.*

"Guilt? Guilty for what? It wasn't me tooling about the Ville with a bloody bone-knife? What the hell kind of guilt could breed this wacky shit?"

*The guilt, Jeremy, that it was more than likely your philandering, uncaring ways that changed the woman you loved from a relatively innocent, gentle-natured person into a ruthless, merciless killing machine, all in the span of a few short months.*

(SHORT PAUSE)

*Before you blow a gasket, those were your exact words to me during one of our taped counseling sessions.*

(LONGER PAUSE)

"Y-yeah. Painful as it is to…think about, those words do right true.

G-go on…"

*In the midst of this devastating breakdown, I suggested we bring you back to the states for continued treatment. Following approval from both the base and wing level, we did just that, transferring you to a facility in San Diego that I myself helped found in nineteen seventy- nine.*

298

*Alas, in the two-plus years that followed, your condition only grew more unpredictable, though individual episodes were a bit less frequent.*

"What…kind of episodes? You mean…situations like this? Waking up in the middle of a… some kind of brain-twisting hallucination…not knowing who the fuck you are until someone shoves a mirror in your face and provides a formal intro to one's self?

*Precisely the type, unfortunately. During your time on the West Coast, we tried dozens of medications and invested countless man- hours on twice as many therapy options. I personally called in every trump card I owned to fellow collogues, at times even passing you off as some sort of freakish 'challenge' in hopes of at least controlling the episodes somewhat. I…truly thought a return to your….to your wife's homeland might serve as a positive in your treatment regiment, though in hindsight I realize I was simply grasping at straws since all other avenues had been well exhausted.*

"You mean, I had…I'd been stateside for…two years before…before this?"

*Twenty-five and a half months, to be exact…yes.*

"Then…how…how long have we been…back here?"

*Six and a half days…the last four and a half of which you've been quite the role-playing fugitive on the run, Jeremy my boy.*

"You mean…but w-where did I go? W-what did I do? Better yet, where the hell did I sleep?"

*Give you a hint: we're standing in the living room as we speak.*

299

"Here? I stayed in…here?"

*There's a certain security in treading familiar grounds. Besides, you hardly had the financial means to seek out the nearest four-star hotel.*

(SHORT PAUSE)

"The back..r-room…right? Behind the stage…"

*Told you the memories would slowly start filtering back in. Yes, upon our initial investigation early yesterday morning, we found a few empty food wrappers and coke cans in what used to serve as the dressing room, not to mention a discarded jumpsuit that the institute had provided. We'd been staking the place out ever since, just hoping and waiting for you to resurface. Obviously you raided someone's clothesline along the way, though I have to say those jeans appear a size or two on the small side.*

"I can… I think I can remember jumping from the back of the van. I recall a traffic jam…side-stepping a half-dozen cabs and buses, almost getting sideswiped more than once…"

*Downtown Seoul no less, in the middle of rush hour. We were hardly expecting such a flare up. Short-sided and careless on our part, certainly, but you'd been so… calm on the flight over, so serene, almost as if it were you revisiting the place of your own birth. Little did I know that was exactly the case, as you were viewing the entire pilgrimage through Sukie's eyes. Rodney leapt from the back of the van in pursuit and only managed to severely twist his ankle. We took less than five minutes to completely lose you in that traffic snarl, though I had little doubt of your final destination. There could be no other place than Sunyon; the Sunyon of*

300

*your and Sukie's time; a place that, three short years later, no longer exists.*

"So I've been….looking for her, right?"

*Jeremy, you've been searching her out practically since the day I met you, be it physically or metaphysically via some cosmic wavelength that will allow you to somehow make atonement.*

"Yeah… yes." (SHORT PAUSE)

"But, it's all seemed so damned realistic. Not like I was some eves- dropping peeping Tom, but like I…*she* was really there…living it.

Experiencing it, living it, *breathing* it on a daily basis."

*It always does, son. Thus far, we've found no effective way to free you or even alter the MO of these mind-treks you're so susceptible to. Believe me, it hasn't been from a lack of effort.*

"I swear, it's… not…it's nothing like dreams. The images don't appear hazy…time itself isn't fragmented like some Beta tape stuck in fast-forward…"

*Yes.*

"The shit seems real. I was…(trails off)..I was…*her* this time, damn it."

*Mind if I give it a go, Jeremy?*

"Give what a go?"

*This isn't meant to be cruel, you understand. I just want to prove to you how unreal it's all been.*

"What the fuck are you talking about, man? Don't think I'm up to any more mental hocus pocus…"

*Let me explain. The thing is, whenever you endure such a powerful episode, one so remarkably*

301

*realistic it has you doubting your present existence, it invariably forces me into the role of naysayer.*

*Jeremy, allow me to outline your latest journey.*

"Say what? *Outline?* So now you're gonna tell me everything I...Sukie and I just experienced? Well, good luck with that, doc. Hope the old crystal ball's had a recent tune-up."

*By all means, feel free to stop me if even the slightest detail rings untrue.*

***

**Part Six:**
*Scripted Madness*

*To begin, your....Sukie's story starts out in...I'll surmise, the Midwestern U.S.*
(SHORT PAUSE)

"I...it was Texas...but it wasn't Sukie...I....it was Lei."

*Jeremy, the character of Lei was merely a stand-in for your ex-wife.*

*Lei "Leah" Chang was Sukie's third victim. A former dancer at the 'Paradise Cove', and a young girl you once confessed to have truly loved, not merely lusted over. You even admitted to giving serious consideration to divorcing Sukie just to marry Miss Chang.*

"Leah was... a real fireplug all right. It wasn't just... the sex with her.

She had a toughness, a grit about her. It just...her personality was so...different from the other girls. So damned dependant at times and so

302

damned…helpless at others. She…in her spare time, she took Tae Kwon do. Had already gotten her blue…no, high red belt. Told me she wasn't gonna stop 'til she earned the black."

*No doubt precisely why you chose her as the avenging angel; the vigilante killer with the special endowment of 'reading the evil' in men's eyes. Certainly Sukie had never shown such an athletic nor physically aggressive side.*

"Leah was…the only one I…I felt…cried for. The others…they were just…lonely and willing. Nice girls, but Leah was the real deal right down the line."

*As for the vigilante's origin, Sukie had once told you that as a little girl she'd prayed for such a special power; to be able to identify and help the authorities track down and catch evil doers as some type of mysterious super-heroine who could stare into a predator's eyes and 'visualize' their past misgivings. You mentioned that such wishful fantasies stemmed from the sexual abuse she'd suffered as a pre-teen.*

"I always felt so sorry for her for the shitty childhood she'd had.

Even when things…started to go sour between us, I'd try to maintain a cover of contentment just for that reason."

*So following several years as this road-weary avenger, Lei is eventually captured by what appears to be a faction of law enforcement and then secretly transported back to her home country. There she is introduced to a brutish 'soldier for hire' who informs her of an internationally approved, Top*

303

*Secret mission for which she's been recruited to play a major role.*

"Charles...Charles Rutherford. Big, tough-talking ex-NCO with a... a patch over...one eye."

*A man who strikes an astonishing resemblance to yours truly, I'd wager, less a few layers of body muscle. Body muscle that, in reality, belonged to one Staff Sergeant Jeremy Whitt, a life-long weight lifter and all-around fitness freak, yes?*

"*Your* face, *my*...my physique?"

*It would appear so, at least with the eye-patch element. In many ways, I' m flattered, though in others, quite flabbergasted as to exactly why I garnered such blatant...miscasting. You and I have shared many a nervous giggle over this in the past, Jeremy my boy.*

"Y-yeah, I'll...bet."

*After a brief but intense in-brief slash training session, Lei is assigned as an undercover dancer at the 'Yellow Fever', where she is to utilize her 'scanning' prowess in hopes of detecting the Ville Ripper amongst all the drunken G.I's and horny locals frequenting the club, while Rutherford serves as her one and only contact.*

"I'm...I' m getting the picture, doct-.."

*During this five to six week misadventure, Lei' s magic 'beacon' goes inexplicably haywire, as she is unable to detect even the most minute 'blip' on the radar. The murders continue unabated.*

*Meanwhile, amidst a tidal wave of muddle emotions concerning such an abrupt return to her homeland, she finds herself falling for the outwardly gruff but 'gentle giant' that is Chunk 'one-eye'*

304

*Rutherford.*

"I've got it, Bennett. I…I see it all now. You can sto-.."

*Once Rutherford rejects her advances in lieu of ruining his happy marriage to a Korean with whom he professes an undying devotion, Lei turns to a locally assigned Sergeant named Jeremy Yeager, who'd been wooing her with 'Kool-Aid' specials and sweet talk at the club for weeks. Meanwhile, the butchered bodies continue to pile up with nary a viable suspect in sight.…*

"Goddamn, I get it.…no need to keep flapping your gu-…"

*With the mission a horrid failure and her future more than likely to be determined by jury trail, Lei realizes the relationship with Yeager is doomed from the beginning, but seduces him for a single night of carnal pleasure, nonetheless.*

"Enough, shithead! I don't nee-.."

*The following day, the last official day of the mission before she is to be cuffed and flown back to the U.S for extradition, Lei is set to greet her mentor and friend, Charles Rutherford in a neighboring city in order to meet his adoring family and essentially say their last, tearful goodbyes. Instead…just when things seem to be screeching to a less than thrill-packed conclusion, the plot thickens substantially…*

"Charles…doesn't show. I…Lei waits for hours, ignoring the puzzling looks and troublesome glances she receives from complete strangers along the way."

*You spent a day in Dwan-Jae, Jeremy. We…interviewed witnesses, including a rather*

305

*nervous waiter at a street side restaurant who confessed to being 'scared shitless' in your presence, which he described as 'creepy'. We figured you had just enough Won to drink a half dozen cups of tea before departing. Otherwise, you've only been sporadically seen roaming about Sunyon the last several days, strolling about the Ville with what was described as a 'dreamy' or 'hazy' expression. Needless to say, with your undersized clothes, bland expression, and building body odor, it wasn't difficult for witnesses to remember you.*

"All right, damn it! I'm…I'm…not in denial anymore, alright? I…can't remember many details, just foggy images, like I was….I don't know, heavily medicated, but I…I know…I accept what you say as….gospel.

What I can't grasp is…why? Why would I… my subconscious, subject me to this *Pink Floyd acid trip* bullshit? You're the specialist, man….talk to me…"

*Jeremy, I'm been treating similar symptoms in you for the past two- plus years. If I possessed either an answer or the solution to, would we really be standing here in this dilapidated old dump discussing it in the first place?*

"Not even a….theory, man? Seems I recall you having…some type of theory you were always keen on….or was that just *another* one of my walking stage plays?"

*I always theorized the possibility that it was merely the guilt complex you'd developed, and that has obviously worsened over time in lieu of healing.*

306

*In one of our earliest sessions, you once told me that Sukie had counted you as the lone positive in a lifetime of struggle and strife, especially when you had taken her to the states for the first time and she was so dependent on your total support in a land so foreign. To... essentially dessert her the way you did upon returning to her homeland had more than crushed her spirit, but permanently spun her very soul into a dark abyss, transforming her into the vile being that...she became Admittedly, within the human condition, there is no more destructively powerful force than guilt. Yet, I have to this day never witnessed a man more dramatically transformed by its negative vibe, driven into hallucinatory-filled realms that aren't dream- driven but carried on in broad daylight as the subject walks and talks and carries on a semi-regular existence.*

"But, it...it doesn't explain all those people....all the individuals I've run across..."

*The usual cast of characters, you mean?*

"Yeah, I know some of those folks were real. I've met them, lived among them for real periods in time, not just minute long blips where the interaction meant nothing. Why can't...I remember them?"

*You will, Jeremy. Again, have patience. Look how far you've come already as we've progressed.*

"Damn it, I'm still not sure what's real and what isn't. If all you say is true, I must be one seriously bent son of a bitch, *Doctor*. Shit, who's kidding who? I *know* I am. But still, some of the images I'm carrying around. I know these people!"

*Yes, you do. No argument there. It's just that, you probably knew of them quite differently than*

307

*what you presently perceive. Here, let me spit out a few names and we'll compare notes, fiction and non-fiction wise, so to speak. I have a folder containing a large listing of your former contacts.*

(SHORT PAUSE)

*Yes, here we are. All right, Jeremy. This should help to clear away a majority of those convoluted thoughts.*

*How about...Kim Sanders?*

"K-Kim...sounds familiar....she... Kim Sanders was an Asian-American officer stationed at Sunyon. A Captain...no! (*SNAPS FINGERS*) A Lieutenant...2^nd Lieutenant who was...k-killed by the Ville Ripper while working...undercover as a dancer"

*Hmmm, fascinating. Actually, Miss Sanders was the wife of a co- worker of yours, a... Technical Sergeant Milt Jacobs. You two served together in your second tour at Sunyon. Last report states they two are still happily married and presently stationed in Arizona.*

"Milt Jac-...she was married to Milt...? (SHORT PAUSE) Y-yes, that's right. Pretty girl with a small frame but big tit...um, breasts for a Korean girl. A real looker, but always seemed kind of shy, demure even. Milt... always figured his family would give him hell for...marrying outside the race. Good....good for him. A good Joe, Ol' Milt. "

*Next I have a....Chow Yun Jung.*

"Chow...Yun... Jung. Oh yeah, that perverted, penny-pinching shit that owned the Yellow Fever, or...used to own, I guess..."

*Or perhaps the Chow Yun Jung who was Sukie's uncle; the one whom she claimed molested her as a child. Sound a bit more feasible?*

"Sukie's….uncle. Yeah, that was the miserable pedophile's name all right. I used to…threaten to look the bastard up and kick his ass, but Sukie would always scold the hell out of me for even bringing it up.

After a while, even the mention of his name was taboo in our household. Can't say I blame her. If I were…the violent type, I'm sure I'd have paid the old bastard a visit by now. Hell, maybe I have and…just can't remember, you think? Might be a stashed body out there with *my* name on it, after all."

*Doubtful, Jeremy. You simply aren't the type. This last one ought to seal the deal, so to speak. Jeremy Yeager.*

"Well, the first name's obvious. But…Yeager? Yeager….(short pause).

The origin escapes me. So who was this Yeager bird anyhow? A long lost lodge brother?"

*You're not that far off, actually. Clint Yeager's been your roommate at the institute for the past year and a half. You two play off one another like a classic comedy team. You've always been the perfect straight man to Yeager's class clown. We've… given serious consideration to the belief that this latest breakdown is partially related to Clint's recent depar-…*

"I know, I…now I *know*. He got his walking papers about a month back. Declared fit as a fiddle and ready to retake his place in proper society, all the cobwebs thoroughly swept from the attic. Hey, I missed the guy...sure. We cracked each other up....liked each other's company, but shit, it ain't like we were swapping spit or anything. No way the Clint-sters taking a hike had anything to do with this meltdown, man. That's a fucking copout from the word go. Better dig a little deeper, doc. Find a shovel with a stouter blade, so...to...speak.

*Now, Jeremy, there's no reason to get mean-spirited. I didn't intend to offend. It's just that....I knew...could see the change in you with Clint's absence. To blame this episode solely on this one traumatic event would surely be short-sided on my part. I realize there are several elements at work here, most of which we might well never fully know. That's why...we're...I'm here. That's why we traveled over nine thousand miles on nothing more than theory. I want to see you obtain a semblance of peace, Jeremy. I want you to begin to heal. I want you to....forgive yourself. Do you understand?*

"Yeah. Yeah, doc, I understand. Sorry for...copping the attitude. I just...I'm just now seeing the big picture, and it...it ain't an easy one to swallow. I sometimes feel...Sukie is still trailing me...haunting me, still...still seeking her revenge. Try as I may, I just can't work up any anger or fear at the thought, doc. Whatever it is she might dish out....I deserve it. Like I said, not an easy pill to swallow. It...never was, you know?"

*Yes, Jeremy, I sure it isn't. Your frustration is fully understood.*

(SHORT PAUSE)

*So... do you now fully accept that what you have perceived as reality these past few days has been nothing more than an elaborate fantasy and not the least bit fact-based?*

"Yeah. I...see it all now for...what it was. Got to admit though, the shit's getting more and more lifelike every time."

*Honestly, I can...only imagine, Jeremy. My promise to you remains unchanged. I will do my very best to see that such episodes will soon be a thing of the past.*

"Believe me, Doctor B, you've got no bigger fan in that particular quest that yours truly."

The two men clasped hands over the bar and exchanged warm, endearing smiles; one born from trust, the other from blind faith.

They then turned to depart the ruins of the former 'Yellow Fever' club, the doctor gently draping an arm over the badly slumped shoulders of his patient, a man he privately deemed the most troubled he'd ever encountered in over eighteen years. The doctor's cohorts stepped aside as to allow passage to the exit just as Jeremy halted in mid-step, the doctor's forward momentum taking him a single stride farther.

"Bingo,' Jeremy croaked in a fearful whisper, his eyes growing wide with either fear or an overwhelming sense of awe.

"What? What is it, Jeremy?" Bennett asked wearily while removing his arm from the larger man's shoulder, 'you're not...zoning out on me again, are you?"

For the initial time in their long history together, the doctor witnessed his prize patient sob; an agony-filled wail accompanied by thick streams of tears

311

that streamed down the young man's pale, unshaven face in a raging torrent.

"This is…bad, doc," he cried, slowly turning about as to rescan the bar, "oh, this is so…*fucking bad*."

\*\*\*

**Part Seven**:
*Fatal Cameo*

"What *are* you…referring to, Jeremy?" Bennett inquired, unable to completely mask the patronizing lilt in his words, "please describe to me whatever it is you're seeing the best you can."

Jeremy's glassy-eyed stare remained focused on the bar's dimly lit interior.

"Well, doc, you see….I…think this here development might fall under the heading of…there's some good news…and some bad news…really…*really* bad news."

"Please clarify, Jeremy. I don't under-…."

"I thought there was an underlying vibe hovering about…..just couldn't place my finger on it in all…the confusion," Jeremy interrupted, gesturing towards the darkened stage with a weak nod, "right under my damn nose the whole time. Actually, under *all* our noses. Then again, I wouldn't expect any of you to be able to sniff it out."

Doctor Bennett and his two cohorts turned as one, following Jeremy's trance-like gaze, the mystery figure floated from the shadows in segmented increments, pulling back the ragged

312

curtain that separated the backstage area from the open spotlight and levitating forward like a dark, billowy cloud.

"Hell of a tracker, oh my yes…one *hell* of a tracker," Jeremy beamed, stepping cautiously forward on legs that seemed on the verge of imminent collapse, "only a matter of time once I got here….simply a…matter of time."

Strolling forward, Doctor Bennett groped with both hands to obtain a firm grip on the larger man's upper shoulders, but was easily shrugged off.

"Jeremy, don't….tell me wh-"

Dashing forward in a clumsy lurch, Jeremy shoved aside two tables and a set of chairs while making a b-line towards the stage area.

"Damn, despite everything, you've gotta admit….what a gorgeous sight!"

Balancing their gleaming, narrow-tipped boots at the stage's edge, the figure hummed in apparent delight at Jeremy's rapid advancement. Dressed exclusively in black from head to toe, the figure blended seamlessly into the surrounding gloom, there initial emergence not unlike watching a section of wall literally come to life.

"Jeremy, don't….come back here!" Bennett screeched, motioning for his two cohorts to retrieve the fleeing man.

The figure reached inside a flowing, ankle-length duster with gloved hands and retrieved what appeared to be a long-barreled revolver.

"Awwww, shiiiiiiiit!" Jeremy yelped, instantly tumbling forward onto his hands and knees while reaching for a nearby table to utilize as temporary cover.

Facing the club's entrance while cowering behind the overturned tabletop,

Jeremy heard a barely audible hissing sound before seeing the first round open a dime-sized hole at in the first man's right cheek, and a second penetrate his left eye, blowing a large, reddish chunk from the back of his skull.

"S-silencer," he mumbled, shaking his head in awestruck wonder with white spittle forming at the corners of his mouth, "efficient as always.".

The second of Doctor Bennett's 'aides', a bald, rotund individual wearing black-framed glasses with impossibly thick lens, kneeled down as to assist his fallen comrade and was immediately pelted forward from a trio of shots, the most fatal of which had impacted directly between his shoulder blades.

"T-two down....t-two to go...," Jeremy cackled hysterically, crawling backwards while pulling the table along with both hands.

"Jeremy, there's no need...," he heard Doctor Bennett plead, turning to see the man standing less than three feet away, posed in a semi- crouch with his arms spread wide as to hug and protect a small, frightened child.

"Doctor B, for Christ's sake, get outta here!" Jeremy shrieked, releasing the table and desperately motioning for the man to either duck down or flee the scene entirely.

"Well, if isn't this one of life's sweeter coincidences?" a seductive, distinctively feminine voice exclaimed from stage level. Jeremy watched Doctor Bennett straighten and place his hands atop

314

his hips.

The man's one working eye squinted and his lips were tightly pursed, like an irritated parent preparing to scold a misbehaving juvenile.

"Drop the weapon, please," the doctor said sternly as his eye darted back and forth from Jeremy to his fallen comrades.

"There's no need for this...animosity."

"Really?" the female voice replied sassily, "damn, I've heard of turn the other cheek, but this is ridiculous, doctor. You're certainly a better person than I. Don't think I could find it in my heart to forgive the individual responsible for stealing one-half of my eyesight."

"Ever peek under that patch, lover?" Jeremy heard her add, the question obviously directed towards him, "ever check out that remaining orb?"

Jeremy started to reply but found his tongue temporarily hung in neutral.

"No matter. You wouldn't be able to see what *I* see. What I...saw in the other eye just before I permanently turned out its pilot light, and what I would've done to the other if given the chance. Tell 'im doctor. Fess up.

Tell your 'prize patient' what you really are. Don't bypass the opportunity, rare that it is, to 'come clean' just moments before officially meeting your maker."

Peaking over the top edge of the table, which trembled and shook from his precariously unsteady grip, Jeremy watched Sukie peel away the soot-colored hood from her face with her free hand, even as the other maintained a remarkably steady aim in

Doc Bennett's general direction.

"Nothing good can come from this, don't you see? Let's…just calm down and talk it out," Bennett repeated, crossing his arms and taking a step back, "let's take a deep breath and calm…down."

"I saw their eyes, you lying, pretentious ass," she growled, "I looked deep into the suffering souls of all those you had sworn to help but instead used for your own sick, demented pleasure. I saw their desperation….felt their fear. How shocking…how repulsive it must have been for them, to discover their chosen 'healer' was nothing more than an ordinary, everyday *rapist*, albeit with a few more diplomas on the wall than the majority of his ilk."

His mouth standing ajar in apparent shock, Jeremy allowed the tabletop to fall away, executing a spastic double-take as he turned back towards Bennett.

"You….you *raped* your…patients?"

"Raped? Did you say…raped?" Bennett asked with a deep frown. "Oh yes, lover, at least a dozen or more over the past decade,"

Sukie spat angrily in response, "hell, who's to say he didn't partake in a little 'mo-les-ta-tion 101' while treating your sick ass? Ever wake up a bit '*sore in the saddle*' and wonder why?"

As Bennett bowed his head in either frustration or shame, Jeremy turned back towards Sukie, who had leapt onto the dance floor and was walking slowly forward with the hand gun's ridiculously lengthy barrel leading the way.

"Two and a half years. Never thought I'd get another crack at you, Doctor *Sick-Fuck*. Though I'm not a religious person by trade, it seems to me a higher power might've had a hand in this particular 'chance meeting', you think?"

"Put…down the weapon…*please*…you don't…know what you're do- doing…" Bennett pleaded, his lone eye having grown wide with fear.

Sukie halted just to Jeremy's left, nervously biting her lower lip as the revolver's sites dipped just slightly.

"They do say…to forget is *holy*…, …to forgive *divine*…"

Jeremy heard Bennett's hearty sigh before turning to see the man slump in apparent relief.

"That's better. That's *much* better. Violence never solves anythi-.." Bennett began, choking on his own words as his hands suddenly arose in a frantic blocking stance in front of his face.

Jeremy immediately twisted his neck about to see Sukie re-aiming the weapon while flashing a hideously sadistic grin.

"Got to confess, my personal favorite will always be '*eye for an eye*' …get it, doc? Of course, in your case I guess that'd be more like 'eye…and *another* eye….'"

"NOOOOOOOOO!!!!" Bennett screamed as the round bore a hole through his left palm before puncturing his eye with a sickeningly moist 'plopping' sound.

Slinking over in a graceful gliding movement, Sukie hovered over the body for several moments, nodding her head from side to side as her thick, shoulder-length hair swarmed and pulsated like ocean waves at first tide.

"No great loss to society here," she announced grimly, whirling about like a predatory beast with eyes lit up like red-hot coals, "man never did anything for you, right lover? No telling the damage the sick bastard inflicted. *Permanent* damage, more than likely."

Despite an unrelenting urge to stand and run to her like the long-lost lover he most certainly was, Jeremy instead found himself backing away, the heels of his boots squeaking loudly as they dug into the tiled floor.

"You...how can you be so...sure about him? I mean...to just...k-kill him and the...others...so damn...casually..."

Sukie tucked the pistol away and pitched forward in an elegant two- step, the duster floating behind her like a wind-blown sail.

"(IN KOREAN) Now, is this any way to act? After all, I just saved you from countless more years of worthless psychobabble. Don't you get it, Jeremy my love? That man was just keeping you around for kicks. You were his pet project, at least until a suitable replacement came along. Fucking amazing how you managed to bamboozle 'em all these years. My compliments, lover...my sincerest compliments."

With his back essentially pinned against the bar, Jeremy crossed his arms across his knees and remained seated. As Sukie fast- approached, he felt his fear magically melt away, replaced by a wave of pity and self-loathing that was sincere as it was cleansing.

"(IN           KOREAN)           Su-Sukie...I'm

318

truly….*truly*….sorry for what I…how things turned out. I… never meant to hurt you….you have to believe that. Whatever happens, I…need to you understand.

I've spent the last several years regretting my actions and…*praying* for forgiveness. It…this may sound…corny and insincere, but I…I never, ever stopped caring for you. Not for a minute."

Sukie continued to dance about, resembling a ballerina from some demonic, Netherworld version of '*Cats*'.

"(IN ENGLISH) Water under the bridge, my love….water under the bridge. Sins of the past should be left there. I've long since forgiven you your trespasses.

In fact, in a strange, 'ain't fate a kick in the teeth' kind of way, I *owe* you."

"(IN ENGLISH) You…owe *me*?" Jeremy asked skeptically, glancing briefly over at the trio of bloodied corpses lying less than a dozen feet away.

"Sounds weird, huh? But…you liberated me, freed me up to discover my true calling in this life. Kind of a roundabout way to do it, true, but the end effect would've been the same, nonetheless."

"You…really believe that?"

Sukie then broke from her dancing jig and knelt down beside his trembling form, placing a gloved hand gently atop his sweat-coated scalp.

"More than believe, lover….I *know*."

"But I….the things I did, and you….you were…"

"Oh, you fucked me over in so many ways, Jeremy Whitt," she whispered through a sad, upside

319

down smile, "no need to soft-soap the issue. To label you merely a traitor to our love…our marriage…is to understate to the extreme. You were a lecherous coward of the highest order, no doubt."

"God, I k-know. I….I considered…..many times over the years I thought about….kill…"

"Killing yourself?"

He bowed his head until his chin rested atop the exposed flesh of his upper chest.

"Never had the…nerve to see it through. Maybe deep down I…didn't want to cheat you out of….this chance, this…opportunity for retribution."

"Foolish Jeremy," she cooed softly, patting his head as a mother would a sulking child, "foolish, foolish Jeremy. My tracking and finding you has nothing to do with something so base as simple revenge."

This time, he openly sobbed, his muscular physique racked with tremors.

"B-but…I deserve it, Suk. I deserve…the cruelest form of vile shit you can….d-dish out, and… and then some. I…deserve…I…crave it. I…need it."

"Maybe so, lover," she scolded, pulling the hair atop his scalp as to raise his head so their eyes could appropriately lock, "but *your* needs aren't the priority here, right? I'm calling the shots, remember?"

Jeremy nodded weakly, reaching up to wipe fresh tears from his horribly bloodshot eyes.

"Damn straight I am. You're taking orders from me now, mister, and I'm here with an offer you simply cannot refuse."

"An…an offer?"

"I need you, Jeremy. Not in the physical sense or merely for companionship. I need a partner in this fight. Who better than the man who pointed the way to begin with, albeit completely by accident via his reckless, *save his own ass by any means necessary* way."

"Part-partner? You and me… partners? You mean…I'll be…doing what you do?"

"*Neh* (Korean for 'yes'), sans any special 'gifts' of course, but I can promise you one hell of a thorough training program before you're subjected to any 'real world' scenarios. Besides, you've obviously displayed a natural instinct for the job, right? Meaning, you've already got *the* major hurdle licked, lover. The rest is just applying practical knowledge and getting your feet wet in the field, and we both know those size twelve's of yours have stepped in their fair share of '*wet- work*' in the past, right?"

"I'd… have to say I've been around the block a few times, yeah. You know all this, Suk," he groaned, "so why rehash known information?"

"Damn fine point, lover.

So, is it even necessary for me to outline the mission in detail?" "No….no, I…I've got it. Deep down, I've always known what really rove me…motivated me," he shrugged, wearing a goofy smile that instantly made him appear a decade younger.

"Hard thing to admit, lover, even for the *stoniest* of hearts." "Never was about love, was it?"

"Anyo (Korean for 'no')." "Or guilt?"

321

"Nope. It's all about the hunt, followed by the orgasmic thrill of the eradication. She's the prototype, lover boy. Face it, the unattainable always makes for the most intriguing quarry."

"I...guess that's right. Thing is, for such a simple objective, it sure makes for one *helluva* complex issue."

"Not really. When push comes to shove, I have all the confidence in the world in you. I mean, look at the progress you've made just in the past several days," she countered, sweeping an arm around in the direction of the fallen trio, "tonight being a prime example. Personally, I think you've gone beyond mere potential right into the big leagues."

"But if...I do find her, will she be as...good...as skilled, as you?"

Sukie smirked, reaching down to hook a hand beneath his armpit as he struggled to stand.

"Not a chance, lover. That hyperactive imagination of yours deemed it necessary to make me some kind of super-human, female terminator. My lookalike/namesake may be damned clever and tough as aged leather, but physical confrontations with a beast like yourself definitely isn't her cup of tea. Consider the night she found you out....if not for town patrol's rude intrusion, we wouldn't even be discussing this particular task, now would we?"

"Still, she did put up quite the scrap. I was bedridden for weeks." "Yeah, but it sure worked wonders in shifting the blame, now didn't it? I mean, the SP's bash their way in to find this naked, stark-raving mad woman waiving around a butcher knife and covered in her husband's blood. Kind of put the focus on Miss Sukie right from the start."

"Hell of a price to pay."

"Hey, beats seventy years of hard labor in Leavenworth, doesn't it?" "The last three in that damned booby-hatch ain't exactly been a free fucking pass, you know. Three years of padded walls and pock- marked butt cheeks from daily 'nerve' injections is far from getting off scot-free, lady!" he barked angrily before quickly turning away as if instantly regretting his tone.

"You're preaching to the choir, lover," she replied with a mild shrug. "S-sorry."

"Accepted. Anyway, congrats on the overall frame-up of the little woman. Damned professional for an amateur, if you'll pardon the word play.

Stashing those knives under that loose board in her closet was a stroke of genius, not to mention the blood-soaked shirt belonging to one of the victims."

"It…wasn't intended…I mean, at first I had no such intention. In the end, all the pieces just…fell into place."

"True. It wasn't as if she didn't have *all* the motive. Once the fuzz found out you'd been…um…servicing the victims, so to speak, the 'enraged spouse' scenario fell into place like the only puzzle piece that really mattered. All that additional evidence just cemented their suspicions. Add to the mix the cold hard political fact that when it comes to the capture and conviction of the infamous *'Ville Ripper'*, it's a whoooole lot easier to pin it on a former exotic dancer *slash* prostitute than Mister All-American G.I. That stalwart *man-of-honor* routine didn't exactly hurt your cause."

323

"Once the evidence pointed her way, there just wasn't any way out…except to confess. In the end, I…just couldn't. Maybe earlier in our relationship, I'd have stepped in and…saved her. I might have…done the right thing. But…not then. We'd grown apart in a big way."

"No shit, Sherlock. Man doesn't just go around screwing everything in sight and then making lampshades out of 'em unless there's a miiiighty big problem at home."

Looking up, the anger returned to his eyes even as his lips parted for a potentially heated rebuttal. Instead, he retained the hangdog look of moments before and fell silent.

"In terms of your…future confrontation with the ex, just remember…" she continued, raising a forefinger into the air, "utilizing the element of surprise is never a bad thing."

Jeremy strolled by her in a noticeably more stable gait, shrugging his shoulders and wind-milling his arms as if warming up for a strenuous workout.

"Well, first things first. Can't leave this mess behind."

He glanced from the bodies back to Sukie, who executed a polite 'curtsy'.

"Its alllll yours, lover boy. You know I'd help if I could."

Stepping over, he titled his head, leaned in and delivered a firm, wet kiss that left her panting in shock from its spontaneous wake.

"Just to let you know, there are…things about you I miss so badly sometimes, Suk," he whispered, his tone husky with lust, "and those memories haunt me without mercy."

"Good to know, Jeremy," she replied, a bit glassy-eyed in the aftermath, "just don't let such... elements weaken your resolve to what must be done. And by the way...I prefer *Lei.*"

Bending down to grip each of the doctor's ankles, Jeremy paused to speak before dragging the body towards the stage.

"Whatever you say...*Lei.* Relax...hang out. I'll be done here in a jif." "No hurry, sweetie. My time is definitely *your* time, after all."

While heaving the limp form onto the stage some thirty seconds later, a large piece of jagged glass sailed clear of the doctor's heavily- seeping neck wound and shattered atop the hard wood finish, garnering a look of utter disgust from the man performing 'disposal' duties. In briefly checking the palms of each hand, Jeremy regarded the half-dozen or more groves cut into his own flesh with casual aplomb, apparently uninterested in the origin of the mysterious wounds.

Soon, a trio of relatively fresh corpses held the top three layers in a six-body monkey pile laid out at the center of the otherwise bare dressing room. The bottom layer consisted of three females, all having expired within the previous forty-eight hours from randomly inflicted slash marks about their scalps, faces, and torsos, though obviously the most fatal had been administered at the base of the throat, where all three flashed eerily similar 'horizontal smiles'.

Pulling the tab from a dust-coated glass fifth of

Barcadi's One-Fifty- One rum, Jeremy generously soaked the reeking pile before gulping down a swallow.

He then used the remainder to pour a narrow trail from the backstage area to the front door, sipping the minute remains from the bottle before shattering it against a far wall with a furious toss.

"Almost there, Su…Lei. You still with me?"

"Whenever you need me to be, lover-boy," came the faint, weirdly muffled reply, as if originating from a faraway distance, 'where ever and whenever you desire the company of the *evil twin*, just pucker up and blow."

Jeremy stood at the entrance with a single match hanging from the left corner of his mouth.

"Well, the, what say we *blow* this Popsicle stand, babe?" he asked, removing the match and striking it against the sole of his right boot.

"By all means, lover. Preliminaries are over. Its game-time," replied the phantom whisper, sounding less like a human voice and more like a charge of electrical current carried past by a gusting wind, "time to seek out and eliminate the last surviving witness. No time for petty sentimentality either, lover-boy. Remember, upon capture, little Miss Sukie didn't hesitate for a second before twisting the blame your way."

"*Game* time," he repeated grimly, though with a sparkling gleam in each bloodshot orb "yep. Time to step up to the plate, I guess, and come full circle."

Pausing to adjust the belt line and collar of his new threads, recently stripped from the largest of the three male victims, Jeremy then buttoned up the accompanying vest as to conceal a dark crimson splatter mark at the center of the light blue cotton shirt.

Grimacing as he fastened the vest's top button near the base of his throat, he was unaware of the reflection cast from a v-shaped strip of broken mirror on an adjoining wall; an eerily distorted reflection that appeared to exhibit two distinctive personas which alternated in two to three second intervals. The first was an attractive Korean female in her mid-to-late twenties with piercing blue eyes, wearing an expression of grim determination. The second was that of Jeremy Whitt, he of the haggard, bone-weary visage, whose own eyes rotated in a psychedelic montage, reflecting the many tragic victims of his inner madness.

"You're out there somewhere, sweet Sukie," he mumbled from between closed teeth while lighting a cigarette he'd discovered in the vest's front left pocket, "all scared and lonely….always looking over your shoulder… frightened of your own shadow. Such a sad, pathetic excuse for a life, really."

Blowing out a perfectly designed smoke ring, Jeremy tossed the still-lit match atop the edge of the spilled liquor and strode casually through the entrance onto the pitch-black street.

"Don't you fret, babe. Yobo's gonna find you eventually, and wipe alllll that pain and misery away.

Well..." he grinned devilishly, picking up his pace as narrow tendrils of smoke began to fill the darkened sky in the background, "all the *misery*, anyway."

# Epilogue
## Re-intros/A Final Wake-up Call

Leaning up and out, he pulled the bill of his cap towards the back of his head as to avoid being spotted while peeking around the base of an ancient oak whose many limbs were predictably bare as late fall mutated into early winter.

From the distance of perhaps seventy yards, he had watched her sip a steaming beverage from the privacy of a wooden-railed front porch, occasionally sitting a large coffee mug aside and hugging herself close in reaction to the early morning chill.

The mailbox leading up to the property had read '**BX 444-M.CHO**' in bolded black lettering. He couldn't help but feel duly impressed.

The woman was nothing if not astonishingly resourceful, not to mention clever as the Western Arizona day was long.

*Then again, so are you, Mister Patrick....so are you. So much in common, still.*

Amazing, he mused, how easily identifiable she was despite the many subtle changes in physical appearance. After a moment, he reconsidered. After all, so vivid were the memories; so deeply engraved the images of the past that he most likely could've picked her out of a bustling crowd with minimal effort.

*My God. She's still so damned beautiful. So damned...alluring. I am indeed the magnet to her steel.*

Monitoring cautiously as to not give himself away prematurely, he watched her sway gently in a front porch rocking chair while nursing the contents of a dark-colored mug, all the while scanning the desolate prairie surrounding her modest homestead. Though a relatively small structure, perhaps no more than twelve to fourteen hundred square feet, the combination brick/siding one-story home appeared recently constructed, meaning she'd probably owned it from the outset.

Crouching back down until his knees balanced atop a thick, above- ground tree root, he saw her rise and re-enter the home. Sighing heavily, he stood to adjust the bulky backpack balanced between his shoulders before trudging slowly forward, the heels of his badly scarred work-boots digging into the loose sand like twin Jackhammers.

Stepping lightly as he neared the front porch steps, he smiled grimly to himself.

*Finally, after all this time....all this insufferable time....D-day.*

*Magical, glorious D-Day.*

He heard a screen door pushed ajar just as his right boot landed atop the lower porch step.

"About time you decided to escape the chill," she said calmly, holding the door open as to casually invite him inside.

Flashing a crooked smile, he nodded silently in acknowledgement and followed her inside, slinging the backpack forward and hugging it to his chest. Once inside, he removed the baseball cap and smoothed the shaggy hair beneath with a quick comb-through with splayed fingers.

Discarding the pack and cap atop the cramped living room's thick shag carpeting, he trailed her into a similarly diminutive but neatly organized kitchen area, where she quietly gestured for him to take one of only two available seats at a circular-shaped table adorned with several bowls of what appeared to be fresh fruit.

"Coffee or tea?" she asked, turning from him to retrieve a matching pair of yellow-shaded coffee mugs from a nearby cabinet.

"Got any bourbon?" he replied with a strained grin while adjusting his hips to fit the chair's severely limited confines.

"Afraid not."

"Soju perhaps? Just for…old time's sake?"

"Nary a drop…sorry. No use for such mind-altering concoctions in these parts. Peace and tranquility are my only vices these days."

"O-kay….make it coffee then."

"Fine. Still take two teaspoons of half and half and three heaping scoops of sugar?"

"Sure do. Amazing memory, that."

"Not really," she countered, turning towards the sink to fill a small silver pot with water before placing it atop a two-burner stove that appeared, much like the house itself, relatively new, "it hasn't been that long, after all."

"Pardon me for taking exception. Thirteen years can seem like fifty, depending on circumstances," he replied, having placed the palm of each hand on the tabletop as the scent of fresh strawberries pierced his overtaxed senses.

Taking the seat across from him, she reached

330

over, cupped a tangerine and began rolling it slowly from palm to palm.

"That's true, I suppose. By thirteen years, you're speaking of the last time…of that *specific* night."

"Yeah, the last time we…spoke. Thirteen years, two months, and sixteen days, to be precise. You know I always was a stickler for details."

"That you were," she laughed, refusing to pull her eyes from the constantly rotating fruit.

A brief silence ensued, only shattered somewhat by the sound of the stove-eye's incessant clicking as heat increased and the water gradually began to boil.

"Pardon my rudeness," he said, reaching over with an open hand, "the names Richard. Richard Lee Patrick. And…you are?"

"Tammy. Tammy Chen," she replied bashfully, temporarily breaking eye contact.

Folding one hand atop another, he flashed a sad, crooked smile. "Ah, Chinese huh? Well, if you recall, we used to talk about how people always thought you were either Filipina or Chinese." After a moment, she re-met his gaze with a casual shrug.

"That's true, we did. Never figured mistaken nationality could ever come in so handy in later life."

"So tell me," he inquired, leaning up while placing his elbows on the table's circular edge, "how long you been answering to Miss Chen?"

"Oh, eight or nine years, I'd say, around the time I left China Town for this desert oasis. What about you, Mister Patrick?"

"Not nearly that long," he replied in a

331

noticeably more subdued tone, "maybe a year tops. It's complicated. Let's just say," he paused, winking playfully, "I've claimed...several identities since our heyday. Honestly, it gets easier and easier to shed one's skin over time. Just a matter of having the right contacts really."

"Very true," she agreed, turning away as the coffee pot's whistle grew gradually louder.

As she rose to tend to the squealing pot, he leaned back with a resounding sigh, placing both hands behind his head.

"Yeah, just a couple of happy-go-lucky fugitives on the run, that's us. Damned if you and I aren't fated to always have something in common, woman."

Busying herself with preparing their respective beverages, her only reply was a brief nod.

"You look good, Sukie. Hardly aged a lick."

"I work out...try to eat right, you know. Don't drink or smoke.

Pretty dull existence, all in all. I see you've added a bit of a spare tire." "Yeah, well," he grinned sheepishly, "it's that damn sea food diet I've been on the past several years."

"Haven't made acquaintance with a barber of late, either..." "Nah. It'll just grow back grayer than it already is."

Each paused to clear their throat at precisely the same moment before exchanging smiles.

"How you supporting yourself way out here, if you don't mind my asking?" he inquired with what at least sounded like a sincere interest.

"The bills get paid, if barely on time," she

answered solemnly, walking over to place their respective cups, "I help file tax forms in the spring and car insurance policies year round. Won't get rich doing either, but at least it lets me work from home."

"Great. Sounds like the perfect career for the reclusive type."

Minutes later, each sipped cautiously from separate cups while falling into a surreal yet vaguely familiar comfort zone.

"So….why are you here, Jeremy?"

"Damn, woman," he answered, peering wide-eyed over the cups steaming rim, "you never were one to beat around the bush."

Tilting her head a bit to the left, she took an additional sip before placing the cup aside.

"Life's too short. Besides, you and I should be waaaay beyond the amenities by now."

"Can't disagree with that," he said with a good natured sneer. "So talk to me. Is this surprise visit all about memory lane or something a bit more…sinister?"

Finishing off his cup with a strained grimace, he pushed away from the table and folded his arms across his chest, resting them atop his ample belly.

"Thirteen long, tiresome years, Suk, including the two I spent in treatment. Tracking you for these past eleven has been quite the universal quest. Think I logged somewhere in the vicinity of twenty, twenty-five thousand miles in-between, not counting the year-plus I spent scouring the peninsula before hopping a bird back to the states."

"You never settled down in-between?" she

333

inquired, rising to pour herself a fresh refill.

"Oh, I lived here and there, getting by on my wits mainly while trying like hell to maintain the lowest profile possible."

"Was it that important to find me, Jeremy? I mean, for what purpose other than to reopen old gashes?"

"I gotta tell you, Suk, over the years my motives have changed more times than we've switched ID's. Ain't gonna bother lying. When the search began all those years ago, it was all about revenge for…killing Lei and…leaving me a raving lunatic for several years after the fact."

"So it… *was* you that left the doctor and his aides inside the burnt remains of the… Yellow Fever," she interrupted, rejoining him at the table, "I…I read about it in a Korean newspaper they print in San Francisco. I know they described a suspect that sounded a lot like you, at least physically."

"Yeah, that was me. I was…pretty damn ill at the time. A 'basket case without handles' as my dear old grandma used to put it. Spent the better part of the next year trying to decipher what was real and what wasn't. Not an easy task without professional help or the proper meds," he replied, running a hand through the lengthy, grayish locks hanging between his shoulder blades.

"Sad thing was, ol' Doc Bennett was just trying to help."

There was a short, awkward pause as Sukie pushed her cup aside with a heavy sigh.

"I'm…I'm sorry, Jeremy, if my…my actions drove you to-…"

334

"Let's not start handing out blame, Suk," he said, waving her off, "we'd have to keep taking turns. Might take all blessed day at that."

Sukie started to speak before merely nodding in apparent agreement while staring down at her own intertwined fingers.

"You...you said retribution motivated you, at least initially. What about... recently?"

"The dreams, Suk," he said wearily, rubbing his face with an outstretched palm, "the nightmares just...wouldn't let up...won't....let go. They wouldn't...won't allow for a normal life. Not that I sleep very well mind you, maybe three or four hours a night if I'm lucky. Gotta say, if I had my druthers I'd keep these baby blues pulled wide twenty-four seven just to avoid waking up in a cold sweat each and every AM."

"I had to figure that...finding you and maybe....settling things between us once and for all might....sever the pattern, you know? I had to at least *try*. No choice, really. It was either that or plant a bullet in my own skull, and I'm waaay too chicken-shit for such drastic, not to mention fatal, measures."

"Dreams....nightmares...." Sukie mumbled between sips before standing and facing the room's lone window and staring between pulled blinds into the vast openness on display, "...sounds painfully familiar."

"You too?" Jeremy inquired excitedly, his dumbstruck expression comically exaggerated.

"Oh yes. Maybe not every night, but most."

"Nightmares? About...those days?"

"Very….creative ones, at that. Real 'period pieces', you might say. Most times, the line between reality and dreamscape blurs to the point of trying to figure out which is which upon waking up."

"Wow," he conceded with a weak smile that reeked of emotional fatigue, "…guess there's some kind of…psychic connection there.

Folks used to say we were connected at the hip…maybe it's more like…connected in the subconscious."

"Lots of baggage stored there, Jeremy." "Isn't there though…"

"Uh…any more coffee?" he asked bashfully, shoving his empty cup across the table towards her.

"Oh yeah," she said, rising after gripping the cup by its circular handle, "I get the feeling we might go through several pots before this day is done."

"Hey, whatever it takes," Jeremy replied with a shrug, "I'm game. Talk about therapeutic; I'm feeling a rush of revitalization already. You?"

She stood with her back to him, pausing in mid-refill.

"I…don't know exactly what I'm feeling, Jeremy. When I saw you walking towards the house, it…at first I thought I was still dreaming. It wasn't until a few minutes ago that I realized…well, that this was really happening. I'm…I haven't exactly been a bastion of stability this last decade."

"Me and you both, lady," he nodded through a blank stare, "Me...and you both."

The pair fell silent until she reclaimed her seat at the table. After an initial sip, Jeremy reinitiated

336

the conversation, his tone noticeably apprehensive, as if he were on the verge of spilling forth some great, earth-shattering revelation.

"I've…got a confession. Suk. I…actually arrived late last night.

Parked my car at the end of the dirt road leading to your place and walked the last several hundred yards. Slept out by that big oak. Even though I didn't see you 'til this morning….somehow I knew I had the right place. Thought about…waking you, but it was way past midnight and I didn't want to scare you. Sounds crazy I know, but I just wanted to…savor the moment…for myself. To understate the obvious, it had been one *hell* of a long journey."

"You could've knocked. I rarely attempt sleep before one AM." "Sleep disorder?"

"Of the severe variety since about the mid-eighties."

"I can relate, believe me. Anyhow, maybe it's just a coincidence, but I slept without dreaming for the first time in years, maybe a decade."

"My God, Jeremy…" "What?"

"Neither…neither did I. Dream, I mean. That's…the reason it took me so long to shake off the feeling that this entire exchange was some sort of…*hallucinatory* state."

They exchanged a hopeful glance before averting their eyes elsewhere.

"Think it's a sign, Suk?" Jeremy finally asked between sips.

"A sign?"

"Like…maybe we've been granted parole from purgatory?" With a sad smile, Sukie rolled her eyes

337

skyward.

"As in…second chances, Jeremy?" "Exactly."

"Well, if daily prayers for forgiveness pull any weight, my personal invoice should be stamped 'paid in full'."

"Me and you both, swee….um, me and you both," he spat, his face instantly reddening.

Rising once again, Sukie placed her own cup in the kitchen sink and stood motionless, staring out the window through visibly moist but unblinking eyes.

"You…really *didn't* come here for revenge, did you?"

Jeremy rose on shaky legs and stood behind her while maintaining a two to three foot distance between them.

"No way. Dropped such thoughts from the agenda years ago. Hate and resentment are pure poison, especially when they're…without any damn merit whatsoever."

"Then…why?"

"Forgiveness, Sukie. I came here to be forgiven. That, and one other reason that's…a little on the selfish side."

"What's that?" she inquired, her voice crackling with emotion. "Pardon the expression, but…you'll probably think I'm crazy."

"Go on…" she chided, backing up a step as if awaiting his embrace. "I came back to see if we….if there's even a chance that….*shit!* Why is this so damn hard to say?"

"Why, Jeremy Stiles, you've changed so. Never knew such a cute, bashful side even existed."

338

Prompted by her subtle gesture, he moved cautiously forward and placed a shaking hand atop her right shoulder, which trembled just slightly in response.

His words gushed forward in a prattling torrent, concluding in a raspy, agonizing sob that threatened to buckle his knees.

"I...still love you, woman. Truth is, I never stopped...despite my actions. I'm so...so sorry for...what I did to you...to *us*. I'd do anything to take it all back. I swear to God I would..."

"Can I...can we...give it another try? I'm not....not beyond begging.

A man with a hollow soul ain't got much to lose..."

Whirling about in what seemed to him to be robotic, gradual increments, Sukie reached up to remove a hair clip that had been holding her shoulder-length locks at bay before stepping forward with outstretched arms.

"Do you know...have any *earthly* idea..." she wept as Jeremy lunged clumsily forward like a new born taking its first steps, "...just how long I've waited to hear those very words?"

Though their initial embrace was cautious and a bit too gentle, it soon transformed into a full-blown, double-barreled bear hug that caused each to grunt in strained exhaustion at its eventual climax.

"Y-you mean that, Suk?" Jeremy beamed, suddenly appearing a decade younger while standing back and wiping his eyes with the back of one hand.

"Well, of...course I do," she replied with a comical sneer, leaning her backside against the wooden cabinet positioned directly below the sink and using the back of a shirt sleeve to clear away the clear mucus pouring from both nostrils, "I wouldn't…bullshit about a thing like that, you s-silly goose."

"Wha-what did you….just call me?" he asked wearily, his eyes narrowing. As Sukie's gleeful expression abruptly transformed to a bland, emotionless stare, he unconsciously backed away a step until his left thigh lightly bumped the kitchen table.

"Call…you? I don't….Jeremy, what's wrong? I say something wrong?"

After a moment's silence, he relaxed his stiffened pose and managed a nervous smile. For the second time in less than three minutes, his lower torso and legs felt akin to slowly melting rubber.

"Oh, nothing….I guess. My mistake. Guess I've still got the jitters.

Overwhelmed is all."

"Just calm down, lover," she cooed, stepping gracefully forward with her head bowed seductively, "we've got all the time in the world to…rediscover each other, right? All the time we'll ever need."

Once again running both hands through his thick, wavy locks, Jeremy closed his eyes momentarily and huffed, a strained, exasperated exhale that reeked of mental exhaustion.

"I…guess you're right. I just…it's hard to believe all this is… happening so fast after…all those years of frustration. I mean, I came damn near committing suicide on more occasions than I care to recall…."

340

"Awww, did you now? Poor pathetic baby…" came the strangely sardonic reply, delivered in an only mildly disturbing tone which rapidly transformed into a vengeful rant, "poor sick pathetic *fuck*…"

Attempting to refocus through vision still blurred from hopelessly overworked tear ducts, Jeremy instinctively ducked down and to the left just as the first blow sailed overhead with a resounding *whoosh,* barely clipping the tip of his scalp in the process.

"Wha-th-*fuc?* Shiiiiit….Su-Suk?" he cried, falling to one knee as an audible growling noise filled the cramped kitchen; an animalistic whine whose decibel level increased ten-fold in a matter of seconds just as the second blow landed dead center at this exposed breastbone with a loud, hollow thump.

Lying flat on this back, his lungs utterly void of precious oxygen, Jeremy raised his head to visualize his ex-wife and one-time serial killer looming overhead like a predatory insect prepping to feed.

Displaying the same wide, toothy, insanity-fueled grin he'd witnessed over a decade earlier, Sukie casually flipped the hair piece from palm to palm like a baseball pitcher in-between tosses. A hair piece with weirdly elongated ends that resembled overly thick fish hooks; a hair piece possessing razor-sharp edges. Razor-sharp edges that gleamed brightly from the sun's blaring rays penetrating the kitchen window's open blinds.

"Sad, pathetic little Jeremy. Your life must've truly been shit since Sunyon, huh lover? How else could you possibly be so damned forgiving? After all…"

As Jeremy began to struggle and squirm, she first dug her bare left foot into his left rib cage before whipping the right forward and essentially pinning his forehead to the hardwood floor.

"I did eliminate your one true love, remember? Miss Lei Park, she of the above average English vocabulary, bubbly personality and perfect little ass. My…replacement, as it were…."

"N-n-n…no…I…it was…its y-you…..I…lo…love…" he spat between labored huffs, his lips having turned a bright shade of purple.

"(IN KOREAN) Now, now…isn't that about the sweetest thing you've ever heard?" Sukie, scrunching down on her hunches and crossing her slender arms across one another in an 'X' shape.

"S-Suk…Sukie…d-d-don't…" he pleaded, unable to muster the strength to raise a single arm in defense, "I….c-came….to….I…came to…make things….b-b-better…p-please…for-forgive…m-me….I…lov…"

"(IN ENGLISH) Make things BETTER?" she screamed, her nostrils flaring wildly and her badly bloodshot eyes saucer-sized, "Make things better, you sadistic SON OF A BITCH? A little late in the game, isn't it, JEREMY? Sorry, lover….this girl lost the power of forgiveness around the same time the only man she ever loved stole her FUCKING SANITY!!!"

He saw her arms uncoil like steel springs and felt a brief burning sensation at the base of his throat.

342

As light turned to darkness and sticky warmth bathed his neck and upper chest, Jeremy heard his wife's agonized cries mutate from low, feminine whimpers to full blown shrieks that echoed in his fading subconscious like high-powered explosives hollowing out his very soul....

*\*\**

Peering through the pitch-blackness, he noted the digital clock read four-thirty-six AM. Rubbing a bare palm over his crew-cut styled coif, he rolled from the mattress with as much stealth as his still-groggy senses would allow. The cool stone floor provided soothing relief as the balls of his feet made contact. Inhaling deeply, he held the air for a few moments before exhaling through pursed lips, again careful not to accidentally execute a whistling sound by mistake. He'd been both relieved and shocked to realize he hadn't screamed aloud just before waking, and just as surprised that his entire body wasn't bathed in cold sweat.

*Jesus crow. Time sure does fly when you're cracking up. Might as well rise and shine...ETA to the main gate is two hours and counting...*

Having arrived home the day before at around three PM following a strenuous thirteen hour shift, he'd showered and eaten a bite before hitting the sack at around five-thirty. He couldn't recall awakening even once in the eleven hours since, and still felt no urgency to urinate despite such a lengthy duration.

*Probably a slight case of dehydration setting in.*

343

*No small wonder, considering I probably sweated away a good ten pounds of body weight yesterday. Damn, I hope the shift's easier today. Can't take too much more of that shit, especially considering my less-than- relaxing nocturnal habits. Shit, what a skull-fuck...like a theme-park ride for the mentally deranged. Guess it's true what they say about a guilty conscience waging war on its host...never really bought into that psychobabble bullshit 'til the last few weeks...*

Rising from the bed like a man executing a set of slow-motion deep- knee bends, he tip-toed from the room, side-stepping through a half- ajar sliding glass door before pushing it completely shut with an equal amount of painstaking caution.

Minutes later, he sat at a small circular table with a mug of steaming black coffee parked between cupped hands. Donned only in a pair of calf-high black socks and green BVD's, he stared straight ahead at a picturesque calendar hanging on the cement wall. Above the thirty-one total days allotted for August of nineteen eighty-four was a photo of a beautiful young Korean girl dressed in the traditional wide-skirted, ankle-length dress, her radiant smile and almond-shaded eyes as surreally hypnotizing as the frosty OB beer she held between two hands was utterly dismissible.

"That's it, man. No more putting it off...." he mumbled, studying the girl's smooth, blemish-free face and neckline through squinting, unblinking eyes, "No more procrastination. It has to end, and end right *now*. Shit's only gonna get worse if I keep ignoring the issue."

The photo's entrancing effect finally shaken, he finished off the cup in three quick gulps before rising and pulling a bulky paper sack from a nearby refrigerator.

*Sweet thing never forgets her man's healthy appetite. Just one in a dozen reasons I have to lay down the law once and for all, before I lose it...lose...her. So much to lose at that.*

*Great cook...damn good lover...damn good friend. Yeah, I've been a grade-A dumb-ass...case closed...no argument... but it doesn't have to lead to a lifetime's worth of shitty choices. I can still make this right...like the others, but it's all about the timing, and the time is definitely now. Not tomorrow. Today.*

*Nope, can't even afford to wait 'til these damn war games end.*

Placing his cup in the kitchen sink, he pulled out a nearby drawer and removed a single object, tucking it tightly against his rock-hard belly as if checking its authenticity.

He dressed in the dark with the seasoned experience of a wily veteran, never missing a button or loophole while donning either the camouflaged shirt or spit-shined combat boots that help make up the required ensemble.

*One thing's for damn sure. The third party in this little triangle ain't gonna be the least bit happy. Not at first, anyhow. Probably throw one hell of a tantrum. Throw some shit around, stomp her feet, the works. These club chicks are all born drama queens. Course, I won't really blame her if she throws a punch or two in my general direction. After*

345

*all, I did lie and say I didn't have a yobo. But, shit...these gals outta be used to G.I's lying through their teeth to 'em by now. She'll get over it...one way or another. Hell, don't they always?*

After a brief equipment check to ensure all mandatory items were indeed present, he proceeded to stack the overstuffed chemical suit bag just inside the three-room hooch's lone exit/entrance. He checked his watch to ensure he still had ample time to make the five-thirty AM bus to the base, then walked gingerly back towards the bedroom.

The morning light had just begun to seep in through the thin curtains, providing him just enough illumination to fully visualize the whole of her as she slept.

*Nope...definitely too much to lose there, buddy-boy. When am I ever gonna get it through this rock-infested noggin of mine that copping a little strange, no matter how good, just ain't worth the eventual price.*

Leaning down, he gave her a light peck on her exposed forehead, receiving a lazy smile and sheepish grunt in reply.

"Love you, babe. See you tonight," he whispered, the faint smell of garlic emanating from her warm flesh.

Stepping out of the hooch and into the chilled morning air, he inhaled deeply, the familiar scent of burning Ondol ever present. Slinging the chemical bag over his left shoulder, he slid his combat helmet on and gave it a quick tug on either side for proper adjustment.

Trudging up the narrow, winding passageway

leading to the bus stop, he pondered the correct approach to use later that afternoon, when he planned on confronting his mistress with the bad news that whatever had been was now over….permanently. It wasn't so much the task of telling her that set his nerves on edge, but her possible reaction to such news. She could yell, scream, protest; even get violent to some extent…such behavior was to be expected. Others had done the same, and worse. That wasn't the main concern. What *was* would be if she threatened to contact his wife with news of the affair. Such a reaction, if only surfacing as a base threat, simply couldn't be tolerated, meaning he would be forced to initiate plan B, effective immediately. So fortunate that she lived in such an isolated area, just off the beaten path from the main arteries leading into the Ville. Easy followed, she was; easily *trailed*. No one would hear, despite the amount of audible ruckus involved. The whole thing could go one of two ways. It all depended on the reaction he received.

*Be smart, Lei. Let it go. What we had was nice, but it was purely physical. Try to wreck my marriage, bitch, and things are apt to get mighty ugly mighty fast. I saw still another nasty vision of my future last night, at least one possibility of it, and I ain't about to let that apocalyptic shit go down. Not on your life, lady.*

Pausing as a steep curve in the road loomed, Sergeant Jeremy Yeager flung the duffel forward and buried his left hand deep into its bulging confines. His hand wrapped around the bone-knife's rough wooden handle. He hoped Sukie wouldn't miss it. If he recalled correctly, she'd planned on cooking a vegetarian dish that evening, Chop Suey Noodles with spinach, he thought she'd said. Besides which, she had an extra meat cutting knife stashed away in another drawer. He'd already checked. As before, he was always one step ahead of the game. As such potentially dangerous games went, it was truly mandatory to do so. Alas, he'd learned so *very* much from recent experience.

*Maybe it won't even come to that. Drastic measure for sure. But, as dear old Granddad Yeager used to say, sometimes in life, drastic measures are a necessary evil in order to maintain the status quo.*

*Yes siree, Bob Barker,* Jeremy mused, Lei Chang *would* listen to reason, by God, or end up worm dirt in some mosquito-infested rice paddy…just as *Mia Park* had a few months earlier…or *Sei Ri Pak* a few months before that…her choice entirely, but there were no other alternatives. The scene would end one of two ways; the easy, or the *extremely* hard.

Repositioning the gear as he'd heard distant footsteps in the background, Jeremy walked briskly forward, feeling strangely rejuvenated. Nearing the bend in the curve that would lead into a paved clearing where G.I's caught the morning bus from the Ville to the main gate of Sunyon Air Force Base, he seemed hopelessly oblivious to either the slightly warped grin he displayed or the barely noticeable tick developing at the corner of his left eye.

"Now, what idiot was it that first said you couldn't learn anything *useful* from dreams?"